C000132375

About th

Andrea Bolter has always of the heart. In fact, she's t for advice with their love l in Los Angeles with her husband and daughter. She loves travel, rock n' roll, sitting at cafés, and watching romantic comedies she's already seen a hundred times. Say hi at andreabolter.com

Annie O'Neil spent most of her childhood with a leg draped over the family rocking chair and a book in her hand. Novels, baking, and writing too much teenage angst poetry ate up most of her youth. Now, Annie splits her time between corralling her husband into helping her with their cows, listening to audio books whilst weeding, and spending some very happy hours at her computer writing.

After earning a degree in psychology, **Robyn Amos** discovered that writing about the suspenseful and romantic lives of the people in her imagination was more fulfilling than writing scholarly research papers. She has since published nine novels. While pursuing her own happily-ever-after with her new husband in Odenton, Maryland, Robyn continues to write about characters from a variety of cultural backgrounds, hoping her stories of romance and adventure will transcend racial stereotypes.

Foreign Affairs

Foreign Affairs: A Parisian Love Story

ANDREA BOLTER

ANNIE O'NEIL

ROBYN AMOS

MILLS & BOON

First Published in Great Britain 2023
By Mills & Boon, an imprint of HarperCollins*Publishers*
1 London Bridge Street, London, SE1 9GF

www.harpercollins.co.uk

HarperCollins*Publishers*
Macken House, 39/40 Mayor Street Upper,
Dublin 1, D01 C9W8, Ireland

FOREIGN AFFAIRS: A PARISIAN LOVE STORY © 2023 Harlequin Enterprises ULC.

Captivated by Her Parisian Billionaire © 2020 Andrea Bolter
Reunited with Her Parisian Surgeon © 2018 Annie O'Neil
Romancing the Chef © 2011 Robyn Amos

ISBN: 978-0-263-31869-2

CAPTIVATED BY
HER PARISIAN
BILLIONAIRE

ANDREA BOLTER

For Megan

CHAPTER ONE

THE EIFFEL TOWER. It had been a long time since Jules had woken up to the sight of one of the world's most famous landmarks. When his eyes clicked open after the heavy slumber he hoped would cancel out his jet lag, he'd used the remote control on the nightstand to raise the blackout blinds and let in the light of the Paris morning. There the tower stood in view through his window, in all its wrought iron lattice glory.

Jules's apartment was an example of the many Durand Properties, his billion-euro real-estate empire, he owned in the city with their mixture of historic architecture and every modern convenience. High ceilings, crown moldings and original chevron wood floors reminded him that this apartment in the Seventh Arrondissement, as Paris's districts were referred to, was over a hundred years old.

His eyes fell shut again. While there was no question that his hometown was one of the most magnificent cities in the world, he was uneasy returning to Paris. Traveling across the globe, buying more and more properties everywhere he went had become his way of life. The last sleep he'd had on land was on the fifty-seventh floor of an ultra-luxury hotel in Singapore. Always on the move, Jules liked living in hotels, anonymous and temporary.

After rubbing his eyelids with the heels of his hands, he reopened them. There was the window again with its spectacular view. The tower, watching over the city as it always did. Yep, he really was back in Paris.

Mindlessly scratching his bare chest, he knew he should get out of bed. Tomorrow, he'd resume his habit of starting the day with an outdoor run. Today, he'd acclimate. A busy morning lay ahead with reestablishing himself at the Durand Properties headquarters and completing the job he'd returned to France to do. It was time to take the reins from his irresponsible mother and father, who had been on their own globe-trot for far too long. Although parenting his parents was hardly how he'd envisioned this chapter of his life, blood was blood and he'd do anything he had to.

As if reading his mind, the buzz of Jules's phone beckoned and one glance at the screen's caller identification let him know it was his mother. He swiped to answer.

"Where in the world is my tall handsome son?" Agathe Durand's singsong led him to believe she was calling from a different time zone, as she was never chipper in the mornings. Her voice was high with that continental-traveler tone she used to fool people, to disguise the fact that she was perpetually discontent with her life.

"My apartment, Mother. You're not in Paris?"

"Tel Aviv."

"Tel Aviv. Dandy." Spending Jules's money, of course. "Dare I ask, is Father okay?"

"Yes, your exasperating pater is fine, although keeping me from properly enjoying Tel Aviv. The man wants to sit in cafés eating falafel all day instead of being out and taking in the sights."

There she goes again, Jules thought. Blaming his father for her own unhappiness. As she did the entirety of Jules's childhood. At their age, Jules hoped their domestic dramas were behind them, especially now that Hugo was confined to a wheelchair after a fall had broken his back. Yet, with his parents, there was no telling. The unpredictability of which drove ordered-and-organized Jules crazy.

"Never mind touring Tel Aviv. You're supposed to be in Paris. That's why I'm here." Arranging to meet them in the same place was often a challenge and Jules had sat waiting in many a foreign train station or airport, eventually receiving the call that they'd missed their departure.

While his parents continued their decade-long knack of finding an antique piece of jewelry to buy and then sell at a high markup, or one of them getting work in some corner of the world at a tavern or on a farm, Jules had been largely footing their bills. Hugo's physical condition now prohibited him from any hard labor. Agathe's bon vivant facade was not what it used to be and she was no longer able to charm her way into dinner or a night's lodgings.

As their only child, Jules felt a responsibility to them despite the dysfunction he'd grown up in. Money was something he had plenty of to give. So while peace and satisfaction were apparently out of the question for his parents, at least he could make sure they didn't disappear somewhere into the abyss. Now their wanderings had become impractical and dangerous. He needed to ground them.

In short, the gig was up for these nomads Jules called parents. It was time they stayed in one place. Paris, where they'd raised Jules in a shoddy apartment on the outskirts of town, long lost to creditors, was where they were born and where they would die.

"Oh, Jules, we'll be there eventually."

A wince reminded him of similar phone calls from years gone by. Only it wasn't both of his parents calling during any hour of the day or night far from home. It was his mother who, at least a dozen times during Jules's childhood, would become bored or angry with her housewifely doldrums. So she'd pack a suitcase and disappear, abandoning Jules and his father. With theatrical vows that she needed to *see* the world and would never return, she'd only get as far as visiting relatives in other parts of France for a few days. Inevitably, she'd regain her senses or outstay her welcome, not having the wherewithal to get any farther. She'd return to her husband and son with promises that she'd never leave them again. Until she did.

In later years, she began dragging Hugo along with her, which gave her the courage to venture greater distances. A bitter and cold man who was never able to maintain steady employment, it made no difference to him where he laid his head at night.

But this move would be final. Once Jules got his parents back to Paris and into one of his apartments where they'd have a safe roof over their heads, he'd base himself here again and look after what their aging health would demand. As laughable as it was to use the term for people his parents' age, it was time for Agathe and Hugo to *grow up*. In the process, Jules would call Paris home again as well, which he had been resisting but knew was overdue.

"If you had seen the way your mother behaved with our taxi driver last night, you'd be as horrified as I was," the voice of Jules's father came through the speaker. Obviously, Hugo had gained custody of the phone in Tel Aviv and was reporting to Jules lest his wife consider herself blameless for their latest row. "She absolutely threw herself at him. The young man was gracious, of course, but even he was embarrassed."

"You're just jealous," Agathe called into the speaker. Why Jules's parents had to fight during a call to him was anyone's guess. There was plenty of other time left in the day for them to badger at each other and then let things subside like they always did, neither of them having the gumption to actually end their marriage. They were becoming more childish every time he spoke with them.

"While I can't think of anything I'd rather do than listen to the two of you argue over the phone, I need to finish the apartment I have for you and run my business. You were supposed to meet me in Paris to make some decisions about the renovation. I'll put you in one of my hotels while we finish the work. Get here." He ended the call, annoyed. Hopefully, he was making the right decision in forcing them back. He couldn't think of another solution.

After showering and donning his uniform of a Savile Row business suit, he found his daily breakfast of a green vegetable smoothie in the refrigerator, which he had instructed the housekeeper to prepare. He readied himself for his workday in what was to become his new routine. Durand Properties occupied an enormous building in Montparnasse. It had been months since he'd set foot in his actual office, the staff spending more time with him on telescreens than in person.

Jules maintained a crack management team to collaborate with him on operations, leaving him free to do what he did best. Seek out real estate to purchase and rehabilitate, resell or lease. He was good at his job, he reasoned, as he'd amassed over two hundred properties on four continents.

He stood at his bedroom window and peered down at the street traffic while he sipped his green drink. People hurried this way and that, many headed to the metro stations where they'd travel underground to their daily destinations.

His eyes fixed on a young couple. The woman had a short haircut and wore a striped dress, gesturing wildly with her hands as they walked. Jules couldn't hear her from his second-floor apartment, but from her facial expressions she seemed to be shouting at her companion. The man, bearded and in jeans, listened silently. At one point, he deftly kissed her on the cheek without causing either of them to lose their stride. From arguing to kissing, their familiarity with each other made Jules guess they were a couple that had been together for a long time. Did interactions with women always have to include commotion?

"Yes, Karim." He turned from the window and paced the wooden floor as he took a call from his personal assistant at the office, who Jules spoke with several times a day regardless of his own whereabouts.

"Jules, I've checked with Lanon in Project Development about acquiring an interior designer to do the apartment for your parents. She tells me that all of our designers are swamped and if we pull anyone away from their current project, we won't make our completion dates."

"I see." Jules contemplated his assistant's report. A few years ago, he had bought a large building in the Second Arrondissement with apartments that would be a good fit for his parents because he was able do the structural changes needed for wheelchair access. Which was not always possible in the stately old buildings of Paris. Plus, it was in a lively neighborhood with plenty of shops and public spaces nearby. His tenant there had moved out, although later than he had expected. So the unit still needed paint, furnishings and decor, and some further accommodations given his father's mobility restrictions.

"I'll be in the office shortly. Please check with Giang in Resources as to how we should go about finding a designer immediately."

Of course, it couldn't be just anyone. Since the designer was to work with Jules as a son of the inhabitants as well as an employer, it wasn't a typical project. He'd want to select this hire himself.

"I already have. He suggested we contact some of our high-end furniture suppliers, as a lot of designers come through their doors."

"Good, then. Kindly get that done."

After the call, Jules knotted his tie in the mirror. He squared himself in the eye. The two little permanent creases between his eyebrows always gave his face a serious demeanor.

This morning, there was also worry in his big brown orbs. Converting abandoned factories into housing for an entire village in India was one thing. But taking charge of his parents' affairs, staying in Paris to be with them in their elder years was going to be his biggest project yet. He was fundamentally as unsettled as they were.

For some reason, he thought of that pretty girl in the striped dress on the street yelling at her man.

Returning to the window, Jules saw the couple far down the block now, as tiny as dolls from his viewpoint. He shifted his gaze to the Eiffel Tower one more time.

Paris.

The City of Light.

Home.

Jules had never felt lonelier.

"I might have good news," Yasmine Jaziri told her roommate, Zoe Gaiman, as she sat down at the outside table of the café on Boulevard Saint-Michel, the longtime haven for young people and students in the city's Latin Quarter.

Zoe nursed her lemon soda as she allowed Yasmine to get settled in. When the waiter approached, Yasmine ordered a glass of red wine.

"Let's hear it." Zoe couldn't wait. She could use some good news no matter who or what it pertained to.

"My boss, Si, told us that Jules Durand is desperately looking for an interior designer."

"Jules Durand? As in Durand Properties?" Zoe bubbled. The real-estate development corporation, which owned dozens of buildings in Paris and many more throughout the world, was founded and led by a certain Jules Durand whom Zoe had read about in a magazine article. The fact that he was much younger than would be expected for someone so accomplished had made an impression on Zoe, and she'd remembered the name. Also, judging from the couple of photos accompanying the magazine story, Jules Durand was twenty-five kinds of good-looking.

"Apparently, he has an apartment he needs work on, and quickly," Yasmine continued.

"What, he asked Si if he knew anyone?"

"Yeah. Si mentioned it at the staff meeting this morning." Yasmine apprenticed for Si Wu, a renowned furniture designer. Trendy and finely crafted side tables that cost more than Zoe earned in a year kind of thing. It made sense that Jules Durand would buy from a studio like that. "I can get you the contact information."

"I doubt he'd consider me qualified." While Zoe was a burgeoning interior designer, Durand Properties was not going to be interested in someone with her level of experience. She'd been in Paris for a year and had only managed to secure a few small jobs. A tiny restaurant that needed a new look on a budget. A nursery school that was updating their two classrooms. The couple that needed to utilize their parking garage for storage. Not much more than what she had been doing in Maupont, the small town near Lyon where she grew up. She had fled to make a name for herself in Paris, not to mention leave painful memories behind.

"What can I get for you two mademoiselles?" the older mustached waiter asked when he returned with Yasmine's wine.

"Thank you, we're just having drinks," Zoe quickly answered. There was no money in her budget for an expensive dinner. She and Yasmine had agreed they'd meet to savor a slow drink and watch the parade of Paris go by. At this point, even that was a treat.

The waiter snarled, no doubt hoping they were going to order food. Zoe shrugged her shoulders at him with a cute smile. It failed to crack his gruff exterior.

"It doesn't hurt to try," Yasmine continued on about Durand Properties. "You have nothing to lose."

"You've got that right."

Zoe had come to Paris on a hope and a dream, and feared that neither were coming to pass. Even sharing a one-bedroom apartment with Yasmine, whom she'd met through a mutual acquaintance, she couldn't afford this expensive city. Something had to give or she'd soon be letting her brothers in Maupont know that she was coming home, defeated.

"Just send an email," Yasmine encouraged. "You have some nice photos from the jobs you've done. Include those. You know what you're doing."

Sweet Yasmine. Always a word of encouragement. She assessed her roommate sipping from her wineglass Her thick dark hair was stick straight, as opposed to Zoe's corkscrew red curls that grew every which way out of her head. Yasmine hailed from Tunisia and had moved to Paris to study, eventually landing under Si Wu's tutelage. Even though Zoe's fantasy of success and a life in Paris seemed to be crumbling, she'd always wish the best for Yasmine.

"I suppose it wouldn't hurt to try and see if I can get a meeting." Not with Jules Durand himself, she hoped. That would be too nerve-racking. He'd probably have an underling interview prospective designers, wouldn't he? The CEO would have much more supervisory tasks in front of him.

What was she even thinking? Jules Durand's company, with some of the most notable buildings in Paris, was not going to hire someone who knew how to make a room look larger by placing mirrors in the correct locations! They would employ designers with CVs as grand as the rooms they'd be filling.

The waiter returned with a tray full of delicious-smelling food for another table. Zoe's nose followed the aroma as far as it could.

"Yasmine, you know what? You're right. I do know what I'm doing. I don't doubt my abilities." She liked saying those words out loud. "Durand Properties might be just the break I need."

"That's the spirit."

The possibility that if she did pursue the opportunity she might encounter Jules Durand himself niggled at her. Staring back at her from those magazine photos with his eyes as dark a brown as hers were as light a blue, he was one intense man. His were the kind of eyes that could take over a girl's thoughts. Make her wonder if the impossible might be possible. Not Zoe, of course. None of that was for her. But it might set someone else to speculation.

"Okay, get me the contact information."

Two days later, Zoe and her portfolio strode toward the Durand Properties headquarters. In her one good black suit with the coordinating silky blouse underneath, she felt professional and terrified at the same time.

Just as Yasmine had promised, the contact person at Durand Properties was easily reachable by email. He, in turn, sent her an e-log from which to choose an appointment time. Several of the slots were already filled, leading Zoe to deduce that other people were being interviewed, as well. Which didn't bode well in her favor as her competition might have more experience than she did.

Nonetheless, she was excited. This was why she came to Paris, to work within the walls of the incredible architectural marvels, both old and new, that graced this remarkable city. She loved it here, where the boulevards teemed with energy. She didn't want to return to sleepy Maupont, where the most she could hope for was the odd job revamping a guest bedroom or small office. Where, walking down every street, she'd see someone she knew who would give her that look of sympathy and pity for what would define her family's name there for the rest of eternity. No, Paris wiped the slate. Gave her a fresh start. And it was where she wanted to live for the rest of her life.

As Zoe neared Durand Properties, a modern glass building that occupied an entire square block, she ducked into an alleyway. Removing the comfortable shoes she'd been walking in, she opened her bag and extracted the business heels that pulled her outfit together. After the switch, she approached the entrance door, *Durand Properties* etched into the glass with a distinct script. An intercom system allowed her to announce her arrival, then the latch clicked and she was able to open the door.

She remembered that Karim Harbi, the man she spoke with on the phone, had told her to check in at the welcome desk before taking the elevator to the fourth floor. The woman who sat behind the counter verified the appointment and pointed her in the right direction.

When the elevator door opened to the fourth floor, Zoe stepped into a central reception area, the likes of which she had never seen before. People bustled to and fro. All the walls were made of glass, affording panoramic views of the city from every direction. The fourth being the top floor allowed Zoe to see that the slanted roof was made of a reflective type of glass and solar panels that could harness the sun's heat.

In the center of the space was a wide staircase with open steps and gray steel railing. Two women descended while engaged in conversation. Off to one side, a long concrete reception desk was staffed by three employees, two women and one man, all stylishly dressed in neutral colors, speaking into headsets. Several seating areas were grouped throughout with blond wood furniture, some with red upholstery, others bare. A cluster of men in suits sat at one talking amongst themselves. Low coffee tables held massive arrangements of red flowers. Abstract stone fountains placed here and there compensated for the lack of artwork given that there were no actual walls other than the glass perimeter. It was, quite simply, the most stunning workspace Zoe had ever encountered.

"Mademoiselle Gaiman?" a young man greeted her as she was taking in the surroundings. His voice served as a good reminder to make sure her jaw wasn't hanging open at the impressiveness of it all. "I am Karim."

His accent and dark skin suggested he was another young person who had come from somewhere else to Paris with a dream in his pocket.

"Nice to meet you."

"If you'll follow me, Monsieur Durand is ready for you."

What did he just say? As it was Karim she had been interacting with so far, Zoe had convinced herself that she'd be having her interview with him. Or with someone in their human resources department. Or someone other than Jules Durand himself.

"Karim," she coughed out, "is it typical that Jules Durand is the first to meet with perspective employees?"

"No, of course, a company of our size has a department devoted to personnel. But this is a special project of a personal nature. Jules will better explain when you meet with him."

Heart suddenly thumping against her chest, Zoe cleared her throat. Karim led her to a massive corner office, private by being delineated with its own glass walls. It was as carefully furnished as the reception area. As they approached, Zoe could see a meeting section with a wood table and chairs. There was also an area with two drafting tables, computer banks and shelves that held architectural blueprints. To the side of that, two white leather sofas faced each other with armchairs beside them creating a conversation space. There was a vase of more red flowers on a countertop beside a sink and refrigerator. A treadmill faced outward to the view. The single office in its entirety was large enough to house a family of four. At the stone desk in the center of it all, a man who Zoe recognized to be Jules Durand sat in a high-backed black office chair speaking to someone through an earpiece.

As she got closer, which for some reason felt like marching toward a firing squad, she could make out the furrows between his eyebrows that she'd taken notice of in those magazine photos of him. They gave him a sort of stern look that was somehow wildly sexy at the same time. In a dark gray suit, white dress shirt and forest green tie, he was as stunning as his office building. His aura, his buzz permeated the air and reached her all the way out in the corridor. This man was over six feet of pure power. Adrenaline pounded through her.

On impulse, Zoe began forking her fingers through her corkscrew curls in hopes that her hair didn't look too unkempt. She threw her shoulders back and stood as tall as she could which, given that she was a shorty, wasn't much.

Cheering herself on, she had this. She was a hard worker, had done nice designs in the past and deserved a chance to move onto bigger projects. Not to mention that the only way she was going to be able to stay in Paris was if she rose up to the next rung on the career ladder.

She was going to dazzle this man, regardless of how imposing he was.

He was going to hire her. No doubt about it.

Karim pulled open the heavy glass door to the private office and, after Zoe stepped in, took his leave.

"It's an honor to meet you, monsieur," Zoe began as she took an uneven step forward, which made one of her shoe heels wobble. Then she heard a cracking sound. But before she could do anything about it, the heel snapped and buckled under, jerking Zoe Gaiman forward and causing her to fall flat on her face into Jules Durand's office.

"Are you all right?" Jules dashed from behind his desk to attend to the interviewee who had just, literally, burst into his office. Presenting his arm for the young woman to use for balance as she stood up, he felt a surprising tingle when she wrapped her small fingers around his bicep.

"Yes, I'm fine," she quipped dismissively, although

nonetheless leveraging all of her weight onto his arm. The portfolio of photos and sketches she had brought along to impress him with was now scattered around her. A quick cheat of a glance told Jules that they were good.

Once she hoisted herself to a standing position, he took notice that she stood not much more than five feet tall. And she had a wild tangle of hair. Had her fall dislodged a more conservative hairdo? Because, at the moment, it looked like a crazed tree straight out of a Van Gogh painting. A wine-induced hallucination of reddish, no, almost orange spirals pointing toward every angle. It took all of his gentlemanly decorum not to reach out and touch one of her curls, so curious was he to know what they would feel like.

She retrieved the culprit that was responsible for her dramatic entrance. Indeed, the pointy heel had almost fully separated from the body of her shoe and dangled limply from its infrastructure.

"Darn it. These are my only..." She decided, flustered, not to finish the sentence. Instead, she slipped the broken shoe back onto her foot and used two hands to smooth down her skirt and jacket before extending her palm for a handshake. "I'm Zoe Gaiman. I hope you can forget what just happened and we can begin the interview over again." She blew a breath upward, possibly in an attempt to send some errant hairs back to their designated place.

As he returned her handshake, Jules couldn't consent to her terms because he had an inkling that he would never forget anything about Zoe Gaiman.

Her fingers were as soft as he'd imagined they'd be. Together, the two of them bent down to gather up the sheets of her portfolio. He gestured for her to take a seat opposite his at the desk. Hobbling on the broken shoe, Zoe made her way to the chair and slid in.

With a tap on his computer, a photo appeared on his screen, the secondary screen that faced Zoe's seat and on the large monitor that serviced the seating cluster to his right. In the past few years, Jules had conducted most of his work from his laptop while ensconced in suites of the world's finest hotels and in Durand Properties satellite offices. Naturally, he'd frequently returned to Paris for meetings and functions. But his highly efficient office here was underutilized. That was about to change, as he'd be basing himself here permanently.

"The apartment in need of design is in this building," he explained about the first photo to Zoe. Five years ago, he'd purchased the building, which had been divided into eight apartments, not knowing at the time that he'd be dedicating one to his parents. "Here are some photos."

To her credit, Zoe seemed to have recovered after her visit with his office floor and she studied the slideshow he presented. "There's an elevator, I take it?" she inquired.

"Yes. Which is critical. You see, this apartment is for my own parents to inhabit. My father is wheelchair-bound."

"Oh, so that's why Karim said this was a personal project. It looks as if the front entrance to the building has the width to accommodate a wheelchair, but the interior doorways have been widened? That must have been a tight squeeze."

"My architects supervised those modifications." Jules was impressed. Zoe was the third designer he'd interviewed today and neither of the other two had noted that obvious need for wheelchair clearance in the apartment's doorways.

He glanced away from the screen to make contact with her sky blue eyes, which had a crystalline shimmer he found very intriguing. She also had an adorable swath of freckles that ran from one cheekbone across her nose to the other. And that hair!

Women and their attractiveness or lack thereof was of no interest to Jules, so he surprised himself in even taking the time to observe Zoe's unique beauty.

"I see from your portfolio pages—" he pointed to what was now a haphazard stack that she'd lain on the spare chair beside her "—that you share my appreciation for blending the old with the new."

"Yes, I like to bring in every functional convenience but make the living space warm and stylish at the same time. And I did a course in special-needs accessibility. Let me show you some photos."

He peered over while she riffled through her pile. One looked like a guest room converted into an office, the other a classroom. Did she have the proper experience for an entire Paris apartment, especially one for his parents where he knew he'd demand perfection? Zoe showed him an unimpressive access ramp leading to a converted garage with a few grab bars installed here and there. Jules's contractors had already done the structural modifications on the apartment. Still, at least she said she'd studied accessibility.

He opened another program on his computer. "Here we have some suggested color combinations for the paint and furnishings in the main living spaces. We can look at the bathroom and kitchen afterward. I assume you're familiar with this software that automatically generates a primary color scheme with complementary shades for accents."

"I don't use auto-generated color combining."

"Excuse me?"

"I wouldn't want a computer to decide a paint shade to match a sofa color for me. That's not how I work."

With two fingers, she twisted a ringlet that fell over one of her ears. Jules had no way to determine if it was actually out of place. It was nothing short of ludicrous how curious he was about her hair. Although, now it was what was coming out of her mouth that alarmed him.

"Mademoiselle Gaiman, as you might imagine, Durand Properties employs every bit of technology available that can assist us in our work."

"With due respect, Monsieur Durand, computer-aided design is, of course, a marvelous advancement. And the furniture placement programs and whatnot on the market these days are timesaving tools. But I also have to feel a project. In my heart—" she paused to bring her fist to her chest for emphasis "—and in my soul."

"I see," he tittered, surprised at this young woman's pluck. People usually yessed Jules Durand, too intimidated to disagree. He wasn't sure whether or not he liked Zoe's assertiveness. Ever so briefly, his mind flashed on a very private way he might show her with his lips who was the boss.

He quickly refocused with, "I'm afraid I don't employ souls. I employ professionals who, in turn, follow industry standards and new developments."

"Does the way yellow spring flowers play against the five o'clock sky rely on a digital approval system?"

"I beg your pardon?"

"When the waves of the ocean ebb and flow, creating a natural rhythm that syncs with a shoreline wind. Can your computer software replicate that?"

Jules was becoming a bit irritated. While there was something mesmerizing about this young woman, he had a job to offer and expected it done his way, and certainly wasn't going to work with someone who questioned his methods.

Especially in dealing with this apartment for his parents, Jules wanted the project done quickly, as he expected Agathe and Hugo back in Paris soon and he couldn't accommodate time-consuming mistakes. He had no leeway for prima donna designers who constantly changed their minds and, for example, repainted several times before being satisfied with their choices.

He needed his parents securely ensconced, not traipsing all over the earth like vagabonds with his father in a wheelchair. It was ironic that Jules himself had called no place home for years, either, although his time away was well spent amassing a fortune.

Everyone was going to stay put in Paris. For all the turbulence of his upbringing, with his mother's abandonments and then returns, and his father's unstable employment history, Jules would ground them now. He'd become the de facto patriarch.

"I thank you for coming in, Mademoiselle Gaiman." He pushed his chair back from the desk, ready to show her to the door. "Obviously, we have an incompatible approach, but I do wish you well." Oddly, the idea of never seeing Zoe again gave him pause and he hesitated.

"Wait…" Zoe threw her palms up, trying to halt him before he stood. "If this apartment is for your own parents, don't you want it to breathe with life? Shouldn't it be a blanket of comfort? That sings in peaceful harmony. Why don't you show me the apartment in person? So I can feel it."

That was the second time she had mentioned *feeling* the apartment.

Jules didn't do feelings. He didn't choose properties based on spring flowers. He relied on engineers and architects and inspectors and financial advisors for whom the tools of the trade brought a scientific precision. Jules liked that. There was no room for gamble in his orbit.

Yet, chance was exactly what was in front of him. He'd get no data collection on how long his parents would live. There was no spreadsheet that could forecast if his mother would finally find serenity within the boundaries of a permanent residence. No analysis would report how good a job Jules would do as their caretaker.

So the last thing he needed was any further unpredictability. While he respected that Zoe was probably a very creative person, and thought he might contemplate for the rest of his life how hair grew out of someone's head like that, he had other prospects to meet with. This interview was over.

"Thank you for your time, Mademoiselle Gaiman."

He stood, hoping she'd follow suit. Which she did, but not before shooting a penetrating look at him that made his ribs rattle. Were there tears pooling in those bright blue eyes? "Good luck with the project," she muttered.

Jules saw Zoe Gaiman to the door with her tottering on her broken shoe heel all the way.

CHAPTER TWO

OBVIOUSLY WE HAVE an incompatible approach.

Jules Durand's words from the day before played over and over again in Zoe's head as she brought two cups of coffee to the teeny tiny balcony of her and Yasmine's apartment.

The window space with its wrought iron railing was barely big enough for two folding chairs and a stool they used as a table, but they loved to drink their morning coffee out there. It was special little things like that which made Zoe hopeful she could always call Paris home.

No matter that their balcony faced out to the rear of their building and overlooked the back of the building on the next street, which didn't afford a view of much of anything. They could still breath in the Paris air and see the way the sunrays cast this way or that, inspiring artists for centuries to capture that special light through their paintbrushes.

"You see the way the sun almost glistens off of the strawberry jam on your toast?" Zoe said to Yasmine as she handed her one of the mugs. "That's what I was trying to explain to Jules Durand. Everything is integrated in the world around us."

"Do you think that Jules Durand, of Durand Gazillion-Euro Properties, needed you to explain *anything* to him?" Yasmine asked before taking a sip of her coffee.

"Apparently not," Zoe snickered, as she maneuvered one of the chairs to the precise angle so that she could sit in it without falling over the railing.

"You haven't told me all of the details of your grand entrance."

"Yeah, I made quite a first impression. The only silver lining is that at least when I fell into his life, my suit skirt didn't hike up to show him my unmentionables."

"Glad you can see the bright side."

"Have I mentioned how much I hate high heels?"

"You say you like them because they make you look taller."

"It might not be worth it."

"So, did Durand give you a hard *no* or was it a *we'll let you know* kind of thing?"

"Oh, it was most definitely a *no*."

Thank you for your time, Mademoiselle Gaiman.

That was a hard *no* if Zoe had ever heard one. Especially with the kingly tone of voice he used and the way he stood up from his desk. Like he couldn't get her out of his office fast enough. She'd been so frustrated she almost ended up leaving in tears. Her shoe, his domineering demeanor, the rejection.

Although one thing not lost on her during their too short meeting was that if she'd thought Jules Durand was nice-looking in the photos she'd seen in a magazine, it was nothing compared to him in person. His thick black hair was cut short but left a little bit longer in front, accentuating the dense eyebrows with those crinkle lines between them. His eyes were deep and very dark, leading to a long narrow nose. With his closely shaven face and knife-blade jawline, Zoe had especially noticed his full lips, which were a pale pink. All united, it was one gorgeous face.

"Why are you smiling?" Yasmine interrupted Zoe's mental recap of the most handsome human she'd ever seen in her life.

"Am I?" She hadn't realized her musings were visible. "No reason."

"Tell." Yasmine chomped on her toast.

"Only that he was, you know, not too hard on the eyes."

"No kidding. I've seen pictures of him. He's tall and has a great build, too."

"He's the long and lean type. Not bulky."

Zoe thought of the impeccably cut suit he'd worn. And how regal he'd looked in it.

"He's always showing up on those eligible bachelor lists. And says he'll never marry, that the institution is not for him."

"He definitely has a way of letting you know he's in charge. Not very equitable."

Zoe looked to the sky. Maybe his arrogance was self-confidence, and that's what had brought him success. Or the other way around, that achievement had made him so sure of himself. In any case, there was more to him than that. A man who had given such detailed thought into setting up a workable home for his parents spoke to her. Maybe because she missed her own parents so much, his care and concern touched her heart regardless of his personal manner.

No matter, though. Zoe had no interest in the man other than professionally. In any man. Men could be distracting and lead to love. Love could lead to loss. She'd had enough of that already.

After she'd fallen into Jules's office, and her portfolio with examples of her work had scattered all over his expensive carpet, she hadn't had a chance to show him one job she had done for a wheelchair-accessible guesthouse in her hometown of Maupont. Maybe it wasn't on the same scale as the apartment he was redesigning in Paris, but if she'd have been able to show him photos of that project, might she have fared better in the interview?

What's done was done. Unless…? Could she call him and try to get another interview? No, that would seem like begging. She'd asked to see the apartment and he'd refused her. He was clearly uninterested in her style. As he said, they were incompatible.

"Do you have any other upcoming interviews?" Yasmine inquired.

"Not a one."

Zoe stretched her spine against the chair back. Still tired, her nights had been fitful lately as she tossed and turned, trying to figure out what to do next. She didn't want to retreat to Maupont, which was not the world's gleaming center of art and architecture where she'd dreamed of vital and fulfilling days and evenings.

Back home, her three older brothers ran the furniture shop that her parents had owned. Returning wouldn't be what she wanted, but they'd put a roof over her head and she'd help at the shop. Where sofas and headboards and lamps had ignited in her a fascination with indoor spaces that she longed to make a career of. And studied to do so.

Unfortunately, there was limited opportunity in

Maupont and its surrounding towns. Rarely was there new construction. Small business owners and residents lived modestly and seldom had money for large remodeling jobs. Or even needed interior design. Nothing there would ever give Zoe the chance to really spread her wings, to exercise her potential. She wanted big clients with big projects and big budgets. Paris budgets.

Plus, every road in her hamlet led to a sad memory. The town square where her parents took her and her brothers to play as children and afterward bought them an ice-cream cone. A small bistro where her parents would occasionally go out to dinner on a date night. How her mother would make that extra effort to put on a nice blouse and lipstick.

Or the train station. Zoe especially didn't want to have to regularly see the train station. When they were kids, her father would take them to watch the trains go by. They'd wave through the windows to the passengers, with Zoe always imagining the faraway places they might be going.

Sadly, the train station would instead come to represent the chilling reality that defined the Gaiman family. When Zoe and her brothers were young adults, their mother and father boarded their train to take the trip to Milan that they had been saving for. Little did the four siblings know that they'd never see their parents again. The train derailment that was the top story in all the local news killed their mother and father instantly.

Because almost no one ever moved to or from Maupont, all the townspeople there still looked at Zoe and her brothers with pity. It didn't seem to bother her brothers, or they didn't notice it as much as she did. The bent neck and mashed lips on people's faces that said

I feel sorry for you even if they were talking about the weather.

When her parents were still alive, Zoe had been reluctant to move away from them, even to chase her ambition. They were a close-knit family. Zoe got her university degree and worked on those small local jobs she acquired through shop customers that only served to make her thirst for the more complex ones. After her parents died, she and her brothers got on with things, selling their childhood home and taking over the shop. But eventually, Zoe knew that she either had to try to make her dreams come true or stop having them. There was nothing keeping her in Maupont. Her brothers supported her decision. And so to Paris she came. Now she feared her hopes had come to an end.

Snatching the last piece of toast from Yasmine's plate, Zoe nibbled on it.

Her phone rang. She glanced at its screen. The caller identification was blocked.

"Hello," she answered with curiosity.

"Zoe Gaiman?" The low voice was familiar. "This is Jules Durand. Would you be available to come see the apartment at one o'clock? I thought we might talk over the project again."

"Hello again, Mademoiselle Gaiman," Jules called out as he saw Zoe walking toward him. He'd arranged to meet her in front of the building where he'd soon house his parents.

"Monsieur Durand." She held out her hand for a shake. It was the second time he'd shaken her hand and couldn't avoid noting, as he had last time, its remarkable suppleness.

"Thank you for meeting with me."

"I have to say I was surprised that you called. I assumed you thought our interview fell flat," she said with a chuckle. "You know, *fell* flat?"

A tiny twitch raised the corners of Jules's mouth. "Yes, I know what you were referring to." He'd almost felt her embarrassment by osmosis when she tripped on that broken shoe and became intimately acquainted with his finely woven carpeting. No one would want to meet a prospective employer in that fashion.

"So, may I ask, monsieur, are you still considering me for the job?"

"I'll be honest with you. I was not impressed with anyone I interviewed."

"I see. I was the best of the worst in your estimation?"

"I didn't mean it that way."

"How did you mean it?"

"I…um…" Why was he befuddled around this young woman whose qualifications were less than he'd expect for this project that was of such personal importance? Something about her threw him off-kilter. Seeing her again made him realize just how much. It would probably be a very bad idea to work with someone as distracting as she seemed to be.

Nonetheless, she really was the best of the bunch that he'd interviewed. When he thought about the six applicants he'd met yesterday, Zoe did stand out. Plus, at least she had a bit of experience with accessibility needs. He thought he should meet with her again.

He watched as she turned her attention to the two wood doors painted navy with their bronze doorknockers adorned with depictions of a lion's head. The handles were original to the 1860 construction of the building. Of course, nowadays, a state-of-the-art coding system facilitated entry.

"I think it'd be a challenge for your father to get his wheelchair across this threshold." She pointed to the bottom of the door where there was a sliver of open space before it met raised concrete. "That wasn't visible in the photos yesterday."

"Yes." Jules liked that she was jumping right into the task at hand and had remembered that his father's needs were of primary concern. "My architectural team is working on some options. Let's go inside."

Jules punched an entrance code into the keypad and the door unlocked with a click. He pulled it open to allow Zoe in. As she breezed past him, sunshine caught that untamed jungle of curls atop her head. It was amazing the way the sun decided which spirals to highlight and which to let serve as contrast.

What was he talking about again? He had projects all over the globe, this apartment to finish while his parents were at present drifting the streets of Tel Aviv. He didn't have time to care about the sun's reflection on Zoe's hair.

If he were honest, it wasn't just his parents' whereabouts he had the most trepidation about. It was the prospect of spending so much time with them, of being face-to-face again with the tumult he'd been embroiled in his entire life. Despite Jules's demand that they return to Paris and *grow up*, as he sarcastically phrased it, he was going to have to keep an emotional distance. The commotion and neglect he'd experienced as a child had been kept at bay by his career and his world travels. Put to the test, those scars had only a very thin skin covering them.

Yet, this was something he had to do. The desperation in their voices during phone calls, the phony suave sophisticated pitch in his mother's tone signaled to him that their roving had to come to an end.

Once in the building's foyer with its marble floor, Jules tapped the button to call for the elevator, an old-fashioned cage style that had been added to the building in the early 1900s.

"Your parents will be able to maneuver this?" Zoe asked in reference to the accordion iron door that needed to be slid back in order to enter the not-so-large cabin of the elevator itself.

"The wheelchair will easily fit and there's room for another person or two to stand."

With no wheelchair inside at the moment, Jules was able to keep to one side of the cage with Zoe at the other as the elevator rose. Which was good, because he'd prefer not to stand beside her if he had the option—she might smell good. His eyes had already betrayed him with their inability to resist inspecting her hair in the sun. Now they were locked in battle with his brain that was instructing him not to look at her legs under that pink knee-length dress she was wearing. His mind lost the fight and his eyes pronounced the legs lovely and shapely. To which Jules almost frowned. Why did she have to be so attractive?

Once they reached their stop, Jules opened the cage and showed Zoe to one of the two apartments on the fourth floor. With another private code, he opened the front door.

"This doorway has enough width, and no threshold," she observed.

"Thank you. I'll let my architects know you concur," he said snidely, though she didn't react. He supposed she was trying to impress him.

The small entry area into the apartment led in one direction to the kitchen and the other to the dining and living room, which they stepped into. The floor-to-ceiling windows with double-glass doors that faced the street, as was typical in so many Paris apartments, would let in lots of fresh air. "Nice light," Zoe commented.

She looked behind her and then retraced her steps. Jules could tell she was imagining the entrance from the point of view of someone in a wheelchair.

"There are no hard turns from the front door to here," Jules confirmed.

"True. I'm thinking about a small shelf beside the front door at wheelchair height—" she gestured to the short wall in the entry area "—with some attractive bowls or baskets where your father could lay down his personal belongings or purchases when he came in. Maybe a painting or a mirror above it."

"Perhaps you'd like to make some notes," he suggested. "Did you bring a tablet or laptop?"

"I don't need to just yet. I'll remember."

"I expect every conversation we have to be documented."

"Yes, Monsieur Durand. I was just tossing out a thought."

"I'd like any ideas to be presented to me in writing or through images and cataloged with a filing scheme so that we might refer to it later."

"Every idea." Zoe gave him a side-eye as if she was

surprised by his request. Was she or was she not a professional? Her licensing and education seemed to be in order when Karim had researched her background.

Jules supposed she hadn't worked for a big corporation before and had a more casual relationship with clients who only needed a room redecorated and so on. It was frustrating that he couldn't find an applicant better suited to how he did business. He assumed that if he hired Zoe, she would want to do a good job and he could train her to use his methods. Although, as soon as he had that thought, it occurred to him that Zoe Gaiman didn't seem like someone who did things other people's way.

"I'm feeling Chopin in here," she said, making swirls with both wrists and outstretched fingers to animate. He noticed how tiny and fine-boned her hands were. "Soothing piano chords for soft hours after your parents have been out and about all day."

Case in point about methods. "May I ask, what does *feeling* Chopin mean with regard to the task? Neither of my parents play the piano."

"No, not literally. It's a mood."

"Is it?"

"Would you like me to write it down?"

He almost laughed. Was this young woman so opinionated with everyone she met, or just him?

The last thing Jules needed in his life was someone to argue with. He'd grown up in one long yelling match. He could remember crying in his bedroom as a little boy because his parents were so combative with each other. It was traumatic.

No, Jules worked conventionally and systematically and he expected all of his employees to do the same. If there was a dispute or disagreement, it was to be handled by one of his project managers. Although, in this case, he was to be the project manager as he would be directing the job given his personal interest in it.

Zoe must have sensed that he wasn't pleased with her little snip because she got that same glassy-eyed look as she'd had in his office when he dismissed her from the interview. Like she was about to cry.

Oh, women! Jules shook his head a little. One minute Zoe was bossy, the next emotional. After growing up in the mayhem of his parents, which was largely triggered by his mother's malcontent, he knew that he had a skewed view of women. He had wanted to believe that most women were not like his mother, full of acrimony and temper. Yet, he hadn't been able to prove his theory.

There'd been no one in his life he'd seen model a healthy relationship. When his parents weren't tearing each other down, they had a dull resignation toward one another. As if they both felt they were stuck in a trap, that there was no other choice. Neither had the guts to leave for good or put any effort into making things better. Agathe did her disappearing act but always returned. She donned a mask to the outside world and could masquerade as an extrovert, one who was apparently at present throwing herself at young taxi drivers in Tel Aviv. Hugo now had his wheelchair to hide in and blame.

Jules had no other relatives or people around him to set a positive example. And the women he'd subconsciously chosen during his university years and in his early twenties were dramatic and needy. It was what he knew. Once he gained success in his career, the opportunists began to descend on him, all sorts of women who would slowly reveal themselves to be only after what Jules could give them.

It seemed absolutely clear that women and Jules weren't a match.

He certainly had normal human desires. So, he developed a three-date rule. Which was serving him well. He could date a woman, but no more than three times lest he or she start to think any kind of connection was developing.

Jules was free to have the company of a female for dinner or drinks or recreation, even followed by physical intimacy should they both want it. He was allowed to repeat up to two additional dates with that same woman. After that, he cut things off, blaming his busy schedule if he liked her enough to explain why he wouldn't be calling again. His system worked like clockwork. He couldn't think of a single time he'd been tempted to break his rule. Zoe Gaiman's sassy and sexy mouth was of no concern to him in that regard. Coupling was not on Jules Durand's schedule.

"Do you think your parents will be doing a lot of entertaining?" Zoe asked Jules as they continued to survey the apartment.

Impress him with something, her brain screamed.

She'd already irritated him by commenting on something his architects were taking care of. Then she let out a little jibe about his rigid approach to work. That led to an awkward silence, which had been blowing like a breeze through the room for an uncomfortable number of minutes.

"I doubt it," Jules stated matter-of-factly. "Why do you ask?"

Hmm. Whenever Jules mentioned his parents, Zoe noticed a change of timbre in his voice. Like he was talking about people he didn't really know, other than that they were aging and his father was wheelchair-bound. Zoe wasn't sure what to make of that.

Don't voice your every thought like you always do, she counseled herself.

While Jules Durand was obviously a difficult man to deal with, Zoe needed to get this job. A reference from him could open doors for her. Her career could really take off if she got this right. The apartment was glorious—it had all the classic Parisian touches with the double-door windows and brass doorknobs. She would adore working on it, and others like it. Maybe she could *yes* him into thinking she agreed with everything he said and then do things her way after all. She'd do such a good job for him, he'd never notice. Although, clearly, Jules was not a man who missed anything.

"I was just wondering about what size the dining table should be, whether it would be frequently used for seating more than your parents. When *we* choose it—" she emphasized the word *we* as if she'd already gotten the job "—we could go with an oval or round shape for safety, no pointy corners. And we could order a couple of the chairs on casters so they'd be easy to roll out of the way if your father wanted to pull his wheelchair up to the table."

"That's worth a consideration."

"I'll make a note of it," she chipped, which earned her a funny double take from Jules, those creases between his eyebrows becoming very pronounced.

Standing next to Jules Durand, coupled with the afternoon sun creating a pleasant temperature, Zoe had a freeze-frame moment. If she got this project, her vision for herself could be coming to pass. By contrast, if she didn't, she'd have no choice but to return to Maupont, at least for a while. Maybe she could save up money and try Paris again in a couple of years. The mere thought of that brought a slump to her shoulders. She didn't want to return to her hometown with her tail between her legs, a failure, and nothing but harrowing memories to look forward to when she got back.

"Is something wrong?"

Zoe subtly dabbed the outer corner of each eye to wipe away the drops that those very thoughts had produced. "No, not at all, Monsieur Durand. This apartment just really speaks to me about the beauty of Paris."

A wistful smile crossed Jules's lips, the first one Zoe had seen. She almost keeled over, and this time it would have been *his* fault.

If Jules Durand was handsome with his serious professional face on, the way he looked while smiling was something from another dimension. Laugh lines defined his mouth, which opened enough to display perfectly straight white teeth. Yasmine had told her she'd seen his photo on those silly Paris's-Most-Eligible-Bachelors lists the gossip magazines did. It was not hard to see why, although she did wonder why this gorgeous and powerful man was still a bachelor.

Zoe didn't exactly know what caused him to grin, but she'd walk ten miles in the snow to be able to do it again. *Make Jules smile.* She'd add that to the list he wanted her to keep.

"I appreciate your enthusiasm," he said by way of explanation. "It is a marvelous property, without question."

They smiled at each other for a minute that Zoe

would swear had nothing to do with architecture. Thinking quickly to prolong the positive interaction she asked, "Can we have a look at the kitchen?"

"Please." He gestured for her to enter ahead of him. He pulled his phone from his pocket.

Standing side by side, surveying the kitchen, Zoe became immediately aware of being in such close proximity to him. He produced an inner heat that she instantly liked and felt drawn to. With him being so much taller, she could have nestled her face against his shoulder and, strangely, thought about doing just that.

Instead, she had to not only discreetly turn her head, but also crane it upward to get a glance of his face in profile while he tapped into his phone. As he concentrated on what he was doing, his strength and potency was tangible. It made the skin prickle all over her body. She'd never been in the presence of someone who controlled the oxygen in a room.

Once she was able to pull her eyes away from him, she saw that the built-in kitchen cabinetry was complete, but doors were not affixed and there was no backsplash as yet.

"I'm thinking of this for the cabinet." He showed her what he'd cued up on his phone. French country wood with intricate arch carvings. She didn't like them. The apartment had enough ornate touches. She'd choose something simpler for the kitchen. But she didn't say anything. Yet.

The client was always right, so the saying went. That was until she could sneak in her own ideas and make clients think they had thought of them on their own.

Just get the job, she advised herself again.

A cream-colored granite countertop was in, which

delineated the kitchen from the front entry area. An idea came to mind that she couldn't resist pitching, even though it would mean redoing work that was finished. "Why don't we lower that granite counter and take the cabinets out from underneath?" Again using *we*. "There is plenty of other storage elsewhere and that would leave open space so that your father could just wheel right up under it. We'll make it a breakfast bar with a chair of the same height for your mother."

"Go on."

"I know it would require a change order and add some cost. But you don't have the cabinet doors yet so at least those won't be wasted."

Jules's heavy eyebrows hitched up.

So, Monsieur Durand was going to be surprised every time she had a good idea? That was fine with Zoe. She had lots of them.

"I can picture that. I'd like to see the specifications. In writing."

"Also, if we go with a style that's less fuss..." Zoe stopped herself again. She wasn't going to tell him that she didn't like the cabinet-door style he'd chosen. There was time for that later. He seemed to be responding favorably to the suggestions she was making for his father's special needs. She should stick with that for the time being. "I'd also like to shorten the length of the counter so that your parents have more room to pass through. And if the stone is cut properly, that extra piece of countertop can be salvaged to create the entry shelf I was talking about."

Jules looked at his watch that Zoe assessed clearly cost more than the salary she made last year. Was she losing his attention?

"I've got an appointment in ninety minutes. Followed by two more. I need to get some lunch."

"Oh," she stuttered after his abrupt change of topic. "I'd love to talk more about the project sometime."

"Yes. We'll have lunch and discuss it further. Was there something unclear about that?"

"Only that when you said you needed to get lunch, I thought you meant… Never mind, Monsieur Durand."

"Why don't you call me Jules?"

"And I'm Zoe."

"Yes. I know."

"I mean, call me Zoe."

"Your name."

Why were they back having so many miscommunications after they had just jived a few seconds ago about the countertop? She didn't understand the way he thought. Although she had the sense that she'd like to.

During the elevator ride down, Zoe observed everything she could about the building's structure. On the street, she followed Jules a few doors down to a bistro he knew. She was thrilled at the moment. Like something from a movie, she was in Paris with a dashing billionaire. It almost wasn't real. They took seats at one of the small tables outside in the fresh air. Everyone who walked by seemed so chic as they went about their business. French women really did knot their scarves a certain way and beard stubble on men never looked better.

When the waiter presented them with menus, Zoe had a moment's panic. She didn't want to assume that because Jules was wealthy he was going to buy her lunch, as he hadn't expressly said so. With her dwindling bank account, she'd need to mind what she ordered.

"Two glasses of the Domaine du Candulon Sauvignon Blanc," Jules ordered before the waiter left. Then asked her, "Is that all right?"

She didn't want to tell him that she'd had so little work she needed to conserve her money. A glass of wine couldn't cost that much, could it? Except that when she found on the menu which vintage he'd ordered, she was wrong.

"I'll take a garden salad with grilled chicken. Would you like the same?" he asked Zoe when the waiter returned. "I'll buy lunch, of course."

Zoe wondered if she was blushing. At how utterly mesmerizing that famous real-estate tycoon Jules Durand was telling her that he'd buy her lunch!

But she wasn't going to bat her eyelashes and let him choose what she'd eat. "No, thank you. I'll have the forest ham and creamed butter on a baguette."

"Really?"

"What do you mean?"

"I prefer a lunch of lean protein and vegetables. That nourishes me for the afternoon."

Another difference between them. Zoe ate anything that was put in front of her and had a special love for the baked goods of Paris.

It shouldn't surprise her that Jules was rigid about his lunch, just as he seemed to be with everything else. Zoe wondered what, if anything, made this man cut loose. Did he have a wild side? Something about the possibility of that rumbled low down in her belly.

She gobbled the first half of her sandwich when it arrived, causing Jules to smirk a bit.

"Were you starving?" he commented on her dedication to her lunch.

ANDREA BOLTER   47

"It's just so delish. Do you want a bite?"

"I don't eat bread early in the day. The carbs slow me down."

She shrugged and took another humongous bite of her sandwich. There was no bread o'clock in her regime. "So I'm guessing you won't want to order dessert?"

Jules ate his salad with vigor while fielding messages on his phone. He shook his head. "I've got to take care of this right now. If you'll pardon me."

"Go ahead," she said, still chomping enthusiastically at her sandwich's salty richness. Should she be pretending she had urgent business to attend to on *her* phone, as well?

"Karim," he spoke into the phone, "set up a meeting for me with Kowalczyk. Today."

After issuing five different sets of instructions to Karim, Jules finally put down the phone and sipped his wine. He made an assessment of Zoe, as if he were sizing her up. "I have a full schedule, and a number of projects that have presented challenges in addition to moving my parents into the apartment. Therefore, I can't spend any more time interviewing for an interior designer. Zoe Gaiman, you have just gotten the job. Effective immediately."

CHAPTER THREE

JULES SIPPED HIS green breakfast drink while gazing out his office window at the morning sky. He and Karim had just finished their morning meeting, the newly in-person chat as opposed to the daily teleconferences they'd been having with Jules checking in from the four corners of the world. There was a lot on Jules's mind, with properties in various states of flux from Kyoto to Morocco to Perth that all needed his review. Yet, he found himself staring out into the distance, longing for something, not knowing what.

"Mother," Jules answered with a tap to his earpiece when his phone's buzz identified the caller. He girded himself before asking the inevitable. "Where are you?"

"Still in Tel Aviv, darling. We met a fabulous French couple last night. Two gentlemen who own inns up and down the Loire Valley. I spent the evening dancing with Gaspard and Louis, while your father sat and drank."

Jules pursed his lips. How like his mother to be critical of his father who, obviously, wasn't the type to be out on the dance floor in his wheelchair.

He could hear over the phone that Agathe was wearing her disguise again, like she was genuinely attacking every day with gusto. He could hear the reedy thinness in her voice, as if she were trying to convince herself as much as she was him.

"At your ages…"

"Oh, heavens, Jules," she cut him off, "you sound like an old fuddy-duddy. When was the last time *you* were out dancing all night?" Ah, so Agathe also had managed a dig at her son.

But with a shrug that no one saw, Jules tried to think of a time he'd stayed out dancing. Never. That was the answer. He did not spend his evenings carousing. Early to bed and early to rise was more his routine. He couldn't say it was fun, but it made sense for his life.

"To what purpose do I owe this delightful update?"

"We're a bit short on funds."

Jules scowled. Not really about the money, which he had plenty of. But his mother's frivolous attitude irked him. "This is the last time. There are plane tickets to Paris already purchased in your names. I've hired a designer for the apartment and unless you want to leave all the decisions to us, you'd better get here." That wasn't much of a threat to her and Jules knew it. She wouldn't care, might not even notice, what style of cabinet door was in the kitchen or the fabric of an armchair.

Agathe was no domestic maven. She always thought she married beneath her and said so at every opportunity, even though her family was of the same working class as Hugo's. They met while he was tending a bar at a local brasserie in the Paris suburb where they both lived. Agathe and some other girls from the neighborhood happened to wander in one night. When Agathe told the story in retrospect, she'd say she was attracted to what she called Hugo's *sad* eyes. The same eyes Jules inherited, according to his mother. Hugo and Agathe began to date and before long she found herself pregnant. Their wedding was held three months before Jules was born.

He remembered as a young boy that his mother spent her days on time-wasting activities like watching television and pouring her first glass of wine before lunchtime, never embracing motherhood or embarking on a career. And Hugo drifted from one job to another, ornery and short-tempered perhaps due to unresolved issues about his own relentlessly critical father.

Jules grew up in a household filled with mood swings that felt like arduous climbs up a steep mountain followed by sharp drops down, wherein the trek began again. And again and again. His parents' fighting might have begun over something as trivial as Hugo leaving his coat on a chair instead of hanging it up. Then the bickering would escalate over several days' time, culminating in his mother packing her olive green luggage and leaving, claiming she'd never return. Jules lost track of how many times it happened, but at least a dozen.

By his teenage years, he was no longer rattled by the abandonment he'd endured as a younger boy, when he'd stick his head out his bedroom window to watch his mother storm down the street away from their dingy apartment, yanking on the handle of the suitcase tottering behind her on its worn-out wheels.

Hugo barely looked up from his newspaper when she left or when she returned. Jules never found an ally in his father. The most Hugo would manage during his wife's absences was to bring home a few groceries at night and sign his son's school forms. There'd never been any commiseration with his father over his mother's behavior.

Jules had his first job by thirteen years old, sweeping the sidewalk for any shopkeeper who would pay him for the task. When he was twenty years old, during his university years, Jules had saved enough money to buy a ramshackle apartment in a downtrodden area. He cleaned it up, leased it and began to learn the ins and outs of being a property owner.

"Toda raba."

Agathe must have thought she was being cute by thanking Jules in Hebrew for agreeing to send money.

He ended the call and returned to scrutinizing the sky. It was a cloudy morning in Paris but the weather forecast predicted it clearing later in the day when he'd be meeting Zoe. The thought of seeing her again brought a smile to his face, which was welcome after he'd just been irritated by his mother. Zoe's orange curls. The petite willowy body that had zigzagged through the crowded boulevard yesterday with snakelike flexibility. The ideas for the apartment that she was so sure and confident about. She'd had some worthy suggestions. That she was full of enthusiasm peaked Jules's interest.

As unlikely and unexpected as it was, something about Zoe had gotten under his skin. He'd thought about her before he'd fallen asleep last night and again first thing when he woke up. He'd even checked his watch a couple of times already, eager for their afternoon appointment. Which was absurd. He kept people at a tidy distance aided by the fact that they were often intimidated by his wealth and position. He served nicely as his own barrier.

Daydreaming about seeing a woman again was not how Jules played the game.

By the time he'd finished having lunch with Zoe

yesterday, he had too much else on his mind to continue looking for a designer and decided to give her the project. Lest his new hire think she'd be given free rein on the apartment, Jules planned to show Zoe some of his other properties in Paris. To make clear what he liked. While he appreciated that she spoke up about her thoughts, he'd make sure that by the end of the day Zoe understood that all final decisions were to be his.

Despite his affirmations about who was in charge, when he saw Zoe coming up from the metro station later that afternoon, Jules felt a lurch in his gut. She was so pretty with her bare legs under a full floral skirt worn with a low-cut midnight blue top. As she got closer, he noticed the freckles that dotted her face were not the only ones on her body. Her collarbone and exposed décolleté were adorned with more of the pigmentation marks that he found oddly charming. For a minute, he found himself almost angry with her for being so lovely. Women didn't sidetrack him, and he was determined to keep it that way. What sorcery was this one carrying up her bright blue sleeve?

"Zoe."

"Jules."

He gestured to the building a few steps away. "Built in 1901. I want you to see an interior design we did in one of the apartments. The tenants are at work and have allowed us to let ourselves in."

She commented once they had entered, "No elevator?"

"No, in this particular building one hadn't been put in over the years, and we couldn't do the structural changes it would have required."

"So it's not suitable for elderly people."

"No, but we've never had any problems leasing it. The stairs are good exercise."

Zoe followed Jules up the steps and by the third floor she was huffing for breath.

"Would you mind slowing down a minute?"

Jules sneered to himself, his face not visible to Zoe behind him. He had indeed been bounding up the stairs. Was he trying to impress her with his physical prowess? So unlike him.

They entered the apartment. It was another well-preserved example of historic Paris interiors.

"Oh, so you went very traditional here?" Zoe commented at first glance.

"Yes, we chose the Tiffany lamps and the rug has details woven in Chinese silk."

"Do you lease all of your properties already furnished?"

"No, just as often they're empty. But here in Paris, our clients tend to be of a standing that utilize the full services we can offer. Expense is rarely a consideration."

"And they choose the design themes?"

"What are you implying?"

"Nothing." Her voice rose an octave. "You've got red walls, gold draperies, the large wood-framed sofas with embroidered cushions."

"I take it you don't like it?"

"Only that I gravitate to more comfortable styles. It's just my personal preference. Again, my opinion, but I think there's opportunity to highlight the period pieces without dominating the whole room in this sort of bordello style."

"Bordello! I'll have you know these fine antiques took a year to locate and cost ten times what it would have to simply recreate the pieces. We used university documentation for authenticity."

For as many times as he'd thought about Zoe in the past twenty-four hours, he seemed to have forgotten that while there was something extremely appealing about her, she was exasperating, as well. Jules did not surround himself with uninhibited people who voiced every thought they had. Squabbling was the last thing he wanted to do with employees, and saw to it that he never did.

Oh, no. His parents were evidence that life was too short to be spent arguing, even for the Zoes of the world who found discourse to be some type of sport. So, it was with a jaw tensed shut that he continued to glare at her, trying to remind himself that her personality didn't matter. As soon as the apartment for his parents was done, she'd be out of his world forever.

"No disrespect intended. I'm sure your tenants love their surroundings. I was just thinking out loud. Isn't an exchange of brainstorming exciting?" she asked in earnest. "You wouldn't have hired me if you wanted someone who would agree with you all of the time."

"And I expect you not to make me regret my decision."

Jules massaged the divots between his eyebrows and began the diaphragmatic breathing a podcaster had been explaining through his earbuds on his morning run earlier.

"Do you have brothers and sisters?" Zoe asked. Was she trying to change the subject?

"No. Why?"

"Only that I grew up battling with three older brothers. Let's just say that confrontation is something I'm quite used to."

So was Jules, but for all the wrong reasons.

Therein lay the difference. Zoe understood arguing as something organic and useful. Jules's parents fought in a way that belittled the other and had no end goal.

Zoe was right, though. Arguing over a bordello— *ha*—lamp did not mean anyone was leaving or being hurt. It was just heated conversation. Jules didn't know why Zoe pushed those buttons in him. Or perhaps it was the apprehension of spending more time with his parents, who hadn't evolved in their thirty-four years together but hadn't parted, either. In their own weird way, they were still very much a couple. Agathe no longer had it in her to leave Hugo's side. But fighting was simply their way, their cycle. Jules had long ago decided it wasn't going to be his. Hence, his three-date rule to be sure he didn't accidentally hope for a different outcome.

As they left the apartment, Zoe swept passed him and he got a whiff of what smelled like coconut shampoo. Without realizing it, his head bent toward the scent as if to follow it through the doorway. He quickly righted himself, shocked by his own actions. Zoe was making him *feel* things. Which was frustrating and baffling because Jules Durand had gotten as far as he had in life by shutting down feelings. At all cost. How high would the price get?

"I don't understand him at all," Zoe exclaimed to Yasmine as they sat cross-legged on their small sofa while watching a cooking show on television. "In one moment he's nice to talk to and then in the next he gets holier than thou."

She reached over for one of the strawberries in the

bowl on the coffee table in front of them. After several hours spent with Jules looking at a few of his luxury properties around town, they'd parted company. He offered to have his driver give her a ride home but she opted for the metro, knowing that she also wanted to pick up some food on the way. She and Yasmine nibbled on the berries, the chicken and loaf of bread she'd brought home. They'd eat the leftovers tomorrow.

The TV chef was shelling a lobster with her impressive knife skills.

"Well, he gave you the job, didn't he?"

"Theoretically. Although he makes me nervous that I could blow it just as easily with one wrong turn."

"Don't make one, then."

Yasmine was right. Zoe needed to keep tabs on her freewheeling style. There was no money left to keep hope churning if she lost this job.

The meeting had gotten off to a rocky start when she likened that first apartment to a house of ill repute. But it was so over the top she'd just blurted out her opinion. Censoring herself didn't come naturally.

"That's probably why he's at the top of his field," Yasmine continued. "By doing things his way."

"How he talks about design choices is driving me crazy. This color matches with that building material, which mathematically coordinates with a certain number of chairs. It all makes perfect sense but there's something so flat about all of his computer software and texture charts."

"At work, we have designers who come into the shop with specifications like that. They want a sofa in blue velvet shade number such and such, and bigger than x but smaller than y. Then just as many come in not certain what they're after but they know it when they see it."

"Right, so I'm the latter, he's the former."

"Just because you're not a high-tech planner like he is doesn't mean he won't be happy with the outcome."

Zoe broke off a piece of the country bread and stuffed it in her mouth. The center was chewy and moist with an airy crumb that made her mouth do a happy dance in response. The chef on TV tossed a large knob of butter into a sizzling skillet.

Zoe thought back to the lunch she'd had with Jules when he told her he didn't eat bread at certain times of the day. While she certainly didn't begrudge anyone healthy eating habits that worked for them, this was Paris! Where even the simplest bread was elevated to an art form. How could he resist the smells and tastes that beckoned to passersby from the storefronts at every turn?

Once again, it was systems and discipline that defined this man's life.

"He can be so annoying."

"Oh, so you're attracted to him! That explains everything."

"What?"

"He wouldn't peeve you if you weren't into him."

"I'm not *into* him." What a silly term that was! "I'm *into* keeping the job and staying in Paris."

"Okay, I'm just saying there's a twinkle in your eyes when you talk about him."

"There is not!"

"Suit yourself," Yasmine said and then wedged a too-big strawberry into her mouth. They both laughed.

On TV, the chef swirled the butter until it was brown and then gently eased the lobster pieces into the pan.

Even if she did find Jules alluring, an elegant billionaire like him wasn't going to be interested in the frizzy-haired little designer he half regretted hiring. For starters.

The second reason for any contemplation of Jules's appeal being ludicrous was that Zoe was never going to get involved with a man. She was never going to love. Nope. That was already decided. The edict signed and certified. Because if there was one thing Zoe had learned the hard way, it was that to love meant to accept the possibility of loss. And Zoe couldn't afford to lose anymore. As it was, the bits and pieces of her heart were barely being held together. She might be willing to take a risk on a paint color, but not with her love.

The phone call she would never forget replayed in her mind.

It hadn't been but an hour earlier when Zoe and her brothers had accompanied their parents to the train station to see them off for their long-planned trip to Milan. Zoe's mother had dressed nicely for travel, an expression of her excitement about the journey to a fashionable city.

Zoe would forever remember the burgundy-colored pantsuit with a patterned blouse underneath that her mother wore. Her long hair was held back with a pretty barrette. She had even convinced their father to sport his black leather jacket and dress jeans so that they looked like a smart couple on the go. Zoe and her brothers had presented their mother with a nosegay as a bon voyage.

At twenty-three, Zoe had long finished growing and

was clearly the short one of the family, taking after her maternal grandmother who had been barely five feet tall and had the same unique red hair. Her three brothers towered above her as they all gave hugs to their departing parents.

After getting on the train, her mother had made sure to blow kisses to her children as they pulled out of the station. They were to be gone for ten days. No one could have guessed that these four siblings waving on the platform would never see their parents again.

Afterward, back at the furniture store, Zoe retreated to the office to do some bookkeeping while her brothers manned the sales floor. When the phone next to her rang, she casually picked it up, assuming it was a potential customer inquiring about an item. Instead, the caller identified himself as a police officer, and from his subdued tone Zoe knew instantly that something was wrong.

Her ears listened but they could barely hear. With each word uttered, the voice on the other end of the line sounded farther and farther away.

Train derailment... Fifty-seven dead... No survivors... Sincerest condolences... Counselor to come by...

What followed was a blur of days upon days of neighbors bringing over soups and casseroles and cakes that had no taste. Coffee was no different than water, midnight was not distinguished from dawn. Relatives Zoe hardly knew descended from both within and outside of France, sharing their sets of remembrances. Psychologists and social workers spoke in the hushed and modulated pitches they no doubt received training for, designed to calm the listener but which struck Zoe as forced and artificial. The questions never ceased about what was going to happen next, to Zoe and her brothers, to the store, to the house they'd grown up in.

There were the tears that wouldn't stop. Like a re-circulating fountain, for as many as erupted from Zoe's eyes, there were still more behind those waiting to spray forward. She'd hardly believed she could cry that much without dehydrating all the liquid in her body.

As the weeks went by, the visitors and stringy meat stews stopped arriving. The spring of tears eventually lost some of its force. It erupted every day, but the flow wasn't as strong and didn't last as long.

What replaced it was something small but heavy that sat on top of Zoe's rib cage and never moved from its spot. It reminded her that her small body couldn't house a second souvenir of bereavement like the one she carried. She'd never ask it to. Yet, the potential for loss was all around. When Zoe caught herself caring too much about anything, that little spot pinged and sent a subtle vibration through her body. A warning sign she relied on.

So whether or not she was fascinated, and pinged, by Jules Durand was a moot point. Obviously, a fling with her boss, and yes his attractiveness was indisput-able, would be a very bad move. And anything more serious was out of the question for her. Not to mention that she had no cause whatsoever to think that he was interested in her.

There was absolutely no reason to keep replaying the moment at that second property they'd visited today, the attic apartment with the steel-framed skylights. It was an innocent gesture of chivalry, the way he placed his hand on her lower back to usher her through a doorway. That it sent a wicked shiver up her spine, snapping her shoulders to arch sharply, didn't mean anything at all. Nothing at all.

It simply wasn't important that she still had the sensation of his large hand on that exact spot, imprinted like a tattoo. When he'd whispered, *Come this way*, he'd meant nothing by it other than to guide her into the room. But his low voice had been so close to her ear it reverberated for the rest of their time together.

Why was she still thinking about that interlude?

Come this way.

Dish completed, the TV chef placed the pieces of lobster onto a serving plate and drizzled the brown butter on top. She then sprinkled on toasted breadcrumbs and chopped parsley, declaring that the most important ingredient in any recipe was quality.

"*What* is that smile about?" Yasmine probed. Were Zoe's thoughts visible on her face?

She stuffed another strawberry into her mouth.

"It doesn't have to be modern, but it should be sleek!" Zoe's voice was becoming a bit sharp as she and Jules disagreed in front of the cabinet door options at the kitchen furnishings shop. "I still say that looks too village cozy. From what it sounds like with your parents' constant travel, I'm sure your mother likes things simple."

"You've never even met my mother."

Jules remembered the kitchen in the dark apartment he grew up in as being plain, with no particular decorative choices. Just as Agathe had no specialties as a cook. Much of what Jules grew up eating was premade food or picnic items.

Nonetheless, he liked what he liked and thought

the more traditional French country style might add a homey feel. Even if his mother didn't care, at least it could look inviting.

Whereas Zoe favored lacquered lightwood doors without any beveling and brushed nickel hardware. "The tone of the wood is warm," she pressed. "I think that will give you what you're after."

"The client is always right," he quipped with what he knew was a cheeky grin. Zoe rolled her eyes in exasperation. That made Jules chuckle. He nudged it further, "Am I correct?"

Zoe narrowed her eyes like she was regarding him with suspicion.

Which goaded him on. He repeated, "Yes?"

She pointed to a space-age turquoise cabinet door made of plastic. "How about these?" She held her smile for a second to pretend she was serious.

Her determination was admirable, if somewhat exhausting. In spite of himself, he'd become tolerant of their friendly dissimilarities about design. They were on their third disagreement of the day, Jules noted as he looked at his watch. At this rate, the apartment should be completed in five years.

"I'm getting hungry. You don't want me to cross over into *hangry*, do you?" He used the made-up word that signified the shift to anger that lack of nourishment could bring.

"That's because all you drink in the morning is that green goopy concoction. You need something that will stick to your ribs."

"What do you suggest, a pastry?"

"Yes, covered in chocolate," she said with an emphatic nod of her head that made a couple of her curls bounce in the process. Jules still marveled that Zoe's hair had a life of its own, falling this way or that as she moved. "I'm kidding but, you know, an egg, a bowl of warm grains, a yogurt. In short, breakfast."

Words were coming forth from her but he couldn't get his attention off Zoe's mouth as it moved. As a matter of fact, studying her lips was a far more intriguing notion than thinking about the dinner party he had to attend tonight. A large development group from Kenya was visiting the Durand Properties headquarters and meeting with a number of Jules's key people in preparation for a large project in Nairobi.

All the negotiations had been already hammered out, and the evening was just to fete the developers by inviting some of Paris's high society for a dinner cruise on the Seine. Jules loathed that part of his job, the socializing and small talk. He should have invited a date to help chitchat and swat away the gold diggers in glittery dresses who always found their way to him at these things.

Jules had a few female acquaintances in Paris, professionals in the industry who were married to their careers. They knew that Jules wasn't open to anything but occasional companionship. In truth, though, while they were polished and accomplished women, nothing about any of them had sparked his fancy. It felt like too much of a chore to reach out.

After Zoe had checked out the shelving in the back of the store, she walked toward him, biting her bottom lip. Out of nowhere, the desire came over him to nibble on that supple lip himself rather than let her continue do it. How might that plumpness feel between his teeth?

As she moved toward him in what he experienced as

slow motion, he imagined himself sitting at his work desk. And Zoe entering his office, this time not flat on her face from the oopsie she'd taken at their first interview.

Instead, she'd be wearing the close-fitting stretchy black dress she had on today that showcased her compact curves and played nicely against the pale skin of her legs. A devil's deliciousness overtook him when he thought of her striding toward his desk. Toward him. To him. For him. He envisioned himself with a press of a button activating the mechanism that would close all the blinds in his office, giving him total privacy.

The hairs on his arms stood up at the possibility. While Zoe sauntered her way across the office, he'd push his chair back from the desk and beckon her close. His hands would take hold of her hips and pull her to him. With a firm grasp, he'd lift one of her legs around him and then the other, raising her until she sat facing him on his lap, straddling him in his office chair. He'd enjoy exploring the soft flesh in his hands, his pelvis thrusting up to meet her.

As a matter of fact, he fought to prevent his hips from making any motion now, in the middle of the kitchen furnishings shop. Covering his mouth with one hand, he continued to watch Zoe browse in the store, his eyelids at half-mast in his arousal.

In his fantasy, once he'd spent a long leisurely time with the parts of her that were, literally, in reach, his palms would move up her spine. One vertebrae at a time up to the back of her neck where his fingers could finally tangle into that glorious head of hair that he was sure would be as silky and springy as it looked.

Grabbing a fistful of those locks, he'd tilt her head so

that her face was close to his and he'd start feathering light kisses down onto that pretty mouth. That wouldn't hold him for long before he'd begin nibbling little pieces of those lips between his teeth, until he heard a moan of pleasure escape from her throat. At which point he'd kiss her with his full mouth.

Over and over. And over.

Until her lips were red and swollen.

Until…

"Are we getting lunch, or what?" Zoe bounced over, startling Jules with her zest. He felt a strain against the zipper of his pants and casually buttoned his suit jacket to conceal any evidence. She said, "You look hungry."

"I am." She didn't know how right she was.

He instantly refocused, shocked at where his mind had been. He couldn't remember the last time craving had come over him like that. Musing about women wasn't on his agenda. Or never had been, anyway.

It wasn't that Zoe affected him in a way that no other woman had, he told himself. He simply wasn't used to spending so much time with anyone. This was temporary. The apartment would be finished soon enough, his parents would move in and bewitching Zoe would be out of his life. That would be in everyone's best interest.

"I've got a business function to go to tonight," Jules said after he guided them out of the shop and to a market café where they could grab a light bite to hold him until evening. Again, he began to dread being *on* for a boat full of people he barely knew. With no stop for reconsideration, the words fell out. "It's a dinner cruise on the Seine. Are you busy this evening? Would you come with me?"

CHAPTER FOUR

"YOU'RE ASKING ME to come with you for a cruise on the Seine?"

Zoe seemed surprised after Jules invited her to the evening with the Kenyan developers so that he wouldn't have to go alone.

"If you'd like. Some notable people in the Parisian property world will be there, too. You might even make some contacts that could be useful."

There. Jules reframed the invitation in his mind so that it made sense to him. Zoe might benefit from the networking. And he'd be more at ease socializing if he had an ally on his arm. He most definitely did not invite Zoe because he'd just spent a solid fifteen minutes at the kitchen furnishings shop fantasizing about kissing her.

"Oh, well, thank you."

"Are you free?"

"Yep. Nothing on my calendar."

Then why was she hesitating?

"So…is that a yes?"

"I'd be happy to. Only, um…"

"What is it?"

"It's only that…what's the dress code for something like that?"

Ah, so that's what was bothering her.

"I suppose the women will be in cocktail dresses. Do you have something suitable?" Jules could tell that while Zoe had a stylish sort of look, her clothes were clearly inexpensive.

"Maybe you'd rather ask someone else," Zoe said as she busied herself collecting the empty containers on the table from their quick lunch. Gathering everything into her hands, she deposited them in a nearby bin. "You know, more from *your* world."

"*My* world?" Jules knew what she meant but couldn't help mulling it over. Yes, he was acquainted with some of the wealthiest and most prominent residents in Paris. But he enjoyed their company no more or less than he did a construction worker he might talk with in Finland or a waiter in Bangkok.

Jules didn't get close to people. Any people. It didn't matter whether they were rich or poor, buyer or seller, old or young, male or female. Although he knew what Zoe meant about his world, it wasn't one he felt any particular place in. After a boy spends his childhood watching his mother pull a suitcase down the street and finds no ally in his father, he learns to go it alone. Jules only trusted Jules.

Strangely, Zoe, tidying up in her budget but body-hugging black dress, was the first woman he'd ever met that caused him to think twice about all the self-protective decisions he'd made. Not that it mattered, though. She was an employee, not a romantic interest. He didn't have those. She was going to accompany him to a business event. That didn't even count in his three-date policy. Plus, there would never be a second or third to make him question his rules.

"Is the issue that you don't have anything to wear?"

"I don't really go to many dressy occasions."

Jules didn't know a thing about Zoe's background. Whether she'd grown up with money, a childhood that was happy or sad. He knew that she was eager to get the apartment job with him. She'd mentioned that she had a roommate, which made him guess that she leased wherever she lived rather than owned.

"If it's all right with you, I'll buy you a dress. We can pop over to a shop on the Champs-élysées right now."

She whipped her head toward his. "*Pop over* to the Champs-élysées?"

"Yes." He texted Karim to find him a recommendation for a boutique.

"Oh, ho-hum, my boss suggested we *pop* over to buy me a cocktail dress."

A belly laugh erupted in him at her intonation. Jules couldn't remember the last time he'd laughed so heartily. He took her hand and said with a tug, "You're quite something, Zoe Gaiman. Come on, I have other things to finish today besides outfitting you for the evening."

On one of the hallowed side streets off the Champs-élysées, in the area where some of the world's most famous fashion designers had their headquarters, Jules's driver pulled to the curb so that he and Zoe could exit the car. People wearing the latest looks walked this way and that, some chic and on trend, others swallowed up by outrageous clothes that seemed fit only for a runway or featured in a glossy magazine. Tourists intermingled with people whose careers were made or broken on these streets. Fashion was in the air.

In the front windows of their destination, a few dresses hung on bald white mannequins. While they were evening gowns, and more formal than was called for the dinner cruise, Jules approved of their understated style. He wanted Zoe to join him for the evening as one of his tasteful young designers, not some flashy arm candy who was going to steal the limelight from his visiting developers.

Karim had phoned the shop ahead of their arrival so they were greeted by the owner as soon as they entered. A tall thin woman with white hair, probably in her sixties, and dressed in a flowing beige outfit introduced herself as Fia.

"Monsieur Durand, it's an honor. How may I assist you today?"

"This is my colleague Zoe. We have a corporate affair tonight, a dinner cruise on the Seine. Cocktail attire. It may get cold so let's include a wrap. Also shoes and accessories."

"Of course." Fia studied Zoe, no doubt estimating her dress size but also her coloring, height and whatever else she could gleam about her. "May I present some options?"

"Please."

Jules noted the airy boutique. Racks of clothes lined the walls with quite a bit of open space in the center save for a couple of tables where small handbags and sunglasses were displayed. It was a well-curated collection, which Jules appreciated, as there was no time to sort through dozens of possibilities.

"Can I offer either of you a glass of champagne?"

"Sure," Zoe wasted no time in answering.

"If you have a mineral water, that would be nice," Jules added.

Fia gestured for them to sit on the sloping black

leather and chrome armchairs that were clustered around a white round coffee table. A previously unseen assistant brought the drinks and then disappeared.

Zoe let out a whistle, then mashed her lips when Fia returned with three dresses. She said, "Let's give these a try. If you'll follow me."

While the ladies departed to, presumably, a fitting room, Jules handled the messages that had come in. There was a voice mail from his father's doctor confirming upcoming appointments. Jules hoped his parents would return to Paris in time to keep them. After a fall down a flight of stairs three years ago broke his back and claimed his mobility, Jules insisted that Hugo be proactive about other facets of his health.

He tagged the message for the file he'd already created called Parents Medical. Others were designated for Residential, Financial and Governmental. If he ran his parents' lives like he ran his business, perhaps he could circumvent the unruly atmosphere he'd grown up in. It was a tall order, but organization was the only thing that kept Jules secure.

Which is why sitting in this dress shop in the middle of the workday suddenly seemed crazy. But not nearly as crazy as that prolonged fantasy he'd had about kissing Zoe and, worse still, the fact that it kept replaying it in his mind. He needed to divert his brain to more productive matters should any future thoughts of that nature arrive.

That affirmation was ticking across his frontal lobe when Fia and Zoe returned to the showroom. Fia had put her in a sleeveless dark orange structural-type dress that had cutouts in the fabric where some sort of mesh was sewn in to cover the flesh that was bared. One slash was across the shoulder while another revealed part of her rib cage, and another still opened across the thighs. It was a creative, fashionable design.

The dark orange color mimicked Zoe's magical hair in a complementary way. But those mesh patches were too sexy. Jules didn't need the extra battle he'd have all evening, trying to avert his eyes from the glimpses of her body under the open weave. Couldn't they just choose something simple and basic?

Fia kept a respectable distance so they could discuss the dress privately.

"I love it," Zoe exclaimed as she approached him, holding her arms outstretched to show off for him.

Her enthusiasm made him want to laugh, like she was the proverbial kid in a candy store.

"Not right for the evening," he stuttered. Deciding not to reveal anything else, he tossed out, "Besides, your exposed bits would get cold. Next."

"Oh, so I don't even get a say," she exclaimed with a cute mock indignation.

"That's right," Jules replied with a wink. A wink! When was the last time he had winked at someone? Never? What was Zoe doing to him?

She returned to the dressing area and then reappeared in the simplest of black dresses with long sleeves and an embroidered band around the high neckline. Boring. Perfect.

"Distinguished," Jules ventured.

"For someone's grandmother." Zoe wrinkled her nose, pivoted and marched back to the fitting room.

While he waited, Jules approved the project schedule for the Miami development. He had several appointments before the cruise and needed to prepare. Hoping the third dress would be the charm, he watched Zoe saunter toward him.

This one was a draped number in a silver metallic fabric. She looked like she was wearing a superhero cape.

"Hate," they both said in unison.

"So, where does that leave us?" He rubbed his palms together. They could continue this all day, actually not an unpleasant proposition, but it really wasn't that important. "Let's get the black…"

"The orange one," Zoe interrupted.

"Fine." Jules could surely control his response to a dress, couldn't he? He waved Fia over and told her of the decision. "Can we outfit her with a coat, shoes, bag… What else do we need?"

"Might I suggest a hair and makeup stylist? Zoe, perhaps you'd like to wear your hair ironed straight for the evening," Fia proposed.

"No, she wouldn't." Both women snapped their heads to glare at him. He must have sounded like an overbearing brute. But he was so enamored of Zoe's nature-defying curly locks that he couldn't stand the idea of them being tamed. Knowing there was nothing he could say to downplay his overreaction, he went for a simple, "I've got to get going. Are we finished here?"

Afterward, he had his driver drop Zoe off at the home decor showroom she wanted to visit for work on the apartment. Jules watched from the car window as she walked away. Shopping had been far more enjoyable than it should have been. Why was doing the most mundane things with Zoe so charged with enthusiasm and vitality? Arguing over a lamp, admiring a purse, seeing her eat a sandwich. As she strode farther away, he inexplicably wished she would turn around and come right back, reclaiming her place beside him in the car. Only when she was finally completely out of view through the window did Jules instruct his driver to pull away.

After the makeup and hair stylist left her apartment, Zoe slipped into the orange cocktail dress and brown stilettos. As long as she lived, she'd never forget the cracked heel that sent her, literally, falling into Jules Durand's office. Navigating a metro station, with all its stairs, in tonight's shoes, would be a recipe for disaster. Fortunately, Jules had sent a car.

Her roommate, Yasmine, wasn't at home so Zoe texted her a quick selfie for feedback on her ensemble. But it was just Zoe and her bedroom mirror to decide if everything was in place. Jules had said a number of influential VIPs in the Paris real-estate scene were going to be in attendance. Making a good impression could lead to jobs that would allow her to stay in Paris. Plus, Zoe had to admit, she wanted to look good for Jules. After all, he'd financed her look from top to bottom.

She couldn't stop thinking about how brusque he'd been when the shop owner, Fia, suggested Zoe straighten her hair for the evening. She had no idea why that had mattered to him but his response had been vehement. And territorial in a way that was shocking at first but very, very, very sexy upon reflection. That take-charge dominance. She'd never met anyone who had such authority over every situation he encountered. Jules's way of doing things was what had brought him success and fortune. He was right to have utter confidence in it.

As to her hair, the stylist had applied several products that accentuated her curls and groomed them into a more tidy pile. A long narrow clip that echoed the slash designs in her dress brought everything together. Reaching for the off-white swing coat that went with the outfit, she reflected on how Jules had made a point to tell Fia that Zoe needed a wrap for the cruise. Yes, it was more evidence of Jules Durand being on top of every little detail, but there was also something so caring about the thought. He didn't want her to get cold. He'd make a fine caregiver to his parents when they returned to Paris.

She had a moment's wonder about his personal life. How many women had Jules made sure didn't suffer an evening chill? She knew from the eligible bachelor lists that he wasn't married and assumed that if there was a woman currently in his life she'd be the one teetering on stilettos to accompany him.

After the driver helped Zoe into the car, she watched out the window as she was whisked through the Paris dusk. It was impossible to say at what hour the city was more beautiful. To her eyes, it was stunning every minute of the day or night. The early evening skies cast a ruddiness on the boulevards as the sun receded. The car crossed over a bridge and Zoe could see the boats of various size and type that were already on the river, most of them with open-air decks and glass-enclosed cabins. Jules's cruise would be joining them shortly.

"You look marvelous," Jules said, as he appeared curbside to usher Zoe out of the car, he and his driver having obviously communicated about her arrival.

"You do, too," she blurted, and then regretted it. But looking good he was, in another exceptional suit. This one was slim-cut and navy, with a navy shirt and a brown tie to match the brown oxford shoes. Everything cut from the finest cloth, constructed with impeccable workmanship and fit to perfection, of course. Zoe couldn't help but take in his personal panache. As she'd thought during every encounter with him, Jules was the most striking man she'd ever seen. It took effort not to swoon.

"Shall we?" They walked a short distance to the dock. He crooked his arm for her to take as he helped her onto the boat's gangway at the riverbank, with the Eiffel Tower as their background. Zoe could hardly believe she was participating in a moment this glamorous. It was like something out of a magazine, dressed-up people on the Seine for an evening ride.

"A pleasure to meet you," Zoe found herself saying over and over again as Jules introduced her to his developers and their significant others who mulled around on the top deck of the luxury boat. The men wore suits and tuxedos while women, both old and young, were dazzling in their fashions and jewels. Bartenders serviced two stations, pouring drinks on order, while waiters passed pretty Kir Royales, champagne tinged with blackcurrant crème de cassis that gave it a red tint. Jules reached for two of the flutes from the silver tray and handed one to Zoe. Hors d'oeuvres were passed on trays lined with flowers and votive candles.

Seating clusters of wooden chairs covered in white sailcloth invited relaxation, but most of the guests stood congregating to keep watch on the Eiffel Tower as the boat pulled away. The captain spoke through a loudspeaker system, pointing out landmarks without sounding too touristy. Audio devices were handed to those who requested translation into other languages.

A thrill overtook Zoe as they passed by the sights, from Les Invalides to the Musée d'Orsay and the Louvre. It was as if she were seeing the Paris attractions for the first time, which she was from the river's view.

She'd be lying if she didn't admit that the moment was profoundly romantic. Paris really was the city for lovers. It wasn't hard to imagine that Jules was her real-life man. That between boat cruises and Michelin-star restaurants and fabulous parties, there was something real and genuine between them. That at the end of every evening out, one more glitzy and exciting than the next, they'd return home to the plush bed they shared where they'd lie down on fine linens to make love and sleep in each other's arms.

Carried away with her musing about Jules really being hers, she barely noticed that she had moved closer to him as he chatted with a guest. Until she distinctly felt her shoulder against his solid arm. She quickly snapped out of it, collected her wits and checked herself and everything around her.

"Do I look like I don't fit in?" Zoe asked Jules once the gentleman he was speaking with stepped away.

"Why do you ask?"

She gestured discreetly with her head at three women across the deck, two blondes and one a brunette, dressed flawlessly from head to toe, all three of their heads craned toward Zoe and Jules. "They keep staring at me."

Jules tipped his flute of Kir Royale in their direction as recognition. "It's not you they're staring at. It's me."

"Why?"

"Haven't you heard? I'm one of Paris's most eligible bachelors," he snickered.

"Oh, my gosh," Zoe quipped. "They're looking at you like you're prey."

"And it feels that way. Nothing but power plays and drama with the likes of them. They're real-estate agents who make plenty of money. But nothing is ever enough. Vultures, indeed."

Zoe decided to inquire on what she'd been curious about. "I take it you're not in a relationship, or else why would you have asked me to accompany you tonight?"

"Most definitely not. Not now and not ever. Three dates is my limit."

He went on to explain about his three-date policy, which was quite sensible, yet the words stung Zoe's face. It wasn't as if she had thought Jules invited her tonight because he was interested in her personally. She knew better than that. He was Jules bloody Durand! He would never date the spunky little designer from Nowhereville.

Not to mention the fact that she was not open to dating, either. There was no way she was ever going to take a chance on adding to the pain that she toted like a piece of luggage. No, thank you. She'd go it alone.

So, she fully understood Jules's three-date rule because it was similar to her body's ping alert system. The little siren that reliably told her she needed to pull back from something that was making her feel.

Yet, somehow, the finality of Jules's declaration about dating was harsh.

The cruise passed by people who sat along the river-banks eating from picnic baskets, and the sweethearts kissing and waving to the passengers in the boats. Jules shook his head as if in disbelief. "I forget how extraordinary Paris can be."

"I've wanted to live here for as long as I can remember."

"Where were you born?"

Zoe described her hometown of Maupont. "The air is clean. People look out for each other. But it's a relic. A couple of historic churches that draw some tourists. Otherwise, nothing ever happens there."

"Did you visit Paris when you were growing up?"

"Just once as a child. And then I came with friends as a teenager. My parents had the furniture shop to run and weren't much for the city. Until they planned their dream trip to Milan when my brothers and I were older and could manage the store for them."

"Did they enjoy Milan?"

"They never got there."

"Why?"

"Look at that." Zoe pointed to a building with an especially elaborate facade. Now was not the time to have brought up her parents. She'd tell Jules about them sometime. But she couldn't take a chance of getting emotional tonight in front of his guests.

"So you decided you wanted to move here..." Jules sensed that she was withholding something and was savvy enough to allow her a segue.

"This probably sounds crazy but it all started with a sofa." Zoe was grateful to move on to another conversation. "A metal-framed sofa covered in a bluish-gray textural tweed modeled after a style from the 1950s."

"You came to Paris on a sofa?" Had he picked up that she was on the verge of tears and was trying to lighten the mood? "Most people use a car. An airplane. Or a magic carpet."

Zoe smiled and peered up to meet his dark eyes that

glistened in the night sky, as reflective as the moon's illumination on the river. What stunning eyes they were. Observant and thoughtful, yet that spark of playfulness that was dying to pry free was evident in their center. His eyes might be one of her favorite sights in Paris, although she'd keep that vote to herself.

"I loved that one sofa we had at the shop so much. My dad put it in the window display with a complementary side table and lamp. It was what got me interested in interior design. I used to imagine creating a whole room, a whole mood around that one piece. To me, it was elegance and flair. I conjured up a lifestyle that went with that sofa. I was devastated when someone bought it."

"And that led you to Paris?"

"In a way, yes. Once I knew I was going to be a designer, I wanted to be in the capital of style. Where else?"

"So wishes do come true."

Zoe let that dangle. She didn't want to tell Jules that it was only because he'd given her the apartment job that she had any hope of staying at all. That she hadn't been able to break in to the industry in a sustainable way. And that she was one paycheck away from having to go back to the furniture shop where, when last she visited, her brothers had put an ugly dining table and chairs in the shop window instead of another beautiful sofa like the one that had inspired her so.

"Now, of course, I want to visit all of the great sights in the world. Where's your favorite place?"

He contemplated the question for a long time. Zoe wondered why his answer was delayed. "Here," he finally stated. "I've been away for so long I'd forgotten how there's something breathtaking around every corner."

The captain announced that dinner was being served. As the guests chose one of the four staircases leading down to the glass-enclosed dining cabin, Zoe was stunned at the lavish appointments. Gleaming polished wood and shiny brass met her at every turn. The dining tables were dressed in iridescent tan-colored tablecloths and white flower centerpieces twinkled with taper candles arranged at different heights. Charger plates at each diner's place were made of copper and the several forks and spoons at every setting promised a multi-course meal. Likewise, four different-shaped stem glasses per guest meant that the wine had been carefully chosen.

Jules sat Zoe beside him and, after the waiters poured the first wine, stood to offer a welcoming toast that earned him polite applause. The starter course was served, smoked salmon atop a cucumber and artichoke confit, drizzled with herbed cream. It was delicious. Over the dulcet improvisations of the jazz trio that entertained from a small stage, Zoe did a respectable job of hobnobbing with the spouse of one of the developers seated on her other side. She wanted advice on where to shop for purses in Paris. Certain that the stately older woman was not interested in the bargain stores she and Yasmine combed through, Zoe mentioned some high-end shops she'd heard of.

The captain told guests that they were passing under the Pont Neuf—the new bridge. Which was a misnomer, he explained, as it was actually the oldest standing bridge in Paris. He pointed out that the structure had twelve arches and, in addition to the equestrian sculpture of Henry IV, almost four hundred stone mascarons adorning the cornices, their grotesque faces originally thought to keep away evil spirits.

During the entrée, which was a choice of spice-rubbed lamb and Greek quinoa or tart Provençal with wild mushrooms, the captain gave a history of Notre Dame. The cheese course followed, a lovely composition on the plate of three varieties and thick triangles of dense grainy bread dotted with dried fruits. After the boat reached its designated turnaround, the captain continued, relaying information about the Place de la Concorde, the Grand Palais and other sights along the route. As stunning as all those locations had been to Zoe when she'd stood in front of them on the street, under the night sky in the boat's glass cabin she felt like she was in a magical place that only existed in dreams. Not to mention the handsome vision sitting beside her.

Dessert and liqueurs were served buffet-style on the upper deck to better enjoy the final landmarks of their cruise. When Jules left Zoe's side to pay special attention to important clients, she had a pleasant conversation with a couple of Paris developers about utilizing small urban spaces. She hoped she'd made some sort of positive impression so that if she were ever to contact them via a reference from Jules, they would remember her.

After the individual almond cakes with apricot buttercream filling topped with warm dark chocolate sauce, the captain began his return to the riverbank. Just as the clock struck eleven o'clock, the boat faced the Eiffel Tower, obviously perfectly timed for the passengers to best see the hourly light display. With the drama that only Paris could incite, the entire tower began to flicker with golden sparkles, shimmering, glittering and as brilliant as a multi-faceted diamond. It was a spectacle to astonish even the most cynical. Like a woman who throws her shoulders back and owns her beauty, the proud monument twinkled. Everyone on the boat, on the banks and, indeed, from views all over the city halted in time to gape.

Jules stood beside her. Zoe almost thought she could see the reflection of the tower in his eyes. With some sort of knowing smile, they acknowledged that they were sharing a moment. Together.

"So we've found something we agree on," Jules said as he led Zoe off the cruise boat toward his waiting car.

"Paris," she answered with a sweeping arm gesture.

His driver opened the passenger door and they both slid into the back seat.

"Are you tired?" Jules asked her.

"Not too tired. Why?"

"Shall I show you some buildings I love?"

"Do you own them?"

"You may be surprised to know that I don't actually own all of Paris."

"Well, there are always career goals."

Jules shook his head at his cheeky companion.

He rattled off a few landmarks to his driver who dutifully nodded.

First was the Musée d'Orsay, which they'd caught a look at from the boat. Jules lowered the car window and pointed to it. "This is my absolute favorite building in Paris."

"Yes, it's amazing."

"It was originally a railway station done in the beaux arts style."

"Talk about renovating and repurposing."

"Apparently, in the 1970s it was scheduled to be torn down before someone came up with the plan to turn it into a museum."

"Thank goodness." Zoe pointed at the building. "How the structural metalwork integrates with all of the ornate details. Incredible."

"When the barrel-vaulted main space and the train platforms were sectioned off with walls inside to hang the art, museum critics hated it at first. They said the building competed with the art."

Jules was enjoying this, chatting with Zoe. Even though he moved fast and accomplished more in a day than others did in a week, a part of him was numb. There was a switch that had never been flipped to the On position. Zoe was in sharp contrast. Her enthusiasm for everything in front of her was such a breath of fresh air, so alive and unfamiliar.

He wondered why Zoe's parents never boarded that train to Milan. She'd changed the subject when he'd asked about it on the cruise. Did they split up? As a child, he often wished his own parents would, although he was never sure which one of them would be worse to live with. Navigating around both of them had taken up so much of his focus from as far back as he could remember.

When his mother was away on her pointless desertions, young Jules would look out the sooty window of their dank apartment on its ugly and nondescript block as if he were searching for her. Or stare, mystified, at the dirty laundry and unmade beds. He worried it was his fault that she'd left, clearly she wasn't a nurturer like most mothers were. He resented his father's inability to put a halt to the situation, or to comfort his son, and considered him weak. Jules never felt loved and never learned to love in return.

He became an angry young man and channeled his rage into becoming hyper-structured, planning out everything from what he was going to wear the next day to how he was going to acquire his next property. He found an ironic comfort in controlling what he could in his life.

After amassing extreme wealth, he started to send money to his parents. He knew it was wrong, that the child should not have to support the mother and father, but he did it anyway as his fortunes grew to the point that the expense had no impact. Blood was blood and he considered it his duty.

When he thought of it all right now, sitting next to vivacious Zoe while they drove through the storied boulevards of the city center, Jules felt a hole in his gut. He was becoming painfully aware that with his chosen lifestyle, he was missing out. That he wasn't leading a full existence, one that deserved some happiness and heart song.

There had to be more than being a parent to parents who were never even good to him, with whom he shared no pleasant memories to coast along on. And more than making billions of euros, most of which sat compounding into more money in never-used investment accounts. The word *enjoyment* had never been on Jules's radar. He was starting to see that if he didn't lighten up inside, darkness was going to cloud over him.

"Now, this works. But how?" Zoe marveled as they approached Centre Pompidou in the Fourth Arrondissement, which snatched his attention back to the present. The high-tech architecture, with its inside-out style where the mechanical systems such as plumbing and electrical were exposed and color-coded on the outside of the building, was one of a kind.

"Some people think it's a monstrosity," he said of the structure that was part art museum, part library and part event space.

"It's a fine line between what works and what doesn't when you do modern on a big scale like this."

"Good point."

Jules was so glad he'd brought Zoe along on the cruise tonight. It was meeting her that had set his mind to wondering about pleasure and about dark shadows. About sharing sunsets. He'd never met a woman he could imagine having a longstanding companionship with, and would never take the chance of ending up in a rancorous union like his parents. Yet, he had to admit the idea of attachment to someone had been crossing his mind, especially in the past few days.

With his face still close to Zoe's as she peered out the window at the Pompidou, he chose instead to study those orange ringlets of her hair up close. They really were a miracle from another realm. Her brain must be filled with some magical powers.

Entranced by a woman's curl?

Yes, Jules definitely needed to bring some diversion into his life. Maybe he should take up tennis.

And what about that dress? He cut his eyes to steal a glimpse of the slash across the shoulder. The design was clever in how it revealed the shapeliness of her décolleté. The hair, the sexy dress, Zoe's peppy companionship at dinner, it had all worn him down. The hour was late and Zoe's seductiveness overtook him. Craving became need before he could restrain it.

As the driver pulled away from the Centre, Zoe turned her head toward Jules, presumably to say something.

Which he didn't allow because before she could speak he leaned over, brought his lips to hers and delivered a long melting kiss. It was better than anything he could think of that had happened in the recent or distant past.

CHAPTER FIVE

In an instant, Zoe was pulled under into a warm and pleasant universe where all she could feel or taste was Jules. While she was able to discern that only their lips were actually touching, it felt like he was all over her, like together they'd merged into one being and she didn't know where she began and he ended. Then, abruptly, he blurted, "My apologies," and jerked backward to his proper place in the car's back seat.

He'd previously instructed his driver to take them to Montmartre, where Jules was intending to show her some notable buildings. With a hand flat against his chest, he emphasized, "How utterly inappropriate. I don't know what I was thinking. I'm so very sorry."

Zoe stilled. Not a cell of her was able to move. She was stuck in an unnatural position, half turned toward the man who had just laid his lips on hers, yet her hips were twisted the opposite direction from looking out the window. Although her brain told her to straighten out, her body wouldn't cooperate.

She'd been hoping to make another clever comment about the architecture Jules was showing her but the words weren't able to make it out because he had covered her mouth with his. His lips had obviously delivered some type of paralyzing potion because all she could do was look into his eyes, perhaps waiting for an explanation. And listening to that constant ping inside her chest confirmed that her emotions were exposed for the plucking. Like plump, ripe fruit from a tree.

"That's okay-ay," she stuttered, adding an extra syllable to her simple words. Zoe most definitely wasn't *okay-ay* but she felt she should say something. Jules looked so pained, the furrows between his eyebrows digging in.

Jules Durand, *the* Jules Durand, had just kissed her, and making billion-euro real-estate transactions was not all he was good at. His kiss was masterful. He slid effortlessly from paper soft to insistent to erotic. From sweet to spicy, nice to naughty. It went on for hours. Okay, it was minutes but it felt like a week. As he finally, abruptly, stopped, Zoe wanted more, internally screaming with a tormenting deficit when he yanked himself away. It was a kiss she would remember forever. And despite his apologies, the kiss hadn't been forced upon her, if that was something he was worried about. No, as soon as the sensation of his firm lips against hers registered, she'd sunk into it, and gave as much as she'd received.

"I promise you that will never happen again," Jules rasped, clearing his throat. "You know I don't generally act in the spur of the moment."

"Of course," she replied in a monotone. "Neither do I." Obviously, it had been a mistake. They were colleagues and nothing more.

So why did his promise that kissing her would never happen again smart like a rejection? Maybe because Zoe hadn't been on a date in a long time and Jules's touch ignited dormant embers of desire that had been smoldering deep within her. She'd had a few dates in Maupont, but no one had ever activated the ping. Not like he just had.

She had to remind herself that even if Jules had any interest in her, which he didn't beyond as an employee, no serious liaisons were in her future. Funny that around him she kept forgetting that decision.

Uneasiness permeated the car like a strange scent as the driver continued whisking them down one street and then another, traffic eased in the late hour. Jules sat up very straight and kept his eyes forward. Zoe finally summoned the ability to adjust her body to face the front, as well.

After a few minutes of traveling in silence, Jules used his matter-of-fact voice. "Zoe, I've noticed that you are a very…what's the word…enthusiastic person."

"Is that a polite criticism of some sort?" She resisted the urge to swivel her head toward him so they spoke with all four eyes focused out the car's front window, privacy glass still separating them from the driver.

"Not at all. I admire it. I've been calculating that the amount I work coupled with what will be my new responsibilities with my parents won't leave a lot of time for…recreation?"

"You mean work and life balance?"

"Work and life balance, yes. Work has been my life. There is no balance."

"So, what do you do for fun?"

"Fun?" He scratched his chin as he contemplated the question.

"To relax, to decompress."

"That was fun."

"What was fun?"

"Kissing you just now. That was fun."

Yeah, she'd have to agree. It was birthday-party-with-triple-layer-cake-and-candles fun locking her lips with his.

"Maybe you should try it more often," she suggested tentatively, not sure if she was being flirted with.

"No. Most definitely not. Kissing, romance, all of that is not an option. What do you think of golf?"

After Jules had his driver take Zoe home, she slipped the key through the lock to her apartment door.

"Yowza!" Yasmine exclaimed as she came in. Zoe's roommate wore red pajamas covered with a graphic design of puppies and she ate ice cream with a spoon straight from a large container. "You look ah-may-zing."

Zoe kicked off the stilettoes that had been killing her but were worth it for the stature they'd given her. After falling into Jules's office, she'd vowed never to wear heels again but the dress Jules had bought her for the cruise seemed to beg for the extra zhoosh. She'd sent a selfie earlier but apparently the ensemble was even better in person. Yasmine leered at her from top to bottom.

"The dress worked, that's for sure," Zoe reported. "I felt good in it and you should have seen me hobnobbing with Parisian VIPs! I can really talk the talk. Maybe something will come of it."

"What about you and the billionaire?"

She wasn't sure that she should tell anyone, even her roommate, about Jules's accidental kiss that would have no meaning tomorrow. Zoe did not want to be quizzed on every move made by Jules Durand.

"There's nothing going on there. He's my boss. I didn't embarrass him so I'd call the evening a success."

"Were there other attractive men there?" Yasmine snooped before spooning a big bite of ice cream into her mouth.

There might have been handsome men in attendance, after all this was Paris and there was the Kenyan contingent as well, but Zoe had failed to notice. She'd barely taken her eyes off Jules other than to exchange pleasantries with the guests he'd introduced her to. They'd been side by side most of the evening. In fact, when he stepped away to greet someone or get a drink, she'd felt the empty space beside her whoosh like a chill.

Zoe took a spoon from the drawer and dug into Yasmine's ice cream for a scoop. She asked wistfully before tasting it, "Have you noticed that this city is a really romantic place?"

"Are you kidding me?" Yasmine scrunched up her face.

"Sometimes I wish I was in love with more than just sofas and paint colors."

"Aha, so maybe a certain someone is making you rethink your no-serious-relationship rule."

"Hardly," Zoe answered too quickly. "In fact, he himself has a *three-date* rule, which I think is very sensible." She explained Jules's rubric.

"Uh-huh," Yasmine replied unconvincingly and licked her spoon.

Zoe had a full day's work on the apartment ahead of her in the morning, so she changed out of the dinner outfit, washed up and went straight to bed. Except that sleep didn't come. Lying on her back and staring up at a shadow across the ceiling, both her body and her brain still vibrated.

Darn Jules for planting that delicious kiss on her! Because even though he retracted it with his words, Zoe's lips were still reacting. How, in a blink, his kiss had sent sensations up and down her like hot blood that coursed through veins parched from drought.

His kiss kindled mental portraits of lovers in Paris. Walking arm in arm, appreciating every bridge over the shimmering river. Strolling down a boulevard, gesturing and animated in their conversations, so much to tell each other. Those same lovers admiring a painting, sharing a pastry, kissing in a dusty bookshop, unable to contain their need for one another. And once they got home, exploring the depths of their desire until the raw sunlight of dawn opened the skies.

Why did Jules have to kiss her? Now Zoe couldn't stop whirling about possibilities she'd forbidden herself to dwell on. She knew herself enough to be sure that she was a person who loved wholly and fully, so casual encounters were never going to do for her. It was all or nothing, and she'd chosen the latter. It wasn't helpful to have her resolve put to the test.

In that way, she was a little like Jules. Having a plan. To protect her heart. And in a strange fashion, tonight he had behaved like her. His kiss was on impulse. Had he thought about it, he certainly wouldn't have done it. Instinct propelled him to her. Instinct was what Zoe usually relied on. What was happening?

That. That was fun.

Jules's earlier statement resonated between her ears.

She scolded his words inside her head to be quiet and to let her fall asleep. Instead, the voice got louder.

Kissing you was fun.

Fun. What a stupid word Jules had used, he reflected during his morning run. He was a thirty-four-year-old billionaire. Obviously, he didn't get this far this quickly in life by having fun. Children in a playground had fun. Frivolous party girls in tiny dresses at nightclubs had fun. Carefree heirs to fortunes lolled about on yachts having fun. Jules worked. Thought. Worked some more.

As was his usual routine for his run, he briskly walked for two blocks in order to loosen up and get his circulation flowing. For the next two, he brought himself to a light jog. Then he stopped for his sequence of muscle stretches to prevent injury. Once he was fully warmed up, he increased his speed to a run and, before long, his breathing rose to meet the exertion.

Images flickered through his mind. Morning runs in the sweltering humidity of Manila. Through the bite of a Chicago winter's dawn. Along beaches in Maui. Yes, he had business in every corner of the earth. He'd toured historic sights. Tasted unique foods. Participated in extreme sports. Been awed by natural wonders. Had interludes with beautiful women. But had he found any *fun*?

This was where he'd take his morning run now. Under the unmistakably Paris skies. These streets were to be his permanent neighborhood, his home turf. Was there *fun* around any of these city corners? What exactly was *fun*, anyway?

Kissing Zoe was *fun*. There was no way he could deny that, even though his brain struggled for a more academic understanding of the word. It was an unfortunate accident that he'd now have to correct by never letting it happen again. He'd told her as much when he apologized for acting on a whim. What was it about her that had propelled him to make that move without self-intervention?

Jules rounded another corner. His breath had reached heaving and he welcomed the perspiration. He checked the fitness settings on his watch to make sure his speed and heart rate were in target range.

Zoe was an underling who'd escorted him to a business function. There wasn't anything personal between them. They hadn't even known each other long enough to be called friends. Absolutely nothing could have predicted that he would claim her mouth like that, fixing his lips to hers until they both had to come up for air.

In all honesty, it wasn't entirely unprecedented. There was that steaming hot fantasy about Zoe striding across his office in her black dress and straddling him in his office chair. When he envisioned his hands grabbing onto everything they could reach as their lips collided in a forbidden middle-of-the-work-day merge that would have shocked his employees on the other side of the glass if they knew what was happening behind closed blinds. Were that little daydream to have come to life, he and Zoe would have spent time on his expensive carpeting, and it wouldn't have been because of a broken shoe.

He hadn't given those images a second consideration. Well, maybe, he hadn't given them a fifth. Or was it a fifteenth? In any case, when she asked him in the back seat of the car what he did for pleasure, apparently he'd shown her. A smile crossed his lips at the recollection, and he lifted the bottom of his T-shirt to wipe the sweat from his face as he finished his run.

After showering, he sipped the green drink the housekeeper had left. Reading over some reports for the condo development in Krakow that was frustrating him with budget overages, his mind kept drifting back to Zoe's sweet lips.

Fun.

Kissing her in the car, he'd acted without premeditation. There was another word he'd been contemplating. *Spontaneity.* Something unplanned. Occurrences that had no place in his world and could, by their very nature, only lead to mistakes. Like kissing Zoe, in case he needed any proof. Worse still, he feared that what he was feeling was more than a sexual charge from his encounter with her lovely mouth and his musings on what her body might feel like in his hands. There was a knocking inside of his gut, like some sort of wake-up call.

He was fighting to ignore it.

Jules didn't need anything more to deal with. For so long without a place he had called home, he'd been able to board intercontinental flights and jet away from any longing that might have made its way under his skin. From uncertainties that had started popping up more and more frequently, about connection and priorities. Contemplations he couldn't shut down.

It was harder here. Jules had never been a lover in this city that celebrated them. He'd spent the occasional carnal night or weekend with one of the exotic women he'd met in faraway locales. Superficial encounters that happened between people who would never meet each other again. After which it was easy to say goodbye.

As he knotted his tie and collected his things for work, that increasingly persistent nagging came at him again, telling him that it was no longer enough.

Grabbing his attaché case and other belongings, he stepped out his door, vowing to stop thinking about saying good morning to Zoe—every morning—for the rest of his life.

"I've been invited to Prague with a lovely family I met who are in need of childcare," Agathe's shrill voice pierced through Jules's phone when he and Zoe were at the apartment a few days later. He stepped into the kitchen out of earshot and left Zoe in the living room.

"Oh, good heavens, Mother." He could only imagine what lies she'd told this family to get them to believe she was capable of looking after children.

"It's not as if your father would care if I..." The strength in Agathe's voice faded, as if she herself were tired of her own script. Jules certainly was.

His loud exhale contained particles of disgust. It was as if a recording that they'd both heard a thousand times was playing. "You are not going to Prague."

"I hate him," she squawked feebly.

"Yes, Mother, I know. You always hate him until you don't." Love was ridiculous. The universe was giving him another reminder to steer clear of it. "Stop this nonsense and get on the plane to Paris."

Jules ended the call and returned his attention to Zoe. She had brought some paint samples and brushed one swath of each color onto the wall. While he really didn't know her well, he could tell that she wasn't like his mother with inconsistent mood swings and a general bitterness, as if life owed her something that it wasn't delivering.

What kind of mother would a woman like Zoe be? Yes, the type who takes her kids to the park and then buys them an impromptu ice-cream cone, eliciting more delight than a planned snack would. But would she also know how to put boundaries on that impetuosity, to raise children who learned how to focus on school exams and work diligently toward goals?

Jules had long ago decided that he'd help the population by not bringing more children with unfit parents into the world. After the instability he grew up in, he was convinced he'd go too far in the other direction and be a controlling and regimented father.

Letting the paint dry, next Zoe analyzed the lighting that had been installed in the hallway that led to the bedrooms and bathroom.

"I wonder if we could better mimic natural morning light with some additional overheads here. Since we haven't painted yet, it wouldn't be too big a job to add on. Let me think on that." She sat down cross-legged on the bare floor in the middle of the hallway. She slowly looked around her, panning side to side, then up and down, as if there was some new information to be gleamed. *Feeling it*. Like she was summoning the dead to vote in.

"Are you conducting a séance?"

"No. But that's a great suggestion. Let me consult my tarot cards. And what are your parents' zodiac signs?"

Jules knew she was joking but his call with his mom had stripped him of any sense of humor he might have been able to muster.

"I have lighting analysis software and you can try your ideas with that," he declared.

He knew his tone was harsh. Still sitting on the floor, Zoe glared up at him. One of her corkscrew curls bounced forward on its own volition and covered one eye. She swept it away with the back of her hand defiantly.

Something in Jules wanted to sit down on the hardwood floor next to her. Maybe take off his shoes. Maybe hold Zoe close. Maybe be in the moment and see what happened.

But he didn't do that sort of thing.

Instead, he offered an olive branch. "Can I take you to dinner?"

The cruise on the Seine was date number one. Except it hadn't been a date because it was a business function. The kiss afterward was a freak accident and he'd already apologized for his mistake. The quick lunches they'd grabbed definitely didn't get logged. Tonight would be date number two, only it wouldn't count, either, as they would be discussing the apartment. It was all figured out. There would not be any more physical contact. Although, dinner would bring him dangerously close to date number three, should they need to spend another evening together in the future. If one was counting these things.

"What do you think of the medium-blue paint?" She stood and led him back into the living room.

"It's bold but the room can take it."

"Jules, did you just make a decision based on preference?" This time she got him to crack a smile. "You'll find it shocking to know that I consulted a color-scheme program. Warm colors advancing and cool colors receding and all those *rules* you like so much."

"Aha! What did that lead you to?"

"Well, at first I was thinking that everything needed to be soothing. Perhaps it's a day that your parents are out and about in the intensity of the city. That they need a gentle cocoon to come home to."

"And then?"

"Then I thought that maybe a home with verve and energy was better for globe-trotters. One that was stimulating in its own right. So I came to this." She pointed to the paint swatch on the wall. "A much darker blue than I would have expected to try. With the main decor colors being forest green, rust and khaki. Something about that feels like the colors of travel."

"Colors of travel? There you go *feeling* again."

"Since they've done so much of it."

"Hmm."

From what Zoe knew, his parents' endless journey was enviable, not a rootless search for belonging and contentment that the Durand family apparently knew nothing about.

"You can't deny that you still have to respond to the suggestions a software program lays out. There are still subjective…"

Jules grabbed Zoe's hand and pulled her toward the front door. "Let's go eat and we can see how the paint colors *feel* to me in tomorrow's light."

Jules led them around one corner and then another and then another, which put them on pedestrian-only Rue Montorgueil in the First Arrondissement. Known as an international foodie paradise, the cheese shops, fishmongers, patisseries and restaurants serving food from every corner of the world beckoned.

After much discussion, they chose a bustling Thai restaurant and took two seats side by side at the counter facing the open kitchen. Zoe opened her laptop and called up a lighting placement program to show him the changes she wanted to do.

"Comes in handy, doesn't it?" he teased again about her use of the computer-aided design, raising an eyebrow in a mock-gloating manner that was adorable. She begged herself to stop reminiscing about that kiss the other night, the one he'd promised never to repeat. Yet, she found herself wishing he would.

If only he wasn't sitting so close to her. Shoulder to shoulder, they both occasionally looked up to watch the chefs in front of them flipping noodles over scorching high heat, the finished products lush with jewels of diced meats and colorful vegetables.

Jules's long muscular arm pressed against hers as they huddled over the laptop screen. Her whole being buzzed when she was close to him. And as they dug into their delicious pad Thai, the rich peanut flavor somehow added to the sensuality. It was a combination of sensations that made her almost light-headed, and had the power to make the loud and crowded restaurant fade into the distance of her consciousness. Zoe wanted to lick the sweet sauce from Jules's lips. Wanted to drop into his arms and press herself against his solid chest. Wanted them to hold onto each other like there was no tomorrow. No one on earth had ever made her feel that way. She hoped nobody ever would. It was really too much.

"I'm not a fool," Jules said as they took a stroll after

dinner. "I know that there's an artistic element to what you do. If I didn't appreciate that, I wouldn't need a designer. I'd simply let the computer make all of the decisions."

They approached the nearby Musée du Louvre. Closed for the evening, crowds still mulled about photographing the world's most famous museum under the moon's glow. Originally a castle, with construction that began in the twelfth century, it became a museum in the 1700s. The campus, its enormous main courtyard and the glass-and-steel pyramid that stood at its center, was instantly recognizable.

"You told me you fell in love with design via a sofa. Did you take art history in school?" Jules asked.

"Of course."

"What kind of child were you?"

Zoe gulped. It was still hard for her to discuss anything about her past without missing her parents so much that the anguish threatened to knock her to the ground. "I suppose I was a happy enough kid. As much as you can be with three older brothers."

"Was your parents' furniture shop successful?"

"Define *success*."

"Touché."

"They made a living in a small town where there wasn't much opportunity. They were in love, so I'd define that as succ…" Her lower lip quivered uncontrollably, leaving her unable to complete the sentence.

"What is it?"

Zoe dabbed away the tears that clouded her vision as they got closer to the pyramid. "One of the last things my mother ever said to me before my parents died was that she hoped I'd someday meet someone as wonderful as my father."

"Your parents died? At the same time? Was there an accident?"

She'd forgotten that she hadn't told Jules about her parents' fate and did so now. "One day they were unlocking the shop door in the morning, turning the old-fashioned sign from Closed to Open and then back to Closed at the end of the day. You go through the motions, thinking you've eked out an existence, that you can count on, that you're content." The ping in her chest hurt so much it could have been a knife blade. "And in the next moment they were gone."

"Oh, my gosh," he responded. "That's an unimaginable tragedy."

"Maybe it's what turned me into the adult I am. I've become one of those *seize life* kind of people, but really it's that I have to be because I'm terrified it can all be taken away in a flash."

"So that's why you're not a planner."

"Touché back to you." She looked out to the courtyard. "There's one thing I'm very organized about. My mom was wrong about wanting me to meet the right person. I'm never going to be with a partner."

"Because they might die?"

Zoe was surprised at Jules's bluntness. Although that was something she liked about him, his way of cutting through to the quick of something.

"Yeah. What are the odds of dying at the same time as the love of your life? Pretty low. So that means there's a fifty percent chance of them dying before you."

"This from a person who says she doesn't bring mathematic systems into her life."

At the base of the Louvre Pyramid, they cranked their necks back to take it in from bottom to top, in unabashed awe.

"What about you, with your three-date rule? Talk about structured."

"I witnessed something very different growing up. Chaos. I can't have that in my life."

"So women equal disorder?"

"Something like that. In any case, it's much easier not to take chances."

"We're on the same page about that. You don't go on fourth dates and I don't get close to anyone."

"Bravo for us. We've figured out our own safety nets."

They both laughed into the night, pretending to be so pleased with themselves.

CHAPTER SIX

"AGATHE AND HUGO, this is my associate, Zoe Gaiman," Jules introduced his parents in the lobby of the Juin Hotel, a boutique inn he owned on the Left Bank. The black-painted exterior outside with its silver awning displaying the hotel name led to the smart interior.

The black-and-white-tiled floor complemented the wallpaper with its design of black pineapples, the fruit a historic symbol of hospitality. Jules had been very pleased when this hotel had gone up for sale a couple of years ago and he'd been able to purchase it. It had been in operation for seven decades.

Zoe shook Agathe's limp hand and bent gracefully down to shake Hugo's from his seat in the wheelchair.

"Jules, you didn't tell us you were seeing someone," Agathe exclaimed in her overly dramatic manner. He hadn't seen her theatrics in person for a while and thought she grew sillier and sillier with age.

"I'm not dating anyone, Mother. As I just mentioned, Zoe is my colleague. She's a talented designer who's assisting me in readying the apartment for you."

"Colleague," Agathe repeated with hiked eyebrows. She retrieved a lace handkerchief, as if something from another century, from her small handbag and used it to blow her nose. Hugo's pallor was gray.

Jules was surprisingly relieved to have Zoe come along for the reunion with his parents, especially after he'd told her more about his childhood, more than he'd ever told anyone. He tallied up just how much time he'd been spending with her. Oddly, the realization didn't displease him. He'd felt comfortable asking her to come along for moral support, although he didn't voice that in as many words.

When he refused to send more money to his parents in Tel Aviv and Agathe's scheme to become a Prague nanny had fallen through, he'd finally squeezed them enough financially to the point where they had no choice but to use the plane tickets he'd provided.

It had been six months since he'd last seen them. On a trip west from Dubai, Jules had stopped in Hungary where they were working as models for a painter who was doing a study on older bodies.

Just the sort of thing his mother had spun into a grandiose tale of adventure, the reality was that the artist in question lived in poverty on a barely operational farm and wasn't paying them a salary. They slept on a haystack in a barn and fetched their eggs every morning from underneath a chicken. When Jules arrived, he found them with dirty bare feet and his father exhausted by a persistent dry cough. Not exactly how seniors, one with health issues no less, should be spending their time.

It was then he'd decided that enough was enough, that he'd need to take charge and prevent any more bad decisions. He needed to look out not only for their well-being but also for their safety.

Had he found them happy and taking good care of themselves, he might have been willing to let them continue their endless drifting. After all, they didn't need employment. He could certainly afford to finance their wanderings. But his father was drinking too much and his mother was, as always, belittling and threatening to desert him, even though it had been years since she actually had. She no longer had the adeptness to run away on her own like she had in years past.

"You're coming home where we'll see proper doctors and you'll live as respectable Parisians," Jules had proclaimed at the painter's farmhouse. "I'm not going to receive a phone call from some remote corner of the world to find out you've been eaten by wild animals or have starved to death."

After that endless row in Tel Aviv, the time had finally come. He'd house them at this hotel until the apartment was ready.

"Monsieur Durand, may I show your parents to their suite?" The hotel manager, who wore a suit and tie with a name tag adorning his jacket's lapel, joined the group.

"Thank you, Huy."

Two bellmen appeared to handle the luggage.

"Zoe." Jules placed his hand on the center of her back to escort her toward the elevator. He wasn't expecting his palm to be greeted with the plushness of the baby pink sweater she wore that seemed to promise something even softer underneath. He supposed it was only natural that his mother would have immediately assumed that Zoe was a romantic interest. That the thought wasn't repugnant was a first for him.

"Shall I push the chair for you?" Jules offered to his father.

"Obviously, I can do it myself." A bark of an answer—not unexpected. Resentment that Jules was controlling their fates. Had his father planned for his elder years, perhaps he wouldn't have been reduced to that. Jules noticed how brawny Hugo's biceps had gotten from their labors. His father speedily pushed the wheels of his chair until he had gotten halfway across the lobby ahead of the rest of the party.

Jules had a moment of terror over what he was embarking on. Bringing these people back into his life who were, for all intents and purposes, dreadful parents. Was he trying to stage a do-over? Did he think that if he cared for them now it would somehow right all the wrongs, salve all of the hurts? How much control did he *really* have?

Once they arrived at the suite, Jules asked Huy to send up some sandwiches, fruit and juice. "We'll see the orthopedic doctor next week to have you fully evaluated, Father. When was the last time the two of you had a complete physical examination?"

"While you're at it, get your mother a psychological exam," Hugo snapped.

Agathe pretended not to hear him as she inspected the suite. "So this is what my prison cell will look like," she stated without looking at any of them. Jules had overestimated his mother's interest in not embarrassing him. Obviously, civility in front of Zoe, who she'd never met, was of no matter to her. Had Jules known his parents were going to be *this* badly behaved, he wouldn't have brought her to witness it.

Jules's forehead became very tight. A headache was developing and he considered taking some aspirin. He hissed in Agathe's ear, "It's only temporary, Mother. I suppose my elite hotel that's fully booked year-round doesn't have the charm of a Hungarian haystack, but you might actually enjoy indoor plumbing."

"Agathe, have you seen the view?" Zoe called from the window. Jules's mother joined her. They looked out to a pretty street with apartments across the way, all the windows adorned with flower boxes. "Isn't Paris lovely?"

"I lived here for too long, dear," Agathe exhaled. "I'm underwhelmed by a few peonies in some store-bought dirt."

"Mother, stop being so rude."

"Soon enough, we'll have the apartment ready and then you can truly settle into your new home," Zoe persisted. "I hope you'll like all the choices we made."

She was clearly trying to help, and Jules wanted to kiss her for it.

His headache was turning into a throb.

"My electricians are installing your hallway redesign this morning," Jules informed Zoe during a FaceTime session. He'd been busy with his parents and they hadn't seen each other at the apartment for a few days. But each morning, she'd met with him on a video chat. Zoe had to admit she looked forward to the early call and was always dressed and ready for him at the designated time.

She'd be lying if she said he wasn't on her mind, but the distance was an important reminder that after this job was finished she didn't know how frequently they'd be in contact. "I'd like to show you some sketches I had for the bedroom furniture placement."

"Sketches?"

"Yes, Jules." She took on a jokey tone as, by now, their different working methods were no surprise to each other. "I had some ideas after I met your parents last week."

"What sort of ideas? That we'll need armed guards to keep the troops in line at their residence?"

Zoe watched Jules through the screen. He was sitting tall at his office desk, the view expansive behind him even through the screen on her tablet. Although Zoe couldn't say for sure which was a better vista to gaze upon, Paris's rooftops or Jules Durand in his brown suit, white shirt and red tie.

It was shocking to think that Zoe had become a part of this man's high-flying lifestyle. Seeing him on the screen like she was watching a television show, he sipped his thick green breakfast concoction, sorted through papers on his desk and fired off messages from his computer. He was a master class in multitasking. She couldn't help but admire how much Jules got done in a day.

She'd also come to know another side of him. Although he made a joke about his parents needing military peacekeepers, she could recognize in his face, in his posture, in his voice, that he was under a lot of stress. She even saw vulnerability in those dark brown eyes.

Zoe could hardly blame him after what she'd witnessed when meeting Jules's parents at his hotel. His mother was ungrateful and unpleasant and spoke without any kind of self-filter. Hugo wasn't much better. Jules was short with them, already exhausted by his caretaking mission.

The more she thought about it, the more it bothered

her that neither of them said thank-you to Jules. For their plane fare from Tel Aviv. For the hotel suite and upcoming apartment. For any of it. She didn't know all of what had transpired between them but it was enough to make her want to protect him. It was ironic that she wanted to don a suit of armor to defend the big tall billionaire.

Studying him on the video call, Zoe noticed how the clench in his shoulder blades made him look stiff sitting in his chair. Analyzing his striking face, the divots between his eyebrows were the most sunken she'd ever seen them. She figured he hadn't fully fathomed what he was getting himself into by bringing his parents back until they'd actually arrived.

She went ahead and voiced her concern. "Jules, you look tense. Did you go for your run this morning?"

He'd told her that morning exercise was vital to his routine.

"Yes." He took another sip of his drink.

"And you have a busy day full of conferences and acquisitions?"

For the first time during the conversation, he looked directly into her eyes on the screen in response to her semi-sarcastic comment.

"Yes, Zoe. I run an empire, you know. And tense doesn't even begin to describe it."

He was having a hard morning, and she was starting to get the feeling that he had come to consider her someone he could talk to, someone who had something to offer him. That he could be real around her, which was rare for him. There was definitely something inside of him that he needed to release. More than strain. It was like there was another man inside the accomplished one she watched through the screen, one who fit in Paris.

A man with a big romantic passion he kept under the surface. Maybe the city itself could eventually set that free for him. Or maybe she could.

What was the good in that, though? Helping Jules unlock his inner spirit was no concern of hers one way or another. She was never going to be the person he'd share that emancipation with. No one was. He'd made that clear. Although, if she were being honest, the notion had popped up in her mind more than a few times. Especially after that delicious mistake of a kiss, the one she was still replaying. What would it be like to be his lover, his best friend, his wife?

It was hard to picture the man who swore by his three-date rule and had spent most of his adult life living in the world's sleekest hotels, participating in domestic pleasures. Would he look forward to coming home to her at night? A designated hour that work ended for the evening? When they would prepare a home-cooked meal, eaten cozily at their little round table for two? Would he stop at the store on the way home to buy medicine when she called suffering from a runny nose? Might there be a beloved pup curled up at his feet while they watched a movie on a lazy Sunday?

No, he had people who went to the store for him. His life was too busy for a pet. A cute little table for two? Absurd!

"What do you have over there?" he commented on what he was viewing from his end of the FaceTime chat. "Is that a toolbox on your table?"

She explained that the hammer, nails and whatnot had been left out as she and Yasmine were attempting to repair a bedroom dresser they'd found broken and abandoned on the street. "We always need extra storage," she explained. "We're going to sand it down to the original wood and then stain it."

"That's what you do in your spare time? Restore other people's garbage?"

"We've never tried it before."

Zoe absentmindedly touched his cheek on her tablet's screen, as if she could penetrate through all the way to his skin.

"What happened?" He reacted to her movement. "Why did you just touch your screen?"

Oops! "Oops," she covered quickly, having forgotten how that move would appear at his end of the connection. "I was just wiping a smudge." While she'd been staring at his face as he spoke to her, it was as if his likeness on the screen rather than in person gave her license to let out some of her own bubbling emotions.

She'd become deeply attracted to him. No doubt about it. What she had initially found irritating about him, she'd come to respect. He'd been able to channel his organizational and decision-making skills into a billion-euro corporation, in spite of an upbringing that offered no encouragement. What he was willing to do for his parents, out of duty and not because they deserved it, was noble. He was a force for good in a world that needed it.

And she wanted to peel away more of his outer layers, to set free the fiery man that she kept getting glimmers of. Glimmers that were keeping her awake at night, so compelling were the *what-ifs* her brain was now constantly ticking with. What if she herself was open to romance, to love? One thing she knew for sure was that if she were, she'd want to be with Jules.

Zoe had been convincing herself for so long now that

she would never enter into a serious relationship. In fact, terror gripped her at the mere thought of something happening to Jules, and they weren't even together.

After her parents' instant deaths, Zoe was despondent for months. The pain of having both parents taken at the same time was a hurt so savage it had the strength to tear her apart limb by limb. She thought she'd never rise up from the sorrow, from the grief.

It was like walking in a daze for a couple of years. To lose her parents was bad enough, but in such a shocking way was too much to overcome.

When she finally did emerge, the lack of opportunity in Maupont was unbearable. She needed change. One day, she visited the cemetery where her parents and grandparents were buried. She had a heart-to-heart chat with them at their gravesites and asked them what to do. It was then she realized she had to come to Paris. She had to pursue her ambition. And at the same time, she decided firmly she could never accept the unknown that getting close to someone would bring. Therefore, she'd avoid it completely.

So it made no sense at all that she was pretending the apartment they were renovating was for themselves, creating a beautiful home that they designed together where they would live in bliss.

Mademoiselle Gaiman pull yourself together, she mentally admonished herself. *Tuck that attraction into the top drawer of the dresser you're repairing and never open it again.*

Nothing useful could come from these musings. Jules had given her a professional boost for which she'd forever be grateful. That was it.

"In addition to the electrician, the painters will be

at work today," he said, while looking down at some paperwork from a different project. "I'll stop by at the end of the day."

Here she'd been having such lofty thoughts about unchaining Jules's more carefree side and about tables for two, while he had his mind on his business. Still, man did not live by green drinks alone, and the recipe wasn't going to keep him healthy if he didn't have some downtime and recreation.

"Why don't we meet there at five o'clock?"

"Yes, five is good," he answered without raising his head.

"After that, what would you think about spending the rest of the afternoon doing something relaxing?" She hadn't meant to ask him that, or maybe she had?

"I don't relax." He was, once again, barely listening as he concentrated on other matters.

"Do you think maybe you should?"

"I'll put *Find Ways to Relax* on my to-do list."

"There you go! I'm sure you'll find something really rewarding if you make it a *should* not a *want to*."

"Are you being sarcastic again?"

He lifted his eyes and his stare shot point-blank right through the screen. Her heartbeat fluttered. She relived yet again that intense kiss they'd shared. What had really happened there? For all his rules and regulations, something overtook him in that moment. She couldn't stop wondering what.

Although she had no reason to, no obligation to, she felt compelled to help him unwind a little. He needed it so. She could safely do that much without too much risk to herself, couldn't she?

"What do you think? Could you shrug off your many responsibilities for a couple of hours?"

"What did you have in mind?"

"I'll show you."

When Jules met Zoe in front of the apartment, he grinned at what he saw. There she stood straddling a bicycle while holding the handlebar of a second, both with white wicker baskets in front that were decorated with artificial flowers. "I borrowed Yasmine's bike for you."

"I can see."

Zoe looked so adorable it took Jules a couple of breaths to settle into the moment. She wore a short and flowing dress made from a fabric with pink, blue and yellow flowers on it. Her hair was tied back with a pink ribbon and she wore retro-style sunglasses and a pair of flat leather sandals. She was a vision of happy, carefree Paris, even though Jules knew by now there was depth and pain beneath her cheery exterior.

He reached for one of the bike's handles and in the process their hands touched each other's. How thrilling the sensation was. After entering the building, they propped the bikes against a wall and did a quick check of the progress on the apartment.

"I haven't ridden in years," Jules confessed when they were back on the street. He held the borrowed bike, amused that he'd be riding with the girly white basket in front. While hotel concierges throughout the world had tried to encourage him to see their fair cities from a bicycle seat, Jules had always refused. He preferred his efficient morning run for his exercise. And a driver to whisk him anywhere he wanted to go.

"Bicycling through Paris, isn't that just a classic thing to do?"

"I used to bike when I was a kid." Indeed, Jules could clearly recall the exhilaration he'd had riding through the streets, pedaling as fast as he could through the outskirts of town where he lived. That was one of the few good memories he had. The wind blowing his hair back, his body leaning into turns or curves he had to maneuver. Whatever challenges the road brought were easy compared to what awaited him at home.

He adjusted the seat to accommodate his height, his fingers remembering the mechanisms of the bike as if it had been yesterday. In fact, Yasmine's bike was so basic it reminded him of a child's. None of the precision advances of sportsman bikes available today. "Where to?" he asked Zoe, aware of how rarely he'd asked that question of someone else, as it was always him making the decisions.

"Follow me."

The long list of things Jules needed to take care of flickered across his mind like news captions ticking across the bottom of the screen on television. But another part of him, one he hadn't seen in a long while, told him it was okay to let everything sit for a couple of hours. His parents were at the hotel and Karim had rescheduled a couple of meetings. The world really wouldn't come crashing down without his constant supervision.

Zoe gestured for them to turn at the intersection and again at a side street, where traffic was light and they could pick up speed.

Deciding to surrender the ride to Zoe's control, he let her stay a little bit ahead of him. Which afforded him a lovely view of her on the bike. Her petite frame was shapely. The thin fabric of the sundress billowed as she pedaled, allowing glimpses of the creamy skin of her thighs. The back of her pale neck was exposed by the ribbon that bound her hair.

Before long he was imagining his lips grazing the back of that neck underneath her hairline. He flashed back to how impossibly silky her pillowy lips were when he kissed her. How scorching and potent his tongue was with his mouth on hers. He wouldn't mind doing it again.

What if he pulled his bike up right next to hers and then at a moment when they stopped at a traffic light, he'd just lean over and touch his lips to hers? He was glad that she was a bit ahead of him so he didn't have to hide the silly grin that swept across his face at the idea.

As he was beginning to suspect, Zoe was leading him to the Luxembourg Gardens, one of the most storied and visited locales in Paris. Not only was it a must-stop for many tourists, Parisians considered it a prime spot to relax and take a break from the active and densely populated streets of the inner city.

"Let's sit by the Medici Fountain," she said as she dismounted her bike once they entered the garden gates.

"My favorite part of the gardens," he said as he gazed at Zoe. The curls that had emancipated themselves from her pink ribbon framed her face. The trail of freckles that traveled from one cheekbone across her nose to the other were fresh and natural in the late afternoon light.

"Mine, too."

They walked their bikes to the fountain with its long rectangular water basin surrounded by shady trees. A place that had been immortalized in countless paintings and photographs. Metal chairs lined each side of the basin, where people had been coming to bask for centuries. The expanse of still water gave way to the fountain with its statues and columns.

"What a nice idea to bring me here," Jules mused, swept into the beauty and peace surrounding him. Were the plane trees fragrant or was that his imagination?

"Let's sit."

They scoped out the available seating. A group of older men occupied part of the space, their chairs turned toward each other in an impromptu circle as they talked using many hand gestures. A woman read a paperback while holding her teeny dog. Schoolchildren, under the watch of a nanny, squealed and played a hopping game. It was almost a step back in time, the tableau set long ago. Jules had to admit he welcomed not being able to spot a cell phone.

He pointed to a couple of empty chairs and pulled them to the basin's edge, the scrape of the metal legs audible as he did so.

Once they sat, Zoe produced bottles of cold water from her bicycle's basket and handed him one, which was most appreciated. Popping the cap, Jules took a sip.

"Look at how much shade these trees provide," she said, noting the way the sunlight broke into shards as it danced on the basin's water.

"Perfect lighting design, right?"

"If you listen for it, you can hear the leaves rustle."

They sat in silence for a few minutes, indeed hearing the leaves' song. Jules could actually sense his heart rate slow, his breath become easy and unrestricted with deep inhales and even longer exhales. It was as if oxygen was reaching cells that had been starved of it for years. A pleasant tingle meandered through his blood vessels. His palms opened and tilted upward. "You were right. A person does need to do a little bit of nothing on occasion."

"This is some darn good nothing, isn't it?"

"Yes," he whispered and fell into a meditative state for a few minutes. His eyes closed. Everything fell away except a gentle wind on his face and the presence of Zoe beside him.

Eventually she said, "Our next destination will be a bit of something, though."

"Intriguing. I'm in your hands." Jules bit his lip. He hadn't meant to say something so flirty—it just slipped out. Zoe was turning him into someone he'd never met. A man he might like to know, to become. Who embraced existence on mental, physical and spiritual levels. Someone open and emancipated. A man who said yes.

After they'd thoroughly enjoyed the fountain and its surroundings, they ambled through more of the garden. Zoe led them to a café within the grounds where people sat savoring an early evening drink or snack outdoors. She chose a shady table and when the waiter approached, Zoe took the lead.

"We'll have a *tartelette des fruits*, a *fondant citron* with Chantilly *crème* and a crepe with cocoa noisette spread. Two hot chocolates and two glasses of champagne. And give the bill to him." She pointed to Jules, eliciting a belly laugh from him and a chuckle from the waiter.

"You're trying to corrupt me?" Another flirt. Not only couldn't he stop himself, he didn't want to. "You know I don't indulge in sweets."

"Exactly. On your relaxation day, you're not going to eat leaves. You're only going to look at them. Although maybe we'll have them with dinner later."

"We're having dinner?"

"If you play your cards right." She shot him a sly smile.

Zoe, he wanted to scream! *Stop saying sexy things!* Bad enough that he was thinking them. She'd already gotten him to ditch all the items on his agenda to go bike riding. And here they sat surrounded by the flora, dirt under their feet. Now she'd ordered desserts! If he didn't watch himself, Zoe might tear down the carefully guarded kingdom walls he'd created. Which, it seemed, a part of him was desperate to let her demolish.

The waiter delivered everything on a large silver tray. Zoe and Jules each put a napkin on their laps and their forks went to work.

He thought surely his eyes were going to roll back in his head at the taste of the warm crepe. He savored the thick hazelnut and chocolate flavor as it swirled around in his mouth. "Oh, my goodness."

"You've heard that expression," she said with a satisfied smile. "Life is uncertain so we should eat dessert first."

As she took a bite of the fondant Chantilly, a bit of whipped cream lingered on the side of her mouth. Jules leaned over and with a swipe of his thumb, removed the swirl from her face. And immediately, without thinking about it, licked it off. Afterward, he was a bit embarrassed at the informality.

She didn't seem bothered by it, though, and they continued peering at the gardens laid out in front of them. Vivid flowers in every shade of the rainbow surrounded the circular lawn with its statuary in front of the Luxembourg Palace.

Time passed at a leisurely pace Jules was so unaccustomed to. Every last speck on each plate was consumed and not a drop of the drinks remained. He and Zoe conversed about books and music and movies. About politics and history. The more they talked, the more he wanted to continue, speaking on any topic that came into their minds.

The moon began to rise when they decided it was time to go.

"Really, we should pick up some salads for dinner after all those sweet indulgences," she decided.

"We could bring them back to my apartment."

Jules hadn't had a guest in his Paris apartment in years, as he had used it so infrequently. He welcomed the idea. Like it was an actual home where he might have friends over. A weak voice in the back of his head tried to caution him that if he was counting, this was his third date with Zoe. And perhaps bringing her to his apartment was a bit too intimate. But his rationalizations and equations were no longer making sense to him.

Zoe gasped comically when she saw the size of Jules's apartment.

"Make yourself at home," he said casually. And then was surprised when she took him literally, unclasping her sandals and tossing them in a corner as she gave herself a self-guided tour. She took note of his upscale furniture and well-appointed office, every cord and cable to his high-tech setup discreetly out of view.

"Can I have a look at the rest?"

He'd have laughed at her lack of pretension if he weren't so charmed by it.

"Have at it, *cherie.*"

She moved to the kitchen, opening cabinets and drawers. Naturally, everything was done with top-notch building materials and craftsmanship.

"Premium quartz," she mentioned as she touched his countertop.

In the master bedroom, she bounced her small hand across the foot of his oversized bed, testing the firmness of his mattress. "Is that a Leon Villar?" she asked about the abstract landscape painting above the headboard.

"It is."

"Did you see his show at Galerie Pauline Caron?"

"I saw the show in New York."

He was glad for the painting discussion as having Zoe in his bedroom was unnerving. Namely, because he couldn't stop picturing laying her down on his bed, and letting his hands, mouth and more explore all of her body that he'd not yet seen. That flimsy little dress she wore would slip over her head in one pull, and whatever was underneath he'd remove with a quick slide.

Jules's feet moved toward her. He called for that warning voice in his head but it had become so faint he really couldn't hear it. It had morphed into a distant buzz that he was easily able to shush.

Her look in response to him moving closer was affirming. Lips slightly parted, the sparkle in her eyes welcomed him.

There was only one thing to do, and so he did it. He wrapped his hand around the back of Zoe's neck and brought her face toward him as he bent down to bring the first of many kisses to her inviting mouth.

It was better than any dream he'd ever had. As Jules

delivered yet another shower of light kisses to Zoe's lovely face, each brush of his lips against her skin presented a dilemma. On one hand, he wanted to slow himself down and register each kiss before he went on to the next. But a conflicting need was ready to devour her with urgency. It was a delicious agony, choosing between the two and settling somewhere in the middle.

Just a few minutes ago, they were picking up salads from a nearby market, after their pastry-fueled sunset at the Luxembourg Gardens. Dinner in tow, they'd brought the bikes to the entrance foyer of Jules's flat. He'd have his driver return them to her apartment later. Better still, he'd also send Zoe and her roommate new bikes with all the latest innovations.

Now he was kissing her at the foot of his bed. He held his lips above hers, just close enough for her to feel his breath and want more. The hiss of her inhale emboldened him.

Both palms cupped her face. He dragged his mouth away from hers, with a tormenting pull, so that he could feather his way down to her jawline. She lifted her chin toward him, a blessing that allowed him to apply his kisses in a continuous line. The journey took him from the plump bottom of one earlobe and down one side of her face. He wasn't done until he traveled her jaw to the other side. The thrum of pleasure that elicited from somewhere low within her prompted him to discover more.

When he brought his face against the cool of her throat, his teeth bared themselves and began tiny nibbles. He reveled in her aura, breathing in her powdery sweetness. With an easy tug, he undid the ribbon that by then had been containing only half of Zoe's physics-defying orange curls. Her hair cascaded down over her shoulders, as shiny and alive as Zoe herself was.

His fingers wove through her locks—something he'd been wanting to do since he'd met her, so mesmerizing were they to him. In fact, he took pleasure from just pressing an individual curl tightly and then releasing it to watch it spring open.

"My hair is fascinating to you?" she asked after he'd performed the operation several times.

"I can't stop myself from touching it."

"Don't, then. Don't stop anything."

Their eyes met, his wearing a dark veil of arousal and hers crystalline with alertness. Jules paused with a moment of clarity. Nothing about this made sense. Why would he want to disrupt his carefully laid-out plans?

Don't stop anything.

She'd just cooed those words straight into his soul, although she might not know the extent of her effect on him. Before he could second-guess himself anymore, his hands glided down to her two shoulders. He caressed them, his fingers taking note of each of her bones and their alignment. His hands were so big they covered her shoulders completely.

He bent to kiss from the bottom of her throat down to the low neckline of her sundress. When his tongue reached the fabric, it flicked under the thin cotton. Just knowing that his mouth had met skin that the dress had been concealing stirred his very core. Her head fell back as she welcomed his exploration, which he continued with focus. His mouth took the temperature of which spots on her throat and her décolleté felt the warmest. Between her breasts was a honeyed heaven where his lips had to linger.

Eventually straightening up, he locked her in an embrace, as he suddenly needed to feel her tightly against him. Although she was petite, he found her not fragile but resilient, her body arching to meet his every move. When he molded her to him, she became pliant. Yet, she was anything but passive. Tender sighs mingled with erotic moans.

"Zoe, you're doing something to me I hadn't planned on."

"You've lit me, as well."

Filled with emotion and sensation and a primal hunger in his belly that wouldn't be contained, he pulled her down onto the bed with him. Climbing on top of her, he acknowledged how lucky his hands and lips were to be roaming over Zoe's velvety beauty. In his eagerness, he kissed her every way his body told him to. A peck on her nose. An assertive bite to the crook of her neck. The taste of the inside of her wrist.

"I haven't felt this much desire in..." Jules stopped himself before revealing what might be his best-kept secret. That he hadn't wanted someone like he wanted her. Not *in years*, which was what he had been going to say. But ever. Ever!

And it wasn't just sexual attraction he was experiencing. She'd opened his eyes to the possibility of a true connection with someone. Something that was honest and fulfilling and sustaining.

After what he witnessed as a child, he'd never trust anyone with his heart, but it was nice to know he could even have those feelings. That he was still human. Zoe showed him an alternate universe where love and beauty were everywhere. She'd changed him. He'd always be grateful for, or maybe tormented by, the gift she had given him.

"What, Jules? What are you trying to say?" Her voice sang out from the avalanche of kisses he was bestowing on her.

"Only that… I'm glad you're here." With that, his mouth found hers again where their tongues met for an extended swirl that pulled Jules into an ocean's tide. His hand began a journey along her thigh, slipping under her dress.

When he leaned his neck back, the passion he saw in her eyes must have been a mirror. He swept Zoe's flowery little dress up over her head and tossed it on the chair beside his bed.

CHAPTER SEVEN

ZOE COULD HARDLY believe she was being seduced by, and for that matter seducing, Jules. She told herself she'd better enjoy this unbelievable moment in time because it would be gone in a flash and was unlikely to ever happen again.

You're doing something to me I hadn't planned on.

His words were spoken in the heat of desire. She had the good sense to not take them seriously. Still, she was a sophisticated denizen of Paris who was free to indulge in a night of impassioned intimacy with an extraordinary man.

So, with the ever-present eye of the Eiffel Tower visible through the window of Jules's bedroom, Zoe pulled him tight, her warning ping screaming from within. She'd never been with a man like him. The few boyfriends she'd had back in Maupont were of adult age but they were still boys, fumbling and tentative, unsure of themselves. Jules was 100 percent man. His power and command as an executive was matched by the strength and confidence emanating from him as a lover.

After he'd taken off every stitch of clothing she wore, he quickly undid the buttons of his shirt and cast it off to the side, as well. Then he was on top of her again, his weight melding her into his bed. She wrapped her arms around his shoulders, his lean muscles defined underneath warm smooth skin.

His hands moved down her outline and then underneath her to bring her body up even closer to him as he pressed his still-clad maleness against her bare and now pulsating center. There they kissed and swayed, embarking toward a destination they didn't yet see.

When craving demanded more, Zoe reached between them to unbuckle Jules's belt and unzip the fly of his pants. Excited by the fullness that she stroked with her palm, her other hand yanked at his remaining clothes. With a devilish grin, he backed away from her to peel off his trousers. He reached for a condom in his nightstand and unrolled it before returning to her arms where their bodies finally truly joined and became one.

Zoe gripped him, wrapped her legs around his waist, as they flew up to the heavens, now knowing where they were going. They ascended higher and higher and higher still until, together, they soared freely as one.

When they landed back down, he collapsed on top of her. Her fingers combed through his hair with a sense of possessiveness, like he belonged to her. It was a heady sensation. Her every breath oozed an earthy, womanly sensuality she'd never known in herself.

After a serene interval of recuperation, Jules announced, "I want to eat."

"We still have our salads."

He separated himself from her, which, at first, was a torturous desertion. It had only been to gather up a few items of clothing. He stepped back into his boxers and black slacks, though he left the top button open, pulled his belt from the pant loops and cast that aside. Zoe slipped on her dress and undies, leaving her bra where it sat on Jules's side chair. He reached for her hand and led her, barefoot, into the kitchen.

As he sat her down at his chrome bar table with its two stools facing each other, Zoe wondered how many women had occupied the second seat at his table, literally or figuratively throughout his world travels.

"Have you ever lived with anyone?" she asked as Jules opened the fridge.

He lashed his head toward her in a way that made Zoe apprehensive that she'd angered him with her inquisitiveness. Instead, the look in his eyes was glassy and sad, especially shadowed by the bluish light coming from inside the refrigerator. "No. I told you. That life is not for me."

Something in his face and the way his response sounded like a question melted Zoe's heart. This man was as precious as the monuments of Paris he so revered. He deserved to be happy, to be able to count on someone. He was worthy of love. How tragic it was that his past was robbing him of a future. Although the same could be said of her.

She studied the movement in the taut muscles of his back as he reached for the salads. Her body went liquid again at the sight, a reminder of what had just transpired in his bed. He flicked on some under-cabinet lighting that gave the whole room a gentle glow, nice for the late hour. After placing the food and cold drinks on the table, he perched at the stool opposite her.

They ate in quiet for an interlude. Zoe's body was still lost in his embrace but her mind had gone to thought. When a little too much time passed, it became oppressive. She believed him when he said that he didn't get close to people and would never couple with anyone. Making love with her had not changed that one iota. Why would it? It wasn't as if she was used to a scenario like this, either. She'd come to Paris to make a career for herself, hopefully to have interesting friends and a full life. Since she'd been here, she hadn't been in a man's bed nor shared hers.

After keeping his eyes on his salad, the awkwardness got to Jules as well and he flicked a remote control on the table to turn on the television. They watched the news together, although she wasn't paying attention to the words coming out of the anchorman's mouth— something about roadwork in the Eighteenth Arrondissement.

There was no denying that an overwhelming yearning had been satiated between them in Jules's bedroom. They fit perfectly together in that respect, as if their bodies were meant for each other's. Only for each other's. But something passed between their hearts as well, something poignant, life-altering. She couldn't have been the only one to have felt it. Although, she had the sense that tomorrow she'd need to figure out how to put all of that to the side and move on with their professional interactions. Jules had made his intentions, or lack thereof, clear from the beginning.

Perhaps they were the cliché of those European types who casually mixed business with pleasure? If so, she should be able to laugh this off, just one night of many free-flowing encounters. After the ecstasy Jules brought her, the heights of giving and receiving pleasure that were new to her, to turn to a self-conscious kitchen snack in the dead of night did not come naturally to her. In fact, for reasons she couldn't coalesce into one explanation, she was fighting back tears.

But it was time to pretend that they didn't care about each other. That's how these nonchalant affairs went. Chitchat was in order and luckily Jules provided. "I'm concerned the two wing-backed chairs for the bedroom are too big in scale." He was referring to the furniture delivery for the apartment that had arrived earlier today. Before the bike ride and the Luxembourg Gardens and her tongue tracing down his spine.

"I'll look at it again with fresh eyes tomorrow," she answered in a scratchy late-night voice, determined to keep up. "It's true that they're more decorative than anything else since it wouldn't be worth the trouble for your father to get out of his wheelchair to sit in them. I'd like to fill in that space, though."

"I still like the idea of a bench. The depth would be so much shorter."

That conversation petered out and they went back to watching the news.

"Well, it's late and I'd like to get some sleep," Jules said after they finished eating.

Did he mean that he wanted *them* to get some sleep or that he wanted her to leave? Again, Zoe racked her brain, trying to figure out how worldly adults who have had sex but aren't together handle these situations. No wonder she didn't do blasé encounters. It was too confusing.

"I… I should be going, then," she managed, figuring that was the safest thing to say.

"You're welcome to stay…" His voice was unconvincing and he cast his eyelids downward. He was feeling as uneasy as she was, so different from the master-of-the-universe persona he usually projected to the world.

On one hand, she wanted to hold him all night long, perhaps including more of the divine lovemaking they had created and then nestling herself into him as they fell into one dream. On the other, she couldn't get away fast enough, to provide herself with a shield before any more affection toward him would promise inevitable disappointment. Being wise, or so she thought, she chose the latter.

After returning from collecting her things in the bedroom, she slipped on her shoes. "Are we still going to see your apartment on the Grands Boulevards later this week?"

"Yes." He tapped on his phone. "I've just called a driver to take you home. Let me walk you down."

At the late hour, Paris was subdued outside of Jules's building but still awake. Some young people laughed loudly as they passed by. A few cars and motorbikes tooled down the boulevard. When the driver pulled to the curb, Jules opened the door and helped Zoe into the back seat. He leaned in to give her a kiss good-night that belied their parting. It was a kiss that informed them, in case they hadn't figured it out yet, that they'd entered the danger zone. Their feelings for each other were anything but meaningless.

"I'll need a phone conference with Kowalczyk and his contractor today," Jules instructed Karim as they walked out of a meeting at Durand headquarters that had his head spinning. "If he doesn't get his materials cost under control, I'm pulling out."

"I let his people know."

"Run me a comparison sheet on what he'd budgeted versus what his estimates are now."

"Yes, Jules."

"And call our legal team and find out what my obligations are at this point."

"I will do that." Karim spoke in a calm monotone that Jules appreciated. Jules would be spending more time in person with his assistant now that he'd be based in Paris. The thought didn't displease him.

"Get the architect on the phone," Jules instructed as he rounded the corner to his office while Karim continued forward.

Entering his office, Jules tossed the file he was holding onto his desk, shrugged off his jacket and loosened his tie. Mounting his treadmill, he set it for a slow walk to help him blow off some steam.

With the city laid out in front of him, he realized that he was overreacting to the work setback. He'd dealt with developers who went over budget many times. His agitation didn't have that much to do with Krakow.

What was bothering him was how uncomfortably things had ended with Zoe last night after they'd made love. It had been so authentic and uncomplicated, spending that time with her at the Luxembourg Gardens and then at his apartment. Like a dance that he already knew the steps to, being with her came easily. He hadn't needed to strategically fortress himself with walls to keep out emotions. Although, maybe he subconsciously had in the end. Because after all the surprising naturalness of them getting out of bed together to eat a late supper in the kitchen, Jules stepped out of himself and saw the situation like someone looking in. And in that instant, the realness he felt turned itself fake in his stomach like rotten food. And he had to get away from it as quickly as he could.

Tucking a woman into a waiting car in the middle of the night. Three-date rules. A vow never to marry. Jules Durand had become the man he'd set out to be. Only now it was someone he didn't like.

"Hello," Jules said with a quick kiss to her cheek when he met Zoe in front of one of his buildings a few days later as planned. Most of the decisions on the apartment for his parents had been made but he'd promised to take her to one of his most show-stopping properties.

He seemed cheerier than he had when they'd parted in the wee hours that night after they'd made love, with her peering out the back-seat window at him as the driver pulled the car away, distress washing over Jules's exquisite face.

"You own this?" she asked, even though the answer was obvious. "The entire building?"

"1869. Haussmann."

Georges-Eugène Haussmann, the prefect under Emperor Napoléon III who redesigned a decaying city into the metropolis and crossroads Paris remained to this day. Haussmann demolished the medieval city neighborhoods that were unhealthy, overcrowded and dangerous, and replaced them with a new Paris. Enormous apartment buildings were built, not to be considered as individual structures but as part of an urban landscape with wide avenues and public squares. That signature architectural style became the look of Paris, the front-facing windows and horizontal designs of similar heights, building-front after building-front cut from cream-colored stone.

Zoe's mind boggled that Jules owned one of those buildings, and at what price it might fetch on the modern market. She shook her head. "I know I'm a small-town girl but it's hard to believe I actually know someone who owns a Haussmann on the Grands Boulevards of Paris."

Jules's mouth twitched. She could tell he wasn't actually smiling at her lack of savvy, only that she'd voiced it out loud. "All right, Mademoiselle Small Town, my property manager arranged for us to see one of the apartments in the building. From what I'm told, my tenant uses a wheelchair and we've made some excellent accommodations for her I'd like to show you."

"Wonderful. Lead the way." Zoe pointed to the entrance door.

So far, so good, she noted of the easier rapport they were managing today. Although, entering the building, she moved close to him and it was all she could do not to lean in. To beg those strong shoulders to encircle her, a return to the magical private universe they'd escaped to in his bed.

All business, Jules used his passcode to enter the apartment.

"Wow," Zoe exclaimed. "Did we just walk into the Palais Versailles? I've never seen anything like this." It appeared that every wall that was not part of the building's intrinsic structure had been removed, artistic pillars concealing foundational beams that were necessary to retain. In doing so, a vast expanse had been created, almost beyond what the eye could see. "I can't believe this is a center-city residence."

"By taking out as many walls as we could, we've

made it easier for Madame to maneuver around the apartment."

"Less doorways and corners. Not to mention the majesty of it all."

"I'm very pleased with how this turned out. And when Madame decides to move out, I'm sure many tenants would appreciate this open plan."

"Ya!" Zoe shrieked, getting a giggle out of Jules. "This has to be the best apartment in Paris. The Grands Boulevards are my favorite part of the city, anyway."

"Come here." He took her hand and brought her to the farthest windows where there was a clear view of the opera house, Palais Garnier.

"Did you know that the opera house was once the nexus of Paris's high society?" she asked.

"What operas have you seen at the Palais?"

"None. I've never been."

"You've never gone to the opera in Paris?"

"I've never been to an opera anywhere."

"We'll have to correct that immediately. Do you have plans tonight?" He didn't wait for an answer as he pulled his phone from his jacket pocket. "Karim, get me an opera box for tonight."

Zoe heart rate sped. Jules was calling his assistant to get opera tickets for them? Just like that?

After the strangeness at his apartment, she hadn't known what to expect today. She'd been working on his parents' apartment independently while Jules was dealing with other properties. She'd updated him during FaceTime sessions but the uneasiness between them had still hung in the air. It was a relief that he was less quirky today.

"I thought you didn't make spur-of-the-moment decisions," she chided him, giddy energy propelling her to make a joke.

"I must be spending too much time with you." He grinned back. "Do you have anything to wear?"

"Can I wear the orange dress you bought me for that cruise on the Seine?"

"You could. But let's buy you something new."

She shrugged her shoulders. "Whatever you say, boss." The quip earned her another chortle from Jules. Their jokey manner was keeping them from dealing with the reality of their night together, both the incendiary lovemaking and the prickly aftermath. But if he wanted to play it that way, so would she. Maybe they could find an equilibrium. In any case, she was going to the opera.

"We may as well go to Galeries Lafayette." Paris's most famous and sophisticated department stores were conveniently located nearby. Jules tapped into his phone again. "Karim, I also need a personal shopper at Galeries Lafayette right away."

After touring the rest of the apartment, they walked the few blocks to the store and entered into its massive sales floor. Each of the store's upper levels, which were flanked with archways, were visible from the center of the ground floor. That drew the eye upward to the styling of the art nouveau multi-colored steel and glass dome. It was another architectural masterpiece. Zoe marveled, "This store is a museum piece in and of itself."

An elevator took them to their floor and they were shown into a sequestered salon. The overstuffed furniture was upholstered in a baby pink and the carpet a pretty caramel. A dais surrounded by mirrors anchored the space.

A young saleswoman introduced herself as Safa. She wore a navy sheath dress with a multi-colored scarf tied around her neck just so, the knot at one side where it magically stayed in place. "I understand you'd like something special for the opera?"

"We would." Jules nodded.

"Did you have something in mind?"

Jules turned to Zoe. "What would be your fantasy opera outfit? I'll wear a tuxedo."

"Old-fashioned romance, I guess. Is black velvet okay?" she questioned. After all, Jules was paying for another dress. She expected he'd want to approve it as he had last time.

"If that's what you'd like."

"I'll be back with some suggestions," Safa said and then exited the salon.

When Jules arrived at Zoe's apartment that night to pick her up for the opera, Yasmine was home, as well. "Ni... ice to meet you," she stammered. Zoe couldn't blame her, as Jules's mere presence seemed to overtake their tiny apartment. It was as if all of the furniture moved out of the way to allow his entrance.

With his substantial height and precision haircut, his slim-cut black tux gave him that look of modern royalty. Every inch of him was faultlessly chic, from the jacket's thin lapel to his luxury wristwatch to his shoes on which a scuff would never dare appear. It was almost comical the way Yasmine's eyes all but bugged out like a cartoon character.

But when Zoe stepped into Jules's view in her ensemble, it was she who drew the approving gaze. As a matter of fact, he cleared his throat in response, which Zoe found adorable. "You look spectacular," he said.

No one had ever called her that before and she almost blushed. Memories of making love with him flooded her. The way his body, his fingers, his mouth had appreciated her and made her feel *spectacular*. Her heart sat heavy with the knowledge that she might never share that glory with him again. Even if she had the opportunity, she'd have to turn it down. Her emotions had already grown perilous. Nonetheless, one of Paris's most attractive bachelors was taking her to the opera, and she was going to turn her mind to savoring every moment of the fairy-tale evening.

So, she quite enjoyed the lustful way he looked her over from top to bottom. He, of course, had sent a stylist to the apartment to help her get dressed, and her unruly hair had been corralled but left curly in a half-up, half-down do. Her smoky eye makeup was dramatic and the most perfect shade of pale lipstick complemented her complexion.

Zoe absolutely loved the dress she'd picked out from the choices the saleswoman at Galeries Lafayette had brought them earlier. Crushed velvet, it had a wide and low-cut neckline. So jet-black it was almost blue. The shapewear undergarment she wore enhanced her bosom, displaying as much voluptuousness as was tasteful. The dress fit her like a glove, hugging all her curves until it reached a lower calf hemline that was flattering on her. And the nude heels gave it a freshness that the more customary black shoe wouldn't have.

"I think there's something missing," Jules stated after his long gander. He stepped closer to her as he removed a midnight blue jewelry box from his jacket pocket. Flipping it open, large diamond stud earrings sparkled from their satin berth. "These are for you."

Yasmine gasped so loudly that both Jules and Zoe snapped their heads toward her. He smiled at her roommate's zest. Jules took one of the earrings from the box and removed its backing. "May I?"

"Yes!" Yasmine blurted. The three of them giggled. With, mysteriously, the knowledge of how to fit earrings onto a woman, Jules graced her lobe with the heavy jewel. His thick fingers understood the task, gently sliding the post in and then affixing the back. The whole process was so profoundly erotic Zoe's eyelashes fluttered and beads of sweat began to form between her breasts. Then he repeated his ministrations with her other ear. She tried to calm herself with slow breaths but to no avail. She was no match for this man's charms.

Pleased with his handiwork Jules decreed, "Perfect."

And divine everything was, as his driver delivered them to the Palais Garnier, one of Paris's most famous addresses for centuries. The ornate building's exterior was decorated at every inch with statues, columns, friezes and sculpture done in stones and metals. It wasn't hard to see why ghostly lore and novels such as *The Phantom of the Opera* were set in amongst such splendor.

Jules escorted her inside and when they reached the Grand Staircase, Zoe could hardly believe she was there. The swooping double staircases crafted of fine marble led up to either side of the foyer. They were even more magnificent in their detail than she had seen in photos and paintings.

"You know, part of the reason these staircases were designed to curve as they do was so that people could get a clear view of who was here and what they wore," she said. "This used to be *the* place for gossip and scandal."

"You've read up, I see."

He crooked his arm to begin leading her up those lavish marble stairs. "Careful with those high heels—" he winked "—we don't want you falling into the opera like you fell into my office. Modern-day scandal as Paris mogul takes adorable klutz to *Madame Butterfly*."

"You're never going to let me live that down, are you?"

"Not a chance."

She scrunched her face but he knew that she appreciated his humor. Still, she took hold of one of the elaborate balustrades and kept her other arm in Jules's. Feeling quite splendid, she reached the top of the stairs, secretly grateful to do it without bobbling.

"My gosh," she exclaimed as they took their seats in the box he'd reserved. The sumptuous horseshoe-shaped auditorium was rich with its red and gold decor. A bronze and crystal chandelier led to the ceiling painting done by Marc Chagall. "I'd read about this Chagall ceiling. I've forgotten when was it done?"

"In the 1960s."

"I think what I was reading said they installed it over the ceiling's original artwork."

"Another example of the old and the new merging in Paris."

When the lights were lowered for the opera to begin, Zoe's stomach twisted. The moment, the splendor of the opera house and her enchantment with Jules should have been perfect. Yet, the extreme discomfort the night after they'd made love still twirled within her like a ballerina's pirouette. She hoped her inner pinging would quiet down enough for her to enjoy the performance.

And Puccini's beauty and poignancy did captivate her attention. She sat motionless and spellbound for the entire first act.

At the first intermission, Jules suggested they visit the Grand Foyer, the long gilded hall with crystal, gold leaf and ceiling paintings that seemed to stretch the length of a city block. The social scene in the Paris of years gone by had gathered in this hallowed expanse, apparently sometimes several nights a week. Zoe could see why. It was opulence rarely seen outside of a palace. Zoe imagined women in the elaborate dresses of centuries past, corsets and gold braiding, tiny shoes with buckles and powdery wigs. Or, later, women with red lipstick and their short hair tucked into cloche hats. The foyer was a history lesson come to life.

"I want to show you something," Jules said as he took her hand. She wasn't able to hide the jolt that his firm grasp produced in her. He took her out to the loggia, the large span of balcony where the night air invigorated Zoe's face.

Tears pooled in her eyes at the sight of everything. The loggia overlooked the Place de l'Opéra, the open public square and the wide boulevards of what was called the Haussmann-Opéra neighborhood. Just as rideshares and scooters now moved people to and fro, she could picture the same streets filled with horses and carriages. Times were different but, in a way, Paris had stayed the same. That was why she'd moved here. To be part of the past and the future of this inimitable city.

"Jules, thank you for tonight. For bringing me here."

"I need to tell you something." He turned his face to

her as they stood in front of the view. "I want to apologize for the other night. I shouldn't have let you leave like that. As I've told you, I don't enter into romantic attachments. My attraction to you got carried away and then after our beautiful lovemaking interlude I...panicked I suppose is the right word."

She girded herself. Here would come the words she was expecting, the words that she knew were in both of their interests. He'd say definitively, lest there be any confusion, that what happened between them was impulsive and that he doesn't *do* impulsive. That they should just chock it up to a mistake, which would never occur again. Just as their original kiss had been.

It really would be for the best. She'd shake her head in agreement. Neither of them were open to falling in love. There was no benefit to continuing a personal acquaintance. They were colleagues and nothing more.

Take a mental snapshot, Zoe.

Because this was all she was getting. This night, this loggia, this stunning and affecting man. She'd cherish and replay all of it until her dying day.

"And?" She encouraged him to finish, wanting her pain served up quickly like a bandage being ripped from delicate skin.

"And..." He lingered before leaning down to take hold of her face and give her a profoundly sensual kiss that snaked all the way down into her belly, coiling in her very soul. "And I want a do-over. I want you in my bed again. And this time I want to hold you all night."

After they returned to their box seats, the tragic longing of Cio-Cio San's famous second-act aria paled in comparison to the music in Zoe's heart.

CHAPTER EIGHT

JULES PLACED A wisp of a kiss on the head of a still-sleeping Zoe in his bed. He grabbed some running gear from a drawer and padded quietly out of the room, not wanting to wake her. After he dressed for his early-morning exercise, he opened the fridge to make sure the green smoothies were there. He and Zoe would have those for breakfast when he returned.

On the street, cafés were open to meet the needs of those already out and about. Shop owners pulled back their safety gates, fishmongers stacked the latest catches on ice. Jules ran past a fruit vendor, the proprietor in a white apron inspecting his offerings, pulling off apples that he deemed unsellable and tossing them into a box under his display stand. Neon lights in a supermarket window looked eerie in the still-sleepy morning, but customers entered and exited. The optometry office, the bank and the pet groomers were not yet open.

Traffic chugged along but few horns honked. In the hum of daybreak, Jules could think. Before demands yanked his concentration from one thing to another to another still. That Krakow project still had him worried. He was missing some information and he'd need to schedule a teleconference as soon as he got to the office.

He increased his running pace. And would his parents be able to make a new chapter of their lives here? Could they manage to set aside their differences, at least some of the time, to grow old together with any amount of grace and respect? Nothing in their past suggested that they would but out of sheer will Jules was hoping against hope that he could create some kind of unit between the three of them that had never existed in the first place.

At the moment, though, he didn't want to think about their issues any more than he did those in Krakow. There was only one thing he wanted on his mind.

Zoe. Charming, vivacious, warm-hearted Zoe. With whom he'd spent a night that alternated from sweet affection to savage hunger. That left them sweating and panting to the point that they could hear each other's breath afterward as they lay spent on his bed. And instead of being satisfied, Jules wanted more.

He ran past his local boulangerie and got a whiff of the yeasty baked goods he was able to see through the shop's open street-facing window.

After he had kissed Zoe so passionately on the loggia of the opera house and stated that he wanted her to come home with him, he waited in a haze of awareness for the rest of the performance, his body flinching and flexing, desperate to be free of his tuxedo. It was an exquisite torment. Their night at his apartment afterward was well worth the wait.

Reflecting on all of it as he ran, oxygen surging through him, one fact caught him by surprise. If one was to be counting, taking Zoe to the opera had been date number four. He'd disregarded his longstanding promise to himself never to go past three dates with a woman.

At the beginning, he'd rationalized that Zoe was a colleague so his tallies didn't even count. Now, he no longer cared. Maybe everything in his world could come together as one big messy whole. Once he stabilized his parents, finally stopped the commotion that he'd been running from his entire life, he'd allow in some joy. And romance. Was anything about that plan realistic, or was he being as silly as a teenager with a crush?

The existence he'd been leading had to change. It wasn't normal, wasn't healthy. When he moved aside the clutter in his brain, he knew that. A man could become nothing but a hard shell living alone, communicating only superficially to his parents or regarding business. His hot red blood would drain, his juices would dry up, the vital force of his solar plexus would shrivel.

Suddenly, while he was running and observing the life on the street around him, it was as if he could see with a bright clarity that had long been hidden. What made existence worthwhile was to spend it amongst other people. Having a shared experience. The ups. The downs. The maybes. Caring and being cared for. And it was Zoe who had opened his eyes.

On a whim, he circled back and started running in the direction he came from. With a ridiculous amount of excitement, he entered the boulangerie whose smells had tickled his nose when he'd run past earlier. The green smoothies could wait. Jules ordered two cafés au lait and four croissants, which were still warm in the bag the cashier presented.

When he got home, he went straight to the bathroom and started pouring a bath in his enormous Carrara marble tub. In his bedroom, he found Zoe just waking, stretching her sinewy arms above her head.

"Good morning."

"You've been out?" she cooed, her voice still subdued from sleep.

"My run."

"Mmm…how ambitious."

"Early bird and all that. Would you join me in a bath?"

"A morning bath, how luxurious. Do you do that every day?"

"Never."

A shy smile crossed her lips and Jules's heart twanged.

He fetched her a toothbrush and gave her a few moments of privacy in the vanity portion of his bathroom suite. Meanwhile, he found some bubble bath his housekeeper must have bought for him and yelled through the door, "Gardenia or citrus?"

"Citrus."

Once she emerged, he helped her step into the bathtub made to comfortably fit two.

"Ah…" she whooshed as she immersed herself in the fragrant bubbles.

Jules lowered himself in, as well.

He positioned them just as he had planned in his mind as he carried the coffee and croissants back after his purchase. With him leaning back against the tub's marble, he pulled Zoe between his legs so that her back rested against his chest and he could be a human pillow for her.

"I can't believe you can see the Eiffel Tower even from your bathtub," she remarked on the view through the picture window that was strategically positioned to afford total privacy. "I'd never get anything done if I had a bathroom like this."

Jules couldn't argue. With the oversized glass shower that had several faucets and jet options, plus the extra-large tub with a whirlpool motor, this room was a special oasis. Connected to the bath and shower suite was a separate water closet, double sinks in cabinets with lots of storage and a dressing table with a lighted mirror. He'd owned this apartment for years but hadn't lived in it for more than weeks at a time. Now that he thought about it, this was probably a woman's dream come true of a bathroom. A measure of his isolation was that he'd never noticed before.

"It does promote relaxation."

"Kudos to your designer on this one."

Jules couldn't remember who had done the renovations on this apartment. He'd been out of the country at the time.

"I've never taken a bath here."

"What? Why?"

"It never occurred to me." He kissed the top of Zoe's shoulder, her skin slick with soapy water. "Until this morning." Wrapping her in his long arms, he fully enveloped her and held her as close to him as was humanly possible.

The bubbles danced beautifully across her bent knees. Lucky bubbles. He kissed the top of her head over and over.

This freeze frame in time was very appealing. It was as if all at once during his run, he *got it*. That the benefits of sharing a bath, a life were well worth any sacrifices of control. His intellectual self knew that most partners didn't walk out on the other and then come crawling back, begging for forgiveness over and over again. None of what Jules grew up in was normal. In a flash, he believed for the first time that history did not have to repeat itself.

A kind of delight came over him, like nothing he'd ever felt before. Sure, there was a rush when a project was completed or an attractive property was acquired. Yet, what he experienced this morning was something different. Better. It was pure and simple optimism.

Almost unwilling to let go of Zoe for even a minute, he leaned over to the tub's ledge and handed her one of the coffees he'd bought.

"Mmm," she sighed after a sip. "Delicious."

"Like you." He dried his hands on a nearby towel so he could open the bag of croissants. Breaking off a piece, he reached his hand in front of her so that he could feed her a bite.

"Croissants for breakfast? I thought you started the day with handfuls of lawn grass or some such."

Jules laughed, his bellows echoing throughout the bathroom. "It was a spur-of-the-moment decision."

"I approve." When he fed her more, she held onto his hand so that she could take the second bite more sensually, her tongue flicking the tips of his fingers.

Their soak was about to take an entirely different turn when Jules's phone buzzed from the bedroom. Because early morning had slid, albeit lusciously, into business hours he felt he should take it.

"I'll be right back."

"Sure. But give me the rest of the croissant first."

Another chuckle made him wonder who he was. Had he learned the meaning of the word *fun*, after all?

He hoisted himself out of the bath, wrapped a towel

around his waist and went to his nightstand to retrieve his phone. His mother's voice tampered the elation that Zoe and bubbles had given him.

"I'm at the Gare du Nord." The train station. Dread thudded in the center of Jules's chest. "I am not wasting one more moment of my life on that louse you call a father. I'm leaving and this time I am truly never coming back. I'll need some money and I'll be in touch with where you should wire it."

"Mother. Stop this nonsense. Do not get on that train. I'll send a car for you. We're not doing this anymore."

"All aboard!" Jules could hear the loudspeaker in the distance.

"Mother!"

"I'm boarding now. Goodbye, son."

Lounging in the bath until her skin was pink and shriveled, Zoe followed Jules's instruction to linger as long as she wanted. As to what was so urgent based on the phone call he'd received, he merely said that he had to go and that it couldn't wait. He'd quickly donned full business garb and his serious face. Zoe assumed it had something to do with the projects he'd mentioned were running over budget. The succulent kisses goodbye he gave her didn't need any explanation.

Zoe could get used to bathing in a huge marble tub with a view. The lazy sunlight shining on the Paris rooftops made the tableau look like a painting. She oozed into some steamy daydreams of her and Jules and bubbles, his big hands making sure every spot on her body was properly soaped. Every. Spot. Those same hands that surely knew what they were doing to her on dry land last night. After the opera and the exchange on the loggia, when he begged her to understand that he'd panicked after they'd made love the first time but that he was sure he wanted her in his bed all night long. She slid underneath the water and allowed the warm cocoon to surround her.

Then, only after she'd eaten every flake of the croissants Jules had surprised her with after his run, she finally got out of the tub and used a thick fluffy towel to dry herself off. With just her black velvet dress from the night before to put on, she quickly left Jules's apartment for her own where she could change into daytime clothes.

Her next stop was Si Wu's studio to approve the living room furniture before having it delivered. Si had previously come to the apartment and, along with Jules, they'd worked out the furniture order there. It was a symbol of respect for Jules that the renowned furniture-maker had paid him a house call. Now, at his studio, Zoe appreciated roaming around his showroom, eyeing the sophisticated yet contemporary pieces Si was famous for.

Since her roommate, Yasmine, worked here, she had a chance to say hi. Yasmine came down from the stepladder she was on, having reached for something. "Didn't hear you come home last night, roomie."

All Zoe did was nod back, a smile breaking across her face.

"Zoe, hi, come, let me show you where we're at," Si cut in. He was a high-strung man with black-rimmed eyeglasses who talked and walked very fast, darting across his large studio. Zoe hustled to keep up with him. Si pointed to the rust-colored button-tufted corner piece that had sofa seating on one side and an L-shaped chaise lounge on the other. He rattled off in his rapid-fire manner of speaking. "I can add another module if you decide you want it larger, button-tufted is always so sharp looking, and wears well, what do you think?"

She inspected the creation and thought about it, picturing it in the place she'd chosen. The fine craftsmanship was evident in every facet. It was a gorgeous piece that would anchor the room. But she did have a question. "As you know, one of the occupants uses a wheelchair." Jules hadn't specifically asked her not to mention that the apartment was for his parents when they started working with Si, but she didn't think it was anyone's business. "Does it have to be so low to the ground? I'd like the tenant to be easily able to get in and out."

"I can do some custom legs to give you a little more height. You don't want to end up with a bed sort of look, especially for the chaise section, unless you do?"

Zoe was almost giddy to be having this conversation with the famous furniture designer, even if he did have an odd way of speaking. This is what she'd dreamt of. Customizing fine pieces, which, together, became a home with personality. There were no price tags on Si's furniture, unlike the showroom of her family's store in Maupont where customers needed that information. At a studio like this, a person couldn't afford his designs if they needed to ask the price.

"The dining table and chairs, end tables, side chairs, bench for the bedroom, nightstands, bed frame, daybed for second bedroom, window table, all being delivered today," Si rattled off the inventory from memory. "Is that okay with you, Zoe?"

That she was here was all because of Jules. Despite her less than graceful entry into his life, he took a chance on her. In more ways than one. She bit her lip, recalling the sensuality they'd shared last night, tuning into each other's pleasure, giving and taking, and bringing the other to ecstasy. With Jules, both professionally and personally, she felt confident and mature. Maybe her inner tide had finally turned.

"What happened *this* time?" Jules barreled into the hotel penthouse where, earlier in the week, he thought things had been a bit calmer with his parents.

"Your mother is up to her old tricks," Hugo said as he wheeled himself closer to his son and then made a dismissive wave with his hand. "It was somehow my fault that the toast got cold and then she was off and running on her tirade. I never provided enough for her. We're reduced to taking marching orders from our son who is locking us into an apartment so we can rot. Her life has been meaningless."

"To which you replied?"

"She's right. With no one to blame but herself."

"Lovely."

"This time she swears she's going to stay away until she dies so she never has to look at my sour face again. Direct quote. Reminds me of the old days."

Jules's brow furrowed, annoyed at his mother's harsh words and at having to endure his parents' theatrics yet again. While her behavior hadn't been better, at least Agathe hadn't been running away from her family the past few years. Whatever the mental process was that triggered her need to escape, with the help of Jules's money, she'd been dragging Hugo along with her. But now her old habits had reared up again, skyrocketing Jules's emotions right back to the old days.

It seemed perfectly fitting that because he'd let Durand Properties make it for half the morning without him, something he so seldom did, and he was getting genuine pleasure from a bubble bath and buttery Parisian pastries with Zoe, that his parents would ruin it for him.

"We'll have to get a nurse in to help you for the time being," Jules voiced as his mind began to spin.

"Don't be ridiculous," Hugo protested. "I don't need looking after like an invalid."

But Jules was already firing off a text to Karim to contact an agency that could find someone suitable. Taking swift action to solve a problem without any sort of debate was what had kept him from falling apart as a child, as a teenager and as an adult. It was his salvation.

No amount of order could make things right with Zoe, though. All the realizations he thought he'd come to this morning quickly burned up in smoke as if they were tossed into a bonfire. What on earth had he been thinking? That happy-in-spite-of-everything nonsense he'd begun believing was just an escape. No one, no woman he'd ever met, not even Zoe, could convince him that partnering with someone wouldn't lead to disappointment, betrayal and despair.

It was pure poppycock that humans were made to share their place in the world with someone. Quite the opposite. The safer a distance a man kept from others and their distortions, the more likely he was to fully develop himself, to find his own way and not be swayed by the needs and limitations of someone else.

Jules saw himself in his father's sneering face. They were survivors, by whatever means necessary. That much they shared in common regardless of their opposite paths. Hugo chose to be alone within a marriage. Jules wouldn't even go that far. Neither should waste time and energy dwelling on how things might be better.

Agathe must have panicked. He'd overestimated her ability to appreciate the stability he was offering. Stronger measures were necessary. For their safety. Jules was the responsible party. He couldn't take a chance that his mother would wander off without him knowing her whereabouts. He would bring in a social worker to administrate and supervise physical and mental evaluations. Bring in round-the-clock care if that's what was called for. Their situation was too much for him to manage on his own. Just like with his properties, he needed a professional team. Organization and logic would prevail, as they always had.

For now, it would be simple enough to get his mother to return this time because, without money, she wouldn't last long even if she did impose herself on some distant cousin for a few days like she used to. After that, he'd bring in a squad.

Jules knew what else he needed to do.

After he'd heard through his mother's phone the train conductor calling passengers for boarding, the desperation in Agathe's voice took Jules back to his childhood. Memories marched along his brain like ticker tape. He replayed all his mother's departure walks down the street outside of their apartment building. How young Jules would stick his head out the window to watch her. He'd rest his arms on the rotted wood of the windowsill that always left scratches on his arms. Agathe's dress or coat might be different from one season to the next, but there was always the olive-colored suitcase.

The rattle of its wheels on the sidewalk was a sound he would never forget.

Before Agathe's call, for a fleeting moment in the bathtub with Zoe, he'd supposed that he could let go of all of that. Convinced Zoe's optimism had changed him. But it turns out, that was as temporary as the bath bubbles that had coated her luscious body.

Because Agathe leaving again had emotionally exhausted him. It was the last straw. He needed to put his armor back on. He wasn't capable of such a big shift as what being with Zoe would bring. It was too late for him. He was actually fragile. Feelings had no place in his world. Shutting down was the only way he could exist. That was what he knew, his lifeline, and he couldn't surrender it. That part of him had to be selfish. The wise part, the overseer, couldn't let him pile on any more disappointment. He was done. What if he put his trust in Zoe and she left him? He wouldn't survive the loss.

Or what if he was the one to leave? After all, as much as he could intellectualize about what had happened to him as a child, it was a fact that history sometimes did repeat itself. Despite his best intentions, maybe he wouldn't be able to go the distance in a long-term relationship with her. He couldn't bear the idea of her hearing *his* suitcase teeter away. Of her poking her head out the window to watch him desert her. He couldn't bear the hurt that his leaving her would cause. He'd had no example on how to do relationships right. Certainly, he'd get it wrong. He loved Zoe too much to take a chance on breaking her heart.

He *what*?

Love. How had that word escaped from the far recesses of his psyche? It wasn't even a word he used often. Was he *in love* with Zoe? Presumably, if a person was in love, they'd do everything in their power to shield their beloved from harm. To not only cherish but to protect. Logically, then, Jules himself was the potential harm to Zoe. Therefore, if he was in love with her, he should safeguard her from him. As a matter of fact, love obligated him to. Yes, he loved beautiful, sexy, talented Zoe Gaiman. So the most important thing he could do, the best way he could demonstrate his love, was to get out of her life.

His mission was clear.

When he'd left her earlier, inviting her to stay in the bath as long as she wanted and let herself out, they agreed to meet later at the apartment to supervise the furniture placement. At this point, perhaps it was going to be his father and a caretaker moving in, but nonetheless the renovation was coming to a close.

The front door was ajar when Jules arrived at the apartment, allowing him to see Zoe arranging some decorative items on the teakwood dining table that had arrived. The light streaming in through the windows added a golden halo to her natural radiance. His stomach clenched at the reminiscence of her satiny lips and of the responsive body that had arched for him over and over during their lovemaking. At the closeness that had formed without him being consciously aware of it, the secrets shared, the compassion for each other, the silly differences between them in the beginning so superficial now.

He'd allowed those forbidden daydreams he'd been having to crystalize into sharp focus for a split second. Them as a couple. His home as theirs. A kiss on the nose. Dancing by candlelight. Sharing an apple.

To have and to hold.

One last look at her through those rose-tinted glasses. Then he had to put a stop to his visions or they might kill him. In that respect, he *had* changed since childhood. Now he knew how to slay dragons, how to decimate obstacles that threatened him. Yes, that was it—love was an obstacle to freedom.

Zoe turned around as Jules entered the living room. "Oh. Hi. I didn't hear you come in."

"Did everything get delivered?"

"Si is doing a modification on the sofa sectional for me. Everything else came."

"Good."

"What's wrong?"

When Jules had abruptly raised himself out of the bathtub where they had been sharing a little slice of heaven a few hours ago, he hadn't explained about his mother's call from the Gare du Nord. While he'd shared quite a bit with Zoe about his past, he wasn't certain how much he should include her in any current matters. Now that he'd recognized what he needed to do, he was glad for that defensive decision.

Obviously, she was able to tell that something wasn't right. He moved nearer to her, though not too close, figuring it was better for him to say what needed to be said if he wasn't touching that honeyed skin he'd been caressing for hours last night after the opera.

"You know," he began, "we've never discussed any ongoing professional relationship after this project finished."

Zoe blinked a couple of times, sensing that the coming news was not good. "Ongoing professional relationship," she rasped the words he'd just spoken.

"I think you're a wonderful designer," he said, gesturing across the apartment. "It turns out all of your instincts were spot on after all, no matter how much I teased you about your methods."

"But..." She squinted.

Jules's lungs couldn't inhale a full breath. What he was about to say would alter the course of both of their lives forever. Compelled, but without the certainty he usually relied on for decisions, he carried on.

"What I'd like to do is connect you with some of the property developers I know here in Paris, who will hire you based on my recommendation. Smart and reliable designers are always in demand."

She nodded in comprehension, sweeping away some curls that had fallen forward. "So you're saying you wouldn't want to work with me again?"

Jules took a step forward but then forced his legs to stay put. Throwing his arms around her was the *wrong* thing to do in this moment. Yet, he couldn't stop fighting with himself about it.

"Zoe, I'm so sorry." *I love you.* "But I know myself well enough that I can't work with you again professionally because I can't see you anymore personally."

She jutted out her chin, choking back emotion. The entire set of her face changed, became drawn. "Oh, were we *seeing* each other?"

"Whatever it is we want to call it. To be perfectly honest, these weeks with you, making love, the Luxembourg Gardens, the opera, made me wonder for the first time in my life if I might be able to open up to a committed union with someone."

"And that someone isn't me."

"No." His Adam's apple pulsed. Frustration wasn't

allowing him to even say what he wanted to. "It is you. I've never felt anything for anyone like what I feel for you. That's the problem."

"I don't understand."

"I've never seen a healthy relationship in action. I wouldn't know what that looked like, how to do it. I'd ruin it. I'd never be capable of trusting someone or letting them put their trust in me. I'm better off as a ship that passes in the night."

"That's right, your three nautical voyages rule. I think with the opera we made it to four."

"You're angry. I'm so very sorry." *I love you.* "You've given me a taste of romance and enchantment. It was a divine state of being. But that's not for me, and never will be." He loathed rejecting her, the very person he'd most like to cherish until his dying day. Hated the words coming out of his mouth, even if they were the truth. For her and for him. His mind knew what his heart didn't want to accept.

Zoe composed herself. She was a survivor, too. He'd see to it that opportunities as a designer would come her way. He'd influence her future to the extent that he could from afar.

"We knew at the beginning that neither of us were intending to enter into anything serious," she stated bravely. "That was something we had in common."

After the loss of her parents, the risk of caring about someone and being cared for was great for her. She'd go it alone, too. Although her face said otherwise. Her eyes couldn't disguise the anguish.

With the weight of the world bearing down on him, Jules said, "I'll treasure this time together for the rest of my life."

Half of her mouth managed a hitch of a bittersweet smile. "Right. We'll always have Paris."

While she hadn't seen Jules enter the apartment a few minutes ago, Zoe surely watched him leave. As he walked out the door, the sight of the back of his head with the sharp swath of his dark thick hair and his slim frame in his pinstripe suit was unbearable in its perfection. She felt that her heart was attached to him and being stretched like a cord that would only go so far and then it would fray and disintegrate. Which it did when he disappeared out of view and she could finally let the tears flow.

After telling her that they'd no longer have a personal or professional relationship now that the work was done, he'd done a quick inspection of the completed apartment and then said he had another appointment. Zoe didn't know if that was true or that he just needed to get away from her. Which she could understand. He was clearly upset and conflicted—it wasn't as if he regarded calling things off with her lightly.

Her eyes couldn't turn away from the open front door as she wiped tear after tear from her eyes with the back of her hand. Even though she was in agreement with him that there was no future scenario that saw them together, the piece of her that had allowed visualizations of a different outcome stung and burned. It proved the point exactly, that Zoe didn't need any more pain, which would only have grown worse if the inevitable came after she'd become even more invested in Jules.

Once every fiber in her being was certain that he wasn't coming back to tell her, like he had at the opera, that he'd made another huge mistake, she pivoted in slow motion to take in the totality of the apartment. Without the strict budget that the clients she'd worked for back in Maupont were bound by, this apartment was Zoe's best career achievement so far. The practicality and accessibility, combined with the furnishings and appointments that announced style, had all come together whether Jules's parents would appreciate them or not.

She had the presence of mind to photograph the apartment for her portfolio. Jules had promised to act as liaison for her to get other design work in Paris, and for that she'd be forever grateful.

In the master bedroom, she'd talked Jules out of the rug he wanted because she was concerned that it was hard to maneuver over with the wheelchair. The bed was cool and inviting with baby blue and white linens. Twin nightstands held lamps and charging stations for electronics, with room for books or drinks. Gauzy curtains flanked the windows, and black-and-white seascape photographs adorned the sidewall. She'd had the wing-backed chairs returned to the shop she and Jules had bought them from, deciding instead on an upholstered bench from Si that would be easy for Hugo to use. There was plenty of passage space everywhere in the room.

Tears still streaming down her face, she snapped pictures of the second bedroom, which had been multipurposed nicely with a daybed that functioned as an extra sofa at an easy height for Hugo if he wanted it for afternoon naps or perhaps to enjoy the state-of-the-art television setup. Or if, in reality, the time came that he'd need a caretaker to spend the night. The long table underneath the picture window could be used for projects or as a desk, without the obstruction of drawers underneath.

The compromise about the kitchen that she and Jules had argued about worked perfectly, simple and clean cabinets painted off-white but with the yellow stone backsplash he'd wanted for a homey touch. Stacks of luxurious towels, storage shelves and artwork finished the bathroom. End tables place-marked where the sofa would fit into a corner in the living room, Jules having promised to send Zoe a photo when it came in.

Room by room, Zoe documented her accomplishments, exhaling loudly with no one to hear her, letting the tears continue to flow as they saw fit. When she was finished, she used the key codes to lock up, knowing this would be her last visit here. On the street, she walked toward the metro station, although not exactly sure of her destination. She didn't want to go home to an empty apartment, and Yasmine was at work at Si's studio.

Zoe descended the station stairs and decided where to go, though only halfway admitting it to herself. On the train, all the seats were taken so she grabbed onto one of the poles to anchor herself. From that position, she observed the fellow passengers surrounding her. That marvelous mix that was Paris, with people of every race, color, belief, orientation, size, age, homeland. Tourists, students, workers, families. Everybody headed somewhere. Stories to be told all around her.

Slitting her eyes to make her spying less obvious, she watched a young couple. The skinny man inked with tattoos up and down his arms held his dark-skinned gal from behind, pressing into her in a very sexual way, leaving no space between their bodies. She leaned her head back against his chest, a glazed-eyed bliss on her face. He whispered something into her ear that made her smile.

A city for lovers.

Zoe had been part of that folklore, ever so briefly. At the breathtaking loggia of the opera house. In the fine clothes and the diamond earrings Jules had bought her. Where her temporary lover kissed her without reserve and told her how much he wanted her in his bed again. How she'd floated up to the chandelier and Chagall ceiling after that, in an opaque trance for the rest of the performance while Jules maintained physical contact. At first, he'd held her hand, the pad of his thumb rhythmically caressing her skin. Later, he put his arm around her shoulder and held her there, the backs of his fingers stroking her neck.

In memory, what started on the loggia was one long embrace that lasted all night long, until they reveled in the morning's bubble bath. Zoe didn't know it at the time, but Jules's phone ringing signaled the alarm that would end the dream.

What would be the fate of the sexy couple Zoe eyed on the train? Happy forever or split by the weekend? Circumstances, wounds, fear, jealousy, fate, destiny. There were so many variables.

She exited at the station and trudged toward her destination. She entered the Luxembourg Gardens to wander around the perimeter of the café where she and Jules had been a pair of those Parisian lovers. Where they talked and laughed. Where she stuffed his face with a warm crepe and gooey pastries. She wouldn't have cared if they'd drunk plain water, as long as she was with him. The most amazing man she'd ever met.

A man of great intelligence and even greater character. Who awakened in her a primordial and grounded femininity that hadn't been unearthed before. Jules made her ping, made her second-guess her commitment to self-protection regardless of the cost. No one, nothing, would ever move her like he had. At least she hoped not.

When her phone rang as she wandered the gardens, she had a minute's hope that it was Jules until the screen identified a number she didn't recognize.

"Hello."

"Is this Zoe Gaiman?"

"Yes."

"This is Dr. Tran at Hospital Sainte-Térèse."

"Yes." Zoe's breath quickened. This couldn't be good.

"Yasmine Jaziri named you as her emergency contact."

"What happened?"

"Yasmine has been admitted into the hospital for observation. She collapsed at her workplace."

"I'll be right there."

CHAPTER NINE

ZOE COULD HEAR the clack of her own shoes as she rushed down the hospital corridor. She wasn't used to the sounds and the smells. Equipment in every direction blipped, dinged and beeped. There was an aroma of cleaning products that, no doubt, were responsible for the sterile whiteness of the hallways and floors.

"Yasmine Jaziri," she asked when she reached the nurses' station after following the instructions the doctor had given her over the phone. She'd left her session of disheartened reminiscing about Jules at the Luxembourg Gardens. As soon as she'd gotten the word about her roommate, she called for a rideshare, not wanting to spend time getting to the hospital on the metro.

Locating the room number the nurse gave her, Zoe poked her head in first, in case Yasmine was being attended to and needed privacy. Seeing that she was alone and asleep, Zoe tiptoed in so as not to wake her and sat down beside her bed in the visitor chair.

It was shocking to see Yasmine hooked up to tubes and wires. Some led to monitoring equipment. Zoe knew enough to note that her roommate's blood pressure and heart rate were stable, obviously a good sign. An intravenous line led to bags of fluids and medications. Yasmine seemed to be breathing normally while she slept. Although her dark complexion was more ashen than Zoe had ever seen it and her lips looked dry and chapped.

Time idled while she waited for Yasmine to wake up or for a doctor to enter with information. Zoe scanned everything in the room from an interior designer's point of view. It was drab but certainly functional, with a wall of built-in cabinets and drawers to organize supplies. Colorful geometric-patterned curtains tried to add some cheer as they flanked the one window. The view was of another building on the hospital's campus but it did allow in desperately needed natural light, as the overhead fixtures gave off a harsh illumination. Zoe thought she might go crazy from listening to the endless buzzing of equipment. Hospitals were not the most pleasant places.

"Well, hello there," Zoe said softly when Yasmine moved her head and slowly flickered open her eyes.

"Zoe," she scratched out, her throat obviously parched.

The bedside tray held a cup of water with a straw. "Are you allowed to drink anything?

"Yes, the nurse brought that before…before I fell asleep, I guess. My memory is a little fuzzy."

Zoe picked up the water and handed it to Yasmine, making sure the straw was close to her mouth and that she had a firm grasp on the cup.

"What happened?" The doctor on the phone said that Yasmine had collapsed but he hadn't had any further details.

After she took a few sips of the water, Yasmine handed the cup back to Zoe who returned it to the tray.

"One minute I was reaching for something on a high shelf and the next I was on the ground surrounded by the emergency medical responders Si had called for."

"Mademoiselle Jaziri, you lost consciousness," a low baritone joined the conversation as a man in a lab coat entered. "I am the attending physician, Dr. Tran."

He turned to Zoe. "You are a family member?"

"No, I'm Yasmine's roommate. Her family are all in Tunisia."

"Doctor…" Yasmine cleared her throat "…what is wrong with me?"

"It appears to have been severe dehydration. Everything looks okay but we'll need to do some more testing to see if there's an underlying condition and to make sure you didn't sustain any injuries when you fell."

"Oh, my gosh, what kind of injuries?"

"It's unlikely there are any based on the examinations and your present condition, but we'll want to do some brain imaging as a standard precaution."

Yasmine's eyes became wide as saucers. Zoe knew she was terrified and reached over to hold her hand. It was cold to the touch.

"I'll be back shortly and we'll get these assessments started as soon as we can. I really don't expect we'll find anything of concern, although we'll err on the side of caution."

"Thank you, Doctor," Yasmine managed as he left the room.

While the situation was serious, Zoe had long accepted that life was full of surprises. A young woman reaching up for something at work wasn't likely to crumple to the ground and need medical assistance. A hardworking couple going on a short holiday in Milan wasn't likely to be killed when a train ran off its track. Stuff happened.

Case in point, that in spite of the devastation Zoe had gone through after her parents' deaths that left her certain she'd never get close to anyone ever again, Jules Durand had happened. And it had shown her a prospect where two people did believe that they could be there for one another through thick and thin. Or were at least willing to give it a try and get by on hope.

Good fortune had actually graced Zoe. Jules called things off between them sooner rather than later. Any more days or nights she might have spent with him would have compounded the already heavy hurt she was towing like a ball and chain. Instead, at least now it was over and done. She didn't have to wait for the sneaky, inevitable stab to the chest. It had already come.

Alone she had decided to be. Alone she was. Everything was according to plan.

"That was a pretty good report from the doctor overall. How did you get so dehydrated, anyway? You did look a little bit off when I saw you at the studio."

"I got busy. I forgot to drink anything. Now that I think about it, it's been that way all week. I get involved in what I'm doing and I don't stop for breaks or lunch."

"That would never happen to me." Zoe smiled to cheer her up. "I eat all the time."

"With the hot billionaire?"

"Not anymore. That's old news."

"What? After the earrings? And the opera?"

Zoe touched one of the two diamonds that hadn't left her ears since Jules had placed them there. "My Parisian affair. That's all it was."

She'd known Yasmine for a year and while they co-existed peacefully as roommates, they weren't best friends. Zoe didn't have best friends. She was on her own in Paris, just as Yasmine was. Young women in a huge city, trying to forge a life for themselves but with no one watching their backs.

Yasmine's eyelids struggled to stay open.

"You should get some rest."

"Will you call my parents and tell them where I am? They're going to be so worried."

"I will."

Needless to say, Yasmine's mother was terribly distraught when Zoe explained the situation. With family and work obligations, neither of Yasmine's parents could immediately leave Tunisia for Paris to be by her side. Zoe promised to call her every time there was anything to report from the hospital. With audible tears, Yasmine's mother said that her daughter needed to move back to Bizerte, that this was the exact type of incident to prove that Paris was too far from home.

Zoe knew that a mother's love was talking rather than a voice of reason. But there was something to what she said, which directly related to the thoughts Zoe was starting to have. She sat back in the visitor's chair and propped her legs up on a corner of the bed while Yasmine slept. She was feeling rather tired herself.

Her fingers twisted one of the earrings. What Zoe had been mulling over was that maybe she should return home. To Maupont, to her siblings. Even though Jules had promised to act as liaison and find her more work, her brief time with him had only served to shed light on how lonely she really was. As much as she tried to outwardly present the idea that she didn't want or need anyone but herself, the lack of connections stared her in the face in this most social of cities. She no longer believed her own lies about choosing to go it by herself.

Boring Maupont. Designing the odd room renovation or workspace. But at least she'd have her brothers. They hadn't felt the ping in their chests, cautioning them not to get too close, not to feel. No warning alarm held them back. Two were married and she liked their wives. Perhaps they'd have children soon. That was something to look forward to. Fate might take any of them from her, but they'd have each other to rely on. She'd never be quite so solitary as she was now.

And as much as she loved Paris, she feared every building, every flower, every croissant would remind her of what she didn't get to have with Jules.

She leaned her head back and her eyelids grew heavy as, amidst the unfamiliar hospital drone, she allowed herself to drift off to sleep.

"I most certainly will not send you money. I've booked you a train ticket back to Paris yet again," Jules had scolded his mother, "and I expect you to use it."

With no options Agathe had, in fact, returned to the city. Jules had a driver pick her up at the train station and shuttle her to what was to be her new home. He and his father joined her there. Hugo greeted his wife with, "You again? I thought you promised never to return."

"This has got to stop!" Jules yelled. "Since you've been financially irresponsible for your entire lives and have no assets saved for your senior years, you are dependent on me. So you will live by my rules. Resent it or not, you've turned me into the parent. It should hardly be a horrible sacrifice to live in this apartment."

"Don't talk to us like we're children," Agathe tossed back with a snub of her nose.

"Yet, that's exactly how you behave."

"You wouldn't be the success you are if it weren't for us."

"You mean in spite of you."

"Don't talk that way to your mother," a gruff Hugo bellowed.

"Oh, have we found something you two agree on? That's a first." Jules frowned, finding himself unable to employ any self-censorship. This endless cycle with his parents was intolerable, and that wasn't all that was bothering him. "I introduced you to the interior designer who did the apartment. Both of Zoe's parents died in a train derailment."

Agathe blinked. "How awful."

"Yes, it's unimaginable. Life is fleeting. I can't understand why the two of you have chosen to live yours in constant opposition with each other."

"Your mother hates me because…"

"Enough excuses," Jules barked, cutting his father off. He'd had it and needed to fully express himself, to finally give voice to what he'd never said aloud to them. "Have either of you ever stopped to think what effect your constant fighting had on me, your only child? What it was like to have your mother leave with a suitcase over and over again, vowing never to return, even though she always did? And a father who couldn't keep a job because he was too stubborn to follow instructions and obey rules?"

A hush fell around them. His words were sinking in, both to himself and to them. It was liberating. To let out what he'd held inside. The words seemed to shock all three of them. After a lull, he found a calmer but pained voice, "Look at me. Really look at me. Beyond the professional success. Your son. Your child." He wanted to scream. For the boy who endured what he had. For the man who was crippled by the damage. "The atmosphere I grew up in of conflict, abandonment and uncertainty has left me unable to form relationships. I don't even have close friends. I've shut down any thoughts of marrying. Or having children. And I've only recently understood how much that has cost me."

Hugo and Agathe looked at each other, genuinely moved by their son's lament.

"I suppose we were too mired in our own strife to notice its impact on you," Hugo admitted.

Agathe shook her head as if she were just coming to a realization herself. "I was a horrible mother."

She was, and Jules was not going to assuage her with a denial. "What's done is done. But this has got to end. Because the craziest thing of it is that deep down you do care for each other. Why else would you, Mother, have always returned home when you left? And you, Father, always took her back? You could have split up. I'd hardly have been the first child whose parents had divorced. Yet, you didn't. And after I grew up, despite your bickering, you've roamed the world together."

"At your expense."

"That's not what matters. Life expectancies have gotten very long," Jules replied, "and even with father's physical limitations, you two could have several wonderful decades together. *We* could."

"What do you say, you nutty old bag?" Hugo threw a guffaw to his wife. "I suppose I must like you a little."

"All right, you good-for-nothing sod," Agathe answered back. "I might actually love you a little. No more drama."

"Let's not ask for the stars," Hugo snickered.

He wheeled his chair over to her and tugged on her arm until she leaned down for him to plant a kiss on her cheek.

Jules swallowed hard at the sight—he couldn't remember the last time he'd seen anything similar.

"You and Zoe did do a lovely job on this apartment," Agathe admitted.

"I know I've probably never said it, son," Hugo acknowledged, "but we're very proud of you." In fact, those weren't words he'd ever heard from his father. And for all of Jules's self-sufficiency, they meant a lot.

"Zoe and you?" Agathe inquired. "There's something between you that's more than just business, isn't there?"

How could his mother have intuited that during the short time they'd spent together at his hotel, when Agathe had been on particularly bad behavior? Was the bond between Jules and Zoe that obvious? Although it was almost impossible to say out loud words he didn't believe, he spat, "There was. There isn't anymore. How did you guess?"

"I can see it in your eyes. A mother knows." All three of them smirked at Agathe's comment as she was, obviously, anything but a typical mother. "I don't think you want to let her slip away."

After he left his parents to acquaint themselves with their new apartment, he got into the waiting car and picked up his phone. He remembered a school professor who'd said that one of the signs of a good leader was someone who would admit when they'd made a mistake. Jules had made the biggest one of his life. Even his mother could see it.

It was time to right the wrong. Witnessing his parents conceding to a reconciliation had moved him greatly. Gave him a new hope. Made him realize he was forever changed. He had a fresh distinction now. He was, and always would be, a man who had loved someone. Did love someone. And his mother was correct. The last thing he should do is turn his back on that precious gift of love. Yes, life came without guarantees. Yes, somebody with no experience in something was bound to stumble.

And yes, one could never be happy unless one followed his or her heart.

Jules's heart was walking around Paris on two curvaceous legs with a remarkable tangle of orange curls on its head. He needed to go claim that heart before it was gone and never to be found again.

When he tapped in the number to his heart's phone, the call switched directly to voice mail. What he had to say was too important to leave on a message. He did ask her to return his call as soon as possible. That it was urgent. He texted the same words and then instructed his driver where to take him.

Jules repeatedly rang the doorbell to Zoe's apartment. There was no response. He knew she wasn't at his parents' apartment, because he'd just left there. There was nothing else that needed to be purchased so she wasn't shopping for any finishing touches. Could she be out on a date? With a man, one who didn't put up barriers?

No, Jules assured himself. Zoe had been as adamant as he was that she would avoid the potential damage of love. He doubted she'd be out with a romantic interest so soon after he'd wounded her. She still might not be open to reconsidering her own rules. She'd been just like him in that respect. But the situation had changed. He'd have some convincing to do. That was okay. Whatever it took.

Not knowing what to do with himself, he went to a sports shop and bought two top-of-the-line bicycles for Zoe and Yasmine, and had them put in his car. He then had his driver return to Zoe's block. Perhaps she'd come home soon. He finished a sparkling water at a café before surrendering and going home. It wasn't until late that night when Zoe called and explained about Yasmine.

"Can I come to the hospital?"

"It's too late for visitors."

"Tomorrow, then."

"Let's wait and see."

Zoe woke up disoriented. Her phone buzzed in her pocket, but she let it go to voice mail. With eyes still closed, a backache reminded her that she'd been sleeping in a chair all night. She was still at the hospital. Although when her eyelids blinked open, she saw that neither Yasmine nor her bed were in the room with her. Zoe's mind whirled, imagining the worst, just as the hospital attendants wheeled Yasmine back into the room. She was sitting up in the bed and had a healthier color to her face.

"They took me downstairs for the brain imaging," Yasmine told Zoe. "I didn't want to wake you when I was wheeled out."

"Do we know anything?"

"No, but the doctor said he'll put a rush on getting the results. He thinks everything will be fine and that if I'm stable I can go home tomorrow."

Zoe stood to stretch. She felt like a twisted pretzel. And she was exhausted. While she'd managed to sleep here and there, she'd woken up many times during the night to the strangeness of the hospital. Darkness had finally opened into dawn. "If it's okay with you, I'm going to get some breakfast."

"You should. Thanks so much for staying with me."

"I'll be back in a little while."

Zoe forced her body into a fully upright posture and exited the room. Walking down the hospital corridor, she recalled the jumble of thoughts she'd had during the long night.

When her parents died, Zoe thought she'd never get over her grief. A black cloud blocked her from the sunlight for months after the accident. Their absence blinded her from seeing any goodness. The pain held her down, trying to strangle her.

That's when it all became certain. When she came to rely on the pings. In case she started to forget, the internal warning would remind her that she'd never let anyone close ever again. While two of her brothers went on to marry, and the other had a steady boyfriend, Zoe couldn't follow that path. Her heart was too soft. The risk was too high. In making her way to Paris, she'd vowed to throw herself into creativity and not people. She'd immunized herself like a vaccination would, preventing love from seeping into her bloodstream.

Over eggs and juice, Zoe was aware of the beeping in her pocket again. A glance at the phone screen told her not only that it was Jules but that she'd missed three of his calls. Why had he initially called yesterday? Something about the apartment, no doubt. Having briefed him last night about Yasmine, these morning calls were probably out of concern.

When she rang, he sounded relieved to hear the doctor's expected prognosis. "May I stop by?"

She didn't want him to come. Or did she? Jules wasn't part of Yasmine's life. He wasn't even part of hers anymore. He'd made a clean break with Zoe, and Yasmine's hospitalization didn't change that. She'd be better off continuing to practice being on her own, experiencing life's ups and downs such as roommates being in the hospital. "I don't think you should."

On the other hand, why wouldn't she want him to come? She didn't have many friends in Paris. Hospitals were big scary places. Why wouldn't someone want to have an ally, or even just a familiar face? How distorted her view of relationships had become. When she got back to Maupont, she'd put some genuine effort into finding a few girlfriends to pal around with, maybe university mates she'd lost touch with.

Solitude suddenly washed over her like an ocean's wave.

Jules said, "I'd like to see the both of you."

Zoe had a moment to protest. She didn't take it.

Zoe was back in Yasmine's room when Jules stepped into the doorway. A sight for sore eyes to be sure, he held a beautiful arrangement of yellow flowers in a glass vase. "May I come in?"

"Of course," Yasmine answered, shooting a knowing look in Zoe's direction.

"These are for you." He placed the flowers down on the stand beside Yasmine's bed.

"They're so pretty. Thank you."

They conversed a bit until Yasmine's eyelids began to flutter. Jules took the cue. He stood at her bedside. "Assuming you're going home tomorrow, can I give you a ride?" He knew that Zoe and Yasmine were alone in Paris, with no family, and he thought of a way he could be useful. That was one of the many things Zoe lo...

"That would be wonderful. Thank you," Yasmine said as her eyes fell shut.

"Step into the hallway for a minute with me?" he asked Zoe, who was on the other side of the bed. She nodded, although apprehension bounced in her stomach.

"What were you calling about last night?" Zoe wasted no time once they'd left the room. To be with Jules in the antiseptic surroundings of the hospital was unnatural. Wrong. And it almost angered her. This was a place for families, for significant others, for lifelong relationships. Where people died or were healed or brought babies into the world. It wasn't a place for Parisian bosses and the underlings they'd had affairs with to chat.

He made contact with her pupils and followed them when they tried to move away. "Do you remember when we went to the opera and I told you I wanted a do-over?"

"Yes."

"I need an even bigger one this time. I've made another horrible error. And I'm here to correct it." He wrapped his hand around her small shoulder, his warmth instantly radiating through his palm into her. "I want to be with you, Zoe. I don't know what I'm doing and I'm bound to take dozens of wrong turns but I love you. And we're going to be together."

Overwhelm had her feeling dizzy. She'd spent the wee hours of the night making sense of his breakup, re-affirming her aloneness. He'd been crystal clear, know-ing himself, stating his mind. Now he'd changed it and she was just supposed to jump in? Her internal ping sig-naled so loud and fast she was sure the nurses in another ward were going to confuse it with medical equipment.

"I can't, Jules. You helped me realize that. I'm not good for anyone."

"You're good for me! Just when I was sure I'd be alone forever, something I wouldn't have predicted in a million years occurred. You. You fell, literally, into my life," he teased her about her first impression, "and you destroyed my ordered world with its rule books and protocols. You've shown me that our hearts can be free. And limitless."

When he'd told her at the apartment that he didn't want to see her anymore professionally or personally, that was news she hadn't thought she could move past. Instead, it was this, the opposite, that was even harder. To turn away from what half of her admitted she so desperately wanted. Yet, she had to. She was the only one there to protect her. Zoe had to be her own knight in shining armor.

"I'm sorry. I can't."

After they stood in the corridor staring silently at each other for as long as they could take, Zoe granted Jules's request to return to the hospital the next day to take Yasmine home. She couldn't deny him that.

"Tomorrow, then."

Time passed with Yasmine undergoing many exams

and tests, and the two roommates making the best of hospital television programming. The nurses were kind enough to give Zoe soap and towels so that she could shower, as she didn't want to go home and leave Yasmine alone at the hospital.

During the artificially lit hours of the night, Yasmine slept peacefully while Zoe's mind whirled. Even though she might have wished for Jules's return, she hadn't been expecting it. Forcing her to face her demons yet again, to reconsider what was real and what she was hanging onto simply because it had become familiar. After endless cups of tea from the kind nurses, and after running down her phone's battery wasting time on the internet looking at furniture, Zoe decided to take a little walk around the hospital ward.

She was used to the blinking lights and identifying sounds by now. There was very little other noises beside a faint and constant buzz. Visiting hours were long since over. A custodian mopped the floor. Someone else restocked bedding onto a cart. Zoe didn't mean to snoop but she glanced into a couple of patients' rooms as she passed them by. A very elderly man, tiny and frail, breathed with the help of an oxygen mask on his face. In the next, a much younger man had bandages on his head. Had he undergone surgery, she wondered? Or had he fallen? Had he been in an accident? Was he the victim of a crime? Her brow furrowed in concern. He couldn't have been much older than twenty.

How unknowable the universe was! Look what had happened even just in her orbit. Yasmine's spell of dehydration could have made her collapse while crossing a street, where she might have been hit by a car, or could have broken her legs or sustained brain damage that left her unable to walk or talk. Zoe's parents might have traveled safely to Milan and be home in Maupont right now. Every moment of existence was a treasurable gift that needed to be treated as such and never taken for granted.

And Zoe finally couldn't deny that however many days and nights she had left on this earth, she wanted more than anything to spend them with Jules. With him, the world could be complete and full and she could belong. She knew that she'd helped him find a little whimsy and delight from within the seriousness of his life, the fallout of his past. But he probably didn't know how much he'd given her, besides just a job.

Without intending to, he made her feel connected to him and part of something larger than herself, something that mattered and was worth having at any cost. Together, they were an interdependent entity. He taught her that planning for the future wasn't to be feared, that it could be a positive thing. His commitment to his parents in spite of what they put him through moved her. In his arms, she'd learned about a joining of souls and bodies far beyond what she'd ever known was possible. And she wanted to keep experiencing that merge for eternity. They sometimes had opposite ways of looking at things but like yin and yang, Jules and Zoe fit together as a whole.

She would never get over the grief of her parents' untimely deaths. Nor should she. Grief was a measure of her love for them. The grief could be welcomed. It could be cherished. And most importantly, Zoe needed to stop using it as an obstacle.

She was in love with Jules Durand. And she needed

to tell him so as soon as possible. Hopefully, it wasn't too late.

Dawn couldn't come fast enough.

With morning cheer, she phoned to let Jules know that Yasmine was being discharged. "Everything is okay. She can go home."

"That's wonderful. I'll be right there."

After he arrived and while Yasmine was collecting her personal belongings to leave, Zoe took Jules's hand to pull him aside. The smile that lit up his eyes told her that nothing had been jeopardized, nothing would ever be too late. She caressed the back of his hand with her thumb. "This time it's me who needs a do-over."

He began nodding excitedly. "Yes. Yes, my love. I think we've got a lot to work through between us. We're going to make many mistakes. Need many do-overs."

"We'll get through them."

"Does Yasmine take good care of herself as a rule? Does she eat plenty of vegetables and take vitamins?"

"I think so. Nice of you to inquire." Zoe's health-conscious man. Was her future going to include icky green drinks and early morning runs? That was okay if that's what he wanted. As long as there were pajama days and plenty of cheese, too. She'd hope to live a long and balanced life. With Jules.

"I'm asking because I want to make sure she'll be okay on her own."

"What do you mean?"

"I was thinking that perhaps she could move into one of my properties."

"Why? Where will I live?"

"I want you to move in with me. And marry me. And be by my side for the rest of our days. Will you do that?"

"I will." The cautioning ping in her gut almost tore her open. That was another thing she'd have to walk with, to accept. She could do it. As long as she was with him. "I love you, too, and I want to be with you forever." Zoe threw her arms around Jules with a force that knocked even him off-kilter. Something she was very good at.

* * * * *

REUNITED WITH HER PARISIAN SURGEON

ANNIE O'NEIL

This one definitely goes out to my readers.

Without you this book literally could not have been made.

You are the ones who built this hero and heroine…

I hope you enjoy their story.

Annie O xx

CHAPTER ONE

SCENT. SOUND. TASTE. Even the air felt different in Australia; so did the sea water he was ploughing through. But as the days had bled into weeks, then months, Raphael had come to know that travelling halfway round the world hadn't made a blind bit of difference. He was still carrying the same hollowed-out heart, weighted with an anvil's worth of guilt. Leaving Paris hadn't done a damn thing towards relieving the burden.

Volunteering had done nothing. Neither had working in conflict zones. Nor donating blood and platelets. He would have pulled his heart right out of his chest if he'd thought it would help. Working all day and all night hadn't helped. And then there was money. Heaven knew he'd tried to throw enough of *that* at the situation, only to make a bad situation worse.

Jean-Luc didn't want any of his money. Not anymore.

The truth was a simple one. Nothing could change the fact that his best friend's daughter had died on his operating table.

He'd known he was too close to her. He'd known he shouldn't have raised so much as a scalpel when he'd seen who the patient was. The injuries she'd suffered. But there had been no one more qualified. And Jean-Luc had begged him. Begged him to save his daughter's life.

Raphael thought through each excruciatingly long minute they'd been in surgery for the millionth time.

Clamps. Suction. Closing the massive traumatic aortic rupture only to have another present itself. Clamps. More suction. Stiches. Dozens of them. Hundreds, maybe. He could see his fingers knotting each one in place. Ensuring blood flow returned to her kidneys. Her heart.

Her young body had responded incredibly well to the surgery. A miracle really, considering the massive trauma she'd suffered when the car had slammed into hers. All that had been left to do when he'd been called to the adjacent operating theatre was close her up.

No matter how many times he went through it, he stalled at the critical moment. There'd been two choices. He'd taken one path. He should've chosen the other. His one fatal error had built to that leaden silence when he'd returned to the operating theatre to see his junior lifting his hands up and away from her small, lifeless body.

They'd looked to him to call the time of death.

Raphael swam to the edge of the pool, blinking away the sea water, almost surprised to see that the sun was beginning to set. He pulled himself up and out of the pool in one fluid move, vaguely aware of how the exertion came easily now that he was trying to burn away the memories with lap after lap.

He was tired now. Exhausted, if he was being truly honest. Coming here to Sydney was his last-ditch attempt to find the man he had once been. The man buried beneath a grief he feared would haunt him until his dying day. He was driving himself to swim harder than he ever had before—churning the seaside pool into a boiling froth around him as he hit one side, dove, twisted, and then started again to see how soon he could hit the other—but his burning lungs did nothing to assuage the heaviness of his heart.

Love could.

And forgiveness could do so much more.

In fewer than twenty-four hours he'd see Maggie…

The years since he'd seen her last seemed incalculable. He remembered her vividly. A clear-eyed, open-hearted exchange student from Australia. Apart from Jean-Luc there had been no one in his life who had ever known him so well, who had seen straight through to his soul.

If, when they met again, she could see a glimmer of the man she'd known all those years ago he'd know there was a light at the end of the tunnel.

After toweling off in the disappearing rays of the sun, he tugged on a long-sleeved T-shirt and headed for the exit, already conditioned to look toward the white fence on the right, leading out of the baths towards the coastal path.

Le petit monstre de la mer.

He was still there. The cock-eared mutt that had been following him from his rented accommodation, along the coastal path to the Bronte Baths and back since he'd arrived in Sydney a week ago.

A reject from former tenants?

There were no tags, no chips. Nothing to identify him or his owners.

It shocked him that he'd cared enough to take the dog to a vet the day before.

At least it proved there was still a heart thumping away in his chest, doing more than was mechanically required.

He huffed out a mirthless laugh.

Or was it just proof that he desperately needed one soul in his life who wasn't judging him? Who still wanted his company?

He winced away the thought. That wasn't fair. After over a decade of virtually no contact, Maggie hadn't merely agreed to meet up with him tomorrow night. She'd found him a job at her paramedic station. She'd gone above and beyond the call of a long-ago friendship.

The memory of her bright green eyes softened the hard set of his jaw.

From what she'd said in her emails, the under-staffed ambulance station sounded like a non-stop grind. Perhaps, at long last, *this* would be the beginning of the healing he'd been seeking, after eighteen months on the run from the pain he'd caused.

He certainly didn't trust himself on a surgical ward. Not yet, anyway. Perhaps never.

"*Allons-y*, Monster." He tipped his head towards the street and the dog quickly met his long-stride pace. "Let's see if we can find you some supper."

CHAPTER TWO

Tick-tock. Tick-tock.

Why had she brought him to a movie?

Raphael was going to think she hated him. But, no, she was just socially inept. And she wasn't quite ready for him to meet the "real" Maggie.

Maggie's phone buzzed in her backpack, adding to her mortification. She dragged the bag out from under her seat and fished around until she found it. Working in the emergency services meant checking your phone every time it beeped or buzzed, whether or not you were sitting next to your teenage crush from the most perfect year you'd ever had.

A year in Paris.

Raphael Bouchon.

Match. Made. In. Heaven.

Not that there'd been any romance. Just a one-sided crush that had come to an abrupt end when she'd boarded the plane back to Australia.

She pushed the button on her phone to read the message.

Dags, Dad needs more of those hyper-socks next time you come.

She speed-typed back.

They're compression socks, you dill.

Her expression softened. Her brothers were doing their best in the face of their father's ever-changing blood pressure. They were mechanics, not medics.

She glanced across at Raphael. *I could've been a surgeon, like you.*

An unexpected sting of tears hit her at the back of her throat so she refocused on her phone.

See you in a couple of weeks with a fresh supply. Maggie xx

She jammed the phone back into her backpack and suppressed the inevitable sigh of frustration. Moving to Sydney was more of a hassle than it was worth sometimes. But staying in Broken Hill forever? Uh-uh. *Not* an option.

She dropped her pack beneath her chair and readjusted in her stadium-style seat, only to succeed in doing what she'd been trying to avoid all night—grazing her thigh along Raphael's.

"Desolé." Raphael put his hand where his knee had just knocked Maggie's and gave it an apologetic pat.

She stared at his hand. Long, gorgeous, surgeon's fingers. Strong. Assured. Not the type of fingers that caressed the likes of her lowly paramedic's knees.

Wait a minute.

Had it been a caress? If it had been then this whole high school reunion thing was swiftly turning into a dream come true. If not…

She glanced across at him and saw he wasn't even looking at her. His bright blue eyes were glued to the flickering screen twenty or so rows ahead of them. Fair enough, considering they were at a movie, but…

"Non, c'est—it's all right."

Maggie fumbled her way through an unnecessary response, all the while crossing her legs, tucking her toes behind her calf to weave her legs together and make herself as small as possible. If they didn't touch again, and she could somehow drill it into her pea-sized brain that Raphael wasn't fabricating excuses to touch her, then maybe—just maybe—she'd stop feeling as if she'd just regressed back to her sixteen-year-old, in-love-with-Raphael self.

Ha! Fat chance of *that* happening.

Tall, dark and broodingly handsome, Raphael Bouchon would have to head back to France without so much as a *C'est la vie!* if she were ever going to give up the ghost of a dream that there had once been something between them to build upon.

The second she'd laid eyes on him tonight Maggie's body had been swept straight back to the giddy sensations she'd felt as a teen.

Two hours in, she was still feeling the effects. Despite the typically warm, late-summer Australian evening, all the delicate hairs on her arms were standing straight up. The hundredth wave of goose pimples was rippling along her spine, keeping time with the swoosh and wash of waves upon the shores of Botany Bay. Off in the distance, the magical lights of Sydney's famed harbor-front were glowing and twinkling, mimicking the warm sensation of fireflies dancing around her belly.

The outdoor cinema in Sydney's Botanical Gardens was the perfect atmosphere for romance. Perfect, that was, if Raphael had been showing the slightest bit of interest in her.

It would've helped if she didn't feel like a Class A fraud. Yammering on about living the high life in Sydney as they'd walked through the gardens toward the cinema instead of being honest had been a bad move. How could she tell him, after he'd achieved so much, that her "high life" entailed a pokey flat that needed an epic cleaning session, a virtually round-the-clock work schedule and quarterly trips to the Outback to tackle the piles of laundry her brothers had left undone.

Hardly the life of a glamorous city girl.

She was such a fraud!

Not to mention all of the appalling "Franglais" that had been falling out of her mouth since she and Raphael had met at the entrance to the gardens. Every single stern word she'd had with herself on the bus journey there had all but disappeared from her head. Including the reminder that this was *not* a date. Just an old friend showing another old friend around town.

Nothing. More.

The second she'd laid eyes on him…

Total implosion of all her platonic intentions.

Whether it was because thirty-year-old Raphael was even better looking than seventeen-year-old Raphael, or whether it was the fact that looking just a little…*haunted* added yet another layer of intriguing magnetism to the man, she wasn't sure. Either way, Raphael had the same powerful effect on her that he'd had the first time they'd met at her host family's home all those years ago.

Jean-Luc. A twist of guilt because she hadn't kept in touch with him either cinched her heart.

She'd had a lot on her plate when she'd come home. She wasn't Super Girl. She couldn't do everything.

She readjusted in her seat and gave herself a little shake. *Just watch the movie and act normal!*

About three seconds passed before she unwove her legs and twisted them the other way round. She'd seen *Casablanca* a thousand times—could quote it line for line and had planned to do so tonight, back when she'd had just the one ticket…

Maggie dropped her eyelids and attempted another sidelong glimpse at the man she'd known as a boy.

His expression was intense and focused, though the rest of the audience was chuckling at one of Humphrey Bogart's dry comments. Smiling was not Raphael's thing.

Not anymore, anyway.

Back in Paris it had been an entirely different story. At least when they'd been together. His laugh had brightened everything, every day. It had made life appear in Technicolor.

Not that his surprise reconnection on social media had come in the form of an emotional email declaring his undying love for her—a love that demanded to be sated in the form of his flying halfway across the world to fulfil a lifelong dream of making sweet, magical love to her.

Quite the opposite, in fact.

His email had been polite. To the point. Bereft of what her father called "frilly girlie add-ons". Silly her for thinking that vital little details like why he'd decided to get in touch and move to Sydney after years of successfully pursuing an emergency medicine surgical career without so much as a *bonjour* were "facts."

Picking a movie as their first meeting hadn't exactly been a prime choice in eliciting more information either. It had just seemed a simpler way of easing back into a friendship she wasn't entirely sure existed anymore.

Back in Paris he might not have had romantic feelings for her, but there had been no doubting that their friendship had been as tight as they came.

Her eyes shifted in Raphael's direction. Seeing the sorrow, or something a lot like it, etched into his features had near enough stopped Maggie's heart from beating when they'd met up earlier that evening. Not that he was the only one who had changed…

She shivered, remembering the day she'd flown home

from France as vividly as if it were yesterday. Seeing her brothers at the arrivals gate instead of her mum…their expressions as sorrowful as she had ever known them…

Leaving France had felt physically painful, but arriving home…

Arriving home had been devastating.

How could she not have known her mother was so ill?

She dug her fingernails into her palms and blew a tight breath between her lips.

It wasn't anyone's fault. It was just…life.

Her breath lodged in her throat as Raphael's gaze shifted from the massive outdoor cinema screen to Maggie's arms.

He leaned in closer, his voice soft as he asked, *"T'as froid?"*

"Cold? Me? No. This is Australia! Sydney, anyway," Maggie corrected, her nervous laugh jangling in her ears as she rubbed her hands briskly along her arms. Just about the most ridiculous way to prove she was actually quite warm enough, thank you very much.

Being in lust did that to a girl.

That, and haphazardly wading her way through a state of complete and utter mental mayhem.

Sitting next to Raphael Bouchon was like being torn in two. Half of her heart was beating with huge, oxygen-filled thumps of exhilaration, while the other half was pounding like the hoofbeats of a racehorse hell-bent on being anywhere but here.

Raphael shifted in his chair and pulled his linen jacket off the back of his seat, brushing his knee against hers as he did. Accidentally. Of course. That was the only way things like that happened to her.

Just like Raphael "deciding on a change" and moving to Australia to become a paramedic. At her local station.

Sure she'd offered to help him, completely convinced it would never actually happen. And yet here they were, thigh to thigh, sitting in the middle of the Botanical Gardens, watching a movie under another balmy summer night's sky.

Raphael held his linen jacket up to her with an *It's yours if you want it* expression on his face. He was so earnest. And kind. Not to mention knee-wobblingly gorgeous.

"Megarooni gorge", as her friend Kelly would say. Kelly would've been slipping into that jacket and climbing onto Raphael's lap in the blink of an eye. Kelly had confidence.

Maggie...? Not so much. Just the thought of climbing onto Raphael's lap reduced her insides to a jittery mass of unfulfillable expectation.

So she waved off his kind gesture, mouthing, *No, thank you,* all the while rubbing her hands together and blowing on them as she did.

Nutter. What are you doing?

"Please," Raphael whispered, and his French accent danced along the back of her neck as he shifted the silk lining of the coat over her shoulders. "I insist."

"Merci." She braved the tiniest soupçon of French as she pulled the jacket and Raphael's spicy man-scent closer round her. She mentally thunked herself on the forehead. *Why* was she acting like such a dill?

As if the answer wasn't sitting right next to her on the open-air theater's bleacher seating, looking like a medical journal centerfold.

Raphael Bouchon, *Casablanca* and the glass of champagne he had insisted upon buying her while they were waiting for the film to start were all adding up to one thing: the most embarrassing exchange student reunion ever. Besides, it wasn't like a first date, when—

Whoa!

It's not a date. This is not a date. You are showing an obviously bereaved, gorgeous friend from high school around Sydney. That's. It. The fact that his arrival coin-

cided with a non-refundable ticket to the Starlight Cinema and the most romantic film ever is sheer coincidence. And practical. Waste not, want not. And that includes Raphael.

At least that was what she'd keep telling herself.

Along with the reminder that this movie ended with a friendship. Nothing more.

She looked down to her fingers when she realized she was totting up the number of short-lived boyfriends who hadn't made the grade over the years. Expecting anything different when everyone had been held up to The Raphael Standard was hardly a surprise. Inaccessible. Unattainable. Dangerously desirable.

And here she was. Platonically sitting next to the man himself. Not flirting. Not reveling in the protective comfort of his jacket around her shoulders. Not trying to divine any hidden meaning behind the chivalrous gesture no one had ever shown her before. Nor was she sneaking the occasional sidelong glimpse of his full Gallic lips. The cornflower-blue eyes that defied nature. The slightly overlong chestnut hair that all but screamed for someone to run their fingers through it. Someone like her.

And yet…

The mischievous glint in his eyes that she remembered so vividly from high school hadn't shown up once tonight. And even though he'd only just turned thirty, the salt and pepper look had made significant inroads into his dark brown hair. The little crinkles beside his eyes that she might have ascribed to smiling only appeared when his eyebrows drew close together and his entire visage took on a faraway look, as if he wasn't quite sure how he'd found himself almost twenty thousand kilometers away from home.

It didn't take a mind-reader to figure out that his relocation halfway around the world was a way to put a buffer between himself and some dark memories. This was *not* a man looking for a carefree year with a Down Under lover.

Not that she would've been on his list of possible paramours. She wasn't anywhere close to Raphael's league. The fact that she was sitting next to him at all was a "bloody blinder of a miracle" as her Aussie rules footie-playing brothers would say, midway through giving her a roughhouse knuckle duster.

Sigh...

Maggie feigned another quick rearrangement of her hair from one shoulder to the other, trying to divine whether Raphael was genuinely enjoying the al fresco film experience. Or *cinema en plein air*, as he had reminded her in his chocolate-rich voice as her rusty French returned in dribs and drabs. There hadn't been much call for it over the years.

She swung her eyes low and to the left. Yup. Still gorgeous.

As opposed to her.

She was a poorly coordinated, fashion-challenged dork in contrast to Raphael's effortlessly elegant appearance. Not that he'd said anything of the sort when he'd first caught sight of her at their prearranged rendezvous point. *Rendezvous?* Get her! Far from it. He'd even complimented her on her butterfly print vintage skirt and the "land girl" knotted top she'd dragged out of the back of her closet. Not because it was the prettiest outfit she owned, but because it was the only thing that was ironed apart from her row of fastidiously maintained uniforms.

Appearances weren't everything. She was proof of that. Freckle-faced redheads were every bit as competent as the next person. Well...maybe not literally, seeing as the person sitting next to her was a surgeon and she was "just" a paramedic. Anyway, her hair was more fiery auburn than carrot-orange. On a good day.

When they'd first met, in the corridors of the Parisian Lycée, she'd shaken off her small-town-girl persona and found the butterfly she'd always thought had been living in her heart. Well…a nerdy butterfly. Raphael had been every bit as nerdy as she back then. Or so she'd thought. But he'd called it…academically minded. He had been the best friend of her host's brother and she'd fallen head over heels in love with him.

Her mother had been right when she'd cheekily told her daughter to keep her eye on the "Nerd Talent." Now, at thirty years old, Raphael was little short of movie-star-gorgeous. His tall, reedy body had filled out so that he was six-foot-something of toned man magnificence. His chestnut hair looked rakishly windswept and interesting. He looked like a costume drama hero who'd just jumped off his horse after a long ride along the clifftops in search of his heroine.

Whether his cheekbones were *über*-pronounced because of the weight he claimed to have lost on his travels or because his genes were plain old superior was unclear. Either way, he was completely out-of-this-world beautiful.

Even the five o'clock shadow that she thought looked ridiculous on most other blokes added a rugged edge to a man who clearly felt at ease in the most sophisticated cities in Europe. Although she would bet her last dollar he'd do just fine in the Outback too. His body confidence spoke of a man who could change a car tire with one hand and chop wood with the other.

Not that she'd been imagining either scenario. Much.

Those blue eyes of his still had those crazy long black lashes…but shadows crossed his clear azure irises more often than not…

As if feeling the heat in her gaze, Raphael looked away from the flickering screen, giving her a quick glance and a gentle smile as she accidentally swooshed her out-of-control hair against his arm. The most outlandish hair in Oz, she called it. If she wanted it curly it went straight. Straight? It went into coils. Why she didn't just chop it all off, as her brothers regularly suggested, was beyond her.

Again she stared at the half-moons her nails had pressed into her hands. After her mum passed it had seemed as if her hair was the one thing she had left in her life that was genuinely feminine. So she'd vowed to keep it—no matter how thick and wild it became.

"So!" Raphael turned to her, with that soft, barely there smile of his that never quite made it to a full-blown grin playing upon his lips. "Did you have anything else in mind?"

Maggie threw a panicked look over her shoulder.

Like holding hands underneath the starlit sky?

Gazing adoringly into one another's eyes in between soul-quenching kisses?

She glanced at the screen and to her horror realized the credits were running. Sitting beside him and not making a complete fool of herself had been hard enough, but— *Oh, crikey*. She hoped he didn't expect her to conduct an actual conversation in French. It had been hard enough when she was in her teens, but now that she hadn't spoken a word in over thirteen years...

All of her tingly, flirty feelings began to dissolve in an ever-growing pool of insecurity.

"Sheesh. Sorry, mate... Raphael. Sorry, sorry..."

She stumbled over a few more apologies. Years of being "one of the guys" at work and growing up as the tomboy kid sister in a house full of blokey blokes had rendered her more delicate turns of phrase—if she had ever had them—utterly obsolete.

She puffed up her cheeks and blew out a big breath, trying to figure out what would be best. A meat pie and a pint?

She took in a few more blinks' worth of Raphael, patiently waiting for her to get a grip, and dismissed the idea. French people didn't go out for meat pies and pints! Why had her brain chosen this exact moment to block out everything she could remember about France?

Oysters? Caviar? More champagne?

Crêpes! French people loved them. Sydneysiders did, too.

There was a mobile crêpe caravan she'd visited a couple of times when she was in between patients. She grabbed her backpack and began pawing around for her mobile to try and find out where it might be parked up tonight.

What was it called? Suzettes? Flo's Flaming Pancakes?

"Actually…" Raphael put his hand on Maggie's forearm to stop her frantic excavation. "As I am starting work tomorrow morning, perhaps we'll take a rain check?"

Maggie nodded along as he continued speaking. Something about heartfelt thanks for her help in getting him the job. The stacks of paperwork she'd breezed through on his behalf.

In truth, it was far easier to stand and smile while she let herself be swept away with the rhythm and musical cadence of each word coming out of Raphael's mouth than to actually pay attention to what he was saying. Each word presented itself as a beautiful little stand-alone poem—distinctly unlike the slang-heavy lingo she'd brought with her from her small-town upbringing.

That year in Paris had been her mother's last gift to her. A glimpse of what the rest of the world had to offer.

She'd found out, all right. In spades.

A glimpse of Raphael's world, more like. And she wasn't just talking about trips to a museum.

For her there was only one Raphael and he was standing right here, speaking perfectly fluent English, his mouth caressing each vowel and cherishing each consonant so that when his throat collaborated with his tongue and the words hit the ether each word was like an individually wrapped sweet.

A *bon mot*.

She smiled to herself. Of course the French had a phrase for it. In a country that old they had a beautiful phrase for everything. Including the exquisite pain of unrequited love.

La douleur exquise. And, wow, was she feeling that right about now. Why had she been so *useful* when he'd written to her a couple of months ago from...? Where was it? Vietnam? Or was it Mozambique? Both?

Regardless, his email hadn't suggested he was intent on coming to Australia. Just "considering a change."

Typical Maggie. She'd just picked up the reins and run with it. Filling out forms. Offering to get the right information to the right people on the right date at the right time.

"Best little helper this side of the equator," as her mother had always said.

And now that he was here...

Total. Stage. Fright.

She'd been an idiot to think—

Nothing. You're friends. Just like Ingrid Bergman and Humphrey Bogart.

"Yeah, you're right. Early to bed sounds good. In fact..." she glanced at her watch "...time's a-tickin'. Best get cracking!"

An image of Raphael tangled up in her sheets flashed across her mind's eye as the rest of her barely functioning brain played a quick game of catch-up.

"Wait a minute. Did you say you were coming to work *tomorrow*?"

"*Oui.* Didn't I tell you?" His brows cinched together in concern.

Again the nervous laughter burbled up, scratching and becoming distorted as it passed through her tight throat.

"Well, yeah, I knew you were coming. My boss told us about it the other day. But I didn't—" She stopped herself.

She'd thought she'd have more time to prepare. To become more immune to the emotional ramifications of working with the one man she'd imagined having a future with. In Paris. On a surgical ward. In a marital bed. *Together.*

"Maggie, if you do not want me working at your station…"

Raphael pulled out the vowels in her name, making it sound as if she were some sort of exotic bird or a beautiful length of stretchy caramel.

Quit staring at the gorgeous man and respond, Mags.

"No. That's not it at all. I'm totally on board with it. You'll be amazing. Everyone will love you. I must've gotten muddled. It'll be nice for you. To hit the ground running, I mean."

"Absolutement." Raphael nodded. "I am completely ready to be a true Australian."

Maggie couldn't help herself. She sniggered. Then laughed. Then outright guffawed. "Raphael, I don't think you could be a 'true Australian' even if you paddled backwards on a surfboard, dropped snags down your throat and chased them up with a slab of stubbies, all with a school of sharks circling round you. You're just too…" She held her hands open in front of him, as if it was completely obvious.

"Oui?" Raphael looked straight down that Gallic nose of his, giving her a supercilious look.

Had she taken the mick a bit too hard and fast?

"What is it that I am too much of, Maggie?"

"Um…well… *French.*" She gave an apologetic shrug. "You know… You're just too French to be Australian."

The warm evening air grew thick. Whether it was an impending rainstorm or the tightening of the invisible tension that had snapped taut between them, she wasn't sure. Her body ached to step in closer. To put her hands on his chest.

"I suppose I will have to rely on you to help me," he said.

Whether he meant it or not was hard to tell.

"No wuckers, Raph," she joked, giving him a jesty poke in the ribs with her elbow, trying to defuse the tension. "I'll give you training lessons on Aussie slang and you can help me with my…um…"

Her vocabulary deserted her as her eyes met and locked with Raphael's.

"Francais?"

It would be so easy to kiss you right now.

"Maggie?"

Oh, God. She was staring. Those eyes of his…

But, again, the bright blue was shadowed with something dark.

What's happened to you since we last met?

Something about the slight tension in his shoulders told her not to push. He had his reasons for giving up his surgical career and zig-zagging around the world, only to land here in Oz. The last thing she was going to do was dig. Everyone had their "cupboard of woes," her mother had often said. And no one had the right to open them up and air them.

Just chill, Mags.

He'd spill his guts when he felt good and ready. Listening to people's "gut-spills" was one of her specialties. But when it came to spilling her own guts…there was no way she was going to unleash *that* pack of writhing serpents on anyone.

When they reached the aisle and began walking side by side the backs of their hands lightly brushed. Another rush of goose pimples shimmied up her arms, ultimately swirling and falling like a warm glitter mist in her tummy.

She was really going to have to train her body to calm the heck down if she was going to be his shoulder to cry on. Not that he looked even close to crying. Far from it.

Had she stuck her foot in it with the whole "you're too French" thing?

"For what it's worth," she said, "I really enjoy working on the ambos, and the fact you have extra language skills is great. Work is different every day. And it was an amazing way for me to get my bearings when I moved to Sydney."

"I'm not sure I'll be at the wheel. I haven't qualified for driving yet. All I know is I'm going to be working on an MIC Ambulance."

Luckily Raphael missed her wide-eyed *No! That's what I do!* response as he scanned the area, then turned towards the main bus stop outside the Botanical Gardens as if he'd been doing it every day of his life. He'd been born and bred in one of the world's most sophisticated cities—acclimatizing to another must be a piece of cake.

"I was actually surprised by how easy it was to get my working papers. Something about a shortage of Mobile Intensive Care paramedics?"

"Yeah, that's right." Maggie nodded, her brain more at ease in work mode. "They've really been struggling over in Victoria. Well, everywhere, I think. The most skilled mobile intensive care paramedics seem to be running off to the Middle East, where the pay is better. Well, not all of them. And it's not because working here is horrible or anything… I mean it's actually pretty great, when you consider the range of services we provide to the community— and of course to the whole of New South Wales when they need it. Like when there are forest fires. Or big crashes out in the back of beyond."

She was rambling now. And in serious danger of sending Raphael packing.

He was one of the only people in her life who had

known her before her mum had passed. There was something about that link that felt precious. Like a tiny priceless jewel she'd do everything in her power to protect.

Maggie looked up, her eyes widening as Raphael's expression softened into an inquisitive smile. The trees behind him were laced with fairy lights and the buzz and whoosh of the city faded into a gentle murmur as her eyes met with his.

A flash of pure, undiluted longing flooded her chest so powerfully that she had to pull in a deep breath to stave off the dizzying effect of being the sole object of those beautiful blue eyes of his. The ache twisting in her lungs tightened into a yearning for something deeper. How mad would the world have to become for him to feel the same way?

Slowly he reached out his hands and placed them on her shoulders. The heat from his fingers seared straight through her light top, sending out a spray of response along her collarbone that gathered in sensual tingles along the soft curves of her breasts. He tipped his chin to one side as he parted his lips.

Was Raphael Bouchon, man of her dreams, going to kiss her?

"I think this is where I catch my bus." Raphael pointed up to the sign above them. "I am afraid I will need my jacket back if we are going to part ways here. Will you be all right?"

"Of course!" she answered, too loudly, tugging off his jacket and checking her volume as she continued. "I'm the one who should be asking *you* that, anyway. Where was it you got a place again?"

It was the one thing she hadn't helped with. Finding him a place. He'd told her it was already sorted, but that didn't stop a case of The Guilts from settling in.

She should've offered him a bed...well, a sofa...while

he sorted something out. Played tour guide. Called estate agents. Cleared the ever-accruing mess off of her countertops and made him dinner.

Not invited him to a movie and then scarpered.

But that level of support would have been slipping straight into the mode she was still trying to release herself from with her family.

The girl who did all the chores no one else wanted to do.

Besides, her home was her castle and there wasn't a chance on God's green earth that she would be inviting him round—or anyone, for that matter. She'd had almost seven years of looking after her brothers and father—enough housekeeping, laundry and "When's the tucker gunna hit the table, Daggie?" to last a lifetime.

"It's a place I found on the internet, near Bondi Beach. I thought it sounded..." he paused for effect "...Australian."

Maggie laughed good-naturedly and leant forward to punch him on the arm. At the same time he leant down to kiss her on the cheek. Their lips collided and skidded off of each other's—but not before Maggie caught the most perfect essence of what it would be like to *actually* kiss him.

Pure magic.

Raphael caught the sides of her arms with his hands, as if to steady them both, and this time when their eyes met there was something new shining straight at her. That glint. The shiny spark in Raphael's almond-shaped eyes that erased every single thought from her harried brain except for one: *I could spend the rest of my life with you.*

The fear that followed in its wake chilled her to the bone.

An hour later Maggie held a staring contest with herself in her poorly lit bathroom mirror. Red-haired, freckle-faced, and every bit as unsure whether she was a country mouse or a city mouse as she had been thirteen years ago.

Closing her eyes, she traced her fingers along her lips, trying to relive the brush of Raphael's mouth against hers. It came easily. Too easily. Especially when she had been in love with him for almost half her life.

Her eyes flickered open and there in the mirror was the same ol' Maggie. The one who would never live in Paris. The one barely making a go of it in the big smoke. The girl born and raised and most likely to return to a town so far from Sydney it had its own time zone. In other words, she could dream all she wanted, but a future with Raphael Bouchon was never going to be a reality.

CHAPTER THREE

RAPHAEL TUGGED HIS fingers through hair that probably could have done with a bit of a trim. He chided himself for not putting in a bit more effort. For not trying to look as if he cared as much as he genuinely did.

Seeing Maggie yesterday had done what he'd hoped. It had re-awoken a part of him he'd feared had died alongside Amalie that day in the operating theatre.

When their lips had accidentally brushed last night there'd been a spark.

He was sure of it.

Enough so that he sorely regretted not kissing her all those years ago. But Jean-Luc's mother's warning had been a stark one. *"Hands off!"*, she'd said, and so he had obeyed.

If he hadn't been relying so heavily on Jean-Luc's family for that vital sense of stability his parents had been unable to provide he would've gladly risked his pride and seen if Maggie had felt the same way.

For an instant last night he'd been certain of it.

This morning... Not so much.

Not that Maggie was taking a blind bit of notice of his *does-she-doesn't-she?* conundrum.

Listening to her now, reeling off the contents of the ambulance they'd be working on, was like being in the middle of an auctioneer's rapid-fire pitch.

From the moment she'd arrived at the station she'd

barely been able to look him in the eye. More proof, if he needed it, that he hadn't meant to her what she'd meant to him. After all, who took someone to a movie when they hadn't seen each other in over thirteen years?

Someone with a life. Someone who'd moved on.

"Raphael?" She clapped a hand on the back door of the ambulance to gain his attention. "Are you getting this?"

He nodded, not having the heart to tell her he'd actually spent the long flight over memorizing the equipment breakdowns and layouts he'd been sent along with the confirmation of his posting.

"And over here we've got your pneumocath, advanced drugs, syringe pumps and cold intravenous fluids. It's not so much a problem this time of year. The hypothermia. What with it being summer. But…" She screwed up her face and asked, "Is hypothermia a problem in Paris?"

She quickly flicked her green eyes towards him, then whisked them back to the supply bins as if looking at him for longer than three seconds would give her a rash.

"Well, you've got snow, so I suppose so," she answered for him. Then, almost sheepishly, she turned back to him and said, "*Neige*, right?"

He nodded, parting his lips to say he was actually ready to head out if she was, but she had already turned back toward the ambulance and was reeling off yet another list of equipment specific to the MICA vehicles.

"Hey, Mags. Looks like the A-Team is being broken up."

Maggie stopped mid-flow, her green eyes brightening as a beach-blond forty-something man came round the corner of their ambulance with a timorous woman who only just prevented herself from running into him when he abruptly stopped.

"All good things must come to an end I guess, Stevo." Maggie heaved a sigh of genuine remorse, then shot a guilty look at Raphael with an apologetic smile following in its wake.

"Raphael, this is my partner—my *former* ambo partner—Steve Laughlin."

"Crikey, Mags. It's only been ten minutes. And no lines have been drawn in the sand yet. No offence, newbie!"

He turned to the young woman behind him and gave her a solid clap on the shoulder that nearly buckled her knees before turning back to Raphael.

"Nice to meetcha, mate." Steve put his hand out for a solid shake. "You've got yourself one of Bondi Junction's finest here, so consider yourself lucky. I'm counting on you to look after her. She can be a bit of a klutz—"

"I'm more than capable of looking after myself, thank you very much!" Maggie cut in.

"Yeah, yeah. *Help me, help me!*" Steve elbowed Raphael in the ribs and laughed. "You know what I'm saying, mate? All these girls *really* want is a big strong bloke to look after 'em. Get a load of these pecs, Casey. This is what happens when your partner doesn't carry her fair share of the equipment bags."

He flexed his arm into Popeye muscles and grinned as his new charge instantly flushed with mortification.

"Yes, Steve. Nothing to do with the hours you spend at the gym instead of helping your wife with the dishes," Maggie answered drily, clearly immune to Steve's *über*-macho version of charm. "And, for the record, I think I can live *without* a big strong Tarzan swinging in to rescue me, knowing that there's a fully qualified surgeon sitting in your old seat. Twice as many patients in half the time, I'm betting."

She gave Raphael a quick *Am I right, or what?* smile.

Raphael winced. Bragging rights over his surgical skills was something he'd rather not be a party to.

"Ah, well, then." Steve gave Raphael a knowing look,

completely missing his discomfort. "If you're not busy curing everyone in Sydney over the next couple of hours, perhaps you'll be able to shake a bit more fun into our girl, here. Tell her there's a bit more to life than work, will ya? When we heard you were a Frenchie we all started laying bets on how long it'd take for you to get her out on the town after her shift. She's got a thing about France, you know?"

He rocked back on his heels, crossed his arms over what looked like the beginnings of a beer belly and gave him a solid once-over.

"You're a better looking bloke than I am, so maybe you're in with a bit of a chance."

"Hardly!" The word leapt out of Maggie's throat, lancing the light-hearted tone of Steve's comments in two.

"Easy, there, Mags." Steve rolled his eyes and gave her a half-hug. "I'm just messing with you. Give the bloke a chance, all right? We're just worried about you. All work and no play…"

"Yeah. I get it, Steve. Don't you have some work you should be getting on with?"

Raphael stayed back from the group, preferring silence to watching the increasing flush heating up Maggie's cheeks.

He stepped forward for a handshake when Steve did a quick introduction of his new junior partner, Casey, before heading for their own ambulance. As soon as they'd left Maggie poured her obvious irritation into filling up all the supply bins in their ambulance.

The idea of spending time with him outside of working hours obviously didn't appeal. Had he said something last night to offend her? Perhaps taking a rain check on a post-film drink had been bad form if it wasn't her usual *mode opératoire* to go out.

Raphael swallowed against rising frustration. Hitting the wrong note seemed to be his specialty of late. Making the wrong move. Insisting upon operating on a little girl he was far too close to, only to have to break the news to his best friend that his young daughter had just died on the operating table because of *his* mistake.

Jean-Luc would never forgive him. Not in this lifetime anyway.

He tried to crush the memory of what Jean-Luc had said to him to the recesses of his mind. A near impossible task as he revisited the cruel words each and every night while trying to fall into a restless sleep.

"You just take! All you do is *take*!"

The medical report had told a different story, had said that Amalie would have died anyway. Her injuries had been too severe. The loss of blood too great. But Raphael knew the truth. *He* was the one who had made the decision that had ultimately led to the little girl's death.

He returned his gaze to Maggie, who had shifted back into her efficient self and was doing a swirly *ta-da!* gesture with her arms in front of the ambulance.

"Clocked that? Are we good? Am I going too fast? Too slow? Should I just stop talking altogether?"

Her eyes widened and he saw that his worries about Maggie not wanting to work with him had been ridiculous. Those green cat's eyes of hers were alight with hints of hope and concern, making it abundantly clear that her nervous energy wasn't anti-Raphael. It was worry that he might not be interested. It was hope that he shared her passion for the job she loved. And, if he wasn't mistaken, there was an underlying pride at what she did for her community.

"All right, Frenchie? How're ya settlin' in, mate?"

Raphael turned at the sound of the male voice, not missing the pained expression taking hold of Maggie's face as her eyes lit on the paramedic behind him.

A tall black-haired man—big—was holding out a hand.

"Marcus Harrison. Fellow paramedic. Friends call me Cyclops. I'll give you three guesses why."

Raphael threw a quick look to Maggie, who shrugged, rolling her eyes rolling as if to say, *Indulge him. It'll be over in a minute.*

When he turned back he was face to face with an eyeball.

"It's glass. Get it? I've only got one eye. Been that way since I was a nipper. Too much rugby, and one day…" Marcus pinched his fingers in front of his eye then made a flying object gesture.

Behind him Raphael could hear Maggie muttering something about *putting it away, already.*

Totally unfazed by Maggie's disgust, Marcus popped his eye back into the empty socket and doubled up in a fit of self-induced laughter. "Oh, mate. You should see your face. Priceless."

"Are you finished?" Maggie asked, her tone crisp, but not without affection.

"Yeah, but…" Marcus bent in half again, another hit of hilarity shaking him from head to toe.

"Marcus, I'm *trying* to show our new colleague the truck."

"What? He'll be all right." Marcus waved off her concerns. "You were a surgeon or something back there in Paris, right?"

Raphael nodded, knowing that a flinch had accompanied the reminder.

"Leave the poor man alone. He's got enough on his plate without you showing off your wares and quizzing him about his credentials."

Marcus strutted in a circle in front of Maggie. "Darlin', let me assure you, you can look at my wares *any* day of the week."

Again Maggie rolled her eyes. This clearly wasn't Marcus's first flirt session. Nor Maggie's first refusal. Clearly having three older brothers had toughened her up.

Marcus crossed to her, leaned in, gave her a loud smack of a kiss on the cheek, then gave Raphael a good-natured thump on the back as he passed, heading towards the tea room whistling a pop tune.

"He seems…"

Raphael searched for a good word, but Maggie beat him to it.

"A right idiot. Except—" she held up her index finger "—when it comes to work. He is a first-class paramedic. Claims he always wanted to be a paratrooper, but the eye thing made that dream die real quick—so he became another kind of para. Paramedic," she added, in case he hadn't caught the shortened term. Something the Australians seemed to do a lot of.

"And you two are…?" Raphael moved a finger between Maggie and the space Marcus had just occupied. "Were you a couple?"

He caught himself holding his breath as he waited for an answer. Was he hoping she would say no?

"Pah!" Maggie barked, her eyes almost tearing up as she laughed at the suggestion. "You have *got* to be kidding me!"

Just as quickly she recovered, throwing an anxious look towards the tea room.

"I mean, he's a lovely bloke, and will definitely make someone incredibly happy, but he's not…" Her eyes flicked to his so quickly there was no time to catch her expression. "He's a really good bloke. I'm lucky to know him. He's taught me loads."

Loyalty.

That was the warmth he heard in her voice. And it was a reminder of why he'd come to Sydney. She was loyal.

She hadn't even questioned why he was here. Just helped in every way she could.

He swallowed. She didn't know the whole story.

He turned at the sound of Maggie snapping her fingers together before displaying a clear plastic bag of kit as if she were a game show hostess.

"Right. Back to work. So, we call these nifty little numbers the Advanced Airway Management Sets—or AAMS if you're in a hurry."

"*Très bien.* It all looks very familiar." He nodded, aware that his attention was divided.

Again and again his eyes were drawn to the fabric of Maggie's dark blue overalls tightening against her curves as she leant into the truck to replace the kit and then, by turns, pointed out the defibrillator, the suction kit, the spinal collars, spine board, inflatable splints, drugs, sphygmomanometers, pulse oximeters and on and on.

In her regulation jumpsuit she looked like an action heroine who donned a form-fitting uniform before bravely— and successfully—battling intergalactic creatures for the greater good of the universe.

Her fiery hair had been pulled into submission with a thick fishtail plait. Her green eyes shone brightly against surprisingly creamy skin. Ample use of sunblock, he supposed. An essential in Sydney's virtually non-stop "holiday" weather.

Instantly his thoughts blackened. As if he'd come here for some R&R after a year and a half of trying to put some good back into the world.

"All you do is take."

There was no coming back from the death of a man's only child.

He scrubbed his hand along his neck, still hearing the heavy church bells ringing out their somber tones on the day they had laid Amalie to rest. Amalie's funeral was the last time he'd seen Jean-Luc and the rest of the Couttards.

It was the first time they had fought. The last time they had had any contact.

"You took from my parents and now you've taken my daughter. No more!"

He opened his eyes to see Maggie waving a hand in front of his face. "Hello? All right in there? Time to jump in. We've been called out. Twenty-five-year-old mother, imminent birth. We're about seven minutes out. Wheels up, mate!"

Five minutes into the ride, Maggie's internal conversation was still running on a loop.

Mate?

What was it with her and calling Raphael *mate*? Almost as bad as Cyclops and Stevo calling him Frenchie.

Grr... Instead of bringing out that Parisian butterfly she knew lay dormant somewhere within her, Raphael's appearance was turbo-charging the country girl she'd tried to leave behind in Broken Hill.

Then again, maybe he didn't care what she did one way or the other. It was difficult to gauge exactly what was behind that near-neutral expression of his. Chances were pretty high that *he* hadn't stayed up half the night reliving their near-miss kiss. How mortifying. She hoped her feelings weren't as transparent as she feared.

Pretending to check for oncoming traffic, she gave Raphael a quick glance.

Still gorgeous. Still impossible to read.

But it went deeper than that. He didn't seem *present*. And that was something he had always been—*here*, engaged.

Could a person change so much that they lost the essence of who they were?

She swallowed the lump of contrition rising in her throat. *She* had. She'd changed a lot since her bright-eyed and bushy-tailed days.

She glanced across again, unsurprised to find his expression stoically unchanged. Not that she could see his eyes beneath the aviator glasses he'd slipped on once they'd strapped in for the blue lights ride.

"You sure you're all right?" She moved her elbow as if to prod him. The gesture was pointless as she was strapped into her seatbelt.

A curt nod was her response.

"This isn't the first run you've had since you left France, is it?"

"No." His gaze remained steadfastly glued on the road ahead of them.

Okay. Guess we're not feeling very chatty today.

Not fair, Maggie. The man's got a lot on his plate today. New country. New language. New job. Old friend...

An old friend she was having to get to know all over again.

The old Raphael would've been laughing and joking right this very second—teasing her about her driving, or about the fact that she couldn't help making her own sound effect along with the sirens and each switch she flicked. He'd maybe even have started quizzing her about why her career had gone to the blue lights instead of the blue robes of the surgical ward.

Not a freaking peep.

When she'd told him to jump into the ambulance they'd done one of those comedic dances, with one person trying to get past the other, that had ended up looking like really bad country jigging. It should have, at the very least, elicited a smile.

Not from Raphael.

Not a whisper as to what was going on with him. Why he was here. Why he had downgraded himself.

The only thing she could guess was that the man was trying to put as much space as he could between himself and some intensely painful memories.

"You know, if you want to talk or anything…"

He glanced across, his brows tugged together. "About the job? No, no. I'm fine."

"Or about other things…" She pulled the ambulance around a tight corner, grimly satisfied to see his expression change from neutral to impressed, if only for a nanosecond.

Why wouldn't he talk to her? They'd once told each other *everything*.

Everything except the fact that she was a born and bred country girl doing her best to believe it wasn't above her station to dream of life as a surgeon in Paris.

Come to think of it, neither of them had talked about their home lives much. Just the futures they'd imagined for themselves. Her host family's beautiful Parisian home had been the base for most of their adventures. And the rest of their time had been spent exploring. With a whole lot of studying on thick picnic rugs in the shadow of the Eiffel Tower thrown in for good measure. After they'd hit the books they would roll over onto their backs, gaze up at the huge steel structure and talk about their dreams for the future.

Raphael had achieved his goals in spades. Resident surgeon in a busy Parisian A&E department. Addressing conferences around the world on emergency medicine. But then there had been an the about-face, eighteen months ago, and he had gone to work in refugee camps and free clinics in developing countries only to turn up now in Sydney.

Mysteries aside, Raphael's life was a far cry from being

a jobbing paramedic in one of Sydney's beach neighborhoods with no chance of climbing up the ladder.

Cut yourself some slack.

She had returned from France only to be told her mother had died while she was flying home. A girl didn't recover from that sort of loss quickly. And then there were the add-on factors: the shock of discovering her mother had known she was ill when she'd handed Maggie the ticket to Paris, the expectation of her grieving father and brothers that Maggie would step into the role her mother had filled—the role her mother had made her promise she would never, ever take.

Cramming her dream of moving back to France and becoming a surgeon into the back of a cupboard, she had cooked and cleaned and washed an endless stream of socks for her family while they got on with the business of living their lives...

It had taken her years to break out of that role. And she had finally done it. She was living life on her own terms. Sort of. Not really... Four weeks of her year were still dedicated to sock-washing, floor-scrubbing and casserole-making, but it was a step. Who knew? Maybe one day she would be the world's first ninety-year-old junior surgeon.

She glanced across at Raphael, saw his jaw tight again as they wove their way through the morning traffic. It wasn't her driving that drew his muscles taut against his lean features. There was something raw in his behavior.

If it was ghosts he was trying to outrun, he looked as though he'd lost the battle. It was as if they had taken up residence without notice, casting shadows over his blue eyes.

If only she could help bring out the bright light she knew could shine from those eyes of his.

A little voice in her head told her she'd never succeed.

You don't have the power to make anyone happy. That can only happen from within.

"So…" Her voice echoed in the silent ambulance as she tried to launch into the work banter she and Steve had always engaged in. "When's the last time you delivered a baby outside a hospital?"

"Is there not a midwife attending?"

Raphael's tone didn't carry alarm, just curiosity. As if he were performing a mental checklist.

"There's been a call made, but it's usually luck of the draw as to who gets there first. We'd be fighting rush-hour traffic to get to the Women's Hospital, so I don't think we'll have time to load her up and take her there. They said the birth was imminent when they rang. That the mum is already wanting to bear down."

Raphael nodded, processing.

She doubted it was the actual delivery of a child that was cinching his brows together.

Maybe…

No guessing. You do not get to guess what has been going on in his life. He will tell you when he is good and ready.

She shot him another quick look, relieved to see that the crease had disappeared from his forehead.

Work would get him on track. It was what pulled *her* out of the dumps whenever she was down. It was what had finally pushed her up and out of Broken Hill.

That twelve-hour drive to Sydney had felt epically long. Mostly because she had known she'd never wanted to go back and that it would be the first of many round trips. They weren't as frequent now…

Instead of saying anything in response, Raphael looked out of the window as they whipped past apartment block after apartment block on their way to the Christian housing charity that had put in the call.

Unable to bear the silence, she tried again. "The mother is Congolese, I think. Democratic Republic of Congo. A recent refugee. My Lingala's pretty shoddy. How's yours?"

The hint of a smile bloomed, then faded on his lips.

"Was there any more information about the mother? Medically?" he qualified.

"Nope." Maggie deftly pulled the ambulance over to the roadside. "We'll just have to ask her ourselves."

A few moments later the pair of them, a gurney, and the two birthing kits Maggie had thrown on top were skidding to a halt in front of a group of men standing outside a door in the housing facility's central courtyard.

"She's in here." One of the lay sisters gestured to an open door beyond the wall of men.

Like the Red Sea in the biblical tale, the men parted at the sight of Maggie and Raphael, letting them pass through, a respectful, somber air replacing the feverish buzz of what had no doubt been a *will-they-won't-they-make-it?* discussion.

Abandoning the gurney out in the courtyard, Maggie grabbed the birthing kits, but stepped to the side so that Raphael could enter the room first. The distant mood she had sensed in him had entirely evaporated.

Inside, curtains drawn, a crowd of women in long skirts and brightly patterned tops shifted so they could see the beautiful woman on a bed that had either been pulled into the sitting room for the birth or was there because of constant over-crowding. Either way, the woman's intense groans and her expression showed she was more than ready to push.

She was pushing.

"I'll do the hygiene drapes if you're all right to begin the examination," Maggie told Raphael.

"Good. *Bien.*"

Out of the corner of her eye she watched as he unzipped one of the kit bags, quickly finding the necessary items to wash and sterilize his hands and arms in the small, adjacent kitchen, re-entering as he snapped on a pair of examination gloves. His movements were quick. Efficient. They spoke of a man who was in his element despite the dimly lit apartment and the crowd of onlookers.

But there didn't seem to be any warmth emanating from him. And that surprised her. It wasn't as though he was being mean, but… *C'mon! The woman's about to have a baby.* A little bedside manner would be a good thing to use around now!

The women, as if by mutual consent, all pressed back against the wall, necks craning as Raphael made his way to the expectant mother's side.

"You are happy with an audience?" Raphael asked the woman in his accented English, and the first proper smile to hit his lips all morning made a welcome appearance.

Finally! So it *is* there. Just hard to tap into.

The expectant mother nodded. *"Bien sûr. Voici ma famille."* She groaned through another contraction.

"Ah!" Raphael gently parted her legs and lifted the paper blanket Maggie had put in place across the woman's lap. *"Vous parlez Français? Très bien."* He turned to Maggie. "You are all right to translate on your own?"

Maggie grinned. Trust Raphael to have his first patient in Oz be a fluent French-speaker.

A seamless flow of information zigzagged from the mother to Raphael to Maggie and back again—including the woman's name, which was Divine.

Maggie smiled when she heard that. What a great name! As if the woman's mother had predestined her daughter to be beautiful and feminine. Maggie was all right as far as names went, but Daggie—as her own family insisted on calling her—made her feel about as pretty as if she were called Manky Sea Sponge.

"Can you believe it?" Raphael was looking up at her, his brow furrowed in that all-work-no-play look she was still trying to get used to.

"Divine? Yeah." She offered the mother another smile. "It's a beautiful name."

"This is Divine's fourth pregnancy."

Ah. That was the vital bit of information he had actually been alluding to. She'd heard. Registered. Moved back to the pretty name. Was he going to be like this all the time?

Three pregnancies without any problems meant this one would likely be a cinch.

Maggie shifted her features into a face she hoped said, *Wow! Impressive!* Not, *Four children before you've turned thirty? No, thank you.*

Her mother had been down that path, and look at all the good it had done her. A life of cooking and cleaning in the Outback before being hit by an A-Grade cancer cluster bomb. Pancreatic. Lymph. Stomach. At least it had been swift—though that hadn't made it any less of a shock.

"First time for a home birth?" Maggie asked, to stop herself from exploring any further her instinctual response to a life of full-time parenting. She'd been down that dark alley plenty of times, and this was definitely not the time or place for a return journey.

"*Non…*" Divine bore down, her breath coming in practiced huffs. "I have never had one of my children in hospital."

"Just as well," said Raphael neutrally, in French, "because you are crowning. I can see your baby's head now."

Cheers erupted from the women around, and to Maggie's complete surprise a chorus of joyous singing began.

Raphael indicated that Maggie should kneel down beside him as he kept pressure on the woman's perineum to prevent any uncontrolled movements while first the forehead and then the chin and finally the child's entire head became visible.

Finding herself caught up in the party-like atmosphere, Maggie beamed up at Divine, congratulating her on her ability to get through the intense moment without any tears or painkillers, and out of the corner of her eye watched Raphael check for the umbilical cord and its location.

"Are you up for one more big push?" Raphael asked over the ever-increasing roar of song. "We just need to get those shoulders out." His voice was gentle, but it conveyed how strong the determined push Divine gave would have to be.

Divine tipped her head back, then threw it forward, her voice joining in extraordinary harmony with the women around her as she bellowed and sang her way through a super-powered push.

Raphael held the baby's head in one hand, turning it towards the mother's thigh, and gently pressed down with the other to encourage the top shoulder to be delivered as Divine bore down for the one final push that…oh, yes… yes…would bring her new son into the world.

"*Felicitations*, Divine. You have a beautiful little boy."

Maggie was shocked to hear Raphael's strangely vacant tone. Why wasn't he as lifted and carried away by the raucous atmosphere as she was? No matter how often she tried to be blasé about moments like these—it was impossible. And to play a role in this miracle of a child coming into the world surrounded by song…

She might not want one herself just yet, but it was just so…so *happy*. One of those truly magical moments a paramedic could have. It brought a tear to her eye every single time.

She swiped away her tears as swiftly, expertly, Raphael suctioned the baby's mouth and nose, giving Maggie a satisfied nod to tell her that the amniotic fluid was a healthy color. Maggie handed him a fresh towel to vigorously and thoroughly dry the baby, then waited with another dry towel to swaddle the infant before gently placing him on his mother's chest.

The cooing and murmurs of delight that followed wafted and floated around them, and Raphael delivered the placenta at the very moment the midwife opened the door with a cry of, "G'day ladies, I'm finally here—no thanks to the traffic. Shall we get to it?"

Laughter, cheers and yet more singing broke out as the midwife's expression changed to one of delighted wonder when the little boy took his first proper wail.

A few more minutes of cleaning up took place while the rest of the women began handing round plates of food.

Raphael and Maggie turned to go, but stopped upon hearing Divine calling for them. Raphael went over to the side of the bed where the little boy was, and after a bit of insistence finally accepted the child into his arms.

Again those shadows shifted and darkened his eyes. It heartened Maggie to see that the shadows weren't so dark as to mask his genuine pleasure at seeing the child was healthy and well, but there was *something* there. Something that colored even the happiest of experiences.

"What is your name?" the woman asked in her heavily accented English. "I am so grateful for your help. For my son, I must know your name."

Maggie shot him a quick look. It wasn't unknown for people to name their children after a person who had helped them in a significant way. She couldn't contain a grin. Barely twenty-four hours into his new life and already he'd brought a child into the world who might bear his name. What a way to make an impression!

One look told her he wasn't nearly as delighted by the prospect as Maggie was.

"Raphael," he said finally.

The answer was reluctant, and his posture followed suit when Divine's eyes lit up at the sound of his name. He gave an almost imperceptible shake of his head, silently communicating that under no circumstances did he want his name to go to the child.

As clearly as Maggie had read the message, so too did the new mother. She gave Raphael's arm a grateful squeeze, then stretched her arms out to him so she could hold her son close again.

"Thank you, Raphael," she said. *"Merci."*

He nodded his acceptance for the gratitude, but remained silent.

"You were amazing. You looked like you deliver babies every day of the year," Maggie couldn't help saying, feeling a puff of pride that her friend had handled the birth with such ease.

She, too, received a silent nod of thanks.

"I think," Divine continued, her eyes brightening again, skidding from Raphael to Maggie and then across to the group of women who were with them in the room, "I will call my son…"

Everyone leaned forward to hear the name of this precious new life, born into an entirely new world, his whole life stretching out in front of him with a perfectly clean slate…

"Walter."

"Walter?" Maggie clapped her hand over her mouth.

A sea of heads nodded in unison, as if it were the perfect choice. Maggie bit down on the inside of her cheek. Hard. She glanced to the side to see Raphael nodding too, as if it were the ideal name for the tiny infant.

Maybe the name wasn't funny in France, but Maggie was straining not to break down in a full fit of giggles.

Walter!

"Shall we go?" Raphael was impatient now, shifting

his run bag from hand to hand as if the incident had unbalanced him.

Maybe it was being stationary that had him so fidgety. He had that faraway look in his eyes again. The unsettled one that needed the immediacy of work to dull its jagged edges.

"Sure." Maggie picked up the other run bag full of supplies, relieved to hear her radio crackling with another call-out.

As she took down her notes she tried to shrug off the disquiet that had formed between herself and Raphael.

This was a *que sera sera* situation if ever there were one.

Whatever would be would be.

Shouldering her own run bag, she received pats of thanks on her shoulder as she passed through the group of men outside with a grim smile, furious with herself—and Raphael, if she were being totally honest—that her joy had been so thoroughly diluted.

Moments like these were her daily gold dust! Unexpected names for children. A singing birth support group. Plates full of exotic sweets being passed around as if it were Christmas Day itself. What other job gave a person access to the most intimate, personal moments in someone else's life? Sure, the bulk of them were horrible—but some, like this one, were pure sunshine.

From the look of his glowering expression, Raphael didn't really seem to "do" sunshine moments. He'd moved to the wrong country, if that was the case. Aussies were optimists. And she'd thought he was one as well.

There had been countless times when they had rolled around on the green grass at the base of the Eiffel Tower in absolute stitches. Imitating a teacher. Trying to outwit each other. Wondering what Jean-Luc was getting up to with his latest girlfriend. Or Raphael finding it hilariously funny that her favorite place in Paris was so clichéd.

She'd insisted it wasn't clichéd—it was essential. She hadn't come to Paris to hang out in burger joints or milk bars, like she could at home. She wanted all her memories to resemble the pages of the tour books she'd read before coming over.

Perhaps this—Raphael's new curmudgeonly persona— was evidence that she was the butt of another one of life's cruel jokes. The man of her dreams had come back into her life, only to be dangled in front of her like a carrot she could never catch. A carrot she wasn't entirely sure she *wanted* to catch.

"You sure you're all right?" she finally asked as they began restocking their run bags.

He shot her a look. One demanding an explanation.

"You did a great job in there. I mean, *obviously*. It's not like you're underqualified or anything…"

"But…?" He scraped a tooth across his lower lip and held it there—as if in anticipation of drawing blood if she said the wrong thing.

"It's nothing, really." She broke eye contact to reorganize the immaculately laid out supply tubs.

"Maggie, if there's something I'm not doing properly you need to tell me. Before we get any more calls." He tapped the face of his watch as if she were holding him back from a super-important meeting. On purpose.

Maggie's lips thinned. Someone had stolen Raphael and replaced him with a robot. She was becoming more certain of that by the minute.

She turned and faced him. "Your medical skills are not in question. Surprise, surprise—you're perfect." *In more ways than one.* "It's just… I thought your bedside manner would be a bit more… I don't know… *French*."

He tipped his chin to the side. "What exactly does *that* mean?"

Nice. Warm. Kind. Compassionate. Letting a woman name her child Raphael instead of Walter.

"Just…you know…a bit more Casanova than clinician."

"He was Italian."

She turned away and rolled her eyes. This was going to be a *long* shift.

Mercifully, the radio crackled, and again she tipped her head to the side to press her ear closer to the speaker on the clipped-on unit at her shoulder.

"We've got a slip and fall about ten blocks away, and then another call after." She picked up her pace to get to the ambulance, forcing herself not to register Raphael's implacable expression.

Whatever. She'd done her bit. Helped him get a job. Taken him out for a so-so night on the town. He was a big boy.

A grown man who looked as if he was truly hurting inside.

The radio crackled again. There was a third call for them to do a hospital transport as soon as they'd dealt with their first two calls. *Good.* No time to worry about feelings. They got in the way of everything. They reminded her of all the dreams she'd let go of in an instant.

An unexpected film of tears fogged her eyes as she opened up the back of the ambulance to put her gear in. She grabbed Raphael's bag without looking and said she'd meet him up in the cab as the sting of emotion tore at her throat. How she longed to share her hopes and dreams with someone. And not just any someone. Raphael.

But he was no longer the bright-eyed optimist she'd known back then. They each bore invisible scars from the harsh realities life had thrown at them and would have to find a new way to relate to one another.

"You ready?" she asked unnecessarily as Raphael buckled up beside her after closing his door with a solid *thunk*.

"Always," he said, his eyes intently focused on the road as she pulled out into traffic.

Are you going to be this stoically bereft of charm forever? Or just when you're with me?

"All right, then."

Maggie tried to shake her head clear of the nagging thought that there was something edgy behind his response. As if he'd missed a step somewhere along the way and it had had devastating consequences. But until she knew what was really wrong, it wasn't fair to judge.

She flicked on the blue lights and siren.

"Let's get this show on the road."

CHAPTER FOUR

STROKE. STROKE. STROKE.

Raphael's arms were a blur the instant he surfaced from his dive into the seawater pool.

She'd been fine when he'd left to attend the next surgery.

As fine as someone could be when their proximal descending aorta had been near enough sheared off the heart and stitched back on again. But he had fixed it. He'd repaired the tear.

He went through the steps of the surgery again.

Traumatic aortic rupture. The tear had been sited near the subclavian artery branch, adjacent to the aorta. Sudden deceleration saw far too many injuries of this type present themselves. Surgery worked sometimes. And that time it had. He had been sure it had.

High blood pressure in the upper body. Very low below the waist. Standard stuff. Renal failure. Internal bleeding in the abdominal cavity. The accident hadn't been kind to the little girl, but he'd gone about repairing each and every tear and shear as if his own life depended upon it.

Again the water foamed and churned around Raphael as he hit the far end of the pool, dove under, circled round, then kicked off to get to the other side, oblivious to the families playing in the sea water around him.

He'd gone through the injuries in order of importance.

He'd focused on her heart first. A partial aortic tear. The possibility of a pseudoaneurysm had lurked. He'd been relieved—elated, almost—to see the outermost layer of the partially torn blood vessel was still intact. This meant her small body stood a better chance of avoiding severe blood loss.

Other thoughts had lurked in the back of his mind as he'd worked his way through the cardiovascular surgery. The possibility of paraplegia. Renal failure if the sluggish blood pressure in her lower limbs was indicating what he thought it was. Renewed aortal tears if a moderate blood pressure wasn't maintained. The ever-present threat of anesthesia taking the child's life.

But if he hadn't called the anesthetist and begun surgery she would have died within minutes of being brought into the hospital.

Two hours in, he'd been certain Amalie's cardiac functions were normal. Or as normal as they could be before he began repairing the blood vessels sheared from her kidney. Stitch by meticulous stitch he had restored blood flow to her kidneys. Renal function would return to normal once she'd had a chance to recover. It would be a long road, but she was a survivor.

He remembered telling himself that when the call had come for another surgery.

All that had been left to do was close her up. Something any junior doctor could be relied on to do.

He'd had to make a choice. There hadn't been any other qualified surgeons available to help. He'd simply had to make a choice.

He gasped for air when he hit the far side of the pool and then began again.

He should have known that even so much as a hint of high blood pressure would exacerbate the tears he'd so diligently stitched back together. That she would go into cardiac arrest. That the junior surgical staff wouldn't be able to massage her poor, damaged heart back to life.

All this while he had been saving a life in the next room. *That* patient had lived. Had told him he was a hero.

Jean-Luc had called him something else. Lots of things he simply couldn't shake.

A murderer. Careless. Reckless.

Raphael knew grief made people say things they didn't really mean, but later, when he'd shown up at the funeral, Jean-Luc had known exactly what he was saying and the damage it would do to their friendship. Making it as irreparable as the injuries Amalie had been unable to survive.

"All you do is take!"

No matter how hard he pushed, how powerfully the blood roared between his ears, Raphael still couldn't drown out the memories.

Coming to Australia had been a mistake.

The Arctic, Brazil, the moon... Nowhere was far enough to outrun the burden of guilt chasing him down like a pack of savage wolves.

He'd thought seeing Maggie again would be the salve he needed. A reminder of the man he had once hoped to become.

She was trying. God knew she was trying her best to elicit a bit of good-natured fun from him as they went from patient to patient, but he just didn't seem to be able to do it. The whole idea of getting someone to the hospital and leaving their care to someone else echoed the situation with Amalie and knocked his response time out of sync. As if his timing was permanently a beat or two behind what it had once been, diminishing his ability to relate to people in real time.

In the refugee camps in Mozambique he had convinced himself it didn't matter. The mass of humanity there had been so overwhelming, their need for care so urgent, that patient had blurred into patient as the weeks had turned into months without his seeming to have noticed.

So he'd moved to Vietnam. The free clinic there—funded by a wealthy French businessman—had been built specifically to allow physicians more time to establish a doctor-patient relationship. There he'd been allowed to have the follow-through he hadn't been able to provide in the A&E. And he'd tried. Tried to make connections. Tried to open his heart.

It had been like tapping blood from a stone in the end. No dice.

He'd told himself it was the language barrier...conveniently forgetting the fact that many of his patients spoke French in some form or another.

He just didn't seem to have it in him to connect anymore.

Not with the beautiful newborn he'd held in his arms. Not with the grandmother who had slipped in the shower and seemed to have bruised her ego more than her hip. Or the drug addict who had, after refusing treatment twice, finally begged them to take him to rehab, give him a chance to start again.

Another chance. That was all *he* wanted. Another chance to prove that he was a good man beneath this ever-darkening cloak of grief he didn't seem to be able to shake. Another chance to look into Maggie's eyes and feel worthy.

He swam until his lungs burned with exertion and then pushed himself up and out of the seaside pool. Without turning back or looking down he began his long-legged stride, with the cock-eared mutt faithfully matching his pace.

What the little monster saw in him he'd never know...

Before he turned down the walkway leading to his rental cottage he stopped and stared at the dog.

"Qu'est-ce que tu veux, eh?"

What is it you want from me?

He stared at the scrubby-looking mutt. No collar. A little ribby beneath the multi-colored wire-haired coat, but not starving. Definitely not a pure breed. A slightly crooked gait, as if he might have had a broken leg at some point, or endured some form of trauma he'd never properly healed from. He would carry traces of that injury forever.

Raphael knew the feeling.

"Life's not fair—is it, *mon petit monstre*?"

The dog shook his head at him, maintaining eye contact the entire time.

The corners of Raphael's mouth tugged downwards in one of those rueful smiles he'd used to see his father give when Raphael had presented him with his latest set of exam results.

"Eh, ça va," his father would say, disguising any pride he might have felt with chastisement. "You'll do better next time, won't you, boy?"

His mother had never looked once—too busy "catching up" with her friends over yet another bottle of red wine.

And his marks had always been perfect.

Raphael opened the low wooden gate and let the dog into the small garden. Everyone deserved a break.

Leaving the dog outside, he went into the kitchen and pulled a takeaway container out of the refrigerator—some grilled chicken he'd bought a couple of days earlier but never got around to finishing.

Back outside on the small veranda he unceremoniously sat down on the steps leading into the garden, where the little monster waited with a patient expression on his little furry face.

"Asseyez-toi. Ici," he said gruffly, handing the dog a piece of chicken once he'd obeyed the command to sit beside him.

A few moments passed in companionable silence until

he felt as if something had begun to thaw within him. Perhaps one day Jean-Luc would see he had done the best he could. Would know a surgeon's life was full of critical choices and that at the time… *No*. He'd had to make a choice and he'd made the wrong one. *He* was the one who would have to own the mistake. Jean-Luc had enough to bear without adding forgiveness to the mix.

Raphael reached out and gave the dog's head a rub. "*Alors, mon ami.* How about I teach you some French?"

CHAPTER FIVE

Maggie held the mobile phone at arm's length and stared at it in disbelief. Had her brothers gone completely mental? Why would she want to drive twelve hours to make a birthday cake…for *herself*? The least they could do was crack a couple of eggs into a bowl and throw in some sugar and flour.

"Aw, c'mon Daggie," her older brother cajoled.

Maggie flinched at the childhood nickname and took a deep breath as he continued.

"You know Daddo would love it. He hasn't had your choccy cake in I don't know how long."

Maggie did. About five years, eleven months and a handful of days ago. The day she'd turned twenty-four, called enough enough and packed her meagre stash of belongings into the rusted-out ute her brothers had refused to drive.

She'd upgraded her car in the years since, but she wasn't so sure how much progress she'd made on achieving her dreams.

"I'll think about it."

"Dad's not getting any younger, Mags," her brother said, his voice completely sober this time.

"I know. I didn't say I wasn't coming, I just said I couldn't believe you're putting in recipe requests."

Maggie swallowed away a thousand other things she

could have said. Facts she could throw back at him. Like the simple reality that Sydney didn't exactly have a fortress wall around it, forbidding them from visiting *her*. They had cars. The ability to book a train. There were flights. Daily.

Who said *she* was the one who always had to rearrange her life to accommodate them? To go back to a place that held so many bad memories?

Her mother's voice rang in her ears, clear as a bell. *"They love Broken Hill, Maggie-moo. Let them. You're my little wandering star. Now, go shine and make the world a brighter place."*

The ache that never seemed to have lessened since her mother had passed tightened in Maggie's chest as her brother continued his campaign for her to make sure she included her birthday in her next trip. There'd be a barbie. And a bonus: the washing machine was broken so she wouldn't even have to worry about catching up on laundry.

Out of the corner of her eye she saw her old ambo partner Steve approach the bulletin board she'd parked herself in front of but had yet to examine.

"I gotta go, Nate. Work."

Her eyes darted across to the new staff rota. Maybe now Raphael had had a bit of acclimatizing he'd be all right with another partner.

"You better mean it, Dags. The thinking about it," Nate said, his voice carrying a bit more warning than it usually did when he made his "time to come home" calls.

"Yeah."

She clicked on the red handset symbol on her phone and felt the weight in her chest sink to her gut. No matter how many times she'd been home since she'd moved to Sydney fear still built in her chest as strongly as it had when she'd boarded the plane at Charles de Gaulle airport.

She'd buckled into her seat thinking she would have

time. Time to tell her mum how much she loved her. How she had, at last, found her place in the world.

She'd disembarked to be told she had to find herself a black dress for her mother's funeral.

She'd been three hours late.

One hundred and eighty minutes short of telling her mother she loved her.

"Looks like you and I are busted up forever, Mags."

"What do you mean?" Maggie followed the line Steve was drawing along his neck before he flicked his thumb toward the new staff rota.

"No more you-and-me squad, from the looks of things. Tough luck. For Casey, at least. You've got yourself a cracking good partner. Not as good as me, of course..." Steve shrugged, shaking his head along with her as she finally connected the dots.

Maggie and Raphael were to be permanent partners.

She stared at the roster in horror. She hadn't protested—much—when she and Raphael had been posted together for the first couple of rounds of shifts, but now it seemed the chief wanted him to be her permanent partner.

Her boss was plain cruel. Hadn't he *seen* how hard she was finding it, working with a man who seemed to elicit every emotion she'd ever hidden from? Lust. Hurt. Complete and total unrequited love.

To name but a few.

Was she still attracted to him?

More than ever.

Was he an incredible doctor?

Hands down the best she'd ever worked with.

Did she want to be stuck in an ambulance with him for the rest of her working days, only for him to discover she hadn't even come close to applying for medical school, let alone got in?

Not a chance in hell.

Whenever Raphael looked at her she felt as if she was being X-rayed. As if he was trying to figure out what had changed. What was different.

She could answer that easily enough. She wasn't the person she'd let him believe she was when they'd been in Paris. And when she'd come home her whole world had changed.

For that one blissful year she hadn't mentioned her Outback upbringing. Not once. She hadn't exactly lied. There had been no fictional sophisticated past she'd had to scramble to remember. But she hadn't exactly been forthcoming about the way she'd really been raised.

Not that she was embarrassed about it. She loved her family. Even if they *were* a bunch of lunkheads. It was just… They were so…*content*. And she'd always dreamed of life being so much *more*. Sometimes she envied how plain old-fashioned happy they were.

Pffft. Well. Stuck in an ambulance together for pretty much three entire days at a time, Raphael was bound to figure out she was a small-town girl whose dreams hadn't really got her all that far.

Already her cheeks burnt with embarrassment at what she would have to admit to.

Years ago she had dreamt of working with Raphael. Scalpel by scalpel, suture by suture, as they approached each and every surgery with the same tenacity and *joie de vivre* they'd seemed to elicit in each other. Countless hours they'd spent talking about it—discussing which classes they'd need to take to get into pre-med programs, quizzing each other on the different disciplines they'd like to study.

Hand on heart, they had even jinxed each other after simultaneously shouting out, "Trauma surgeon!"

Jinxed was right. For her, at least.

That day as they'd sat near the Eiffel Tower—at her insistence, of course—she and Raphael had crossed their hearts and made up a silly handshake to confirm that they would each do everything in their power to work together as surgeons one day.

She'd truly believed all her dreams would come true. But when she'd returned home it was as if she'd never had them in the first place.

She'd remembered getting almost dizzy as they'd tipped their heads back and tried to see all the way up to the top of the Eiffel Tower, making a promise that in ten years' time they would come back and compare notes. Then again in twenty.

Little had he known she was hoping they'd also be seeing each other every day in between.

Little had he known how the bubble of perfection she'd woven into her heart had shattered into a thousand irreparable pieces when she'd flown home the following day.

She watched now as her old partner made his way to his ambo, prepping it for the day's jobs.

She sternly reminded herself that being a paramedic *wasn't* second best. She loved it. Much more than she'd anticipated. It was a way of reaching people who often had no one else in their lives. She'd seen it countless times—particularly with the elderly. She loved knowing how a simple chat, a moment of human connection, was often all they were after. And she was more than happy to be the person to bring a smile to their face.

Besides, she was good at it. The human touch part. After she'd finally moved to Sydney she'd considered going to pre-med night classes, but life had got busy and she was always knackered at the end of her intense shifts.

At the end of the day, *she'd* given up on her hopes and dreams and Raphael hadn't.

He was the most driven person she had ever met. Lycée. Pre-Med. Med School. Surgical Intern. Surgical Resident.

He'd hit every one of his goals as if his life had depended upon it.

There wasn't a chance in the universe he'd ever want to be with someone who had given up at the first hurdle. Even if it was the biggest hurdle she'd ever had to leap. This whole "slumming it" thing on a paramedic crew was obviously a blip on his timeline. Something he would look back on and wonder, *Why did I do that?*

"Maggie?"

The sound of Raphael's voice threw Maggie's tummy into its usual tailspin of swirls and loops. "I'll meet you at the truck in five," she called across to him, heading to the station chief's office.

Masking how she felt about Raphael was getting harder and harder. Not only had it thrown her long-dormant feelings into full-on active volcano mode, but his brooding presence was also starting to impact her ability to treat her patients with one hundred percent focus.

That was a line she was completely unwilling to cross. And she wouldn't leave her boss's office until he understood her, loud and clear.

"Everything all right?" Maggie smiled across at Raphael as she clicked open her door, but the note of anxiety in her tone was echoed in her green eyes.

He nodded. He was the one who should really be asking *her* how she was doing. As if he didn't already know.

She jumped out of the ambulance and closed the door with a solid clunk.

"I think he hates me."

The words were still ringing in his ears nine hours into their shift. He'd overheard Maggie speaking to the station chief before they'd started work this morning. This was their third round of three days on, four off, and it looked as if she'd had enough of him. Perhaps coming to her favorite food truck was her way of letting him down gently. Sugaring the pill before letting him know that things simply weren't working out.

He hung his head and gave the back of his neck a rough scrub. This wasn't right. Just letting things fall apart. He had tried to make things right with Jean-Luc but it had been too soon. Too fresh. He saw that now. But he had the ability to change the here and now.

"Stay with my little girl."

He shrugged his shoulders up and down, then climbed out of the ambulance. He had to rid himself of the toxic emotions that had been feeding on each other, multiplying instead of diminishing. It was an unhealthy pattern and it needed to be broken.

The thought of losing Maggie was the spur he needed. He knew he wasn't a barrel of laughs to work with, but *hate*? He didn't *hate* her.

He admired her.

More than that.

He lifted his eyes up to the heavens for inspiration.

He was *grateful* to her. Grateful to this woman who'd unquestioningly helped him when he'd written to her from Vietnam. She hadn't asked a single question. She'd simply helped. And when he'd arrived she hadn't pressed, not having the remotest clue why he had changed from the laughing, trivia-obsessed pre-med student she'd met all those years ago to this darker version of the man he'd hoped to become.

She wasn't the only one who'd stopped writing when they'd said goodbye all those years ago in Paris. But she was the one who had kept her heart open. The one he'd come to when his own heart had been worn raw with effort to atone for a mistake he could never change.

The simple truth was that Maggie Louis was the only person left on earth who treated him with respect.

A vinegary twist of guilt tightened in his gut. Not telling Maggie about his past—what he'd done that awful day at the hospital—was akin to lying to the one person who deserved his honesty more than most.

A shot of energy surged through him and gripped his heart.

He couldn't lose her. Not now.

He hadn't travelled around the world only to let her slip through his fingers. He'd lost Jean-Luc's precious friendship. And Jean-Luc's parents'. Not that the Couttards had spelled it out for him, but he knew there was no coming back from the loss of a beloved child and grandchild.

Well, he was damned if he was going to let Maggie slip away. Not this soon. Not without letting her see the real him.

She needed to know about the Raphael who'd grown up in a wealthy neighborhood—not in a beautifully appointed home like Jean-Luc's, as he'd let her believe, but a few blocks away on an estate for low-income families. She needed to be told about the teenaged Raphael who had fallen head over heels for her but only offered friendship after Jean-Luc's family had cautioned him to keep things platonic.

Maggie deserved to understand why he'd honored the request. How Jean-Luc's family had all but raised him, virtually adopting him after his own parents had passed away the summer he'd finished Lycée. He couldn't have compromised that level of support. Support he'd known he'd need if he were ever to come good on his dream of becoming a doctor.

The near-impoverished upbringing...the less than loving parents. They were things he'd been able to put behind him. And now he had to find a way to learn from the experience of Amalie's surgery and put that behind him, too.

Maggie needed to know he'd become the man he'd

promised her he would become one day. But now he'd lost track of that man. And he'd sought out the one person he thought could help find him again.

He closed the ambulance door behind him with a renewed sense of purpose. He would tell Maggie everything. And when the slate was clean he'd live with the ramifications.

She would either accept him or say goodbye. But he would not let her believe he hated her. Or let her "dump him" over a gourmet sandwich across the street from the beach. Not until she knew the truth anyway. After that, the decision was solely hers.

Raphael rounded the ambulance to where Maggie stood, glanced across at the brightly colored food truck, then back to Maggie. "So, this is the best food in Sydney?"

Start small. Aim high. Earn this. Earn the place in her heart.

She nodded. "I think so, but I suspect your standards may be a bit higher."

"I'm always open to trying new things."

Her eyebrows shot up, then cinched together. "Well… I like it, anyway. Hopefully you will, too."

Lead. Balloon.

He was going to have to ramp up his conversation skills. "Do you remember that last day we were in Paris?"

Her brow furrowed. Okay. It was a bit of a non sequitur, but he could see it so clearly.

"At the Eiffel Tower?"

She gave an embarrassed laugh. "I made you go there loads, didn't I? You must've thought I was a right nutter."

"Remember it was raining?"

She'd been twirling round one of the lampposts as if she was in a musical. It was the most free-spirited he'd ever seen her. There had been a fraction of a second when the ache to pull her into his arms and kiss her had been almost overwhelming, but he'd made a promise to the Couttards. That friends-only promise had been one of the hardest he'd ever had to keep.

"Yeah, well, that was a long time ago. So…" She sucked in a big breath and pasted on a smile. "Now it's all sunshine and tucker trucks! Who would've thought it, eh? From Paris to…uh… Tuckerville."

He arched a perplexed eyebrow.

"Tucker truck? Not heard of that? Food. Food is tucker. So…" She tipped her head toward the truck and gave a shy grin. *"La cuisine…c'est superb!"*

She exaggerated her French accent—a habit, he noted, that she fell back on when she was unsure of herself. The ache returned. The desire to kiss her. Hold her. Be the man she wanted to swing round lampposts and sing in front of.

He had to tell her. Tell her everything.

Together they took another step forward in the admittedly impressive queue, and after a moment she asked, "Don't you have food trucks in France?"

He nodded. More with each passing year if memory served. Food might top most French people's list of Important Things About Being Alive, but it hadn't been anywhere on *his* radar during those last six months he'd been in Paris. Food had become merely something he had to consume in order to stay alive.

Maggie took in a big breath and popped on that nervous smile of hers again. "I probably should've brought you here the first day we worked together, but—" She stopped herself short.

He knew what she was going to say…what she *should* say. *I would've brought you here earlier if you hadn't had such an enormous thundercloud hanging over your head since you arrived.* Or, as a more straightforward Australian would've said, *If you hadn't been so bloody rude after all the hospitality and kindness I've showed you.*

"They say good things come to those who wait."

His eyes drifted to the menu hung alongside the service windows of the silver caravan. He'd have to meet those cat-like green eyes of Maggie's soon. Answer her questions. Tell her the truth.

"Well, I know it's just my opinion, but Betty's Big Baps is totally worth the wait." She grinned as she said the name. Then giggled. "I just love saying the name of this place. I don't know if I love the name more, or the sandwiches."

He tried to return her smile—the first genuine one he'd seen on her all shift.

Maggie didn't miss the fact that the smile didn't make it to his eyes.

She turned away and feigned interest in a couple of surfers joining the queue. They were laughing, regaling one another with stories of the waves they'd caught. Light. Free.

The two words caught his attention. He hadn't felt either one in eighteen long months.

Driven. Determined. Committed. Those words worked.

Driven to do penance for his mistake? Determined to do—what? Go over and over a surgery he couldn't re-do until the details eventually began to blur? Committed to staying out of Jean-Luc's path to avoid any more painful confrontations?

That was a coward's way out.

And he was no coward.

As his gaze returned to Maggie he was suddenly struck by the delicacy of her features. The smattering of freckles across her button nose. The gentle angles of her high cheekbones. The delicate swoop and dip at the apex of her upper lip. One that was begging to be traced with a finger. With a tongue. She was a beautiful woman. And he hated it that he was the reason behind the uncertainty in her gaze when their eyes finally met.

It's not brain surgery. Start a conversation.

He nodded at the ten or so people in front of them. "What if we get a call?"

Nice one. Très bien. *You really have mastered the art of embarking on a meaningful* tête-à-tête, *Raphael.*

"No worries on that front," she replied. "The station chief has promised us half an hour off before sending any more calls our way since we've been flat out all day. It's worth the wait. Honest. You won't have tasted anything like it before. *C'est magnifique!*"

A soft smile softened the usual hard set of his mouth. Maggie had been dappling her conversation with French with increasing frequency, but she was still twisting her forays into his native tongue into a comedic parody. As if she didn't quite trust herself to just…*speak.* She'd been practically fluent when she'd left. Had all the confidence she'd gained over the course of her year in France disappeared?

The thought detonated another black hole in his chest. He knew how easily confidence could take a knock.

When he'd walked out of that surgical room he'd been one hundred percent certain Amalie would make a full recovery. He had told himself that hanging around just to make sure was an instinct he wouldn't have had if she'd been a stranger. Walking away was what he would've done with any other patient.

But ten minutes later it was as if he'd entered a different time and space continuum. He should have stayed. The instinct hadn't been a case of emotional involvement. It had been a surgeon's decision—and he'd gone against it.

His team of junior surgeons had tried their best to resuscitate her. He'd come as soon as he'd heard the Code Blue had been called. And it had still been too late.

As a group, the surgical team had looked up to the digital clock and they'd all waited for him to call the time of death. Then they had each followed suit, as per protocol.

The same protocol that had dictated he had been too close to the patient to be her surgeon.

Hearing the collective confirmation that Jean-Luc's only daughter had in fact died in his care had been akin to receiving an axe-blow to his heart.

A part of him had died that day too. And the quest to find it again—that vital spark that had made him courageous enough to believe he could perform surgery on the most critically injured people and give them another shot at life—had brought him here. To Maggie.

A gentle sniggering at his side brought him back to the present.

"I still can't believe you let that poor child start going through life being called Walter." Maggie was shaking her head in disbelief.

"Sorry?"

"The baby from our first call-out? The other week?" Maggie prompted. "He was adorable. Absolutely gorgeous, with chubby little cheeks and a little round belly. He would've been even more adorable if he'd had your name. *Walter?* You really think he's going to be down with the kids with a name like that?"

"Raphael isn't exactly a guarantee of a gilded life."

Maggie sucked in a sharp breath, rolled her eyes to the cloudless sky then swore softly under her breath. Not something he'd ever heard her do.

"*Desolé.* I'm sorry, Maggie." He tugged his fingers through his hair. "I seem to be hitting all the wrong notes lately."

She gave him a sharp *no kidding?* look, her features instantly melting with a wash of remorse. "Don't worry. We all have off days."

Days. Months. Years, almost.

Everyone in Paris had eventually drawn back. Not that he blamed them. Until he made things right with Jean-

Luc and his family he was no good to anyone. He'd gone to their homes to try and explain, to apologize, each time knowing whatever he'd say wouldn't be enough. Could never be enough.

All you do is take!

There was truth in those words. He'd taken their love. Their hospitality. Their kindness.

Their daughter and grandchild.

Every single time he'd raised his hand to the door to knock, he'd turned and walked away.

"What'll it be, mate? Big Bap? Little Bap? Cardboard box?"

Without his having noticed, they'd reached the front of the queue.

Maggie was tipping her head toward the rotund sandwich vendor. "You're up, Raphael. I'm having the Pie-Eyed Pastrami. What'll you have? My shout."

His heart softened at the hopeful expression playing across her features. He owed her kindness. The kindness he seemed to be able to show the little mutt who still followed him faithfully from the seaside pool and back every night. But extending it to a *person*… Too risky. Too painful.

"Raphael? Your order?" Maggie gently nudged his arm.

"Yes, of course. Um…cheese. A plain cheese sandwich with be fine."

"We don't do plain old cheese, mate." The counter clerk looked at him as if he'd grown an extra head, then changed his disbelief into a suggestion. "We've got a Buttie Brie Blinder. Would that float your boat? It's got horseradish and some properly ponging brie in it. I can stick some beetroot in there for you if you like. Adds sort of a vinegar twist. A real ripper."

Raphael blinked up at the vendor, not entirely sure how to respond.

"Smelly cheese," Maggie prompted, her brows cinching

together. "You know… Brie. Just like at home, in France. You always said cheese wasn't any good unless you could smell it a block away." She laughed at a sudden memory. "That's how you taught me which cheese was which. The smell-o-meter."

He looked at her, almost confused as to who she was referring to. Had he *ever* spoken with her about cheese in such a light-hearted way?

"He'll have the Blinder," Maggie told the perplexed-looking vendor, and then, after collecting their drinks, steered Raphael over toward an empty picnic table under the shade of a large tree a few meters from the van. She handed him a cold bottle of water. "Here. You don't seem entirely with it. Probably dehydrated. You've got to remember to keep drinking water. It's really easy to dehydrate here. Even in the winter."

"You shouldn't be working with me."

The words were out before Raphael could stop them. And they had the opposite effect to what he'd been hoping for.

Maggie's body language instantly shifted from open to closed. A woman protecting what was left of her dignity in the wake of an excruciating dressing-down. She pushed aside the packet of crisps she'd bought unopened, and began toying with the lid of her water bottle.

"Um… Raphael. I've actually already spoken to the chief. You're obviously in a different league to me, so it shouldn't be too hard to get you transferred to a different station or working with a different partner. It's pretty obvious you and I aren't exactly a match—"

"Non."

Her eyes widened as he held his palms up between them.

Fix this. Now.

"No, no, Maggie—that isn't it at all."

"Look, there's no need to try and cover up the fact that things have not exactly been relaxed between us." She looked away for a moment, swallowing the emotion rising in her throat. "I know we were friends back in the day, but things change. People change."

He had to stop this before it went too far.

"Maggie, it's *me* who is not worthy to work with *you*."

"What are you talking about?" Her green eyes widened again, this time in disbelief. "You're a qualified surgeon. You've worked around the world. All I've done is my paramedic training and then managed to move from a small town to a big one."

He shook his head and lifted a hand to stop her. "Please, don't do that."

"Do what?"

"Put yourself down. You are..." He reached across the table and took Maggie's hands in his before she could withdraw them. "You are, hands down, one of the kindest, most qualified medical personnel I have ever met."

She huffed out a disbelieving laugh. One entirely bereft of humor. "If you're going for flattery to let me down easily, please don't bother. Look." She threw a look over her shoulder. "The sandwiches will be ready in a minute. We've not eaten all day, so let's just get our blood sugar back to normal, get through the rest of our shift and then I'll ask the chief again for one of us to be transferred. They need people everywhere in Sydney, and with someone of your caliber it shouldn't be a problem. Easy-peasy."

She looked as miserable as he felt. And that was when it hit him. She cared for him. And not just as a friend.

Hard-hitting waves of emotion bashed against his chest, one after the other. Disbelief. Concern. Regret. And then, like the smallest ray of sunlight penetrating a sheet of pure darkness...hope.

Hope that if Maggie could still see something good in him there might be a way for him to redeem himself.

He moved the crisps and their drinks to the side and reached across the table, tipping Maggie's chin up with a finger so that her gaze met his. The sheen of tears glazing her eyes didn't come as a surprise. But his response to them did.

He had nothing to offer Maggie right now and she needed to know why.

"I killed a child, Maggie. I don't know who I am anymore. I think I came to you so I could remember who I once was. To see if I could be that man again."

CHAPTER SIX

MAGGIE STARED AT the foil-wrapped sandwiches the vendor had deposited on their table, swiping at the tears spilling freely onto her cheeks. The ability to breathe had been snatched from her. She forced herself to meet Raphael's gaze, knowing it hadn't left her since he'd dropped his bombshell. She didn't recognize her own voice when she finally spoke.

"A child? What do you mean?"

Raphael tipped his head into his hands for a moment, and when he raised it again those dark shadows all but obliterated the blue in his eyes.

"Her name was Amalie," he began, his voice hollow with grief. "She was my best friend's daughter."

"You mean Jean-Luc?" Disbelief was icing her veins. "But... I don't understand. You would never do anything like that. *Never.*"

"She was in an automobile accident," Raphael conceded.

Maggie felt the pounding of her heart descend from her throat to her chest as he continued in that same, painfully toneless expression.

"It was a motorway pile-up. One of those multi-car incidents that happen when everyone's in a hurry and a thick fog descends. One minute everyone was driving at the national speed limit and the next—" He made a fist and rammed it into his other hand.

The gesture was so finite that Maggie flinched against the suggested screech of tires and clashing of metal on metal as one car ran into another.

"Were you in the car?"

Raphael shook his head. "*Non.* It was Jean-Luc's wife, Marianne, and their daughter Amalie who was three."

Maggie's curiosity flared. This was the first time she'd heard him mention Jean-Luc, though she'd tried raising the topic a couple of times. Pressing for details would have meant explaining that she'd dropped the ball too, so she hadn't pursued it.

She'd stayed with Jean-Luc's family for her student exchange year and they had been unbelievably kind and generous. Over the year she had wanted to write to them so many times, to tell them how grateful she was for that incredible year in Paris, but apart from the quick thank-you note she'd forced herself to write she had ceased all contact.

She should tell him. She would. But this was *his* time.

"What happened?"

"Marianne suffered superficial injuries and a couple of broken ribs, but was fine. Thank heaven. But Amalie—she suffered massive internal trauma when another vehicle hit theirs from the side."

Maggie's fingers flew to cover her mouth. "I am so sorry."

Raphael's brows cinched together as he huffed out a frustrated sigh. "Don't be. Not for me, anyway."

"What are you talking about?"

"We were all going to go for supper after Jean-Luc and I had finished work. You know he's become an amazing lawyer?"

His sad smile was in direct contrast to the pride in his voice that his friend had done so well.

"I don't see why this means I can't feel sorry for the loss you suffered. You two were so close. Amalie must've been like a—"

He shook his head. He didn't want her to say the words. *Like a daughter.*

Had he wanted children? Lost one of his own?

"Going out was my idea. We'd moved to different areas so didn't see each other socially as much. Nothing fancy. A walk along the Seine... Amalie always enjoyed watching the boats, so we had picked a little restaurant on Ile Saint Louis."

Something flickered in his eyes. Was it the same memory that had popped into Maggie's mind? Of that bright spring day when he'd taken her for some of the famed ice cream on the little island in the middle of the Seine? She'd somehow managed to get ice cream on her cheek, and he had leant forward and swiped it off with his thumb. His eyes had linked to hers for one moment longer than she would have expected of a friend...

Maggie forced the thought away. This wasn't about her. Nor was the blame for that car accident something Raphael should shoulder. She could see where he was coming from. The number of times she'd asked herself whether or not her mother might have had just a few more months if she'd been the one at home caring for her...

She pressed her thumbs to her eyes and did her best to squish the thoughts away. She watched Raphael tease at the aluminum wrapper holding his sandwich hostage. He looked about as interested in having lunch as she was. *Not very.*

She ducked her head and tried to catch his eye. "You know, people organize going out for supper all the time.

That hardly makes you culpable. Road traffic accidents are just that. Accidents."

Raphael continued as if he hadn't heard her.

"Jean-Luc's wife and Amalie had been out of the city for the day and, as they were running late, had decided to drive in. Normally they would've taken the Métro." His voice grew hollow. "And then the accident happened."

"How did you find out?"

He looked her square in the eye. "The casualties were brought to our hospital. When Jean-Luc arrived I said he must stay with his wife in the recovery ward while they waited on news of Amalie. He was so frightened. I've never seen a man more terrified in my—" His voice caught in his throat.

Maggie dug her fingernails into her palms, forcing herself not to reach out for him. Every pore in her body ached to console him. To tell him it would be all right. But he didn't want comfort. She would have had to be blind not to see the torture that had become all but ingrained in his cell structure.

"He knew the protocol. He knew I was too close to Amalie to be her doctor. But he begged me to look after his little girl. To do everything I could. There were only junior surgeons available, and she had suffered severe internal trauma as well as massive blood loss by the time she reached the hospital."

"So…you were following his wishes." Maggie gave a little shake of the head. "I don't understand why you're torturing yourself."

He widened his eyes in disbelief, opened his palms wide and slammed them down on the table, sending shudders through their untouched meals. "I should have said no. I was too close."

"So why didn't you?"

The look he shot her told her he had asked himself the same thing again and again.

"We were short-staffed. Most of the other doctors on duty that day were less experienced—fresh out of medical school—and casualties from the accident were flooding in, one after the other. The senior surgeon on staff told me to find someone else, if I could, but there was no one I trusted with that precious life. My best friend's child."

The anguish in his voice was palpable, and despite the heat of the day Maggie wrapped her arms around herself to fend off the wave of shivers trickling down her spine.

"Had you been specifically told not to operate on her? Before you took Amalie into surgery, I mean?" Maggie wasn't sure why she'd asked the question, but getting everything in order seemed essential if she was to understand why Raphael was blaming himself for something that had patently been an awful accident.

He shook his head. No. He hadn't.

"I was a surgeon. A good one, I thought. I had vowed to do my very best—promised my dearest friend I would save his child—and when it came down to it I failed. I failed as a friend. I failed as a doctor. I failed a child. It is *my* fault his little girl died and I will carry the weight of that burden until the end of my days."

"And that's why you came here?"

He shook his head, not entirely understanding.

"To try and unload the burden...with distance?" she clarified.

He tipped his head back and forth.

"No. It's not so simple. I just—"

This was the moment he'd been over again and again. Doing the checklist. Ensuring he'd done everything he could to stabilize Amalie.

"My instinct was to stay, to see the surgery through right to the end, but there was another patient in the next room. They needed me to operate straight away. All that was left to do with Amalie was close up. An easy enough job for the junior surgeons."

"But…?"

"She went into cardiac arrest."

From the look on Maggie's face he knew he didn't need to spell out the lengths his team had gone to in their vain attempt to keep her alive.

"If I'd made the decision to stay in the room instead of rushing off to the next surgery she might have lived."

"*Might* have?"

"I'll never know."

He rattled through Amalie's injuries in detail. The surgical procedures he'd followed. The gut instinct that had told him to stay. The pragmatic override that had pulled him from the room.

"And the other patient? What happened with them?"

"They lived." He corrected himself. "*She*. She lived."

She'd even sent him flowers, with a note expressing her gratitude.

"So…" Maggie pressed her fingertips to her lips for a moment. "Africa? Vietnam? What was that for? Were you atoning, or something?"

Raphael considered Maggie for a moment before answering. He should tell her what Jean-Luc had said and the cutting effect his words had had.

All you do is take!

He'd felt… He'd actually felt *orphaned* after the Couttards had made it clear they weren't ready to see him and Jean-Luc had dismissed him with a flick of the hand. More so than when his actual parents had died. That was how precious his friendship had been. Jean-Luc and his parents had been his family.

"Go," Jean-Luc had said. "Go show what a big man you are somewhere else. You obviously know what is best.

Who deserves your magic surgeon's hands. Your time. It must be so precious, your time. Please…" He'd stepped in close and said the last words so quietly Raphael had had to lean in to hear him. "Don't let me take one minute more of it."

And then he'd shut the door. Hadn't taken his calls. Raphael had no idea if he'd read the letters he'd written or torn them to shreds still in their envelopes.

"Things were difficult between me and Jean-Luc. His parents, too."

"What?" Maggie laughed. "They didn't banish you from France, did they?"

The black look that swept across his features suggested she wasn't far off the mark.

Raphael cleared his throat. "I needed to prove to myself I could still do it. Make a difference as a doctor."

"And did you?"

He shrugged. He'd been so emotionally absent he knew he hadn't made a difference on any sort of personal level, but as a doctor…yes. Yes, he had.

"So why are you here?"

He gave her his best Gallic shrug.

He wasn't ready to explain that it was Maggie he had sought. That she was the one person he believed would give him the most honest perspective on the type of man she thought he was. Mortal or monster.

He heard her muttering something under her breath.

"A quelque chose malheur est bon."

She remembered. It was a saying equivalent to *Every cloud has a silver lining.* Or, the more French interpretation, *Unhappiness is, at the very least, good for something.*

He'd used to say it when, inevitably, it had rained on one of their outings and they were forced to seek refuge under a small awning or in a tiny alcove. He'd always wondered if she'd ever cottoned on to the underlying meaning… Though it had rained, it had meant he could be closer to her.

"So." He clapped his hands together, the sound sharp against the white noise of the late-afternoon activity surrounding them. "I understand why you wouldn't want to work with me anymore. If you need to transfer me out, please… I completely understand."

"You have got to be absolutely joking me." Maggie shook her head back and forth.

This was a lot of information to take on board, but it certainly answered the bulk of her questions.

Raphael had been through the wringer. He'd changed, all right. But he was truly trying to make himself a better man than he had been before this tragedy. He was living with an unanswerable question and it had obviously been hell.

Would the child have lived if he had made a different decision?

As little as she knew about surgery, she knew enough about the traumatic injuries Amalie had suffered to imagine the answer would be no. And he'd returned to medicine. That wasn't something a man who doubted his skills would do. There *had* to be something more. Something he hadn't yet come to terms with.

"It's okay." Raphael's accent thickened. "I wouldn't want to work with me either, after knowing the truth. I am sorry I wasn't more honest before I came—"

"No." Maggie stopped him with a hand gesture. "Are you *mad*? Now that I know what you've been through there isn't a chance in the universe I'd let you work with someone else."

He bridled and it pleased her to see there was still fire in his spirit. He wasn't beaten. Just lost.

"Cool your jets." She took a deep breath and put her hands up so she could take a moment to put her thoughts in order. "I'm not keeping you pinned to my side because I think you're a bad doctor. Or a liar. Or a disappointment. Or whatever other words you attack yourself with. I want to work with you because what you need more than anything after what you've been through is a friend."

A quizzical look passed across his features. "Why would you want to work with me after this? Trust me? You said at the beginning of this that people change. I am proof of this, Maggie. I have changed."

"Raphael Bouchon." She fixed him with a stern expression, hoping he was reading affection in her expression rather than someone passing judgment. "I know it's been a long time seen we've seen each other, but a man can't change *that* much. That young man I met in Paris was the most honest, honorable, kind person I had ever met. And, though an awful lot of water has passed under the bridge since then, I still believe that's true. You're still that young man. But with maybe just a bit more of a distinguished air."

She pointed to her temples trying to indicate that she liked the salt and pepper look working its way through his rich chestnut hair.

"No, Maggie. You are kind, but..." Raphael opened his water bottle and took a long draught before continuing. "I thought when I saw you I would see the old me again. That I would find him somewhere buried in here." He made a fist and thumped it on his chest as he shook his head. "Now that I'm here, I see that you're just the same. But I don't think that seventeen-year-old Raphael you met all those years ago exists anymore. I'm not fun to be with. I can't see any point in looking forward to the future the way I once did. I don't even see the point of dreaming about the future. I failed my friend. I have the blood of a child on my hands. My best friend's child."

She shook her head—no, no, *no*—as a powerful rush of energy charged through her bloodstream.

If Raphael believed in their friendship enough to tell her about his darkest moments, she would show him just how strong her love for him was. Unrequited or otherwise.

If he needed a friend, he had one. If he needed a shoulder to cry on, she had two. If he wanted to believe in the possibility of love again...

She swallowed. That might be pushing things.

Baby steps.

She sucked in a deep breath of air and parted her lips. It was time to be as brave as Raphael.

"That's where you're wrong."

Wide blue eyes registered incredulity at her statement. "Maggie! I was *there*. I failed as a surgeon. I was the one who let Jean-Luc down. Let all the Couttards down."

"First things first."

She gave the picnic table a solid tap with her index finger, then wove her fingers together in front of her heart.

"I am very sorry for your loss. It must've been horrible for you. But you surely must see it was an impossible situation. And who's to say another surgeon might have made a different call? However cruel and personal it must feel, these things are random. It wasn't like you willed the fog to appear on that motorway or anything. And secondly—" she held up a hand so he would let her finish "—how exactly did you let Jean-Luc down? He asked you to do your best. To look after his little girl. I can't imagine you did anything other than try and save her."

Raphael looked at her, his features wreathed in disbelief. "Amalie *died*, Maggie."

She sat back and eyed him silently for a moment before taking another drink of her water.

Her heart ached for him. He was seeing the world through a distorted lens. One that showed him branded as a failure for not being omniscient. In that respect, yes, he *had* been too close to the patient. But in terms of deciding he didn't cut it as a surgeon…he'd just made it all up.

And then it hit her. All of the insecure dark thoughts she'd been having about Raphael not liking her, or thinking she was a loser, had also been a complete fiction. She'd seen what scared her most instead of stepping outside of herself and facing facts. It was something Raphael needed to do, too.

In that instant Maggie knew she would do everything in her power to help Raphael take off the blinkers that seemed unrelenting in their mission only to let him see the dark side.

The thought stopped her cold.

Had *she* worn the same blinkers with her father? Her brothers? Instead of being sexist, demanding, nineteen-fifties throwbacks, on a mission to keep her in a pinny, had they actually been as blindsided by her mum's death as she had?

They hadn't been in tears, or lost in faraway thoughts or anything. It had seemed on the surface that everything was business as usual. But men were good at disguising things. Raphael being a perfect case in point.

But there was something else that was torturing him. Something beyond the failed surgery that he had yet to set right.

There were things *she* needed to set right as well.

When she'd come home to find her mother had been ill the entire time she'd been away, only to die while Maggie was flying home, Maggie's world had been turned upside down. At the time it had felt as though she'd been drowning in the past she had only just begun to escape. Blinded with grief and frustration, she'd blamed her brothers and her father for pushing her into the vacant role their mother had left behind. Carer. Cook. Cleaner. The very roles her mother had made her promise she would never take on.

But could it be that instead of being pushed she had willingly stepped into the spot her mother had once filled in their lives? That she had naturally found herself filling that void because she was the girl and that was what girls—*women*—did? Instead of it being a weak decision, perhaps she had been the only one strong enough to make sure their lives somehow returned to normal in the wake of their collective grief.

A strengthening weave of resolve unfurled within her. Raphael needed to believe he had been the only one strong enough to step into an impossible situation. If he could see that—know it in his heart—he would finally be able to forgive himself. He would finally be able to believe that, no matter who had operated on that poor little girl, her fate had already been decided when their car had been struck by another.

And if she wanted Raphael to believe that about himself she would have to take the same risk—and see her own life from another perspective.

"Maggie, please." Raphael raked his hands through his hair. "Put me out of my misery."

She looked at him as if seeing him for the first time. She'd been miles away. About a twelve-hour drive, in fact.

Maggie tipped her head to the side and wove her fingers together under her chin. "After this shift is over we've got four days off, right?"

He nodded.

"How would you feel about making it a bit longer?"

Maggie held her breath, waiting for his answer. Taking him home to meet her family was akin to unzipping her chest and handing him her heart. And then throwing some warts on top of the whole mess for good measure.

Raphael didn't look too pleased about the invitation.

"This isn't about you wanting me to be transferred to a different paramedic station, is it?"

"No! Crikey! No, not all."

"So we're good on that front?"

"Yeah! Of course. Now that I understand why you've been such a downer— I mean…"

To her relief, Raphael gave a self-deprecating laugh and held up his hands. "I *have* been a downer. But…" again that Gallic shrug "…now you know I have my reasons."

"I know. And it's a pretty big reason." She played with the edge of the aluminum wrapping on her sandwich and then, feeling a sudden hit of hunger, went ahead and unwrapped it. "Now that I know what's been going on in that head of yours…" she pointed her finger between the pair of them "…you and me? We're solid."

Maggie took an enormous bite of her sandwich and then grinned at him, a daub of sauce teasing at the crest of her upper lip before she swiped it away with her tongue.

He didn't deserve her. The open-hearted way in which Maggie had absorbed the worst thing he'd ever done in his life and simply…*accepted* it, forgiven him for the transgression and moved on.

It was humbling.

Maggie munched on a few crisps, then took a gulp of water. "So, back to me. Have you had your fill of being a tourist in Sydney?"

Raphael shrugged. The only reason he'd come to Australia was to see Maggie. So saying yes was an honest enough answer. And honesty was the only way forward. He saw that now.

"I think you and I need to go on a road trip. Get you out beyond the black stump."

Her tone was decisive. As if hearing his story had given her a new course of action. More to the point, her entire demeanor had changed…as if they were actually friends again.

"Black stump?"

"City limits," she explained, a soft flush coloring her cheeks. "If you say yes, there's a whole lot more Aussie slang waiting for you outside of Sydney. If you're feeling brave enough, that is."

Something in him softened. She was trying. He'd been making this whole reunion thing tough. More than tough. And yet she was still trying.

"Are you sure this isn't some attempt to take me out to the desert with a flint and a bottle of water to see if I make it out alive? A survival of the Aussie-est?"

She shrugged and smiled. "We-e-ell…" She drew out the word. "Nah. Of course not. Look. I have to go out there. Family."

He lifted his eyebrows. She hadn't mentioned her family. Not once.

"A reunion?"

She shook her head. "No. But let's just say you're going to see a whole side of me you never knew existed if you say yes."

"Sounds intriguing." Was she trying to ease his guilt? Prove he wasn't alone?

Her features darkened.

"It's not a reunion, but… You've been incredibly honest with me and I appreciate it." She pressed her hands to the center of her chest. "From the very bottom of my heart. It proves to me our friendship meant as much to you as it did to me."

Raphael locked eyes with her. "It did. It still does."

He watched as she sucked in a tight breath, then made the decision to speak.

"I don't think you are responsible for Amalie's death."

He scrubbed his hands along his legs. "Maggie, you weren't there—"

"No. I know. But I know *you*. You made the best decision you could at the time. I've been watching you work and you have it. That ability to make a split-second decision about a patient that is going to be for their benefit. No matter what you think of yourself now, I know without a shadow of a doubt that you simply do not have it in you to let another human's life pass through your hands if it doesn't have to."

The words struck so deep Raphael knew they would be embossed on his heart forever. But Maggie didn't owe him this: an easy out. She didn't owe him anything.

"*Tu es trop gentile*, Maggie. I am so grateful to you for not…for not thinking the absolute worst of me."

"How could I?"

There were countless answers for that one. He began totting them up before answering, then stopped himself. Holding back from Maggie had only meant making himself his own worst enemy. Could this be the first step in forgiving himself? Finding a way to claw himself out of the black hole he'd all but swan-dived in to?

He met her clear green eyes and saw nothing but compassion in them. Empathy. Her unfiltered gaze was the oasis of peace he'd been seeking all these months.

"I'm glad I came." He reached across and took her hand in his, stroking his thumb along the back of it.

"Me, too." She gave him a shy smile, thought for a minute, then winced. "But I do think…perhaps…you need to decide if your heart is really in the paramedic world."

"What?" He feigned affront. "You don't think I've been doing a good job?"

She gave a melodramatic sigh. For his benefit entirely.

"Quite the opposite. And you know that." She tugged her hand out of his and poked him in the arm. "But it's not where your *heart* is. A blind man could suss that one out. And although running around the world and showing off your medical prowess is an amazing thing to do, I don't think that's what you're doing. You're more… It's more like you're living life on the run. Waiting for that one medical save that will put you back to the place you were before that night. From where I'm sitting, what you're feeling is grief, not guilt. And you're not letting yourself be good old-fashioned sad. Maybe you should do that, instead of all this globetrotting."

She put on a dramatic television presenter's voice. "'*Dr. Raphael Bouchon has been spotted in yet another country. Paraguay this time. Or was it Brazil? Will he keep interested parties guessing as to his whereabouts for years to come? Or will he suck it up, go back to France, and have a weep and a talk with Jean-Luc? Will he finally make peace with his dearest friend?*' Apart from me, of course." She smirked.

Despite himself, he smiled.

"This isn't—" He stopped himself. It *was* running. All of it. He hadn't even fully unpacked his suitcase and he'd been in Australia over a month. Even "his" dog wasn't his. Just a stray he'd called Monster who helped him eat his leftovers.

He shrugged, accepting her comments as fair, and finally picked up his sandwich. "Are you saying you don't like the idea of me living as an outlaw in your fair city?"

She laughed and when their eyes met he knew she liked the idea of something, all right. But he was guessing it wasn't the outlaw thing.

A sting of regret that he hadn't kissed her all those years ago resurfaced.

An even bigger hit of remorse could so easily follow in its wake if he didn't get his act together and start to actively live his life. With purpose. With passion. With *love*.

Maggie put her sandwich down and took a sip of water.

"So, if you can scrape the bottom of your soul and put your darkest moments on display, why don't you take a break from beating yourself up about it and come out and see a bit of mine? The soul stuff I mean. The black parts."

"Just because I've done something awful it doesn't mean you—"

"Uh-uh!" She held up a hand. "I'm not done yet. I think this trip will be good for you. Maybe help you see life isn't always the way you think it is."

"You're talking in riddles."

"Yeah, well… I didn't exactly think I'd ever be telling you any of this."

"Any of what?"

She shook her head. "It's a show and tell sort of thing. You have to be there to understand."

Her eyes shifted up to the tree above them and glassed over. She shrugged her shoulder upward to swipe at the single tear snaking down her cheek and took another bite of sandwich. A poor disguise for an obvious rush of emotion.

When she'd finished chewing she swallowed, waved a hand as if erasing a whiteboard, and said, "Forget about all the 'feelings' stuff. It's a road trip—plain and simple. You are under no pressure to say yes. But at the very least, after we get past the Blue Mountains, you'll see first-hand that there is a whole lot of nothing in between the coasts of this fair isle. Besides, I need someone to keep me awake. It's a long drive."

There was something else. Something she wasn't saying. But he didn't press. He'd wanted a change and Maggie was delivering.

Maggie.

A life-affirming electrical current shot through him and the first undiluted desire simply to say yes to life took hold of his heart.

Maggie was the difference. He'd just told her about the worst moment in his life and already he felt…not lighter, exactly, but less alone. If Maggie could believe that one single shred of the man she'd met still existed...

"What?" Maggie's features scrunched up as she tried to interpret his expression. "You haven't gone soft on me, have you? Not up for a bit of rough and tumble out in the Woop Woop?"

"Quoi?"

"The Outback," she explained with a laugh. "The middle of nowhere."

He crossed his arms, narrowing his eyes in a dubious squint.

"Is this some sort of Australian ritual? Bringing a poor, defenseless Frenchman to the Outback to see if he can make his way back to civilization as a means of proving himself?"

"Something like that." The hint of a mysterious smile teased at the corner of her lips. "Or it could just be to prove you can survive a couple of days with my brothers. Believe me—if you can make it forty-eight hours straight with the Louis brothers, you can survive anything."

A warmth hit Raphael's heart, and with it came a sudden hunger. Nothing to do with being invited to meet the family of the girl he'd always wondered *What if?* about, he told himself drily.

He began unwrapping his sandwich, abruptly stopped and locked eyes with her.

"One question."

The change in his own voice surprised him. It reminded him of the man he'd used to be before the harshness of grief had turned him irritable. It was the voice of a man who *cared*.

"Can I bring my dog?"

Maggie's eyed widened and stayed wide as her radio crackled to life and a rapid-fire stream of instructions rattled through. "Code Twenty-one," she whispered, her green eyes locked on his as she continued listening.

Can I bring my dog?

What was *that* all about? It wasn't like Monster was actually *his*. Or that he needed a buffer between him and Maggie. She was...she was *Maggie*. The sunny-faced, flame-haired girl—

Who was pressing herself up and away from the picnic table, grabbing her half-eaten sandwich and making a "wheels up" spin with her finger as she continued to take down the details of their call-out.

It was at that moment that he truly saw her for who she was. Maggie wasn't the lanky, shy, still-growing-into-her-skin teen he'd met thirteen years ago, who'd tied an invisible ribbon round his heart.

She was a woman.

And a beautiful one at that.

He'd been so preoccupied with shaking off the ghosts chasing him around the world that he hadn't stop to breathe her in. This past year he had felt as if he'd only just been holding on to the back of a runaway train, and now Maggie had leapt on and hit the brakes. Showed him there was more than one way to handle the grieving process he knew he had to go through.

"We've got a broken arm, a possible neck fracture, and a few more injuries."

"All for one patient?" He grabbed his own sandwich and drink, following her at a jog.

"No. Cheerleading pyramid gone wrong."

"Cheerleading?"

"Cheerleading. Or not, as the case may be," she added soberly, before jumping into the ambulance.

When they arrived at the high school they pulled into the car park at the same time as another ambulance. Maggie's mate Stevo and his new partner Casey. Raphael rolled down his window as a man ran between the pair of vehicles, waving his arms and identifying himself as the headmaster.

After a quick conference with the headmaster they drove the ambulances round to the school's large playing field to find a huge group of people gathered in several circles.

"I'll grab the tib-fib compound," Stevo called, heading for a group already opening up to let him and his pale-faced junior through. Those injuries had the potential to be pretty gory. Raphael felt for Casey.

"She looks horrified, poor thing." Maggie made a sympathetic noise, then grabbed a run bag and a spine board. "Oh, well. There's only one way to learn and that's by confronting the tough stuff. Can you grab a couple of extra collars and a pile of blankets? It looks like you and I are over here."

Maggie tipped her head at the pair of girls in cheerleading outfits running toward them.

Confronting the tough stuff.

Precisely what *he* needed to do.

"Over here!" One of the cheerleaders arced her arm and pointed toward a nearby group. "She says she can't feel her legs!"

Raphael shouldered his run bag and set off in a jog alongside Maggie, hoping the situation wasn't as grim as it sounded. At the very least, the patient was alert. Speaking. From what he'd heard, cheerleading injuries could be catastrophic, with all the gymnastics involved.

Words whirled round him—"flyer", "base holders weren't there", "on her head"—as they approached the circle around a sixteen or seventeen-year-old girl. A hush fell upon the crowd.

"Hello, love." Maggie dropped down to her knees behind the girl and immediately stabilized her head by bracing her elbows on the ground and holding her temples steady. She shot Raphael a quick look, then shifted her gaze to the girl's legs. They were lying at peculiar angles and, whilst alert, the girl had an entirely mystified expression playing across her face.

"Looks like someone took cheerleading to some new heights—oops. No, no. Stay still, darlin'. We want to make sure we don't move anything we're not supposed to."

Maggie gave Raphael a nod and he ran a series of quick checks for additional injuries, keeping a sharp eye on the patient as he moved the teen's legs into place. No response.

"Have you seen anything your end? Spinal injuries? Brain?" He asked his questions in French, and a swift murmur of approbation followed from the teenagers behind him. If they knew he'd spoken in French to keep potentially bleak news from them, they wouldn't be saying such nice things.

Maggie shook her head. "Protocol says we should use the stiff neck braces for precautionary immobilization, but I think they're too much for her." Maggie held her hand alongside the girl's neck, as if measuring it.

"I think the vacuum mattress would be best. It will keep her entire body stabilized without any unnecessary jarring—particularly if she has a pelvic fracture."

Maggie's eyes flashed to his.

"We won't be able to see any internal bleeding, so the best we can do is stabilize her as much as possible."

Raphael's mind had ticked over to automatic pilot—which didn't second-guess his every decision. And it felt good. It felt like being a trauma doctor again.

Maggie tugged a couple of blankets off the pile Raphael had placed on the ground and started rolling them into boomerang shapes. "I'll use these to stabilize for now, while you do the rest of the checks."

After examining the girl for any immediate evidence of neck wounds or the potential for underlying hematomas, Raphael ran to get the mattress.

When he returned he saw Maggie checking the girl's vitals again. "Have you looked for signs of neurogenic shock?"

Maggie shook her head. "I've only just started. I've done a quick pulse check—doesn't seem too low. Or high, for that matter." She smiled down at her young charge. "All right, there, love? Seems as though your ticker's all right." Then, in a lower voice she continued. "Amazing…good. Not bradychardic in the slightest."

"What does that mean?" the girl asked.

"It means your body seems to be doing its best to help you recover." Maggie brushed her fingers along the girl's cheek, then rattled through a few stats with Raphael.

In between all the medical speak with Raphael, Maggie continued to keep up a steady flow of fact-gathering in the guise of casual chit-chat with their patient. This was her forte. He could see that now.

Being calm, warm and conversational kept the patient relaxed, the atmosphere less stressed, and significantly reduced the patient's potential for panic. His quest to be as exacting as he could had all but turned him into an automaton. A patient's worst nightmare.

He smiled as Maggie continued.

What was her name?

Jodi.

How long had she been a cheerleader?

Four years, and this was to have been her last as she was planning on becoming a veterinarian.

Any favorite animals?

Dogs. Definitely dogs.

Maggie shot him a quick look, so he threw in a comment about dogs being wonderful.

What pyramid routine had they been practicing?

The Eiffel Tower.

A pair of amused green eyes met his.

"Well, isn't that a coincidence?" Maggie put her hand directly above Jodi's eyeline. "Can you move your eyes toward the handsome chap over there on your left?" Maggie used her finger above the girl's face as a guideline.

Raphael smiled. That was a clever way to check her responses.

Wait a minute... *Handsome?*

"He's a genuine Frenchman, and—would you believe it?—the very same man who took me all bright-eyed and bushy-tailed around Paris. The first day we met he took me to see the Eiffel Tower."

Maggie's eyes flicked up to Raphael's and for a microscopic instant they caught and locked. Something in him flared hot and bright as he saw Maggie in full, glorious high-definition. The flame-colored hair. The beautiful green eyes. The milky white skin, flawless save a tiny scar at the corner of one of her eyes.

How had he not noticed that before? Had someone hurt her? Another swell of emotion built in him. A feeling of fierce protectiveness. If anyone had hurt Maggie he'd—

"Raphael?"

He cleared his throat and looked up at the sea of expectant faces. This was definitely *not* the time for flirting or thumping his chest like a he-man.

Had Maggie been flirting or just being nice?

"Um, Raph?" There were questions in Maggie's eyes, and not all of them were about work.

"*Alors*...shall we get Jodi onto the spine board?"

Raphael moved the board to Jodi's right, ensuring the vacuum mattress was in place, and on his count they rolled her onto the board and secured her with the series of straps attached to the mattress.

"How's your breathing, Jodi?" Raphael asked.

The teen stared at him, wide-eyed. "Say that again."

"How's your breathing?"

He shot an alarmed look in Maggie's direction. Breathing problems indicated much more serious injuries that might require intubation, the need for a positive-pressure bag-valve-mask device—though there were issues that went along with that as well. Distorting the airway could impair breathing, then circulation…

He was surprised to hear Maggie giggling.

"I think her breathing's just fine, Raphael. It's your accent. She likes it."

"And his name, too." Jodi's voice was positively dreamy and her expression fully doe-eyed.

"Oops! Easy, love—let's keep you looking straight up. Even if it's just *my* old mug you're looking at."

Maggie quickly pushed the blankets back into place, realigning Jodi's head to a neutral anatomical position. She widened her middle and index fingers between the girl's chin and suprasternal notch to get a measurement.

"Maybe we'd better slip an extra-small soft collar on her for the journey. Especially…" Maggie dropped a teasing wink at Raphael "…as you're the one who's going to be sitting in the back of the ambulance with our girl, here."

Raphael laughed and together, with the quick efficiency that usually came from years of working together, they inflated the mattress, lifted Jodi onto the wheeled gurney and loaded her into the ambulance for their ride to the hospital.

A few hours and several patients later they were sitting in companionable silence at the front of the ambulance as they headed back to the station.

Raphael's thoughts returned to Maggie's invitation.

"Did you mean it?" His voice sounded more intense

than he'd anticipated. Pulling back the emotion, he clarified, "About the road trip?"

Maggie threw him a quick look, the bulk of her attention on the rush hour traffic she was battling. "Yeah, I suppose…"

"That doesn't sound as if you've entirely made up your mind. If it was a charity invitation—"

"No, no." She batted a hand between them. "That wasn't it at all. It's just that it's a long way. *Aussie* long. I thought it might be part of your How-to-be-an-Australian training, but if you don't plan on sticking around it might be too much bother."

He dropped his head and looked at his hands.

Why was he here?

To see Maggie.

Why did he want to see Maggie?

To find out if a human heart still pounded in his chest.

What happened when he was with Maggie?

Blood charged through his veins.

"Sounds good. I'd like to do it."

She threw him a quick glance. "All right, then. Well, in that case, the invitation is still open—but it comes with a warning."

"Are there venomous snakes where we are going?"

She laughed. "Loads. But they're everywhere in Australia. The warning is much bigger. My brothers can't cook for toffee. Chances are you're going to have to eat whatever I manage to rustle up—and let's just say most of the takeaways near my flat would go out of business if I moved."

"Didn't your mother cook?"

His mother's cooking was one of his better memories of his home life, but from the chill that instantly descended between them, it was obviously not the right question to ask Maggie.

"She did." Maggie's voice sounded hollow. "Best cook in town."

"Did?"

"She passed a while back."

"I'm sorry to hear that."

She made a small noise, her gaze fastidiously trained on the cars in front of them, each battling for those few precious centimeters taking them that much closer to home.

Home.

Such a simple word, but one laden with the power of a nuclear bomb.

He didn't know where home *was* anymore. He'd rented expensive modern apartments in Paris. A total contrast to the cramped, low-rent housing he had grown up in with his parents. A tent in Africa. A tiny beach house here in Sydney.

Nothing seemed to fit.

The thought twisted and tightened in his gut.

Would anything? Anywhere? Would yet another trip finally give him some answers?

He looked out of the window as they crawled past one of Sydney's most famous beaches. It was mid-week but the shore was packed with families, couples, surfers, sun-worshippers. The sky was a beautiful, crisp blue. The air was tinged with a lightly salted tang. It was heaven on earth, and yet he still felt as though being a part of it all remained out of reach. Impossibly so.

He looked across to Maggie, startled to see her swipe at the film of tears blurring her clear green eyes. The moment was over so quickly he wondered if he'd imagined it. And in its place was her bright, ready smile as the radio crackled to life with a call-out to an asthma attack.

She flicked on the blue lights.

"Let's hit one more before we call it quits, shall we?"

CHAPTER SEVEN

Don't forget the socks, Dags.

MAGGIE GROWLED A response at the text message, half tempted to throw her phone out the car window. But she knew she'd go to the store. Buy the socks. Take the washing powder. Make the meat pies. Enough to put in the freezer for later.

She could already see herself rolling up her sleeves and cleaning up the three months' worth of detritus that had no doubt accrued in the Louis household.

It was what she did. It was what *they* did. Annoying as they were, at least she *had* a family. It was a lot more than Raphael had.

Losing the Couttards had genuinely seemed to set him adrift.

Not that she'd gone over the reasons he'd chosen to seek her out a thousand times, or anything, but...had he come to fill a void? One that Jean-Luc and his parents had filled when they were teens?

Losing Jean-Luc as a friend must have been devastating for him.

When she'd lost her mother she had felt as if the world had disappeared from beneath her feet. But that was cancer. Just one of life's cruel turns.

Losing a friend...losing a child.

The thought gave her chills. Raphael's loss was a vivid reminder that, even if they *did* drive her bonkers, her father and brothers had been there for her all along. The proverbial wind beneath her wings.

She glared at her phone for a minute, then felt her features soften as she punched in a reply.

I've already put holes in the big toes. Just the way you like 'em. x PS Don't call me Dags. I'm bringing a friend. Who has manners.

Another message pinged straight back. Something about bringing extra "talent" into town for the brothers' pleasure which she chose to ignore. There was no chance she'd bring a *female* friend out to meet that lot of larrikins. Kelly had once begged her and she'd flat-out refused.

Besides, if she explained to her brothers that her "friend" was actually the man she was trying to convince herself she wasn't head over heels in love with, her phone might blow up with their responses.

And it wasn't as if it was reciprocated. If Raphael had actually come to Oz because he was in love with her it would've come out by now.

So it was Just Friends, then. And that was the way the biscuit was bashed.

The instant Maggie laid eyes on Raphael the next morning her tummy went all fluttery butterfly park, and she knew the talking-to she'd given herself about the whole Just Friends thing had been entirely unsuccessful.

He was already out on the street, lit by a single lamppost in the pre-dawn gloaming, his hair scruffy, blue eyes still a bit sleepy, his trousers hanging on his slim hips, a soft navy blue chambray shirt making the most of his shoulders and trim build—well, it *looked* soft. Not to mention the just-about-as-adorable-as-they-came dog by his side.

Raphael with a hang-dog pooch? That image all but nailed Raphael's place in her affections for evermore.

If he hadn't spied her—unleashing one of those bright smiles of his that had the power to make the world a better place—she would've spent a few minutes banging her head against the steering wheel. Doomed! That was what she was. Doomed to be a spinster forever. Lost to an unrequited love that would never blossom in a million years.

What had she been thinking? A fourteen-hour road trip with the most gorgeous man in the universe and his dog? If she came out of this with one single shred of dignity left intact it would be an out-and-out miracle. Particularly once he met her family.

Oh, *cuh-rikey.* This was a Class A brain failure.

She dropped her head to her steering wheel anyway, little flashes of ominous foreboding appearing in her mind's eye. One of her brothers' huge workman's hands crushing Raphael's beautiful surgeon's hands in a friendly *How-ya-going? Don't-you-dare-mess-with-my-sister* handshake. Their unrelenting passion for burnt snags on a barbie. The coolbox filled with a fresh slab of tinnies "just in case" it was a scorcher. It was *always* a scorcher.

Raphael would catch the first flight out of Broken Hill. If there even was one that day.

Was it too late to talk him out of it?

"*Salut, Maggie. Ça va?*"

The man had a voice like melted chocolate. What was she meant to say?

Why, yes, Raphael. I would be perfectly well—if inviting the only man I've ever loved to my crazy Outback family home were not the type of thing to send a girl stark raving mad. Which it is.

"Maggie?"

"Oui, ça va."

Sigh. Swirl. Flip. Loop-the-loop. A pop song clicked on in her head... If she could turn back time, indeed.

Raphael walked round to her car door and handed her a coffee through the open window. *"Un café* for my chauffeur..."

Before she could thank him, he passed her a beautiful eggshell-blue box with a cream ribbon around it.

"And a little something special for you."

An image of opening it and finding a diamond ring flicked into her head, instantly unleashing a ridiculously huge explosion of tingles. Maybe fairy tales *did* come true...

"You didn't have to do this—"

"Of course I did." He waved away her protest. "I couldn't have you driving all the way across the state without some of Sydney's finest croissants."

His lips twisted into the inevitable Gallic *they're-not-French-but-they'll-do* twist, then melted into a smile.

"Yeah!" She rubbed her tummy in a show of gratitude, her heart sinking straight through to the foot well of the car.

Idiot.

Diamond ring.

Croissants. Of *course* the box had croissants in it.

Ah, well. Being a well-fed spinster was better than being one with a grumbling tummy.

She popped the box and the coffee into the central console between their seats and climbed out of the car.

"So this is Monster?" Maggie nodded down to the scruff-muffin who hadn't left Raphael's side.

The dog looked up at the pair of them, as if he knew he was the topic under discussion.

"Oui." Raphael hooked his fingers onto his hips and

looked down at him with a warm smile. "He seems to have adopted me."

"Smart dog," Maggie said before she could think better of it.

Nice one, Mags. Why not just out-and-out tell the man you're completely in love with him?

Oh, mercy.

Was she?

Was the Pope Catholic? The sky blue? The earth beneath her as red as the blood pumping through her heart?

Yes. *Yes.* Near enough.

She hid her grimace of embarrassment as best she could as Raphael turned to her, his expression suddenly shadowed with sadness.

"Perhaps he is a little foolish. Pinning his hopes on a man who doesn't know if he is coming or going is never a wise investment."

Thunk. There went her heart. Plummeting straight down to the very center of the earth.

Her eyes lit on the harness in his hand. "Looks like you've made a bit of an investment in him."

"This?" Raphael held up the safety restraint and smiled at it. "Yes. Perhaps it is me being hopeful."

"Hopeful is good." *Hopeful means you might stay.*

"Oui."

Raphael nodded, and their eyes connected so completely that Maggie was sure he could read her thoughts.

"Hopeful is good."

"Guess we'd better hit the road, then." Her voice came out more as a croak then a chirp. "You'll want to make the most of the time you two have together."

She scurried to the rear passenger door and opened it up so Raphael could secure Monster to the buckles and harness, all the while thinking, *Nice cover.* Way to show the man it would be a dream come true if he stuck around. Stayed a while.

And by "a while" she meant forever…

Raphael was marveling at how different the landscape was already. Fewer than a handful of hours outside of Sydney, they were working their way through the Blue Mountains. The vistas were utterly breathtaking. Unlike anything he'd seen before. And the atmosphere in the car was nice. A bit of chat. A bit of silence. Repeat.

"Maggie, this may seem like a silly question, but with a trip this long…in France we would fly or take a train. Why do you drive?"

"What?" Maggie shrugged away his question. "You never drove anywhere in France?"

"Of course—but not almost twelve hundred kilometers for a short visit."

Maggie tipped her head to the side and considered her response.

He smiled. She'd done that as a teen as well. Usually the questions had been about algebra or advanced chemistry. Those two thick fire-red plaits she'd always worn had shifted across her shoulders as she'd tipped her chin up to the left, her green eyes following suit until she gave her answer.

"I suppose… Oh, I don't know… It gives me a sense of being in control of my destiny."

"Driving for over a thousand kilometers?" He laughed. "So *that's* the answer to taking charge of your destiny. *Bof…*" He let out a low whistle. "If only I'd known."

If only it was that simple. He would've driven ten…a hundred thousand kilometers if it would have changed things.

A thought struck him. He couldn't change the past. But he could change the future.

He reached his arm back between the seats and gave Monster a scratch behind the ears. The dog nestled into his hand. Trusting. Believing there was a future.

He looked across to Maggie, her eyes firmly on the road. He had a dog and a friend. A dear friend who...who maybe held the promise of something more?

"Holding the steering wheel of destiny is a personal thing." Maggie tip-tapped her fingers along the steering wheel, as if divining good advice. "Everybody's got their own thing, right? The thing that lets them soar. Perhaps you just haven't found yours yet. Besides..." she laughed "...it's not as if driving from Sydney to Broken Hill a dozen times has landed me a gold-plated mansion by the sea and the love of my life or anything!" She gave another horsey laugh, then quickly swallowed it.

"Is that what the goal is? A gold-plated mansion?"

She huffed out another laugh and gave him a look as if he'd just turned into a stranger. "Yeah. That'd be about right. You read me like a book."

Raphael turned in his seat and looked at her. She was obviously being sarcastic. Of course she had zero designs on a gold-plated mansion, but...the love of her life? Something told him she meant *that* part. She was ready for love.

He was tempted to say something—crack a feeble joke and tell her that if a slightly the worse for wear heart was what she was after, his was all hers—when Maggie picked up the conversation again.

"Buses, trains, airplanes...they're just...you can't *do* anything if they're running late, you know? If you're driving then you get to be in charge. Pick your speed. Choose the route. Stop. Start. Do what you like, when you like, so you can get where you need to go exactly when you want to."

"Is that why you like driving the ambulance?"

"A little bit." She tipped her head back and forth, letting the idea settle, then smiled broadly. "A lot, actually. Even more so than my 'civilian' car, because I've got the lights, the siren. If they invented one that would let me drive above the traffic I'd be the happiest girl in Sydney."

She looked just like a little girl as she imagined the scenario. Which made him wonder if the answer wasn't, in fact, a simple one. "Does your desire to be mistress of your own time spring from always being late for things as a child?"

"No." She shook her head emphatically. "But I was late for something once…"

Maggie's sentence trailed off into nothing and the vibe coming from her distinctly said, *Time to back off,* mon ami.

He understood that feeling well enough, so he settled back into his seat and scanned the views spreading out beyond them—a rich palate of rusty cliff-sides, greens and blues still alight with the golden glow of the morning sun.

"If the rest of the journey is anything like this, I completely understand you wanting to be the master of your own destiny."

"It's pretty beautiful, isn't it?" Maggie said proudly.

"I didn't realize there were so many wineries near to the city."

Maggie nodded, much more relaxed now they'd shifted conversation topic. Playing tour guide suited her, and it was enjoyable to see her visible pride about all that her nation had to offer.

"We could've gone through the Hunter Valley, but that would've added a couple hundred kilometers to the trip. Really we could travel for weeks—months, even—and not get across to Perth. Australia's awash with wineries. Maybe not as many as France, but Aussies definitely like their wine." She laughed at a sudden memory. "Do you remember when you took me to that one cafe?"

They'd been to a lot of cafés and bistros, but a picture

sprang to mind of a little corner café they had visited early on in her trip. It had been the French cliché. Cast-iron tables—a bit wobbly, with green tops. Rattan-framed bistro chairs with a blue and cream weave. A sun-bleached red awning beneath which the ubiquitous rude waiting staff jostled between the tightly packed tables. He'd been showing off. Acting the sophisticate for his New World charge.

Falling in love.

"Do you mean the café where we were served wine by that waiter who thought he was a model?"

"Exactly." Maggie laughed again, her green eyes sparking at the memory. "I was too embarrassed to tell you, but I'd never had wine before. Only stolen a few sips of my brothers' beer. I loved those little glasses so much…you know, the bistro glasses…but I didn't have a clue if I was doing anything right. I was amazed it was even legal!"

She sighed, and from the expression on her face he imagined even more memories were flooding in.

"Want to hear a confession?"

"Definitely. Yes." She shot him one of those bright smiles of hers that always seemed to land in the center of his heart.

"It was my first time, too."

She turned to him, features wide with astonishment. "*No.* I don't believe that for a second. Compared to me, you were so suave and sophisticated."

"Were?" he teased. He'd never felt suave or sophisticated for a single day of his life.

"Are," she parried solidly. "Believe me, when you see where I've come from you will see for a fact that you are, hands down, the most sophisticated person I know."

"Maggie Louis," he reprimanded her playfully. "You are being ridiculous. I am just a kid who was lucky enough to be born in a beautiful city. I wanted to show it off to you."

"You did that all right…" Her voice drifted off. "But I

don't agree with you about the 'lucky kid' thing. You knew everything about Paris. I never felt for a single moment that I wasn't with the perfect person."

Her eyes flicked across to him and then quickly returned to the road, her upper teeth taking purchase on her lower lip as if she'd admitted more than she'd wanted to.

"I had a wonderful time showing you Paris."

He meant it to his very marrow. Going home to two parents more interested in the next bottle of spirits or who would win the inevitable fight over who'd spent the last of the welfare check had been a lot less fun than seeing Maggie's eyes light up when he showed her the nooks and crannies of Paris he'd discovered on the endless walks he'd taken to avoid going home.

"The truth is…" Maggie began slowly, then continued in a rush as if she'd dared herself to finish. "I think I was always a bit in love with you."

The instant she'd said it a thousand memories fell into place. The gentle looks. The soft smiles. Those moments when their hands or fingers had brushed and it had felt as though time itself had decided to stand still.

It was blatantly obvious that Maggie couldn't take it back fast enough. Words began tumbling out to erase what she'd said.

Of course only in a schoolgirl kind of way…a teenage crush…ridiculous…nothing to worry about. He mustn't think he was trapped in the car with her…she wasn't a stalker or anything."

"Maggie! *Arrêts.* It's okay. We were kids. Besides, even if I'd wanted to I couldn't have done anything about it."

Her lids lowered to half-mast and she shot him a look.

"Jean-Luc," he said as a means of explanation.

Tell her! Tell her you felt the same way!

She lifted a finger and rolled it round. *Keep on talking,* it said. Clearly just saying Jean-Luc's name wasn't enough.

He sucked in a deep breath. Talking about Jean-Luc in any capacity was tough. Going back to the "good old days" was the hardest. Because they seemed the furthest out of reach.

"He told me he'd give me a black eye if I even so much as *thought* of kissing you."

"He did?"

Raphael nodded. "He did."

"And you listened to him?" Maggie gave him a quick glance.

"Let's just say Jean-Luc was acting at his mother's behest."

"Um…" Maggie's voice sounded dubious. "Since when do teenage boys listen to their mother? I grew up with three brothers, remember?"

"If one of your brothers had threatened someone who had designs on you with a black eye, would the boy have listened?"

Maggie obviously didn't need long to work that one out.

"Most likely—but that's small town stuff. Jean-Luc was your best friend. And he already *had* a girlfriend. Surely he would've just ignored his mother and told you to go for it?"

"Is that what you would have liked?"

"Raphael." Maggie threw him a stern look. "This is already immensely embarrassing. I'm not going to beg you to explain to me why you never kissed me."

There were a thousand reasons why. How did he explain to her that the Couttards had been his second family? That they had provided the structure and the balance—and sometimes the square meals—he had needed throughout his teens.

It had been out of loyalty. Maggie would understand that. And yet every part of him wished he had taken the risk.

"I know it sounds a bit pathetic, but think about it. Would *you* have disobeyed Madame Couttard?"

Maggie's features stayed static as she considered the question. "No. Definitely not. She was lovely, but she was a stern woman. I remember every time I asked why they ate so late she would fix me with an astonished expression, pop her hands on her hips and say. *'Je n'aime pas manger avec les poules, Margaret!'*"

"Exactly." Raphael tapped the dashboard soundly. "She saw being your host mother as akin to being your *own* mother. Looking out for you. Caring for you. Making sure errant teenage French boys didn't get any wayward ideas. The only change she wanted in you when she returned you to your own mother was speaking better French."

Maggie nodded and made an undefinable noise. "Yeah, well…my French certainly improved, all right."

She pushed a button on the display panel and turned on the radio.

Topic. Closed.

A brick wall to bang his head on would be useful about now.

Ça me soûle!

He scrubbed a hand through his hair and looked out of the window. Well, that had been about the quickest way to go from awkward to awful. The perfect tone to set for a road trip lasting over a thousand kilometers. *Très bien.*

Just say something to make her feel better about you not kissing her when you should have.

"It was a long time ago."

Nice. Exactly what she wanted to hear. That her feelings were silly and adolescent.

"Yeah. It *was* a long time ago." She nodded, cheeks flaming with embarrassment. "Would you—? Would you just…just forget I said anything? All right?"

She was gripping the steering wheel so hard her hands were trembling. Her eyes were glued to the curve of the mountainous roads ahead of them as if her life depended on it.

With every pore of his body Raphael ached for things to be different.

And that was precisely the moment when Raphael knew why he'd come to Australia.

Not to find himself. Not to make peace with his past. It was to find Maggie. To see if he could put a name to that elusive *something* that floated around in his heart whenever he thought of her.

She'd named it first. It was love.

Maggie held up her ice cream cone and tipped it towards Raphael's wattleseed flavored scoop for a "cheers" bump.

"So this is the world's best ice cream?"

"Don't look so dubious. This town may not look like much, but when you're about five hundred kilometers from civilization it's the height of sophistication."

Maggie took a satisfyingly cold lick of her saltbush and caramel cone. Ice cream fixed everything. Even incredibly awkward atmospheres in a car after you'd confessed to the man of your dreams that you've loved him since you were a teen and he's told you that someone's mom told him not to kiss you.

What she *should* be taking away from the whole mortifying scenario was the fact that Raphael had, for at least a nanosecond on the universe's timeline, *wanted* to kiss her. Not be sulking about having great French and no mother to show it off to. It wasn't as if she could change anything now.

Besides, if the *chaussure* had been on the other foot and *her* mother had laid down a similar order…

No pashing on the French exchange student, love. We've got to return that boy to his mother the way we found him. Pffft.

She would have obeyed, too. Small town kids knew that parents talked. Nothing was a secret.

Except that her mother had already been dying of cancer the day Maggie had boarded a plane for Europe.

Raphael "clinked" her ice cream cone again. "You're right. This is excellent. I have to confess, finding a gelateria in a petrol station is not something I thought would happen today."

He was handing her an olive branch. Trying to get rid of the weirdness as well. So it looked as if they'd be friends forever.

If it was good enough for Ingrid Bergman and Humphrey Bogart...

Maggie gave him a *Strange things happen in Oz* shrug and a grin. "There are loads of Italians who settled in Australia, so the country definitely does good ice cream—wherever you are."

"As good as France?" Raphael arched a prideful brow.

Ruddy French. Not *everything* was better over there!

"I would bet you any amount of money in the universe they don't have wattleseed ice cream in Paris."

Raphael laughed. "You are probably right about that." He took a lick and made *mmm* noises as he swirled the entire tip of the cone between his parted lips.

Maggie tried not to stare. *Too much.*

"It's good. Tastes a bit like coffee. Would you like to try?"

"Yes, please." She leaned forward and took a lick, vividly aware of Raphael's eyes upon her. Was there something...*different* about the way he was watching her? Something softer?

The man was now aware that she'd been in love with him forever and a day...

Or maybe she had dirt on her face.

Whatever it was, his gaze was making her flush.

"Mmm. That's good. Want to try mine?"

Maggie held up her cone, felt her eyes going into some sort of crazy blinking fit as once again—almost in slow motion—his lips parted before surrounding the top of her cone and taking a small taste.

Her breath caught in her throat as she imagined the cold ice cream hitting his warm tongue, melting and swirling in his mouth. Hot darts of desire shot across her more intimate regions as he made that delicious noise again. He looked up at her through dark lashes with those beautiful blue eyes of his, and in that instant she felt as though her skin was on fire.

He wasn't even *touching* her and she was on fire.

Gulp.

She still loved him.

No, she didn't.

She *lusted* after him.

Loving someone meant knowing them, and she was about as far from knowing what made Raphael tick these days as she was from knowing how to fly a jumbo jet.

Road trips were fun only if you weren't dying of humiliation at the same time. This was obviously a mistake.

Even if Raphael *was* still gazing at her with that beautiful soft smile on his lips.

She started when he reached forward and tucked a wayward strand of hair behind her ear, his fingers softly grazing the side of her neck as they passed. It was all she could do not to groan with pleasure.

What would she do when they finally kissed?

You're not going to kiss!

Madame Couttard had made sure of that.

Pah!

If they kissed then she'd be completely in love with him—which was stupid because they were heading for Broken Hill and her mad-as-a-sack-of-frogs family.

When they arrived Raphael would find out who she was and what sort of place she came from. A universe away from his own background. The whole charade of being someone she wasn't would come to an abrupt end, her heart would break into a million tiny pieces and then they could all get on with their lives. Which would be a good thing.

Except right here, right now, Raphael was licking a little bit of wattleseed off of his lip and was inches away. If she moved her ice cream cone a tiny bit to the right and went up on tiptoe...

"Maggie? Is that your phone ringing?"

The hum and rush of desire dropped from Maggie's internal soundtrack and was replaced by the very clear chirruping of her ringtone.

Mortified that she'd been staring at Raphael all goofy-eyed and lovestruck, she turned away and pulled her phone from her small bag. It was Cyclops.

"What's up, mate? I'm out in the Woop Woop."

"Yeah, I know."

Cyclops' voice was in full business mode. *Uh-oh.*

"There's been a car crash reported between Cobar and Wilcannia. Coupla lorries and some secondary vehicles. Quite a few, from the sounds of it."

She listened intently as he detailed the location.

"You anywhere near there?"

Maggie closed her eyes and pictured the road. "We're about ten kilometers east, give or take. Is anyone else on the way?"

"Yeah. They're sending a chopper out from the Blues, but it'll take at least an hour to get it crewed up and in the air. The fire crews in Cobar are all out on other jobs, but I'm coming in a chaser air ambulance. Probably two hours out. The coppers are on their way. I think they're trying to send a fire crew in with some Jaws of Life, but they'll all be volunteers. Not sure how up on first aid they'll be.

It sounds serious. Any chance you can get to them and help until we arrive? Got any gear on you? Is Frenchie with you?"

"Yes, yes and yes." She looked at Raphael and gave him a tight nod. "I've got a small run bag in the boot, but not much else. Hang on a second, Cyclops."

She took the phone away from her ear, tugged a couple of notes out of her pocket and handed them to Raphael.

"Do you mind grabbing a few extra bottles of water from the guys in the shop? Loads, in fact. And as much paper toweling as you can get. Tell them it's for a medical emergency. Car crash up the road."

Raphael's features tightened instantly, and the all too familiar clouding of the bright blue in his eyes shifted into place.

This was difficult terrain for him, given his recent history, but it was an emergency. And it was what Australian paramedics did. They mucked in when there was no one else.

He was gone before she had a chance to ask if he was up to it.

Good.

Maybe working on the ambos was helping take the edge off the guilt he felt.

You couldn't save everyone, she thought as she signed off with Cyclops, grabbed her medical kit from the boot and threw it in the back alongside a perplexed-looking Monster.

But you sure could try.

CHAPTER EIGHT

RAPHAEL SAW THE smoke before the vehicles came into view. These weren't his first crash victims since he'd left Paris, but it was the first time he'd been on-site at a multi-vehicle accident. Adding scent and sound to a scene he'd imagined again and again might be torture. Or it might be the first step in putting the past right.

A couple of kilometers down the road cars were already starting to tail back on the wide highway.

"I don't suppose you have a spare set of blue lights in your car?" Raphael asked rhetorically.

Maggie shook her head. "No. But I do have a red and blue top in my bag on the back seat, if Monster hasn't turned it into a bed. Do you mind digging through my things to find it? Hopefully it's not too near my undies." She shot him an apologetic smile.

He shook his head and smiled. Trust Maggie to problem-solve her way out of a situation other people would duck out of at the first hurdle.

"Here it is." He held out a red shirt with blue polka dots.

"Right. Your job is to hold that thing out of the window."

"What for?"

She yanked the car brusquely out of the slowing traffic and onto the hard shoulder. "Tell Monster to cover his ears. You're the lights. I'm the siren."

Clamping her lips together with a determined expression, Maggie pressed on the horn of her car with one hand and gunned the car down the hard shoulder with the other.

It was impossible not to be impressed.

He ventured a guess. "Older brothers?"

"Got it in one." She flashed him a smile. "As I said, there wasn't much to do in Broken Hill as a girl."

When they were close enough to start picking out details, Raphael's gut told him the next few hours were going to be grim.

"You ready for this?" Maggie's tone suggested she didn't really care if he was or he wasn't. Either way, he'd be rolling up his sleeves and getting to work.

"Of course. You can count on me."

He meant it, too. Medically, of course. But also to support Maggie. The last thing he wanted was for her to have to worry about if he'd be all right on the accident scene.

"Why don't you have a dig around the medical kit and familiarize yourself with what we have? From the sound of things, we'll have to make it last for about an hour. Criticals first." She gave him an apologetic smile. "Sorry. I forget you're hardly a stranger to trauma. Talking it through before I arrive always helps me calm down."

"*Bien.* Talk away."

He secured the blue and red top between the window and the window frame, keeping half an ear on Maggie's ideas for the best tactical approach as he pulled her medical kit onto his lap and had a quick run through it. Rather than the handful of plasters and couple of bandages he had been expecting, it was a proper first responder bag, full of wound dressings, burn gels, eye gels, thermal blankets, Epi-pens—the lot.

"I like your version of a 'small' kit."

"Things happen out in the Woop Woop." Her eyes remained glued to the road. "There's also a couple of picnic rugs in the back. No doubt some of the other drivers will have them as well. Blankets are going to be our stretchers, our braces...just about everything until the choppers arrive."

Raphael nodded. Though it wasn't as good as having an ambulance's worth of gear, for some of these people the difference between no equipment and this soft bag could be critical.

Maggie slowed as they approached the jack-knifed road train. Its accordioned cab was enough to produce shivers. The trailers lay sprawled across the highway amidst a tangle of combis, caravans and utility vehicles—or utes, as the Australians called them.

When they pulled up at the apex of the crash Maggie was pure business.

A police car was already on the scene and she quickly identified herself and Raphael, offering to start setting up a triage area on the side of the road farthest away from the smoking vehicles.

"That'd be great." The officer introduced her to a nearby female in uniform and pointed them toward a spot they'd already pre-identified as being appropriate for triage. He lifted his chin towards Raphael. "You're a doctor?"

He nodded.

"Good. Come with me."

After rolling down the windows of the car and pouring Monster a bowl of water, he shouldered the medical bag and jogged along after the policeman to the other side of the road train.

"We need as many people as possible. There's a motorcyclist who landed under a ute when he was skidding to a halt. Bloody miracle he's still alive. Don't think he's conscious, though. Hasn't said a word."

They rounded the corner. About ten people in crouching positions surrounded a mid-sized car still smoking from a recently doused engine fire.

"Quel desastre!"

The officer shot him a sideways glance. "You're not from around here, are ya?"

"France."

He let out a low whistle. "Well, this is a far cry from France, mate. Prepare to get sweaty. If we lift this ute on a three count are you good to pull him out?"

The officer had a couple of people shifting the vehicle, including the ashen-faced male driver who looked close to fainting. Raphael made a quick mental note to find him later and check for symptoms of shock or whiplash, then knelt down to see where the motorcyclist was. His lips thinned when he saw just how much of the vehicle's undercarriage was resting on his chest. He slipped two fingers beneath the man's helmet to check for a pulse. Thready. But it was there.

"Okay." He looked up at the officer, feeling his adrenaline kick in. "Whenever you are ready."

The three count came fast.

"Now—*lift!*"

Amidst the groans and grunts of exertion Raphael channeled his strength into a swift and fluid move, pulling the motorcyclist out and away from the undercarriage of the ute.

Leaving the biker's helmet on, he flicked the visor up, unsurprised to see the man was unconscious, a blue tinge appearing on his lips. Raphael dropped his gaze to his chest, taking in the depth, rate and symmetry of his chest as he struggled to breathe. The shallow, jagged breaths suggested a pneumothorax or flail chest.

It was difficult to tell what had happened without taking off his leathers. But taking off the leathers would come with its own set of complications. In a worst-case scenario the motorcycle gear might be the only thing holding together compound fractures and preventing massive blood loss. But palpating the man's chest with them on was pointless.

His brain kicked up to high gear.

"Can I get a couple extra pairs of hands, please?"

Protocol in France dictated leaving the helmet on, so he did. On his instructions, a pair of bystanders rolled the man onto a thermal blanket from Maggie's medical kit and, with their help, he carried him away from the site to the triage area Maggie had magicked out of nothing.

Most of the color coding seemed to come in the form of pieces of colorful fabrics secured to the white road reflectors on the edge of the hard shoulder.

Maggie appeared by his side. "What've you got?"

"Possible pneumothorax. Do you have any fourteen-gauge needles in there?" He nodded to the run bag. "His lung will need decompressing. It'll keep him stable—"

"For up to four hours," Maggie finished for him. "When you've done that are you happy to attend the patients still in their vehicles?"

Raphael nodded, taking a fraction of a second longer than he needed to search her eyes for any doubt in his ability. But, no. She was already pawing through the medical kit for the equipment he'd need for decompression.

Faith. Loyalty.

Two of Maggie's standout qualities. A shot of pride surged through him. Maggie believed in him. She trusted him in spite of everything she knew about him. It meant more to him than he'd expected. All he wanted to do now was make sure he kept it. Earned it. Sustained her belief in him as a doctor. As a man.

With the help of one of the women who'd carried the man over he quickly rolled thick supports to place on either side of the motorcyclist.

Once satisfied the patient was supported, he unzipped his leather jacket and inserted the fourteen-gauge needle, his head tipped to the man's lips as he waited for the return of steady breathing.

Beat. Beat. And breathing returned.

"Is he going to be all right?" The woman who had helped carry him over was still kneeling on the other side of the motorcyclist.

"He should be." Raphael did a quick scan of the man's abdominal area. No blood. No obvious sign of other injuries. A miracle, really.

"Will you be all right to watch him?"

The woman nodded, yes, still wide-eyed from seeing the quick-fix release of air from the man's chest cavity.

With a renewed sense of determination Raphael set out again with the police officer, who seemed to have a good handle on all the people involved in the accident.

The rest of the afternoon passed in a blur of serious traumatic injuries and quick fixes.

Supplies were severely limited, forcing him to come up with an innovative way of stabilizing one particularly bad compound fracture.

"Oooooh...*maaaaaaate*! That really, *really*—"

Raphael blanked out the stream of blue language coming out of the middle-aged man's mouth.

He was lucky to be alive. He was lucky the volunteer fire crew had been able to cut him out of his car.

Raphael's features tightened as he tried to stem the flow of blood with the pile of assorted clothing and towels other drivers had been bringing to him.

This man would be lucky to keep his leg. Keeping the area clean, blood loss to a minimum and the rest of his organs functioning properly was paramount.

"Incoming!"

Calls signaling the arrival of the first helicopter began to ring out. Raphael used himself as a cover for the man, steeling himself for the screams of pain he knew would follow as he continued to keep pressure on the open wound.

"What you got here, mate?"

A uniformed doctor appeared by his side, with another doctor running behind with a stretcher.

"Compound tib-fib. Possible comminute fracture—but that's just from what I can see."

"Right." The heli-medics gave him a short nod and turned their focus to the patient. "We're gonna get you into town, cobber...take a look at that leg. Hope you're all right with— Whoops! He's losing consciousness. Let's get him on the chopper. On three."

Raphael helped with the transfer and, satisfied the man was in good hands, felt clear to move onto the next patient.

Steadily, swiftly, he worked his way through each of the patients who were unable to leave their vehicles—or hadn't done so yet.

The generosity of spirit amongst the drivers who were uninjured amazed him. Each time he brought a new patient to the triage area there were more sets of helping hands.

"Easy. You don't want to put any weight on it if you can help it." Raphael was helping a teenaged boy hobble towards the lower-grade triage area in the hope of getting some ice.

"Do you think I crushed it? I've got a footie match tomorrow. Do you think I'll be able to play?"

Before Raphael could answer a couple of men ran and scooped the lad into an actual armchair.

"We gotcha, mate."

They caught the surprise in Raphael's gaze.

"We've got a lorry-load of furniture we were moving to a charity store. Figured it would come in handy for you lot."

"What else you got in there?" the teen asked. "Is there

a couch or a bed? I'm going to need to elevate and ice this baby if I'm going to play tomorrow."

Raphael couldn't help but laugh. "I don't think you will be playing tomorrow. Even if you ice it."

He knelt on the ground and lifted the boy's ankle up onto his knee, noting as he did so the sharp wince the boy tried to hide.

A quick examination and Raphael was close to certain the lad had suffered a pilon fracture. It would compromise his footie career for a while—if not forever—but without an X-ray there was no point in diminishing the boy's clear fighting spirit.

He rose to his feet as the other "furniture man" appeared with a footstool.

"Here you are, mate. Best we can do. The sofas are going for the ladies."

Raphael jogged over to the edge of the triage area where people who had portable ice boxes—including several huge ones—had made ice, tea towels—whatever they had to hand—available.

He brought a tea towel full of ice over to the boy.

"Who have we got here?" Maggie appeared from behind the chair with a notebook and pen in her hands.

"Charlie Broughton."

Raphael grinned as he watched the boy turn into a young man before his eyes, ratcheting up his flirt factor. Gone were the winces and groans of pain, and in their place was a broad smile and an extended hand.

"And you are…?"

Maggie gave him a quick smirk. "The woman who's going to get you a lift into the city. What do we have here? Sprain?"

Raphael shook his head. "He will need X-rays, definitely, but his injury is not critical."

"What? *Mate*..." Charlie looked at him, aghast. "The footie team is going to be absolutely furious if I'm not on the field—"

"The footie team is going to have to learn to do without you for a match," Maggie cut in as she leaned over and took a peek beneath Charlie's icepack. "Even if it is a sprain, there's no chance you're playing tomorrow."

"Well..." Charlie managed to make the word sound flirtatious. "Yes, ma'am." He gave her a wink and another smile.

Maggie laughed good-naturedly and started taking his details.

Raphael took a moment to grab some water and take in the scene.

People were handing round water and food. Their own small but increasingly useful first aid kits. A young girl had even "adopted" Monster to make sure he didn't overheat in the vehicle.

With rapidly dwindling resources, Raphael was being forced to rely on the spirit that had compelled him to choose medicine in the first place. Compassion. Skill. Dedication to helping people through their most vulnerable moments.

He felt like a doctor again.

And there was one person he had to thank for that.

A freckle-faced, green-eyed, redhead whose attention was now solidly with the newly arrived air ambulance teams and helicopter crews from Sydney.

She was pointing out the triage areas, handing across her notes as well as giving verbal hand-overs for each and every patient and details of the medicine they'd been given. Florence Nightingale had nothing on his girl.

His girl?

Mid-flow, Maggie looked across the crowds of people gathered on the roadside, met his gaze solidly…and smiled.

"Here." Raphael held out a cold bottle of water to Maggie as they walked back to her car. "I hope you have been taking your own words of wisdom to heart and staying hydrated."

"Oh, brilliant. And *cold*!" She pressed the bottle to her throat and gave a sigh of relief. "I always forget how much hotter it is out past the Blues."

She shifted the bottle to one sunburnt cheek and then the other, only to realize Raphael had been watching her the entire time. She swigged down a few grateful gulps. When she lowered the bottle from her lips there was something in his gaze she hadn't seen before.

Curiosity.

And not a brother-sister, friend-friend curiosity either.

A rush of goose pimples rippled across her entire body.

"That was pretty intense. Are you all right after all that?" Though it was a dodge away from what she was really thinking, the question had been playing in the back of her mind all day. She might as well use it as a cover for the fact that all she wanted to do was jump the man and snog him senseless.

He nodded with an assurance that put her at ease. She'd seen a change in him today. Glimpses of the "old" Raphael. Assured, confident. And more than that. There had been genuine compassion in the care he'd provided for those people today. Not that frightening hollow look in his eyes.

Today he had been *present*. Today he had been the man she'd always imagined he would become.

She balanced the water bottle on the car bonnet and rubbed her hands along her arms. "Whoo! You'd think I had a bit of heatstroke from my body's reaction to that water."

She tried to laugh, but when her eyes caught with Raphael's again it died in her throat.

"Do you think you might? You were pushing it today."

Raphael took a step towards her that caught her by surprise. So much so that she stumble-stepped backwards, only to bump into the car.

"Do you feel dizzy?"

Again, Raphael closed the distance between them, his eyes searching hers for answers. Or for dilated pupils. Which he would definitely see. And that wasn't just because the sun was beginning to set behind him.

"Maggie," he persisted, "are you feeling unwell?"

Dizzy. Weak-kneed. And a bit dreamy-eyed.

"No." She tried to shake her head, but couldn't.

Raphael reached up and cupped her face between his hands, searching her features for symptoms. She knew he'd feel heat in her cheeks. An acceleration in her heart-rate. Her breath had become shallow, her lungs impossible to fill, because everything in that instant was... *Raphael.*

And then he was kissing her. Softly at first. Tentatively. As if asking for permission to continue.

He didn't need to ask twice.

Her lips parted as his kisses gained confidence. And when she felt the initial sweep of his tongue along her lower lip a soft whimper of pure longing hummed from her chest. As the kisses deepened their breath intermingled to exhilarating effect, as if they were at long last joined as one.

One of Raphael's hands dropped to Maggie's waist, firmly tugging her closer to him as he wove the fingers of his other hand into the thick fistful of hair at the base of her neck.

For thirteen years she'd wondered what it would be like to kiss him... It was even better than she could ever have imagined.

The kisses…his touch. Everything about him was sensual. Erotic in its simplicity of purpose. The culmination of a day's intense work was pared down to these perfectly intoxicating expressions of desire and pent-up longing.

At last she knew in her heart that he felt it too.

The kisses came in so many variations it was impossible to keep track. Some were so passionate she thought her heart wouldn't be able to keep up and others were so exquisitely tender she could hardly breathe.

The world had long since blurred around them, but traffic was beginning to make its way away from the crash site.

Snail's pace? Lightning speed?

She didn't have a clue. All that mattered was Raphael. The sweet taste of his lips. The tang of salt on his skin. The rough bristles of growth upon his cheeks shifting past her fingertips as she swept her hands into a loose cinch behind his neck.

She was half tempted to sling a leg up onto one of his hips when a sharp wolf whistle broke through the thick heat of the afternoon air.

They pulled apart, surprised to find themselves the object of an entire fire crew's attention. More wolf whistles began to ring out from passing cars, along with cheers and cries of, "Good on ya, mate!" and "Nice one, cobber!"

Maggie didn't know whether to shrivel up and die of embarrassment or laugh and scream, *Finally!*

Feigning a demureness she knew she didn't possess, she sought her cue from Raphael.

But instead of withdrawing in horror, Raphael rested his hands on Maggie's hips—protectively, almost—and smiled, tipping his chin toward the firemen and drivers before returning his gaze to her. And that bright twinkle in his blue eyes was alight for the first time in… It had been a while. And a long time coming.

"Do you mind? The attention?" he asked, his gentle accent adding an extra level of sensuality to the question.

She shook her head—no. It was a lot better than being the center of attention because she was the only one who knew how to get grease stains out of work overalls. Better by a mile.

She squinted at the setting sun, the brilliant wash of colour doing its magic behind him. Though she would have happily stayed on the roadside, woven into Raphael's arms, absorbing the full impact of just how incredible it was—how incredible *he* was—practical Maggie kicked into gear.

"We'd probably better hit the road. We're going to be driving all night from the looks of things."

"It's too far, Maggie. Especially having worked flat-out today. *Non.* Is there not a town nearby where we can stay?"

"What? You mean like in a motel or something?"

OMG! One room or two? One room or two?

Raphael pulled back and examined her, his fingers hooked on her hips with a sense of familiarity that unleashed another thrill of expectation in her heart.

One room. Definitely one room.

That was what his eyes were saying...what his hands were saying. The lips just about to meet hers—

"Maggie!" The police officer who had been coordinating the accident scene—Scott Roland—was jogging towards them, waving something vaguely familiar-looking in his hand. "Don't forget your knickers!"

Flames of embarrassment streaked across Maggie's cheeks.

Why, why, *why* had she used her superhero panties as triage color tags?

Scott slowed to a halt in front of them, eyeing the pair of them with a smirk. "I'm not interrupting anything private, am I?"

"Hardly!"

Maggie scooted out of Raphael's loose hold on her hips and reached out to grab her knickers.

"Not so fast, little lady." Scott's features broadened into an ear-to-ear grin. "I think the press might be interested in hearing about the real-life superhero of today's accident."

"I don't think so. *You're* the real hero and no one's interested in your undershorts!" Maggie ground out, trying again—unsuccessfully—to nab the brightly colored bits of cotton that no one was meant to know about apart from her.

So what if she wore superhero knickers to give herself a little private motivation as she worked her way through the inevitable piles of debris and gunk that had built up at the Louis household in her absence? Her secret little charwoman's outfit. Fit for no eyes other than her own!

"Let's see…" Scott was relishing her discomfort. "What do we have here…?"

From perfect moment to perfectly mortifying…

This was the cringe-worthy material nightmares were made of.

If she could just grab them before Raphael—

"I particularly like these ones, Maggie," Scott said, holding up her favorite pair—the Wonder Woman knickers—for one and all to see.

"Stop it!"

"What? Or what about these? Don't you want the world to know you've got Cat Woman panties? I wouldn't mind a glimpse of you in these, if you don't mind me saying."

He put his fingers at either end of the black knickers with sassy cat's eyes on them—one for each buttock—and tipped them back and forth like a cat about to pounce.

"*I* do."

Raphael reached out, took the knickers, handed them back to Maggie and then pulled her close to him, snugly wrapping an arm around her shoulders.

If swooning was still a thing she would be doing it. And

then crawling beneath her car and crying fat, hot tears that said, *Why, oh, why can't I be the cool one? Just once!*

"I'm guessing these are Bat Girl?" Scott pulled one final pair out of his back pocket.

Raphael held out his hand for the panties and made a *put 'em here* gesture as Scott held them out: black, with a bright gold bat embossed on the behind.

Unfazed, Scott gave him a wink. "I suppose you've got the matching Superman boxers, then, big boy?"

Raphael tipped his hand back and forth in a move that said, *Maybe I do, maybe I don't. Superheroes don't tell.*

If Maggie hadn't thought she was in love before, her affections were cast in stone now.

"Right!" Maggie pulled the car into a huge dusty rectangle that served as a car park. "This is us, I guess."

Her state of mind was the same as Raphael's: one part *Why are we still wearing clothes?* to one part *Are we really ready for the next step?*

The hour-long ride to the motel had seen the sun set and their expectations of what was to come rise.

Now that they were here...

In unison, they looked up at the large neon sign blinking in front of them. With its blood-red lettering and handful of blown-out letters, the level of invitation to come on in and stay the night was questionable.

Big Pe e's Road use & ottleshop

Monster made a noise expressing his doubts from the back seat.

"Do you think they have room service?" Raphael asked.

Maggie laughed, then echoed Raphael's dry tone. "If you're after a hunk of cheese stuck between two bits of bread and an ice-cold stubbie I think you might be all right."

"That's more than I grew up with most days." He shrugged nonchalantly, before remembering Maggie still didn't know that side of his upbringing.

She squinted at him, hands still braced on the steering wheel as if she hadn't entirely decided whether or not she was going to let go. "What are you talking about? Compared to me, you had a *lovely* upbringing."

Something instinctive and fierce rose up in Raphael. From what he could remember, *her* upbringing had been similar to Jean-Luc's. "What do you mean, compared to you?"

Maggie rolled her eyes. "No, no… Nothing bad. Just… no fancy Parisian neighborhood with all the trimmings." She tipped her head toward the back seat. "Shall we give Monster a bit of a stroll?"

Raphael agreed, grateful for the chance to stretch his legs and enjoy the cooler night air.

After a few moments of strolling around Raphael tried again, adding as much of a light-hearted tone to his voice as he could. "What was so bad about your upbringing? If I should have brought my sword to your home, you could have warned me."

Maggie laughed and shook her head. "Honestly, it was nothing like that. My family are goofballs, but they're all very loving. It was more…what the town *wasn't*."

"What do you mean?"

She huffed out a laugh. "Suffice it to say Broken Hill doesn't really throw a patch on Paris. Trust me. You're in for a bit of a shocker tomorrow."

He sucked in a breath. Was she ready for the real Raphael? Warts and all?

He reached across to her and took one of her hands in his, tracing along the lines written into her palm. Before things went any further—and he knew in his heart he wanted them to progress—he owed her this much.

"If you think back," he began softly, his eyes trained on hers, "you never actually came to my house."

Maggie's lips parted in protest, but just as quickly she screwed them into a little moue and thought. "It never really occurred to me…"

Her fingers covered her mouth and she drummed them along her lips for a minute—lips he would do anything to be kissing again.

"We did everything at the Couttard's or around Paris, didn't we?"

He nodded.

"Why was that?" She looked utterly baffled.

"My parents were both…how do you say?…fond of a drink. Or eleven. Do you understand?"

Maggie's eyes widened. "It's not strictly a saying, but I get your drift."

She wasn't judging—just listening. She'd been that way when they'd met. He should have trusted her with this information back then.

The fog cleared in his head. How pointless it had all been! To disguise part of himself from her. Maggie's affection for him wasn't attached to wealth or status or—he looked round the dusty car park outside the motel—to Paris. Paris hadn't been a factor. She'd simply cared for *him*.

"They didn't hurt you, did they?"

Raphael shook his head, no. They hadn't been that bad. Most of the time. The odd cuff to the ear. An arm gripped too tightly. Impossible to fulfill their expectations because they simply weren't happy people.

"They weren't horrible—just poor. And not terribly motivated." He shrugged again. It eased his heart to realize he'd let go of that anger long ago.

"So…how did you and Jean-Luc—?"

"Become friends?" Raphael finished for her. "We met

at school. My parents had a small apartment—subsidized housing—in the same neighborhood where the Couttards lived, and at school we were seated in alphabetical order."

"Bouchon and Couttard," Maggie murmured, as if saying the names helped her picture the scene. "And they basically...what? Adopted you?"

Raphael gave a soft smile. The Couttards had opened their hearts and their home to him as if they were his own parents.

"Without the formalities, I suppose you could say they did. Jean-Luc didn't have any brothers or sisters and, as you may remember, both his parents were lawyers so they worked a lot. It was one of the reasons Madame Couttard accepted foreign exchange students."

"Someone for Jean-Luc to hang out with?"

"Yes—precisely. And they had always wanted a large family. The year you came, you had the fortune—or misfortune, depending upon how you look at it—of being lumped in with me. If you remember, that was the year Jean-Luc discovered girls?"

Maggie laughed at the memory. "It was impossible to keep track of them all."

She gave Raphael's hand a squeeze, then gave him a *C'mon buddy, we've just pashed in front of a thousand cars* look.

"I suppose you've figured out by now it was a real hardship being 'lumped' in with you." Her eyes brightened with another thought. "So...when Madame Couttard asked you to do something—"

"If you mean something like *not* kiss the beautiful Australian girl even though it would have made me very happy? Yes. I obeyed. I owed them so much."

"I get it now," Maggie said, nodding as she connected the dots. "I would've done the same thing." A twinkle hit her green eyes. "Even if it left a poor Aussie girl heartbroken that she'd gone all the way to France and hadn't been kissed."

Raphael made a noise to protest, but he could tell from her relaxed demeanor that she wasn't chastising him. The past was in the past.

It was a powerfully healing thought—leaving the past where it was and doing everything he could for his future. And he wanted his future to be with Maggie.

"Well, you know…" His voice dropped an octave. "I didn't fly halfway across the world to stand outside a neon lit motel and talk about the past."

"Oh, no?" Maggie's lips curled into a flirtatious smile as her lids dropped to half-mast over those green eyes of hers. "Why *did* you come?"

"I came for you."

If someone had thrown a lightning bolt straight into her heart it would have had less of an effect.

"Me?"

Raphael nodded. "It's taken me a while to figure it out." He shot her a sheepish look. "Sorry for all the glowering and thunderous looks back in Sydney."

She waved off his concerns, her insides still recovering from the glitter storm of emotion swirling in her chest. "You were fine. You were just really…"

"French?" he filled in for her, and they both laughed.

Raphael took a step closer towards her. The air grew taut with expectation. With promise.

Monster barked. He wanted his tea.

"What do you say we check in? Get this guy fed and then…bed?"

Yes, yes—yes, please. If I don't die of anticipation first.

She nodded as nonchalantly as she could. "Good idea."

A few minutes later they'd met the owners and reassessed their dodgy motel as a quirky work in progress. The owners were a young couple who offered them the "spa room" before showing them a fenced outdoor area complete with dog house where Monster could stay the night.

"Alors." Raphael held up the large room key, a mischievous twinkle in his eye. "Shall we?"

"No time like the present!" Maggie chirped too loudly, and she grabbed her bag and smiled, just a little impressed that she could even walk. Her legs were wobbling like jelly.

The second the door to their room clicked shut behind them all Maggie's nervous energy disappeared.

She barely saw the dated bedcover. The art that looked as though someone's grandmother had won it in a tombola with poor pickings. The lampshades she was certain she'd seen at a car boot sale flanking either side of a queen-sized bed that already seemed too far away even though it couldn't have been more than a few footsteps away.

Raphael clearly felt the same way. He backed her against the door, dropped their overnight bags where they stood and cupped her face with his hands, his lips descending to hers for the most beautifully intimate kiss she'd ever known.

Not five minutes later she realized her entire body had shape-shifted into molten lava.

They'd managed to kick their shoes off, but not much more. Her blouse seemed to have lost a couple of buttons. So had that chambray shirt of Raphael's, she noted with a wicked grin as she gave the sweet spot at the base of his throat an entirely out of character lick.

Each moment in Raphael's arms—touching him, being held by him, caressed by him—was lifting her to another level of sexual revelation. Her body responded to his every touch as if she had never known a man before. And, in his arms, she knew there would never be another.

His fingers slid along her sides as he dropped heated kiss after heated kiss onto her neck. The tips of his fingers dipped in at her waist, eliciting a shiver of response along her belly. Her hands sought his, weaving their fingers together, and as one they turned toward the bed.

"Es-tu sûr?" he murmured, his thumb skimming along one of her cheekbones and shifting a stray strand of hair behind her ear.

"I've never been more certain of anything."

And she meant it. It was as if her whole life had been leading to this point. To Raphael.

When they had checked in to the motel they had giggled like the teenagers they had once been.

All that giddy effervescence was gone now.

In its place was electricity. Fire. The building blocks of desire that had begun to form so long ago leading them to this one erotically charged night of discovery.

Before she could sit on the bed Raphael held her at arm's length, looking at her as a man who'd not drunk water in a hundred days might view a clear running mountain brook.

He wanted her. Knowing that in her heart emboldened Maggie.

Where she had once felt timorous and incredibly body-shy with the two or three other boyfriends she'd had, with Raphael she felt...*beautiful*. Powerful, even. Sensual.

It was surprising, considering just how filthy she must be from the day's hard work.

Which gave her an idea...

"Would you like to take a shower?"

A gleam of heated expectation hit Raphael's eyes. It was a look that said, *Yes.* And, *Why aren't we there already?*

Again he took her hand, and they practically raced to the next room.

Much to their surprise, the bathroom *wasn't* a relic of the previous century. It had been updated into a large wet room, with beautiful earth-tone tiles on one wall, thick slabs of hardwood on the controls wall, a gorgeous cobalt-blue-tiled floor and a huge waterfall shower head. A long olive tree plank held an invitingly pristine pile of thick bath towels.

It was perfect.

"Why wait?" Raphael asked, reaching across to the controls, and then pulling her close to him, still completely clothed, he turned on the water.

Maggie lifted her head to the cascade of water, closed her eyes and let it pour down over her. When she opened her eyes she met Raphael's blue gaze, and in that moment she gave her heart to him completely.

Slowly, assuredly, he undid the remaining buttons of Maggie's blouse, dropping kisses on her bare salty skin as he peeled the cotton away first from her shoulders, then her breasts. Her fingers flew to his hair, clutching thick handfuls of the rich chestnut curls as he took one of her nipples into his mouth, slowly swirling his tongue round and round before sucking and caressing her breast as if time were no factor.

And it wasn't. Not anymore.

All that existed was Raphael.

Her second nipple tightened in anticipation of his kiss. A soft moan vibrated the length of her throat when his lips gained purchase. Her entire body responded—lifting, swelling and aching in feverish suspense, waiting for his touch.

Her knee-length skirt suddenly felt too tight. Her knickers too constricting. Every thread of cotton on Raphael's body was in the way of what she really wanted. Skin to skin contact.

She surprised herself by pushing him back against the wooden wall of the wet room, water still pouring over them, taking each side of his shirt in her hands and tearing it in two.

Raphael laughed.

Shock? Surprise, maybe?

Their eyes met and meshed.

No.

Desire.

Up until this point their movements had been slow, sensuous. Each touch, kiss and caress had carried with it a note of precaution, speaking of a wish to ensure they were pleasing the other.

But now a switch had been flicked.

Now their movements became assured, laden with sexual intent. Down went his jeans. One of them kicked them in a heap to one side. Who knew where his boxers went? Not Maggie. Her skirt hit the far wall. A blink of an eye later her lace-just-in-case knickers were history. And her brassiere…? *What* brassiere?

Raphael pulled her against him and as one they groaned with the pleasure of skin-on-skin connection. Hot. Wet. Insatiable.

They soaped one another with beautifully aromatic body wash, teasing, playing as they did so. Her hands swirled through chest hair. His fingers teased along the soft curves of breasts.

When Raphael parted Maggie's legs with one of his own and trailed his hand up and along Maggie's inner thigh she thought she'd scream with pent-up frustration. When his fingers slipped inside her she did scream. Her thighs instinctively clamped tight onto his hand as she begged him to stop. She wanted to reach her peak with him inside her. She wanted to share the exaltation of that ultimate intimacy as one united soul.

A moment later he took her hand in his and filled it with shower gel, lifting his eyebrows, taunting her to have as wicked a way with him as she could imagine.

Maggie didn't have to imagine. Having the real Raphael here and now was all the inspiration she needed.

Bathed in soft light, warm water and the gentle gaze of the man she loved, Maggie enjoyed the slick sensation of shifting a soapy hip along one of Raphael's solid thighs, her soft belly against his well-defined stomach, then moving lower…to the hard, taut, evidence of his desire.

The temptation to wrap her hands round his neck, lift her legs to his hips and lower herself onto the solid, velvety thickness of his erection nearly blinded her to any other option.

The scenario played itself out as they moved from the drenched wall behind them to the beautiful rich blue tiles beneath their feet. The need for protection shifted the immediacy of her desire into the tantalizing prospect of toweling him off and starting all over again on the bed.

As if reading her mind, Raphael turned off the water and reached for the pile of thick bath towels. He unfurled one of the towels, wrapped her in it, and swiftly secured one around his own trim hips.

Just two seconds of being hidden from him and already Maggie felt deprived of all six foot two inches of Raphael's beautifully toned body.

Depraved, more like.

But not indecently so. More as if she'd found the key to a special door—*une porte magique*. A portal that gave her access to the richness of carnal desire with someone who was safe, someone who cared, someone who loved her as much as she loved him.

A few long-strided steps later and Raphael was ripping the covers off the bed. He was right. They didn't need anything to hide from each other.

She ran towards the bed and launched herself at it, laughing with sheer delight.

Raphael turned back from his overnight bag and held up an easily recognizable foil packet.

"You came prepared?" She feigned shock.

"I came with hope," he parried, a naughty choirboy expression playing across his features.

"Good answer." She crooked her finger and beckoned for him to join her.

Once he'd stretched out to his full length on the bed and begun reaching for her she shook that finger—no.

Plucking the packet from his hand, she straddled him, saying, "Now it's my turn to drive *you* wild."

Raphael was astonished at Maggie's transformation.

Temptress. Tactician. *Femme fatale.* All wrapped into one flame-haired package of feminine beauty.

She smiled above him, her feline eyes weighted with desire as she lowered herself just enough to give him luxurious kiss after luxurious kiss. Then, slowly, she began to work her way down.

Her lips grazed his nipples, her tongue darting out for hot, quick licks as she ran her fingers along his chest as if it were clay she was about to mold into a thing of beauty.

"You're beautiful," he whispered.

"You're all I've ever wanted." She lifted herself so that her lips shifted across his own as she spoke.

"Je t'aime."

Maggie's eyes glassed over and a single tear dropped onto his cheek.

"Je t'aime aussi."

He loved her.

At long last he'd found her, and he would never let her go.

Maggie shifted so that she was straddling one of his legs.

She looked like a goddess. Her damp hair tumbled down in waves and curls along her shoulders. Little drips of water were wending their careless way along the curves and dips of her breasts. When he tried to reach out and touch them she tsked at him and wagged a finger—no.

She lifted up the condom and smiled.

It was time.

Mieux vaut tard que jamais.

He might be thirteen years too late for the kiss he should've given her as a teen, but something told him the timing was exactly right for making love to this woman he'd always held in his heart.

Maggie's hands shook as she unwrapped the small packet. When she touched him, he met her hands with his own, helping her guide the protection along the length of his erection.

And then he couldn't wait anymore.

"*Maintenant.*"

"Now?" She smiled, lifting herself up from his leg as she did.

"*Oui. Mais doucement.*"

Taunt me. That was what he was saying. Fast. Slow. She could do what she wanted, but he needed to be inside her. *Now.*

Teasingly at first, hinting at the warm depths that would surround him, she lowered herself in excruciatingly slow increments, occasionally raising herself up again so that the cool night air hit him, until he couldn't bear it anymore.

He placed his hands on her hips and teased her down the length of him until she covered him completely. Together they moaned as she began to rock her hips back and forth, back and forth, until he thought he would go mad. Pressing his fingertips onto her hips, he encouraged her to set herself free. To abandon herself to the desire they felt for each other.

He lifted his hips, pressed them towards her with a drive and desire he'd never known before. Again and again their bodies met and sparked, sending waves of pleasure through him in such heated blasts that he couldn't restrain his longing for her anymore.

"Be with me!" he cried, his eyes connecting with hers more powerfully than they had ever done before.

It was impossible to tell if she'd heard him or not. Maggie glowed with exertion and desire.

He lifted himself up, wrapped an arm around her waist and flipped her over so that he was on top.

Her smile spoke volumes. *Take me,* it said. *I'm all yours.*

He thrust into her with renewed vigor. Hips meeting hips. Maggie's legs wrapping around him and pulling him in closer. Her thighs, breasts, belly—every touch was hypnotic and energizing. When her fingernails dug into his shoulders and scored the length of his back he knew he couldn't hold back any longer.

He met her green eyes and as if by mutual agreement they allowed themselves the luxury of the ultimate mutual release.

The detonation of pleasure was initially so powerful that he couldn't even see.

Pulling her close to him, he rolled to one side, still inside her, feeling their breath intermingling as they each floated back to earth.

"Well, that was nice," Maggie said eventually, her full grin making it obvious she had just made the understatement of the year.

"Comme-ci, comme-ca."

He played along, tipping his hand back and forth between them, letting it come to a rest atop her rapidly beating heart. He placed her free hand on his own chest, proof that his heart was pounding in time with hers.

They both knew there was nothing so-so about what had just happened between them.

They lay together in silence, wrapped in one another's arms. Gathering their breath, their thoughts, enjoying the simple pleasure of gazing into each other's eyes until eventually Maggie asked, "Do you fancy room service?" before dissolving into another fit of giggles.

CHAPTER NINE

"WELCOME TO BROKEN HILL!"

Maggie used her best tour guide voice, hoping the anxiety building in her chest wasn't bleeding through.

The morning had been magical. Of course. How could it not have been when she'd woken up to sweet kisses being dropped onto her lips by Raphael as he held her close to him?

Leaving the motel room had proved tough, so they'd opted for a late check-out and made the most of it.

Eventually—reluctantly—Maggie had answered her brothers' building number of texts and said they'd be there by teatime.

The closer they got to home, the harder the Cinderella syndrome struck.

Cinderella the morning after the ball.

The further away from the roadhouse they drove, the less she believed it had really happened.

No glass slippers anywhere. Just a girl and a guy in a car on the way to her childhood madhouse.

Raphael had gone very quiet over the last few hours of their journey. Rather than ask him what he was thinking, she had let the all too familiar fingers of doubt begin niggling away at her confidence.

Did he regret telling her he loved her?

Was making love to her and meeting her family in a twenty-four-hour period too much, too soon?

Perhaps the whole thing had simply been a release after the accident.

He'd never attended a huge pile-up like that. And it had to have unleashed some pretty dark memories.

He'd told her he *loved* her. That wasn't something that just slipped out.

"It's not as big as I expected," Raphael said as the town came into view.

His tone was hard to read—not a hint of anything other than general surprise in his voice. No disdain. No, *Have mercy upon me—I just had sex with a girl from the Woop Woop.*

Not yet, anyway.

"Well, you're probably going to see a lot of things you didn't expect over the next couple of days."

She offered him an apologetic smile, then returned her gaze to the road, chiding herself as she did.

Just because she'd entered the town's limits it didn't mean she was submitting herself to a life of servitude. All she'd have to do was unearth the kitchen counters from who knew how many weeks of washing up, scrub the floors, air the place...

Raphael would understand if she had to do fifteen loads of laundry before they headed back to Sydney, right?

To buy a bit more time she took "the scenic route", pointing out an enormous red bench someone had built eons earlier near one of the old mine sites.

"What is it for?" Raphael asked.

It was a reasonable question, considering there wasn't really anything else near it. It was just a giant bench in the middle of the desert.

"No idea," she admitted. "Aussies like big things. If you had enough time on your hands you could visit them all. The country is full of them. A ginormous banana, a guitar, a sundial…"

She forced herself to stop, surprised at how long she could have prattled on. As if her country's super-sized objects were part of her. Which, of course, they weren't. But the culture was—the landscape, the air. They were *all* part of who she was. Who she would become.

Would Raphael stay and become a part of that too?

He peered out of the window and made one of those French noises that meant, *Peculiar, but I like it*.

It made her smile. But it made her a little sad, too. This was probably the first and last time he'd ever be here.

"We used to come out here all the time. To see the bench."

Why she'd loved it so much was beyond her. But she had begged her parents and her brothers to help her clamber up onto it countless times. They'd done so gladly, climbing up themselves after they'd hoisted her up, and then they'd all sat and watched the world go by—excepting the time a dust storm had blown in and they'd high-tailed it home so her mother's asthma didn't kick up.

Little had they known her coughing was actually lung cancer.

Raphael refocused his gaze on her, his smile shifting into a concerned frown. "Are you happy to be home?"

Maggie shot Raphael a quick smile she knew looked more nervous than chirpy.

Excited?

Not really.

Nervous?

Completely.

"Sure…" she said finally.

It wasn't much of an answer, but it would have to do. Although hightailing it back to Sydney had a certain appeal. There was so much she still hadn't told Raphael—so many reasons he might begin to regret last night.

She bit down on her lower lip and trapped it tight.

Why was coming home so painful?

It didn't take a surgeon—or indeed a paramedic—to figure that one out.

Coming home reminded her of all the dreams she hadn't realized. And having Raphael next to her was a double reminder. *He'd* gone and done it—he'd fulfilled those teenage dreams of becoming a surgeon.

She glanced at her road trip companion, unsurprised to see him looking bemused as they passed the mismatched series of houses that made up Broken Hill's eclectic aesthetic.

Wood. Cinderblock. Corrugated metal sheets rusted the same color as the iron-red earth they sat upon—and, of course, the centerpieces of the ever-shrinking town's main street: two traditionally built brick and stone hotels. Glorious yesteryear structures that sang of a golden era when precious metals had all but sprung from the earth.

Now the town was doing its best to reinvent itself as a tourist destination, but with water in short supply and not much to do if you weren't into collecting Outback art or looking at solar panels...

The place was about as far a cry from Paris as you could get, short of a village made of igloos.

Sitting at a traffic light, Maggie stared at the grand old structures. When she was little she'd thought they were the most beautiful buildings she'd ever seen. When she'd returned from Paris...well, a lot of things had changed after she'd returned from Paris.

Maggie's knuckles emptied of blood, her grip tightening on the steering wheel as she drove on a few more minutes and eventually pulled the car into the familiar covered carport.

It had been haphazardly tacked onto the family property years ago, when her brothers had flirted with the idea of becoming construction workers before finally settling upon becoming auto mechanics and setting up their own garage. The fact the carport roof was listing indicated they'd chosen wisely.

There were few signs of life in front of the wooden house, but that wasn't unusual. With their house situated only a couple of streets away from the main street, her brothers often shifted from their auto repair business to the hotel a couple of doors down for a few drinks—and, she imagined, since she was no longer there to cook for them, some dinner.

She stared at the entryway to the house, surprised to see that the trim had been repainted from a mysterious orange to a rich blue that matched the sky. In fact the whole house had been repainted.

The façade of the four-bedroom bungalow had been peeling under the desert-strength heat of the Australian sun for as long as she could remember.

So what?

A paint job didn't mean anything. It was just the same thing as if she'd taken herself out for a manicure. Superficial changes—nothing more. Hardly proof her family had changed after all these years. She stared down at her unpainted nails.

"Are you all right?"

"Yeah, sure." Maggie smiled at Raphael, almost surprised to see him there. He looked so out of context here. "Just…adjusting."

She made a fuss over tidying up a couple of serviettes left over from their trip and finishing off her water as Raphael unclipped Monster's harness and put him on a lead.

She squinted against the afternoon sun as the pair of them walked toward the house, with Monster bimbling around, sniffing this and that, as Raphael soaked in the atmosphere.

Would he stay in Australia? Make Monster a permanent part of his life? Make *her* a permanent part of his life?

She pulled her fingers through her hair and teased it into a loose plait. This wasn't the time to be asking herself questions like that.

"Maggie?" Raphael gave her a questioning look. *"C'est ta maison, n'est-ce pas?"*

"Oui, oui." Maggie confirmed on automatic pilot, then checked herself.

This wasn't Paris. Or Sydney. This was the Woop Woop and the only way to fit in was to go back to being the girl who hadn't known the difference between the Louvre and the loo.

"Prepare yourself," she said to Raphael.

"For what?"

The meaty revving of a quad bike drowned out anything she was about to say, followed by some very familiar whoops and hollers. She rolled her eyes. Sounded like another Louis Brothers experiment.

"You'll see."

Very little could have prepared Raphael for the scene unfolding in front of them as they walked through the carport and around to the back of Maggie's childhood home. Instead of the postage-stamp-sized garden he had been expecting there was a huge open sprawl of land that at one point might have been destined for another row of houses.

Two men were on the back of an all-terrain vehicle, pulling something attached to two enormous elastic bands which were, in turn, attached to two unused telephone poles. Just off to the left another man was holding up a video camera, feet propped on an Esky, a broad smile on his face.

Only when the men on the ATV released the "object" did Raphael realize it was another man. As he flew through the air and bounced back and forth against the rubbery pull of the super-sized slingshot the group collectively dissolved into fits of hysterical laughter and self-congratulation.

So this was Maggie's family.

"I told you Aussies like big toys," Maggie said dryly, her eyes rolling as if this was an everyday sight in the Louis backyard. She put a hand to the side of her mouth and called above the roar of laughter, "Get Dad down from there, you lot! Are you trying to get yourselves a Darwin Award? No prizes for proving you are idiots by vaulting father into the strastophere!"

"Daggie!" As one, the two men on the ATV turned around, leapt off the vehicle, ran to Maggie and picked her up and squished her into a big brother sandwich.

Une baguette de Maggie, Raphael thought, a smile hitting his face as Maggie laughed and protested in equal turns. Her protests gathered strength when the other two men joined them and followed suit with a second, more rigorous hug and a proper knuckleduster.

This boisterous homecoming was a far cry from anything he could have expected. A hit of emotion gripped his heart and squeezed. It wasn't envy he was feeling… *Longing.* That was what it was. Longing to be part of a family. The sensation hit him hard.

She was part of a family. He didn't have anyone to offer her. Two years ago he would've had the Couttards…

"Let me down, you oafs!" Maggie finally shouted.

"Where's your girlfriend, Dags?"

"I didn't bring a girlfriend." She looked across at Raphael. "I brought…um… I brought Raphael."

The men—all tall, strongly built alpha males—turned to him with narrowed eyes and flexing hands. Maggie looked like a china doll next to the four of them. A china doll with a killer left hook.

"But…" One of the men shot her a bewildered look. "He's a *bloke*."

"Yeah, glad you figured that one out on your lonesome." Maggie's expression was decidedly…*mixed*. Annoyed. Embarrassed. Hopeful. Anxious.

"But…" One of the other brothers took a step forward. "You didn't say anything about bringing a *bloke*."

"I didn't say anything about bringing a girlfriend either. What does it matter?"

Hmm… Not a straightforward case of "meet my new lover", then.

"Well, it doesn't, Dags." The final brother stepped even closer and said, "Except…"

"Except what?" Maggie snapped back. "Except you've forgotten your manners and how to say, *G'day, nice to meet you, Raphael. Can I offer you a cold drink after your long journey?*"

"We've got plans tonight."

"So? We include him in them. What's the big deal?" Maggie glanced across at Raphael and gave him a *See? I told you they were a pain* look.

"Who are you, anyway?" asked the younger brother, lifting his chin as he gave Raphael a sidelong glare then moved his eyes to his sister. "We thought you were bringing one of your girlie friends from the big city to show her how real Australians get on."

Raphael was certain he saw the man's biceps twitch in anticipation.

"Raphael is…" She drew out the word, obviously struggling to find the best way to describe him.

There were a number of options she could choose from.

Colleague?

Friend with benefits?

Love of her life who couldn't make any promises?

"Raphael. Dr. Raphael Bouchon. He's testing the waters over here in Oz for a bit. We're on an ambo together. He was sort of my host-brother-type-of-thing when I lived in France." She shot him another apologetic smile.

Or that.

Her description stung. But what else was she meant to say?

He hadn't even told her whether he was staying in Australia.

He didn't know himself.

The part of him that knew he loved Maggie wanted to.

The other part—the part that couldn't keep at bay the memories of the day Jean-Luc had told him to leave his family's home, that all he did was take—that part still wasn't at peace with his past.

"Well, then, welcome, Frenchie." One of her brothers kept his gaze solidly on Raphael as he spoke. "So, Dags... what sort of sleeping arrangements are you after for your friend?"

All eyes turned to Raphael.

Though the sun had long passed over the yardarm, it still burnt down on them with a fierceness completely unlike the summer heat in Sydney. Or perhaps it was the family's heated glares that had Raphael pulling himself up to his full height.

With their Wild West demeanor, he would not have been the tiniest bit surprised to see each of the Louis men shift aside their jackets—if they'd been wearing them—to reveal sheriff's badges and holstered pistols in preparation for running him out of town if he so much as suggested he would very much approve of sharing a bed with Maggie.

It looked as if he was back to being a teenager. Looked as if he was back to being judged.

"For heaven's sake, Ed." Maggie punched one brother in the arm. "Could you not call me that anymore?"

The tension lessened as Ed relaxed his pistols-at-dawn pose and looked at the rest of his family and Raphael in disbelief. "What's this I hear? My kid sister doesn't like being the Dagster anymore? What's wrong with being our little Digga-dagga-doo?"

He cooed and gave her a little tickle under the chin, all the while calling her Dags. Whatever that was.

"I know this might sound completely mental to you lot..." Maggie crossed her arms defensively over her chest, a smile twitching at the corner of her lips "...but now that I'm a big girl, I think I might actually like to be called by my *real* name in front of our guest." She ground out the last part of her sentence and flicked her eyes in Raphael's direction.

"Oh, I doooo beg your pahhhdon." Ed put on a faux, hoity-toity English accent and bowed. "Did you bring *royalty* from the big city, Princess Margaret?"

Ed received another punch from his sister without so much as a blink.

Through gritted teeth Maggie turned and grimaced. "Raphael, I have the very obvious *dis*pleasure of introducing you to my feral family. Boys, this is Raphael. He was my best friend when I was in Paris and is a proper badass on the ambo. Not to mention a surgeon who is completely capable of removing all of your internal organs. Come along, then. Line up."

She clapped her hands together and in a well-practiced maneuver they lined up alongside her.

"This is my father, Joseph."

"Any friend of Maggie's is welcome here, mate." Her father reached forward to give Raphael a bone-crushing handshake before giving him a quick wink. "And Daddo or Joe'll do just fine."

"This is Edward," Maggie continued, pretending not to listen to the correction.

"Eddie, Ed or Big Fella work for me."

Raphael braced himself for another über-macho handshake, only to receive an abbreviated military salute instead, followed by a display of dark-stained hands the size of pie pans.

"Sorry, mate. My mitts are covered in grease. Wouldn't want to get your city slicker clothes all mucky straight off the bat, would we?"

Maggie gave an exasperated sigh and quickly introduced her other two brothers—Nate and Billy—both of whom seemed to be quite happy to be called Nate and Billy and to shake hands with Raphael in a straightforward, if slightly suspicious fashion.

"You made good time from—where was it you stayed last night?" asked Billy.

Maggie flushed bright red and muttered something about the roadhouse and the accident scene.

Billy nodded, clocking his sister's pinkening cheeks, then cocked his head to the side and crossed his arms over his gym-toned chest. He looked as if he was deciding whether or not to give Raphael a black eye.

Raphael pressed his heels into the ground. He'd take a shiner for Maggie. It was the least he could do, considering he had no answers to give her about a future together.

"Be honest with me, mate," Billy began, "did Daggie tell you we were a bunch of half-witted losers or did we get better billing?"

Raphael looked to Maggie, hoping for some sort of cue on how to respond to the question. Another eye-roll answered his raised brows.

"What is a Daggie?" he asked instead.

Her brothers fell about laughing so hard they were near enough swiping tears from their eyes.

"Please." Maggie drew in a deep breath and shook her head. "Do not pay attention to the cave people in my life. A 'dag', if you must know, is an Aussie term for a person who is a bit…" Her green eyes flicked up to the sky as she sought the right definition. "Someone who is a bit like we were in high school."

"She's trying to say an A-Grade nerd," Nate jumped in, giving his sister another friendly knuckleduster.

"Aw, mate! So you were a *nerd*?" Billy's friendliness shot up a notch. "Got it. One of the book squad. Makes sense."

Maggie flushed a bit. "No, boys. *I* was a nerd. But Raphael…he was…" For an infinitesimal moment their eyes caught and then her brothers started gabbling away again.

What had she been about to say? The flush on her cheeks suggested she was glad she hadn't said it. The cinch in his heart wished she had.

"Who's this little creature, eh?" Ed knelt down and called Monster to him.

Raphael unclipped the lead, surprised to see Monster run to Ed, tail wagging, virtually jumping up and down with anticipation of getting scratched behind the ears.

"His name's Monster. He's looking for a home."

Ed sent him a sharp look. "What? This little guy's not yours? What'd you do? Kidnap him?"

"He adopted Raphael back in Sydney," Maggie jumped in giving Raphael a curious look.

Monster lay on his back and wiggled his paws in the air, easily wooing Ed into giving his furry belly a good old scrub.

The dog was obviously drawn to him. And Raphael couldn't blame him. By all appearances Ed was a settled, happy, solid guy. A man content with life and his place in it.

The type of man *he* needed to be before he took the

next step in loving Maggie. And he wanted to take that step. But with one foot still firmly cemented in the past he didn't know how.

"It looks like Monster's affections have changed..." Raphael lifted up his hands, as if to add, *He's yours if you want him,* but instantly he felt the loss of his little four-legged companion.

Now it was Maggie's turn to shoot daggers at him.

He swallowed.

What was he *doing*? Giving away Monster was akin to saying *au revoir* to Maggie in the crudest way possible. Bidding her farewell by proxy.

"Hey, Mags..." Nate sidled over to his sister's side and gave her a poke in the ribs. "I don't know if Frenchie is going to like our plans for dinner."

"Why?" Maggie shot an alarmed look between her brothers, then leveled her gaze at her father. "Dad...what have you let these larrikins dream up? Wait a minute!" She held up her hands, her jaw dropping. "You're not actually telling me you've made dinner all by yourselves."

They all laughed uproariously.

Raphael guessed that was a "no" on the homemade supper, then.

Maggie's father smiled mischievously and stroked his stubbled chin. "I think I'd better let your brothers explain about your birthday pressie."

"Birthday?" Raphael sent her a questioning look. "You didn't say it was your birthday."

Ed, or maybe it was Billy, slung a congenial arm across his shoulder. "She's a sly one, our Dags. Doesn't say half of what goes on in that big ol' brain of hers. That's why we thought she deserved a bit of TLC from her big brothers."

"What? TLC in the form of letting me clean your house, do your laundry and make my own cake?" Maggie's hands flew to her hips and an indignant expression that ought to have elicited steam from her ears hit her face. "Yeah. You guys *really* know how to treat a girl."

Nate guffawed. "Laundry's all done, Mags. All you have to do is get yourself scrubbed up for a night on the town. And…" he flicked a thumb at Raphael "…your mate here can tag along if he wants, but I don't know if it'll really float his *bateau*."

Raphael smiled. Not as much of a country bumpkin as he let on, then. He'd have to be careful. He'd have to win her brothers over. Without their approval he didn't stand a chance.

Maggie eyed the lot of them skeptically. The lot of her family, that was. Her eyes failed to connect with Raphael's.

If he'd known it was her birthday…

He would've what? Bought her a diamond ring and asked her to marry him?

"What have you boys planned?" Maggie's eyes crackled with impatience.

Some of that ire had to have been fuelled by him. Surprise parties were usually met with a smile.

"It's a secret," Billy said, tapping the side of his nose and then giving his sister a scan. "Got anything a bit more girlie than what you're wearing right now?"

Maggie's lids lowered as she evil-eyed her brothers, who collectively started kicking at the dirt and looking at the sky as if they weren't hearing a word of the conversation.

"Again, I ask you. *What* have you planned?"

"Perhaps you should head on down to the hotel and get changed. For tonight."

"Hotel? What happened to my room?"

"Aw, yeah…about that."

"Yeah, *that*."

Maggie's heart was thumping so hard in her chest she wouldn't have been surprised if it had started ricocheting around under her blouse. What on earth was going on? This morning Raphael had been the picture of an adoring…what? Boyfriend? Lover? And now that he'd met her family he was giving them his dog and looking as if he'd rather be anywhere but here.

Terrific.

Just as she'd predicted. Who would want to take on a family as mad as hers?

No one. That was who.

And, to make matters worse, she didn't even have her childhood bed to throw herself on and sob away her loss.

"It's been a while since you've lived here, Mags…" Nate scrubbed his hands through his short strawberry-blond hair. "We reckoned you weren't coming back so we sort of made it into a storeroom."

A level of hurt she hadn't expected to feel filled her gut.

"A storeroom?"

"Yeah. You know—extra parts for cars and suchlike. Billy put in some shelves. It looks good." There was a note of apology in his voice, but not enough to say, *Welcome home, sis.*

Maggie knew she didn't have the right to protest. She'd been gone a long time. Years. And had given no indication that she would ever be moving back.

"Don't pull a face like that, Mags. As I said, there's no need to throw your swag blanket under the stars or anything. We got you a room at the hotel."

Ed picked up the "no worries" mantle and gave a carefree shrug. "Ralph can stay here."

"Raphael," she ground out. "It's Raphael." Her eyes widened. "Wait. Why would he stay here?"

"Well, there was only one room left at the hotel." Her brother gave her a no-brainer face. "And that's yours."

"Yeah, well, I—"

I'd rather stay with Raphael?

She shot him a *Help me out, here,* look, not a little worried about his response. Or lack of one. Was he going to stand up for her, as he had with the knickers and the policeman at the crash site? Throw an arm around her shoulder with a she's-with-me attitude emanating from his every pore?

A hit of regret that she hadn't put on her Super Girl knickers that morning jagged through her. This morning she'd felt so *sure*! So certain of herself. Of Raphael.

Before she had a moment to process the expression developing on Raphael's face Billy was elbowing past Ed while pulling something out of his back pocket.

He presented her with a pink envelope with tiny little strawberries laced around the edges. All of the breath left Maggie's lungs in an instant. When she saw her name written in her mother's delicate script tears blurred her vision.

"Here, Mags. We found this when we cleaned out your room."

"What is it?"

He shrugged and stared at it, as if seeing it for the first time. "Well, I dunno, do I? It's addressed to you. We found it behind your headboard." His voice turned a bit gruff as he continued, "Mum must've put it under your pillow, or something, before she—you know. She must've left it for you."

He held the envelope out and shook it in a gesture for her to take it. With trembling fingers she reached out, took the envelope in her hand and pressed it to her heart.

"Right." Billy clapped his hands together and shook the obvious swell of memories from his expression. "Since no one seems particularly keen on changing into their fancy duds, whaddya think about heading into town and getting this show on the road?"

CHAPTER TEN

AFTER AGREEING TO leave Monster at the family home while they headed into town, Raphael and Maggie climbed into the car. As he clicked the door shut Raphael felt the confines of the vehicle make Maggie's mood significantly more pronounced.

Whether it was the unopened letter, his insensitive behavior, her brothers or all three was difficult to divine. The least he could do was start setting the record straight in *his* corner. He did love her. He did want her. But he needed to put some things right in his own house before he could offer her full access to his heart.

The wheels screeched as she turned a corner.

"Thank you for inviting me here. It's wonderful to see where you grew up and meet your family."

"Well, it's not over yet," Maggie grumbled, her eyes flicking to her rearview mirror to see where her brothers were following in a Louis men convoy.

"Your family seem to love you very much," he tried.

"If treating me like a twelve-year-old virgin is the definition of *love* then—" She stopped herself. "Well, yeah, they do love me, but…" Her tone suggested familial love wasn't the problem.

If only she knew what it felt like to have the people you loved most—the people you saw as family—withdraw their affections, she would understand what he was going through. But until he had it completely figured out he didn't want to muddle things more than he already had, so he lumbered ahead, trying to make a light joke of things.

"You don't like surprises?"

The look on her face indicated that he shouldn't be looking to start a career in stand-up comedy anytime soon.

"Not when I've just opened my heart to someone and they go and offer to give their bloody dog away because they don't even know if they're sticking around, I don't," she snapped.

"I shouldn't have done that. With Monster..." he admitted. "And nothing's set in stone."

"So." She clapped a hand against the center component of the steering wheel. "What exactly does this mean? Will you be coming back to Sydney with me or will you be flying back to Paris straight out of Broken Hill?"

"You can *do* that?"

The second the words left his mouth he knew it was the worst thing he could have said. And the one thing he needed to do.

The ominous mood around Maggie grew and multiplied until it all but developed into a force field around her.

"Maggie, please."

"Maggie, please...what?"

Maggie's emotion was barely contained. Her eyes were glassed with obvious frustration as her foot became a bit heavier on the pedal. Not exactly the ideal mood for driving.

"Please pull over the car. Let's talk about this."

"We're here anyway," she snapped, abruptly yanking the car into a space in front of one of the traditional hotels that dominated the main street.

"Maggie—" Raphael reached out to touch her arm and she pulled it away.

"Don't." She turned in her seat to face him. "Don't do

that if all you want to do is to leave. I've missed enough in my life because of you!"

She covered her mouth and gasped, tears immediately cascading down her cheeks.

"I'm sorry," she sobbed. "I shouldn't have said that. It wasn't your fault. That was a horrible thing to say. It wasn't your fault at all."

"*What* wasn't?"

The over-familiar sensation of dread—of guilt—began creeping into his bloodstream.

"Missing my mum. Not seeing her before she died."

A buzzing began in his ears as he struggled to make the connections. Maggie had never told him the whole story. Though she rarely alluded to it, he knew her mother was no longer alive, but he hadn't pressed, well aware that his own ghosts were hard enough to contain without forcing someone else to release theirs.

He pulled a fresh handkerchief from his pocket and handed it to her. It was one of the few lessons he'd learned from his own mother before she'd succumbed to the temptations of drink—*"Il ne faut rien laisser au hazard,"* she would say, pressing a single, freshly ironed square of cloth into his hand each morning.

Leave nothing to chance.

It had been their one moment of true connection each day. The last thing she'd said to him before she'd passed away. And Maggie had missed that own moment with her mother.

Leave nothing to chance.

The words lodged in his heart.

They spoke of action. Risk.

Was opening his heart to more rejection a risk he was prepared to take?

Maggie steadied her breath and began to speak. "We'd

planned... Well... I'd been dreaming of a trip to France ever since I read *Beauty and the Beast* when I was little."

She went on to detail how she and her mother had planned the trip in meticulous detail. How her mother had been secretly scrimping and saving ever since they'd first read the fairy tale and Maggie had become transfixed. A dreamy-eyed country girl going to the most magical place in the world...

"Going to Paris was a dream come true."

"And your mother? What happened while you were away?"

Maggie swiped a few more tears away and sniffed, unable to meet his eyes. "I didn't know it, but she had lung cancer."

Conflicting emotions threatened to split him in two.

Half of him ached to reach out and touch her, hold her in his arms and tell her how sorry he was for her loss. The other half respected the determined look on Maggie's face, her need to tell the story once and never again. He nodded for her to continue. He'd hear her out and then he'd leave. He'd face his own demons head-on, as she was doing here in Broken Hill.

"She was pretty far along when I left, but we all thought it was something else. Something curable. She told us her cough was asthma-related." Anguish filled her voice as she continued, "We didn't *know*! *I* didn't know. My brothers eventually made her tell them the truth, and she started to get treatment while I was away, but she swore them to secrecy."

A sob escaped her throat.

"She told them they weren't to do or say anything that would interrupt my year. I finally figured it out the day I was flying home."

"How?"

"She hadn't come to the phone in over a fortnight.

She'd sent emails and little notes, but her handwriting had changed. Had become weak and scratchy. When she wouldn't come to the phone to wish me a good flight I finally demanded that my brothers tell me. I wasn't getting on that plane until I knew what was going on. They said she'd just been admitted to the local hospice."

Her green eyes shone with streams of tears but her voice sounded dull when she finally spoke.

"I presume I don't need to spell out why she was there."

He shook his head, no, grateful that her mother had been given appropriate palliative care. He was astonished at the strength of a mother's love.

"That plane couldn't move fast enough," Maggie said. "It was the longest journey of my life."

"And when you arrived?" He already knew the answer, but he had to hear it from her.

"She passed away three hours before I got here." Maggie stared at him, strangely dry-eyed, as if something inside her had died all over again. "My brothers and my father had been with her the whole time. I was the only one who wasn't there for the one person who had sacrificed so much for me to reach my dreams."

A sharp series of knocks sounded on the side of the car.

"Dags! Let's get a move on. Time to celebrate, birthday girl!"

Maggie swooshed her sleeve across her eyes and rolled down her window with a huff. "Quit rushing me, you big drongo."

She gave her hair a bit of a princess shake and shooed her brother away with her fingers. A little-sister-in-charge-of-her-big-brother move that would have made him laugh if Raphael hadn't known she was hurting so much inside.

"It's my birthday, I'll come in when I'm ready."

"You all right, Maggie?"

Raphael clocked Eddie's use of his sister's real name. Genuine concern. Family love.

"Yeah. Fine. Just…you know…getting myself prepared to enter the hotel after who knows how long. I'll be there in a minute."

"Raph? Are you not coming in to celebrate Maggie's big three-oh?"

This one was up to Maggie. He wasn't going to prolong the torture if she didn't want him there.

"I don't know." She looked across at him, with nothing but questions and defiance written across her features. "*Are* you coming in?"

This wasn't a win-win situation. It was lose all the way. But leaving was the coward's option and he didn't want to be *that* guy anymore. The one who walked away when the going got tough.

Don't leave anything to chance.

This time he'd see it through.

"Of course, Maggie."

She held out the handkerchief towards him, then pulled it back. "I'll wash it first."

"Keep it." He gave her hand a squeeze, doing his best to ignore the flinch that followed in its wake. "I want you to have it."

"Terrific." She gave the handkerchief a wry smile, and as her brother opened the car door for her she muttered, "Something to remind me of the best and worst birthday I've ever had."

"Why are we going in the back way? Where's Dad? You haven't put him in your slingshot to get him here, have you?"

Maggie knew she was being irritable because things were being yanked out of her control again now that she was back home.

Little sister mode.

Doing what she was told.

Correction.

Doing what was expected of her.

Which was following in her nutty big brothers' wake and then, most likely, cleaning up the inevitable mess.

Despite her determination to stay grouchy, her heart softened as she followed her brothers into the hotel. There were the usual shout-outs to the lads, all of whom played locally for an Aussie Rules footie team. Of course. The "When in the blue blazes are you going to get my car fixed?" questions were followed by a friendly laugh and a promise to buy them a drink if they went to the bar.

And there were a few other comments Maggie didn't quite understand.

"When do you want us to have the bits and pieces in place?"

"Are you sure you got the right music?"

And, the most disconcerting of all, "I've told the wife to bring her camera. This is going to be legendary."

That one she *couldn't* let go.

She skipped-ran to catch up to Nate, aiming for casual but landing on high-pitched panic. "Nate, my dear big brother, if this is some strange thing like being hit by thirty cream pies in front of the whole of Broken Hill, I am *out*."

Raphael caught up with them, but met no one's eye. He had reverted straight back to being the brooding, mysteriously enigmatic man who had met her at the Sydney Botanical Gardens all those weeks ago. The one she wasn't entirely sure she knew anymore.

Well, now she knew a lot more than she'd bargained for.

Yes, he was an incredible doctor. And he had suffered a deep loss. It seemed to have made a permanent mark on him—one that wouldn't allow full access to his heart. Unless he was able to forgive himself…

She tried to swallow the frustration building in her throat.

Why hadn't she been enough?

This was buyer's remorse at its cruelest.

He might have made sweet, intimate love to her. He might have whispered his innermost feelings. But there hadn't been any promises. Only some ridiculously unsubtle back-pedaling the second he'd got an eyeful of the real Maggie Louis.

Just what a girl needed on her thirtieth. Not that she'd forewarned him of that. Becoming an official spinster was traumatizing enough. She'd thought she'd cracked it on the eve of her birthday... Cinderella Syndrome, indeed. Only this time the handsome Prince had figured out that Cinders wasn't really all that and was going to hightail it back to his castle. Sooner rather than later if the expression on his face was anything to go by.

"All right, Mags." Billy turned around when they reached one of the lounges that were usually used for private parties. "Can you just wait here with Raphael for a minute?"

She nodded.

Billy threw a couple of looks between the pair of them, then leaned in and whispered, "He's not the jealous type, right? You're just mates?"

Less than twelve hours ago she knew her smile would have been from ear to ear. She would have told her brother that she was off the market, that her heart was Raphael's and his was hers.

What a difference a road trip could make.

She nodded her head and reluctantly whispered back, "Just mates."

"Good. Hey, mate..." He dug into his pocket, pulled out a couple of notes and handed them to Raphael. "You wouldn't mind going to the bar and getting a round, would you?"

Raphael said of course he wouldn't mind, but refused the money saying this one was on him. He was polite and sophisticated and perfect. He asked them all what they wanted, told Maggie he'd find her something with bubbles in it, then disappeared around the corner.

Would he even bother coming back?

Eddie rejoined them and gave his brother a discreet nod. Not so subtle that she didn't catch it. And, even though she felt her guts launch into Kid Sister Attack Mode, there was a comforting familiarity about it. They all knew their roles. They all played their parts. It was an upside to coming home that she hadn't really considered before. Even if it *did* most likely mean she'd be back in her pinafore and acting the spinster sister and housekeeper until she was an old, shriveled, apple-faced lady. Wrinkled. Hunch-backed, no doubt. Miserable. Alone.

"Cheer up, Dags. It's your party!"

Eddie tried to tickle her and she batted at his hands, reluctantly succumbing to the giggles until he stopped.

"What are you boys cooking up? You haven't got Dad jumping out of a birthday cake or anything, have you?"

Nate shook his head and laughed. "Nah. But I wish we had thought of that." He crossed his arms, swayed back on his heels and gave her a cheeky grin. "I think you're going to like what we've got planned for you. It's one of our best ideas *ever*."

She gave him a wary look. "You mean like slingshotting our father across a vacant lot? Yes. What a terrific idea *that* was. Making us orphans on my birthday."

"Easy, there, little bear cub." Nate gave her shoulder a gentle rub. "Your brothers are looking out for you as you launch into womanhood."

"What, precisely, do you think I have been in these last ten years?"

They laughed. "Mags! Your twenties are just a warm-up for the big stuff. Trust us."

"Not ruddy likely," she grumbled, but they told her to stay put, wait for her drink and they'd come and get her in a few minutes.

She peeked round the corner and saw Raphael, waiting politely for his turn at the bar. Looking completely gorgeous. Of course.

She dug around in her handbag for some lip gloss. Might as well at least remind him of what he was missing.

Her fingers made contact with some paper.

The envelope.

Her heart cinched tight.

Sinking into a nearby chair, she decided to take advantage of the few minutes she had alone and read the note her mother had written to her all those years ago.

The back of her throat grew scratchy at the sight of the handwriting. When she lifted the letter to her nose to smell it hot tears fell in splatters on her skirt.

Forcing herself to take a deep breath and focus, she opened the letter and read.

My darling Maggie-moo,
By the time you get this letter I will have been unable to say goodbye in person. Don't let a single solitary second pass with you thinking I didn't love you with every cell in my body. You are my beautiful green-eyed, red-haired dream come true, and it was my mission in life to help you reach your goals. Or at least give you a nudge in the right direction.

Dry your eyes, love. I know it was a selfish decision not to tell you, but as well as being a dreamer you're also a realist. If you'd known... Well, it was

*time for your brothers to help out around the house
a bit, and for you to go out there and see the world.
A bit of it, at least. The bit that I hoped would in-
spire you the most.*

*Your letters were like a window to Paris. Through
you I was able to go to the Louvre. Have ice-cream
by the Seine. Climb the Eiffel Tower. Especially the
Eiffel Tower! I felt as if I was right there beside you.
The icing on my cake.*

*Your father once even made us crêpes based on
the recipe you sent. They were awful. But he tried.
And that's what I am going to ask you to do.*

*Please try and let those moments—the "icing"
moments—be your lasting memories of our time together. An adventure. And never let anything stand
in the way of following your beautiful heart. Wherever it wants to take you, near or far, your family
will always be with you, no matter how many kilometers lie between you.*

I love you so very much, my little Maggie-moo.

*Always think of me as being with you, in your
heart, for you will always live in mine.*

*Don't let your brothers boss you around too much.
They're protective. They love you, even if they lack
the ability to buy socks. Keeping you near to them is
the only way they know how to keep you safe. But I
know you're strong. You'll do just fine on your own.*

Bisous, *my darling.*
Love, Mum

Maggie's hands dropped to her lap and she looked up
to the ceiling, physically opening herself up to the waves
of emotion hitting her.

Bittersweet relief at having the letter, seeing her mother's writing again, being able to cherish her scent.

This letter was the link—the farewell she'd never had.

Most of all she felt love—unconditional love—for her brothers. Sure, they lacked finesse, but they tried. Their campaign to get her to move home had never abated. Not once…until now.

That thought unleashed sorrow. All the frustration and sadness that had gone with the initial loss. Dreams unfulfilled, ambitions unrealized. Had she lost or gained more in the years following her mother's death?

It was something she'd never know.

She looked up, sensing someone approaching.

"Maggie, are you all right?"

Raphael quickly slid the tray of drinks onto a nearby table, tugged a small pile of serviettes from the tray and sat beside her, his hand halfway to wiping away her tears when she stopped him.

He was an unrealized dream. She needed to take this letter as a sign that it was time to move on. Some dreams came true—some didn't.

Her brothers appeared at the end of the corridor, bursting with excitement.

She grabbed the serviettes and scrubbed them across her face, almost relishing the scratchy pain that accompanied them. It was a marked contrast to Raphael's soft handkerchief and the love she had thought she had felt.

Well, she wouldn't rely on him anymore. Or on his love. It was her birthday, and she was going to ruddy well enjoy herself. She had her brothers here. *Family*—who, despite everything, had been there for her all along.

"C'mon." She spoke in a low voice so her approaching brothers couldn't hear. "They've gone to a lot of effort. We should at least try to look happy."

Against his better judgment, Raphael picked up the tray of drinks and pasted on what he hoped passed as a smile.

When Maggie's brothers led them down the corridor and flung open the double doors of a private lounge any hint of happiness dropped from his lips.

In front of him was a huge banner.

Broken Hill Bachelors Got Talent! Who Will Win Our Maggie's Heart?

Her brothers kept looking at the banner, at the pre-lit stage area, and back to Maggie for signs of delight.

She laughed. Punched them in the arm. Then threw Raphael a look that said, *It could've been you*, grabbed her glass of Aussie fizz from his tray and followed her brothers to the throne-like chair they had set up in front of the stage.

What followed was the most painful hour of Raphael's life.

And not just because of the ample talents of the men of Broken Hill.

The Maggie who had opened herself up to him less than twenty-four hours earlier had all but disappeared.

Whether she was the real one or the one protecting herself from the world's most idiotic Frenchman was tough to tell at this point. He'd lost his perspective.

The one thing he *was* certain of, he decided, between a live chainsaw juggling act and a fairly impressive bit of "condiment art", inspiration courtesy of legendary local artist Pro Hart, was that until he went home and made peace with his own "family" he would never settle. Never be able to offer Maggie everything she so richly deserved.

"Mate!" Nate appeared beside him, tickled pink with the evening's showcase. "Isn't this brilliant? I don't think I've ever seen Maggie have more fun."

Together they looked across at her. She was accepting a vividly decorated rain stick from a suitor who had just performed a rain dance in the hopes of "growing a life together" with Maggie.

She looked completely delighted. If not a little unconvinced.

"We should've asked you, but as Mags said you were just mates we didn't bother. Do you want to go up and do a jig or something? You're looking a little bit as if the green-eyed monster has come to life inside of you." Nate's voice was genuinely concerned and then his eyes widened. "Wait a minute. You're not in *love* with her or anything, are you?"

Raphael just stared at him. Was he that transparent? Luckily Nate wasn't waiting for an answer.

"It's unrequited love, isn't it? Poor bloke. You flew all the way Down Under to get our Mags, only to have her turn you down?"

Again he didn't wait for a response, just blew out a low, *Sorry, pal* whistle and shook his head.

"Rough. She's a bit of a treasure, though. Worth fighting for. You *sure* you don't have a little tune or something you could sing *a capella*? Dad plays the accordion if you need a bit of back-up."

Maggie *was* worth fighting for. But a song wouldn't cover what he needed to do to win her heart.

At the very least, he knew she would be surrounded by people who loved her if he didn't get the answers he was hoping for in Paris.

"I think Maggie looks very happy here."

Nate looked across at his sister. Her green eyes were glistening, her hair lit by the bright stage lights as yet another suitor pulled her up onto the stage only to perform a traditional Maypole jig around her—Maggie as the Maypole.

He did want her.

He didn't yet deserve her.

But he was going to do everything in his power to do just that.

There was only one way to be worthy of the love she so openly gave him.

Go back to Paris and prove he was the man she had once believed him to be.

Though she was doing her best to look entertained by the dance, Maggie's eyes kept darting towards the dark-haired, blue-eyed man who, despite everything, still drew her like a magnet.

Halfway through the courtship dance that felt more like an endurance contest she saw Raphael whisper something to her brother, then get up and leave.

Her mouth went dry as tingles of fear whispered across her skin.

History was repeating itself.

Why did the people she loved most in life refuse to say goodbye to her face to face?

The thought didn't settle properly.

Her mother had done her best. The letter had been there. It had just… Maybe it had been waiting for the perfect time to surface—to serve as a reminder of the girl she had once been. The woman she had hoped to become.

Raphael stopped at the doorway and turned to look back at her. Every cell in her body ached to run after him, to demand an explanation, to ask why her love wasn't enough. Why *she* wasn't enough.

Steadfastly, she held her ground. She had her mother's faith living in her heart again. She had the knowledge that at least one person in her life had believed she was strong enough to make a go of things alone, to pursue her dreams—at least some of them—until she achieved them.

Medical school wasn't out of the question.

Nor was international travel.

It simply wouldn't be with Raphael.

Defiance and strength replaced fear. She didn't need anyone by her side to confront the future. She just needed to believe in herself.

She was thirty, single, and ready to dream again.

She forced a smile back to her lips as Darren O'Toole and his steel-toed work boots continued circling around her in a proud display of peacocking. Pounding. Thumping. Clomping round her like an elephant aspiring to be a ballerina. Okay, perhaps her future wouldn't be linked to Darren O'Toole. But there'd be someone out there.

One day.

She looked toward the back of the room. Her eyes connected with Raphael's like an electric shock. There was fire in his gaze. But it was impossible to tell if the flames burnt for *her*.

When he turned and walked away she knew she had her answer.

She'd be facing the future on her own.

CHAPTER ELEVEN

RAPHAEL HAD STOOD in front of this door so many times and never once hesitated. Not like this.

He blew on his hands, chiding himself for not remembering how cold it would be in Paris. Chiding himself for even caring. There was so much more at stake than chafed skin if he didn't take this chance.

A family.

A future.

A heart that would never break again.

He gave the door a sound knock.

When it opened he was face to face with Jean-Luc.

His friend's eyes widened with disbelief as he took a half-step back…then opened his arms and pulled Raphael into a tight embrace…

An hour later, Raphael's only regret was not having come sooner.

Jean-Luc had apologized for flinging blame in Raphael's direction. He'd been angry with the world. Now he knew, no matter how painful, that his daughter's death had been simply an awful truth he'd had to absorb and live with. Whether Raphael had stayed or left, the end result would very likely have been the same. He saw now that Raphael had been put into an impossible scenario and he no longer felt it necessary to blame anyone.

It had been no one's fault.

Just a cruel turn of events.

"I should have stayed." Raphael shook his head at his own folly. "Stayed with Amalie. Stayed with you. Given you a human punching bag. I just felt so responsible. When your parents said I had to give it time, give you some space—"

"They said that?" Jean-Luc cut in. "Give me some *space*?" He laughed drily. "You took that a bit literally, didn't you? Africa? Australia? You couldn't get much further than that."

"They aren't yet sending commercial passengers to the moon," Raphael riposted, grateful to be engaging once again in the banter that had once fuelled their friendship. "No free clinics to volunteer at in outer space. Yet."

Jean-Luc laughed again. "Well, perhaps they were right. Perhaps we both needed some space, eh, my friend?"

Raphael nodded. He knew now that living as he had been—in the eye of the storm—had been painful and scarring. Now that it had passed he thanked the heavens above for showing him how strong his friendship with Jean-Luc truly was.

"Hang on a minute," Jean-Luc said, slipping the pair of coffee cups off the table and setting them beside the sink. "Would you be able to stay for supper? There is some extra news you should know, but I would like Marianne to be here when I share it."

"*Bien sûr*. I would be delighted."

"Excellent." Jean-Luc crossed to him and gave him a solid hug. "My parents would love to catch up as well. Shall I call them? Make it a proper family meal?"

Emotion caught at Raphael's throat.

A proper family meal.

There was only one person who would be missing—one person who would make the evening perfect.

Twenty-four hours earlier...

"Wait. You *what*?" Maggie stared at her brothers in disbelief.

"We banded together and bought you a ticket to Paris." Billy pressed it into her hand. "Go on. Get out of here."

"I don't understand."

Eddie fuzzed his lips. "C'mon, Dags. Anyone could see that the Broken Hill bachelor brigade didn't hold a single iota of interest for you. You only had eyes for one man in that room, and he was *not* a Broken Hill man."

Maggie laughed at her brother's affronted tone.

"You can't help who you love." Her shoulders hunched up round her ears and she sheepishly scanned them all.

"Love?" Her father gave a pointed look at the wall clock, distractedly scratching a curious Monster behind the ears. "If you don't begin to get a move-on you're going to miss the connecting flight. If I have to get the chief of police to put you in the back of a van to get you there on time, I will."

Tears sprang to her eyes for the millionth time that day. Well, they'd hardly been dry since she'd insisted on going back home with her brothers after Darren O'Toole had finally finished dancing.

She'd made a mistake. She'd let pride stand in the way of her heart and that was the last lesson she was meant to have learnt from her mother's letter.

Her mother had told her to follow her heart. Not her cerebral hemispheres. Or her hurt feelings.

She loved Raphael, and when he'd got up to leave—

Her thoughts froze. Before he'd left he'd spoken to Nate. She fixed her brother with her sternest gaze.

"What was it Raphael said to you before he left?"

Nate scuffed his work boots along the ground. "Aw, it was nothing, Dags. Just go get your plane, wouldja?"

"Nathaniel Louis! Your mother did *not* raise you to obfuscate."

"Margaret Louis," her brother countered solidly, "your mother raised you to follow your dreams, and it might have taken us a while to figure it out, but we're pretty bloody sure they're not here in Broken Hill."

He grabbed her keys from the kitchen counter and put them in her hand, then pointed to the carport.

"Now, go out there and get your man. Or become a surgeon. Or both. Otherwise the lot of us are going to have to gaffer tape you up, put you in the boot and get you on the plane ourselves."

Hands on hips, ready to give back as good as she'd got, she suddenly burst into laughter.

She had the *best* family.

She opened her arms wide and pulled them all into a group hug, in which *she* ended up getting squished. Amidst the sprawl of arms and chests and poorly shaved chins she finally managed to elbow enough room for herself to shout, "I love you lot!"

"We love you too, Margaret," her father said, opening a pathway for her to get to her car. "Now, go make us proud and make some dreams come true. And if they don't go the way you thought they would, we'll be right here waiting for you. Monster included. With enough laundry to keep you busy until you're ready to joust again."

Keep on trying.

That should be her family's motto.

And today she was emblazoning that motto straight onto her heart.

"Puis-je...?"

Maggie didn't even have to look up to recognize the man asking if it was all right to sit on the patch of grass next to her.

Her entire nervous system knew his voice.

Her memory banks were covered in images of the two of them in this exact spot.

It was next to her favorite bench. Which was situated at her favorite angle to tip her head back and…

She watched as his legs bent at the knee, then his waist came into view, and his long fingers, pressing into the grass alongside her.

"How did you know I was here?"

Maggie could barely look up, her heart was thumping so rapidly. When she did, the Raphael she'd seen that night in the motel met her eyes. Blue irises, pure as the uncharacteristically clear spring sky. Lips parted in a half-smile that all but invited her to jump into his arms and kiss him.

He pulled his phone from his pocket and shook it. "Your brothers. I believe you just sent them a picture message of yourself at the Eiffel Tower."

Maggie frowned. She had, but… "How did they know—?" She stopped. "Is *that* what you told Nate. You gave him your phone number?"

"Non." He looked a bit confused himself before crossing his legs and sitting beside her on the ground. "I said if you hadn't heard from me in three days to hold another talent show. And another. Until you found someone who deserved you."

"Why would you have said that?" The note of defensiveness she'd hoped to keep from her voice leapt to the fore.

"Because I wasn't sure I would ever have anything to offer you."

"What? I don't want things. I want *you*!"

The words were out before she stood any chance of preserving her dignity. She stood up and gave the ground beneath her a stomp, reminding herself she hadn't flown halfway round the world to make idle chitchat.

Raphael stood up and met her gaze straight on.

"Good," he said, a glint of anticipation lighting up his eyes.

"Good?" she parroted.

"*Oui.* Good. But I have two questions before I tell you why."

Maggie tilted her chin to the side and gave him her best suspicious look. The one that said, *If you are messing with me I am turning around and flying back to Australia whilst ensuring every single person on that plane, and perhaps the whole of Australia, knows just how much of a jerk I think you are. Even if you're gorgeous. And I love you.*

"I love you," Raphael said.

"I just said that!"

"What? No, you didn't. You haven't said anything."

"I did. I said I loved you." She pointed to herself. "In my *head*. Which means we're connected. And that means you should stop running away from things, and stop jumping onto planes when people shout or yell. Or when you are forced to watch your girl be the guest of honor at incredibly ridiculous talent shows."

"Maggie." Raphael lifted a finger to her lips. "Will you just listen for a minute so I can explain? A bit of clog hopping is not going to keep me from loving you."

She tried her best not to give his finger a kiss. She was still supposed to be angry. Defiant, even. But she couldn't resist. Not when his touch unleashed a wash of glittery fireworks inside her that would have lit up the Eiffel Tower if it hadn't been broad daylight.

She kissed his finger. "See?" She grinned. "Proof I love you."

"And I wanted to get *you* proof."

"What? Why would you have to—?" She stopped herself. "You've been to see Jean-Luc?"

Raphael nodded. "And, if you would care to join me, you and I are invited to dine with them tonight."

Maggie's heart exploded with relief for him. "That's amazing, Raphael. I am so happy for you. *All* of you."

He nodded, his smile truly lighting up his face. "And, even better, his wife is pregnant. They are expecting twins!"

A wash of pure gold heat warmed her body. "That's incredible news. I'm so happy for them. For you."

"And perhaps for us?"

A tiny part of her wanted to play the coquette. To make him suffer just a tiny bit for all the nail-biting her poor fingers had endured during the long flight over. But he'd been through the wringer these past couple of years. And besides, if she'd learned anything at all in the past forty-eight hours it was that life was too short to dither. She'd flown here to get answers.

"What exactly are you saying?"

"I am saying, or rather I am asking, Margaret Louis, if you would accompany me to dinner with the Couttards as my fiancée. And then, perhaps another time, as my wife?"

"Perhaps?" she yelped. "Perhaps! You mean definitely."

Raphael's smile was unfettered. "Is that a yes?"

"You bet it is."

She could barely speak, she was so happy. And then the questions flooded in.

"Where are we going to live? Do you still want to work on the ambos? Do you hate Australia? Love it? How would you feel if I went to medical school?"

"Right now I have no idea. All I know is wherever I am, I want it to be with you." Raphael pulled her close to him and her hands naturally slipped up and around his neck. "Now, my beautiful Maggie, would you allow me the pleasure of kissing my fiancée?"

"I think that is a most excellent idea."

Maggie rose up on tiptoe and, with a fully open heart, accepted the very first kiss from her future husband.

EPILOGUE

"ARE YOU SURE it looks all right?" Maggie squinted at her reflection and shifted the white lab coat collar to the left.

"You look perfect, Dr. Bouchon. What time is the flight going to leave?"

Maggie glanced at her watch. "Probably in an hour." She laughed, her eyes connecting with Raphael's in the mirror. "I still can't get used to this."

"What? The flying doctor part or the Dr. Bouchon part?" Raphael slipped his hands round his wife's waist and dropped a kiss onto her neck.

"Either." Maggie turned and gave her husband a kiss. A hit of emotion clouded her eyes for a moment. "I wish my mum could see this. I wish she could know I've finally become a doctor."

Raphael smiled at his wife's reflection in the mirror. "She does. Because she's living—"

"In my heart," Maggie finished, knowing full well that it was true. "I wonder what she would think of our lives now."

"What? Living in Broken Hill and taking our winter holidays in France?"

"Yeah." Maggie giggled. "Part of me thinks she would tell us we're absolutely bonkers…"

She looked out of the window to where her brothers were building a super-sized swing set for their toddlers.

"The other part thinks she might've known this would happen."

"As long as you are happy, *mon amour*. That's all that matters."

She turned around in her husband's arms and embraced him tightly. "I have everything I have ever dreamed of here and now."

"Très bien." He dropped a kiss onto her cheek and took her hand in his. "Shall we make sure your brothers aren't planning to trebuchet our children over to the next-door neighbors?"

"How well you know them." She gave him a wink and, hand in hand, they headed out to be with the rest of their family.

* * * * *

ROMANCING
THE CHEF

ROBYN AMOS

Chapter 1

Veronica Howard stretched her aching muscles. Her step aerobics class had been especially rigorous today, and she knew she'd pay the price tomorrow.

Ronnie was thirty years old and a former couch potato. So when it came to exercise, her body was in a constant state of rebellion.

"After you've done it for a while, you'll start to love it," her best friend, Cara Gray, a former fitness instructor at the trendy Tower Vista health club, had often told her. But Ronnie had been working out seriously for over a year... and she still hated it.

Ronnie headed from the locker room to the club's juice bar, The Big Squeeze, where she and Cara hung out after their workouts. The state-of-the-art gym in Bethesda, Maryland, was a bit of a drive from her new town house in Washington, D.C., but it was worth it to keep up their tradition. Without Cara's constant pep talks, Ronnie would have quit a dozen different times already.

Even though Cara was now helping her husband, A.J., run their computer consulting business, the women still met at the gym three times a week. But her best friend didn't need the workouts. Cara's years of physical fitness had apparently made her body fat resistant even after three kids. But Ronnie, who worked with food for a living, needed to exert herself to stay fit.

As Ronnie entered the juice-bar area, she saw that Cara was already waiting for her. Cara had placed a shot glass filled with a ruby-red juice at her seat. It looked like blended berries, so Ronnie picked up the glass and filled her mouth. As soon as the thick liquid touched her tongue, she nearly gagged.

"Ugh. What the heck is this?" she sputtered. "It tastes like...beets."

Cara laughed at Ronnie's yuck-face. "And hello to you, too." She nodded to Ronnie's half-empty glass. "It's a special blend of carrots, beetroot and grapefruit juice, so good call on the beets."

Ronnie wiped her tongue on her napkin. "And you thought I would like this *why?*"

"Because it's good for you," Cara said with a mischievous grin. "I figured you were ready to kick things up a notch."

Ronnie shoved the glass across the table. "Well, I guess I'm not, because I'm not drinking any more of this."

"Ron-nie! You're a chef. Your highly trained palate should be able to handle a little beetroot."

"Honey, I may have a newly skinny body, but that doesn't mean I have skinny taste buds." She swiveled her neck, feeling her curly ponytail swinging at her nape. "If there's one thing I've learned in the last few months, it's everything in moderation."

She eyed the offending glass. "And some things in *nada-ration*."

Cara rolled her eyes, having finally learned to ignore Ronnie's affinity for making up words.

Ronnie caught a glimpse of her reflection in the mirrored panels behind the bar. It still shocked her to see that her round frame had been replaced with an hourglass. As a chef, she'd worn her extra weight as a badge of honor—a testimony to the quality of her food. For years she'd told all who would listen, "If I lost weight, people would think my food wasn't any good."

She'd been a member of Tower Vista for as long as her friend had worked there, but it was only recently that she'd gotten serious about working out. The good old days had been all about massages, dips in the hot tub and fruity juice-bar drinks—all the perks of belonging to an upscale gym without the perspiration or sore muscles. But after coping with some harsh realities in recent years, Ronnie had realized it was time for a few drastic changes.

Her dream of opening her own restaurant had finally come to fruition, and she'd lost nearly eighty pounds. But the most significant weight she'd lost was the one-hundred-eighty-pound no-good ex-boyfriend she'd finally cut loose.

Now she was happily single, and the only male she needed was her German shepherd, Baxter. Baxter provided affection, security and above all…loyalty—the one thing she'd never been able to get from a man.

"Fine. You're off the hook for today." Cara took back the red shot and downed it in one gulp. "But I'm not giving up the battle. I'm going to turn you into a health nut sooner rather than later."

It's never going to happen, Ronnie thought, but she kept that fact to herself. When she'd decided to get in shape,

Cara had been beside herself with glee. Even though she no longer trained professionally, she'd taken Ronnie's weight loss on like a job, mapping out a strict regimen of diet and exercise. Now, even though Ronnie was happy with her current figure, Cara was still trying to push her further and further into the realm of fitness fanaticism.

"Yeah, good luck with that. In the meantime, I've got some news."

Her friend's eyes lit up. "What kind of news? Are you ready to start dating again?"

Ronnie rolled her eyes. Sure, three years was a long dry spell without a man, but she still hadn't reacquired her thirst. And the time on her own had done her a lot of good.

"Believe me, this has nothing to do with any man. I've been invited to participate in another Gourmet TV *Food Fight*."

Cara blinked. "That's great, Ronnie, but you do those all the time."

Ronnie smiled. "Yes, but this one is special. It's the first ever *All-Star Food Fight*. They're taking the top winners from the last two years and pitting us against each other in a three-part challenge. The prize is one hundred thousand dollars!"

Cara's eyes widened with surprise. "You're kidding me. That's ten times what you usually win."

"I know, and that's not all. Each round takes place in a fabulous place—Las Vegas, Hawaii and Paris."

Cara clutched a hand to her heart, her almond eyes taking on a dreamy expression. "You lucky girl. I've always wanted to visit Paris."

Ronnie's posture collapsed. "Well, there's no guarantee that I'll make it to Paris. The challenge starts out with five contestants. With eliminations after the first two rounds, only the top three will get to go to Paris."

Her friend, loyal to the end, waved off her concerns. "Oh, don't worry. I know you'll make it to the final three. One, because none of those chefs have the creativity and flair you have. And two, because I'm so going to visit you in Paris for the finale."

Ronnie released a tense breath, and Cara reached across the table to give her hand a reassuring pat. "Crave has been open for almost two years, and it's already received four-stars. You have nothing to worry about."

"Thanks for the vote of confidence, but there's going to be some pretty stiff competition. In fact, against most of these celebrity chefs, I definitely qualify as an underdog."

"Really? Who *are* the other chefs?"

"First, there's the queen bee herself, Etta Foster."

Etta Foster, a cross between Martha Stewart and Sarah Lee, was a household name. She had the most extensive line of cookware and frozen foods of any chef in the business. That was aside from her franchise of cooking shows on Gourmet TV. Yet despite her vast culinary empire, she still evoked the down-home image of a Southern grandma baking in her country kitchen.

Cara shrugged. "Etta Foster is a powerhouse, but she's old-fashioned. Your modern approach will blow her out of the water."

"Okay, but I'll still have to face off with Ann Le Marche and Stewart Compton."

Her friend, who only watched GTV when Ronnie was on it, was unimpressed. "I've never even heard of them."

"Well, I'm certain you've heard of my biggest competition, Ace Brown."

Cara gasped. "Ace Brown? The Sexy Chef himself?

Now you're talking. Finally a chance to prove yourself against your old culinary-school rival. Wiping the floor with him will put the icing on your victory."

Ronnie laughed. She and Ace had always been friends, but there had been an air of unspoken competition between them. They'd gone head-to-head many times in school, but unfortunately he had more points in the win column than she did. Since graduation, his career had grown to overshadow hers entirely.

Ace had been on the fast track, landing himself a show on Gourmet TV called *The Sexy Chef* soon after building his reputation on the Manhattan restaurant scene. His show had focused on romantic meals prepared from ingredients considered to be aphrodisiacs. Despite the show's popularity, when his contract was up, he'd decided to leave television to travel the world.

Ronnie hadn't seen Ace in nearly two years, and she couldn't help but feel a tad excited to show off her recent successes.

Every woman in culinary school had had a crush on Ace, herself included. But since she'd had a boyfriend at the time, Ronnie had been able to pretend she was the lone female on earth immune to his charms. As a result, they'd become good friends.

Ace's face flashed in her mind. Back then he'd had a full head of curly hair, a clean-shaven baby face and a leanly muscled body. When Ronnie had started catching *The Sexy Chef* on GTV, she'd noticed that Ace had become so buff he'd needed to cut the sleeves off his chef's jacket to free his massive guns. He'd also shaved his head and grown a neat mustache and goatee.

Combine his smoking hot physique and his natural charm in front of the camera, and you had the recipe for sexy. His show had been aptly named, and Ronnie suspected that when it had been on the air, his female viewers tuned in more for the tasty sight of Ace than for his romance-inspired haute cuisine.

Ronnie had never really been immune to his charms, but a guy like Ace had his pick of women. So why would he have gone for the pretty but pleasantly plump version of her? There were plenty of men who'd appreciated her voluptuous curves. But judging by the swarm of skinny women that had surrounded Ace, she didn't have any reason to believe he was one of them.

Therefore, it had been easier for her to pretend that she wasn't interested. To sell the lie she'd joked that she was more woman than he could handle.

"Wow—" Cara said, snapping her fingers in front of Ronnie's face "—the mere mention of Ace Brown sends you into a dream state."

"I wasn't daydreaming. It's been a while since I last saw him. I'm hoping he'll be thrown off his game when he gets a load of all this," she said, presenting her body with a flourish worthy of Vanna White.

Cara laughed. "I'm certain he'll be so intimidated by your hot body and restaurant success that he'll lose all ability to function. Then you can whisk the floor with him."

"How can I expect him to be impressed with my one little restaurant opening? He has two bistros in New York, a television show in syndication and a new cookbook coming out. The only way I'm going to earn his respect is by kicking his butt in the *Food Fight*."

Ace Brown stacked his canapés, delicately balancing Serrano ham, roasted tomatoes and shaved Parmesan cheese on thinly sliced crostini. He garnished each layer with a leaf of cilantro and carried the platter out to his guests waiting in the living room of his Manhattan loft.

He'd spent the majority of his career creating dishes for two, but tonight his apartment was filled with six of his closest friends—all of them foodies and one of them his sous chef for the upcoming competition.

"I can't believe you've just returned to the country, and you're already running off again," Devon said as Ace held the tray out to her. A polished hotshot lawyer, she wore her short hair slicked to her scalp, light makeup and a casual pantsuit.

"That's right," her husband, Ace's oldest friend, Spence, said. "We've gone almost six months without a decent meal. Now you're asking us to hold on for another three weeks?" A light-skinned pretty boy, Spence had done his friend a favor when he'd married Devon. Ace did a lot better with women without the added competition.

Ace offered the tray to the remaining couples in the room, his sous chef Marcel and his wife, Simone, and Garett, his publicist, and Garett's date du jour.

"Relax. Tonight I've planned a feast that should tide all of you over until Marcel and I return home from battle."

Garett squirmed in his seat. "I still think we should have accepted the television deal. Gourmet TV offered you a minimum of six episodes to cook your signature dishes in front of a live audience. You're getting too big for these little competition shows." Garett slapped the knee of the girl he'd brought. "Talk some sense into him, sweetheart."

Ace exchanged smirks with Marcel and Spence because he knew they were all thinking the same thing. One, Garett had called his date sweetheart because he probably didn't remember her name. And two, he'd chosen a perfect stranger to reason with Ace over a roomful of friends he'd known for years.

The beautiful Asian woman smiled at him tentatively.

"I'm sorry, Garett—" Ace said, letting her off the hook, "—I'm just not ready to commit to another TV show. I want to promote my upcoming cookbook, and then see what happens after that. I've been driving in the fast lane for so long. It would be nice to take some time to regroup."

"I thought that's what you were doing on your extended vacation," Garett said, raking his fingers through the dark locks that hung just below his ears.

"That was work. In addition to researching my book, you had me doing press everywhere I stopped." Garett always wanted more, and he always wanted it now.

The two men had become friends years ago when they were both starting out their careers. Back then they'd had two things in common—skirt chasing and a driving hunger for success.

Since Ace had returned from his travels, he'd changed considerably. He'd visited some of the most romantic cities in the world, and even though he'd experienced good times, his share of romance and a lifetime of culinary inspiration, he'd never been more lonely. For the first time, he wished he could have shared those things with someone special.

That fact had never been as clear as it was tonight. He'd invited his closest friends over, and it wasn't until they'd walked through his door that he'd realized it—they were all couples…and he was single.

Although Garett didn't count. He *was* part a couple, but with a different woman for each occasion.

After returning to his empty apartment, Ace had to face that he was tired of avoiding long-term relationships. But thanks to the memories of his parents' rocky marriage, he still wasn't sure he could make one work.

"At least we'll be able to watch you two on television," Marcel's wife, Simone, said, helping herself to another hors d'oeuvre. She and Marcel were both French Creole from Louisiana. Marcel had joined Ace's staff when the couple had moved to New York after Hurricane Katrina.

"We're going to record every episode on our DVR," Spence said, "so we can watch you win as many times as we want. Who are the other chefs in the competition?"

Putting down his serving tray, Ace sat on the arm on the sofa and looked toward Garett. "I'm not sure."

"Didn't you read the information packet I sent you? Everything you need to know is there."

Ace got up and pulled the thick packet of Gourmet TV paperwork from his desk drawer. He started flipping pages until he saw the list of names of the other competitors. He read them aloud, pausing for a second when he got to the last name. "Veronica Howard."

"Ronnie Howard? Didn't you two go to culinary school together?" Marcel asked.

Ace nodded. During those four years, they'd had a lot of fun together—despite doing their best to one-up each other. He frowned, realizing it had been almost two years since he'd last seen her.

"The good news is," Spence said, "there isn't anyone on that list that you can't take."

"You think so?" he asked, hiding a cocky grin. "What about Etta Foster? She's an icon. In fact, for this show all of my competitors have multiple wins under their belts. It's not going to be a piece of cake."

While his friends debated the strengths and weaknesses of each competitor, Ace went back into the kitchen to check on his braised beef. As he stirred the hearts-of-palm risotto, his mind wandered back to Ronnie.

He wondered what she'd been up to. They'd been close in school, but hadn't spent much time together in the years since then. His career had taken off quickly, sending them in opposite directions. But now Ronnie's career was starting to pick up momentum, setting them back on converging paths.

It would be really good to see her again, he thought, turning off the heat beneath his copper saucepan. Her sassy wit always made him laugh. Hanging out with Ronnie in a great city like Las Vegas or Paris was a good time just waiting to happen.

She was the only woman he'd gotten close to without being romantically involved. Of course, if he'd had his way, they would have hooked up long ago. But Ronnie wasn't having it. She'd always blown off his flirtations with the taunt that she was too much woman for him.

Even though she was full figured, he'd never taken her words literally. Tall, short, thick or thin—he valued variety in women the way he valued variety in fine wine. And Ronnie had voluptuous curves and a pretty face that had always reeled him in.

But she'd also had a jerky boyfriend back then who'd made his skin crawl. In fact, for as long as he'd known her, she'd been in one relationship or another. Last time they'd spoken, she was dating a food critic whom Ace had always despised.

Taking out seven square serving dishes, he began plating his beef and risotto. For all he knew, Ronnie could be married by now, he thought with a grimace.

But, he thought, carrying the first two plates to the dining table, there was always the chance that she was free. If that was the case, anything could happen.

With that flicker of hope, Ace realized he was looking forward to this competition more than ever.

Chapter 2

After a busy night's service at Crave in trendy Georgetown, Ronnie looked over her staff, who'd gathered to see her off.

"Now, you all know the rules. Even though I won't be here in person for a while, you'd better maintain my standards. My spies are everywhere."

Though she pretended to scold them, Ronnie felt deeply grateful for the predominantly female talent she'd been able to assemble for her first restaurant. It was a man's world, and she'd taken a gamble scouring culinary schools for female chefs.

Fortunately, she'd hit the jackpot. Even though they'd been untried, she'd been able to train the eager staff to her satisfaction. Ronnie had confidence in them, even though this would be the longest she'd ever left them on their own.

"Don't worry about a thing," her restaurant manager,

Callie, assured her. The petite blonde was a business dynamo. "All you have to think about is bringing back that hundred-thousand-dollar check."

"We've got it in the bag," said La Quanique Collin-Silverberg, her top sous chef, who would be at her side throughout the competition.

Despite her unconventional name, La Quanique, or LQ as Ronnie liked to call her, was the only person Ronnie trusted in a high-pressure situation because she was genuinely invested in Ronnie's success. Second-generation African and newly converted to Judaism for her husband, she had skin the color of dark espresso, was Amazon tall and wore her hair in a tightly braided updo that sprouted out of her crown like the spikes of a sea urchin.

Her staff took turns cheering the team on with words of encouragement, until one finally interrupted the love fest for an announcement. "We got you a little something for good luck."

Ronnie felt her skin heating. "You didn't have to do anything special for us," she said, in a rare shy moment as Callie gave her and LQ gold lapel pins embossed with Crave's art deco logo.

Ronnie thanked her staff profusely. "These will come in handy. With the competition we'll be facing, we're going to need all the luck we can get."

LQ shook her head, pushing up her square black frame glasses. "We don't need luck. We have everything we need right here," she said, tapping Ronnie's temple.

Ronnie felt her eyes welling up as she took in the confident smiles of her staff. She just hoped she'd be able to live up to their expectations.

On the day of her flight, Ronnie arrived at the airport early. *Check,* she thought, ticking off an item on her mental list. She'd eased one fear in the barrage that made up her flight anxiety—would she miss her plane? Would her baggage arrive on time? Would the plane land safely?

Even though she hated to fly, it was a necessary evil, and she refused to let it get the best of her. But it was a process, and she was still working through it. After clearing security without getting stripped naked or carried off in handcuffs, Ronnie crossed another worry off her list. Now her stomach was making an audible plea for breakfast.

Heading to a coffee shop, she was immediately assaulted by the smell of her favorite treat, a tall whipped-cream-laden mocha latte. The barista put it in the waiting hand of yet another temptation, a tall chocolate-skinned man in an expensive suit.

He saw her looking and nodded. "You should try one. It's delicious."

In a moment of whimsy, she imagined asking the barista for a dark sexy gentleman with a good job and no emotional baggage.

In the real world, Ronnie smiled and shook her head no. In the past she would have ordered that mocha latte, filled it with extra sugar and then drank it alongside a warm, buttery Danish. Today she told the barista, "I'll just have a small black coffee and the fruit cup."

After she received her breakfast, Ronnie perched herself on a stool at a long counter that faced the airport traffic. Seconds later, the sexy guy in the suit parked himself next to her with his latte and Danish.

"Where's your flight headed?" he asked, flashing a flirtatious smile.

Ronnie had to resist the urge to give her answering smile its full wattage. "Las Vegas," she said in a neutral tone.

"What a coincidence. I'm going to Las Vegas for business, too."

Ronnie wanted to bat her eyelashes and sweet-talk him. Handsome and well dressed was just her type. But sweets weren't the only things restricted from her diet these days.

So she just nodded politely, not encouraging further conversation.

"Since we're both going to be in town, maybe we could—"

Ronnie was already shaking her head. "Sorry. I'm going strictly for business, and there just won't be any time to socialize."

Picking up her coffee and fruit cup, she slid off her stool with her heart hammering in her chest. She felt awful, but she had to believe she was doing the right thing. No sweets because they were bad for her health. No men because they were bad for her heart.

Once in a while, she allowed herself to eat something sinful, but Ronnie didn't know when she could trust herself with a man again. Like food, she loved men, and when left to her own devices, she always picked the ones that were bad for her.

Ronnie stumbled off the plane in Las Vegas, feeling rumpled and irritable. It had been a miserable flight, and now all she wanted to do was get her luggage and go.

She made her way to baggage claim, then watched the carousel circle, trying to stay back from the fray of elbowing passengers hauling their bags away.

After several minutes, she spotted her navy-blue bag. Timing her approach carefully, she made a grab for it. But, at that same time, a large man who'd been talking on his cell phone with his back to the carousel spotted the bag and went for it.

The bag slipped from her fingers as he pulled it out of her grasp.

Temper spiking, Ronnie said, "Watch it, man! That's mine. See, I wrote my name on the label in neon-green ink."

"Oh, sorry, ma'am," he said, immediately setting the bag down in front of her.

Ronnie shot a glaring look upward and froze in place. She was staring at none other than The Sexy Chef himself.

Pressing her fingers to her lips in surprise, she said, "Oh my gosh, I can't believe it. Ace Brown."

He flashed his perfect white teeth. "Well, yes. It's always a pleasure to be recognized by a fan."

The smile died from Ronnie's lips. She searched his face to see if this was some sort of joke. Instead she saw a friendly distance in his eyes.

Ronnie had been looking forward to seeing Ace's reaction to her new, slimmer figure, but she doubted she looked *that* different from her former self.

Instead of being flattered, Ronnie found herself getting ticked off. She'd finally come face-to-face with her old friend Ace Brown, and he didn't have a clue who she was.

Chapter 3

Preoccupied, Ace had given the woman before him only a cursory glance. He'd been trying to reach Garett because he couldn't remember if GTV was sending a car, or if he was supposed to take a cab.

Even in that brief look, he'd noted that the woman was attractive, and he was always happy to meet a fan of his show.

Not having any luck reaching his publicist, he tucked his cell phone into the back pocket of his jeans. Ace looked up in time to see the woman's face go from pleasantly surprised to angry.

His brows knit. Why on earth would a perfect stranger be mad—

Then it hit him. She wasn't a perfect stranger. He might not have recognized her right away, but after *really* looking at her face for a few seconds, he began to see those familiar espresso-colored eyes, her juicy plum lips and her pert little nose.

"Oh my God. Ronnie? Is that you?"

Her features were just about the only things that hadn't changed. Somehow his friend had gone from cuddly cutie to buxom bombshell. Her round face was more narrow and her waist more slim, but, thankfully, she still had those voluptuous curves where it counted.

She'd always been attractive, but facts were facts. Now she was hot. He had to force himself to look away before his ogling became cartoonish.

Her lips twitched, but not into the smile he was hoping for. "Oh, so now you recognize me."

He sighed sheepishly. "I'm sorry. I was distracted. It's been a while since I've seen you, and I wasn't expecting to run into you just now. But, you look fantastic and...I'm rambling, aren't I," he said, when her expression remained impassive.

She simply nodded.

Her rumpled clothing and slightly mussed topknot suggested that she'd had a rough flight. But Ace still couldn't stop staring at her. The new Ronnie was a slice of perfection.

Dressed in hip-hugging caramel slacks, a scooped cherry-red tank and a butter-soft leather blazer the color of roasted peanuts, she looked good enough to top a hot fudge sundae. Her form-fitting clothes showed off her feminine curves.

She cleared her throat, and Ace pulled himself together. "I guess we were on the same flight. I should have realized when I made my connection at Dulles, but I didn't see you on the plane."

Ronnie rolled her eyes. "That's because I was in coach."

He frowned, confused. "Didn't the show fly you—"

"Yes, but it's a long story." She picked up the handle on

her rolling luggage and searched for the exit. "I guess I'll see you at the hotel."

Surprised by her dismal mood, Ace stared after her. Was she so upset just because he hadn't recognized her right away? No, it had to be something else. Even though they'd been out of touch for a while, they'd been too close for something so petty to come between them.

Grabbing his luggage off the carousel, Ace headed toward the exit. To his relief, there was a driver outside holding a sign with his name on it. The man led him to a black sedan waiting at the curb and opened the door for him.

He slid across the seat and found a pleasant surprise. Ronnie was already in the car. "And we meet again."

She nodded without her usual enthusiasm, and Ace knew he had to get to the bottom of this once and for all.

"It's a short drive to the hotel. So you'd better talk fast."

She frowned. "What are you talking about?"

"Your long story. What happened on the plane? I can tell it's put you in a bad mood. And Vegas is a party town. I can't let you show up with the wrong attitude."

With a heavy sigh, Ronnie said, "I've always been a nervous flyer, but I was actually looking forward to this trip. But when I boarded the plane and tried to claim my seat in first class, some guy was already sitting there. We called the flight attendant to sort it out. Apparently the flight was overbooked, and we were both given the same seat assignment."

Ace shook his head. "So why didn't the guy move?"

"Because of the age-old rule that applies in these situations."

"What's that?"

"Finders, keepers." From there she described an uncomfortable ride in coach, wedged between a snoring business-man and a mother cradling a cranky newborn. "It might not have been so bad if the guy next to me hadn't passed gas in his sleep during the entire fight."

Ace reached for the complimentary bottle of champagne in the minibar in front of them. "Sounds like we need to put this trip back on the right track, starting with a glass of bubbly."

He popped the cork, filled two flutes halfway and clinked glasses with her. "Here's to a fantastic journey. And to winning."

Ronnie clinked his glass, flashing her eyes at him mischievously. "It's so kind of you to drink to my victory."

Ace grinned, happy to see the sassy girl he knew returning. "Oh? You think you can beat me?"

"I know I can. I've changed a lot more than my dress size since I saw you last."

Not sure if he should broach the subject, Ace couldn't resist asking, "So what *did* make you decide to…get so fit? You always used to say that if you lost weight people would think your food wasn't any good."

"That's another long story. One we don't have time for now. Suffice it to say it was time. Besides, I've finally gotten to the point where my food speaks for itself."

Ace saluted her with his glass. "I heard you opened a restaurant in Georgetown."

"Crave. You should come by next time you're in D.C. I might even give you a professional discount."

"You don't need to give me a discount," he said, teasing. "I'll just pay for my meal out of the prize money when I win."

She cut her eyes to him. "Honey, I don't know if you're aware…but, there is no prize for second place."

Ace threw his head back and laughed. He'd forgotten just how fiercely competitive they'd been in culinary school. Hearing her talk smack the way she used to was arousing his drive to win, among other things.

Winning hadn't been his strongest motivation when he'd agreed to do the competition. He'd been more interested in trying out the new techniques he'd picked up on his European travels. But after five minutes in Ronnie's presence, he suddenly wanted nothing more than to win just for the bragging rights.

"You're so confident *now*," he taunted, "but you may have gotten in over your head. It's not just me you have to beat. You have the culinary queen, Etta Foster, to compete with. Not to mention Ann Le Marche and Stewart Compton. Are a fledgling restaurant and a couple of *Food Fight* wins enough to back up all your big talk?"

Ronnie drained her champagne glass. "Don't you worry about me, Ace. My biggest advantage is that I'm the underdog. Underestimating me will be your downfall."

Ace knew first hand not to underestimate Veronica Howard. She'd always been tenacious and eager to learn. He had no doubt that she would be good competition. But his reputation spoke for itself.

"I just want to make sure you haven't forgotten just how things went down in culinary school. Soufflés, marinades, knife skill—I got better grades in all those areas. Plus, I've been honing my craft with some of the masters around Europe." He popped the collar on his polo shirt. "You don't want none of this."

"And? I got better grades in pastry and desserts," Ronnie said, waving him off. "Plus, I've got a lot of new tricks up my sleeves. And your chef's jacket doesn't even *have* sleeves."

Caught off guard, Ace laughed. When he'd started doing

his show, *The Sexy Chef,* it had been Garett's idea to take the sleeves off his jacket.

"Europe or no Europe," Ronnie continued. "I've seen what you do, and I'm ready to take you *and* the others on. We'll prove ourselves in the kitchen soon enough. But for now I just want to salvage what's left of this day and enjoy being in Las Vegas."

With their obligatory trash talk out of the way, Ace swiveled in his seat, letting his knee touch hers. *Damn she looked good,* he thought, resisting the urge to say it out loud.

Was she single? No ring on her finger. He hoped she wasn't still dating that jerky food critic.

Unable to ask what he really wanted to know, he asked instead, "Is this your first time in Las Vegas?"

"Yes, I was supposed to come for a bachelorette party once, but I got the flu and had to stay home. The girls told me all about the fun I'd missed. Gambling, Chippendale dancers, staying up all night—"

"So much for What happens in Vegas stays in Vegas."

She sighed. "I know. I'm still mad that I couldn't go."

"Then you'll just have to make up for it this time. I don't know how much you'll be able to squeeze in, but there's the rest of today and part of tomorrow."

"There are three things I want to accomplish before I leave Vegas. First, I want to gamble in the casino—not just slot machines like I've played in Atlantic City—but some real table gambling. Then I want to see a show. I love Cirque du Soleil."

"And the last thing?"

"I just want to perform well enough to make it to round two," she said, showing vulnerability for the first time as she rested her forehead in her palm. "Ugh, I don't want to be the first to go home."

"That doesn't seem like too much to ask for."

Ace smiled, both happy to be with his old friend again and excited by the crackling tension he felt between them. Was it mutual this time?

It could be. Her eyes had taken on a coy slant as she lowered her lashes to hide her normally direct gaze. When she raised them again, he saw her eyes trace his body from where their knees touched slowly up his frame.

Time to make his move. "Ronnie, are you—"

Before he could ask if she was seeing anyone, the car stopped. They had arrived at The Venetian hotel, where the first leg of the *All-Star Food Fight* would take place. The chauffeur pulled open their door just as things were getting interesting.

Bellhops instantly appeared, and the two of them were ushered off to check in. Unfortunately, Ace didn't get the opportunity to finish his question.

On the elevator ride to his room, he made a silent vow.

If they were both as good as they thought they were in the kitchen, they would have up to three weeks together on the road. Ace decided it was finally time for him to take a shot at romancing the chef.

Chapter 4

The bellhop let Ronnie into her luxury concierge suite. As soon as she saw the giant, king-size bed, a huge smile spread across her face.

Thankfully Ace had helped her dispel the gloomy mood that had developed during the flight. Now her arrival at the hotel pushed her back into full elation.

After quickly unpacking her clothes, she walked over to the window to discover she had a fantastic view of the gigantic pool. Instantly, Ronnie craved a swim in the cool water.

Even though she had to run down to the event gallery to make sure the boxes she'd shipped had arrived, there were two motivating factors calling her to the pool. One was the hot Las Vegas sun, and two was the promise she'd made to Cara that she'd work out regularly while she was away.

After confirming that her shipment had arrived safely,

Ronnie changed into her bathing suit and headed out to the pool. But old habits died hard, and she covered her suit with a T-shirt and shorts as well as a long terrycloth robe.

Grabbing some towels, Ronnie set herself up in a lounge chair. The water was calling to her, but on such a hot afternoon, the pool was packed. Even though she'd lost a lot of weight since the last time she'd been swimming in a public pool, she still couldn't bring herself to undress.

"Wow. I'm getting hot just looking at you."

Ronnie looked up and found Ace standing over her. She silently caught her breath. A towel was slung around his neck and his chest was bare, showing every bulging muscle, from his abs to his pecs and biceps. His red swim trunks were wet and clung to his large, muscular thighs. Ronnie had to school her eyes to stay away from his lower body.

But there was no safe place for her eyes to rest when there were big muscles and sleek brown skin everywhere she tried to look.

"Ace. I guess we had the same idea about how to spend the rest of our afternoon."

He laughed. "I don't know about you, but I was actually *swimming* in the pool. Did you forget you're in the desert? Because you're better dressed for the Alaskan tundra."

Feeling embarrassed, Ronnie shook her head. "No, I just got here. I'm planning to get in." A bead of perspiration slid down between her breasts under all her layers of clothing.

"Well, come on. Take off your snow suit and get in with me."

Ronnie's skin became even hotter under Ace's watchful gaze. It was one thing to show off her new figure under a carefully chosen outfit that complimented her shape. If she undressed now, there would be nothing left to the imagination.

"You go ahead. I'll be there in a minute."

He shook his head. "What are you waiting for? Come on in. The water is perfect. I know you're roasting under that robe."

Ronnie realized that if she protested any further she'd sound foolish, so she bit her lip and stood up. Untying her robe, she slipped it off and took her time folding it on her lounge chair.

Ace immediately snickered. "I can't believe you have even more clothes on under that robe."

Swallowing hard, Ronnie took off her shorts first, letting the length of her T-shirt cover her suit. Suddenly, she was overwhelmed with nerves. Even though her mirror showed her a thin person when she looked in it, she still felt like an overweight person on the inside. She'd always made a big show of confidence and bravado when it had come to her body in the past.

But now that Ace was standing there waiting for her to disrobe, all that confidence eluded her. All she could imagine was the disappointment in his face when he saw her in her modest black tank suit.

Trying to come up with some witty distraction to hide her insecurities, Ronnie whipped her T-shirt over her head like a child ripping off a bandage.

But her witty remark died on her lips as her gaze raised to Ace's. Before she could utter a sound, he said, "Very sexy."

Then she was scooped up in his arms and summarily dumped into the swimming pool.

When she came up sputtering water, the tension of the moment had been broken. Ace was suddenly next to her splashing water in her direction.

"You were moving too slow. I didn't have the patience to watch you dip one toe, then the other before you declared the water too cold. So I thought I'd help you along. You're welcome."

"You—" Without thinking, Ronnie jumped on his back and pushed his head under the water.

Ace burst to the surface, laughing. He quickly grabbed her around the waist and held her so she couldn't get at him again.

As her own laughter began to subside, she began to realize that only a thin, wet layer of bathing suit separated her bare skin from his. Feeling her self-consciousness returning, Ronnie began to kick her feet and flail her arms, sending wave after wave of water at Ace until he dumped her back into the water.

She felt safer, hidden under the surface of the water. "I'm free," she said, goading him to chase her.

They played a cat-and-mouse game around the pool, carefully dodging the other occupants. Ronnie was able to evade Ace's grasp for quite some time, until she made the mistake of feinting left when she should have feinted right.

"I've got you now," he shouted, as she found herself locked in his arms.

Before she could stop herself, she said, "And just what are you going to do with me now that you've got me?"

"Whatever I want, of course." His tone was light and playful, but she could see heat rising in his eyes.

Suddenly it was more than Ronnie was prepared to handle. She didn't come to Las Vegas to have an affair. Especially not with the ridiculously hot Sexy Chef.

Immediately Ronnie began squirming in his arms. But that only made the situation worse. Ronnie applied a little pressure against his muscular embrace and quickly realized there was no escape. Ace's arms were like bands of steel holding her against him. And her struggles caused an exciting friction between their bodies. Suddenly the heat in his eyes wasn't the only thing rising.

Clearly a bit startled himself, his grip on her loosened and Ronnie wriggled free. In a full panic now, she dove under the surface and swam to the nearest ladder. She didn't care that she had to now walk halfway around the pool to get back to her things.

Barely taking the time to fully cover herself, she gathered up her clothes and started heading for the hotel entrance.

"Ronnie!" Ace called out from somewhere behind her.

Darting a quick look over her shoulder, she waved in his general direction. "I'm going to go back inside," she called to him. "I'll see you later."

Ace stood on the pool deck, watching Ronnie literally run away from him. Granted, things had progressed faster than he'd intended, but he hadn't expected this kind of reaction from her.

Ronnie had always been sassy and confident. Ace couldn't quite wrap his mind around it, but it seemed that since Ronnie had lost weight, she had become self-conscious.

It was obvious in the way that she'd dressed for the pool in layer after layer of clothing. It had seemed as though she was avoiding disrobing in front of him. From the way she'd been acting, he'd half expected to see gruesome burn scars or massive stretch marks, but her body had been tight and toned. The only thing wrong with her shape had been that matronly tank suit that covered up too much of it.

He'd wanted to stare, openly admiring her new figure, but, on impulse, he'd decided to drop her into the pool. He'd gotten the desired reaction. She'd been too angry to focus on her hang-ups…at least at first.

If only he'd been able to keep his hands off her, she might not have run from him. But that only made him more determined than ever to let her know how he'd been feeling about her.

"There you are. I've been looking all over this place for you," Ace heard Garett say, walking toward him, looking like a fifties throwback in his straw fedora, white cabana shirt and pale plaid pants.

"Get a load of you, Frank Sinatra," Ace said, looking his publicist up and down.

"Hey, if you think I'm not going to make the most of my time in Vegas, you're crazy."

"And here I thought you traveled all this way to give me moral support."

"Why don't you dry off and come inside, Ace. We have work to do. The press junket is tomorrow, and I want to do a little prep."

Ace started across the pool deck to the lounge chair where he'd left his things. "I do press all the time. I really don't think I need to prep."

What he really wanted to do was go after Ronnie. He had a feeling that the more time he gave her, the more she'd be able to convince herself that nothing had happened between them.

"Of course we have to prep," Garett said, coming up behind him. "We need an angle. Something that will make you stand out from the other contestants."

Ace shrugged, drying himself off with his towel. "I'll stand out from the others when I win."

"We can't wait until then. We need to find an angle now. Something that will make them follow you for the entire competition."

Ace pulled his on T-shirt over his head. He should have been used to Garett's push for publicity stunts by now.

Instead, he chose to ignore him most of the time. And it wasn't lost on his friend that Ace was distracted at the moment.

"You're not focused. Does this have anything to do with the girl I saw hurrying away from you just now?"

"She's not just some girl. That's Ronnie." At his friend's blank expression, Ace continued. "You know, Veronica Howard. She's in the competition."

"Are you kidding me? I didn't even recognize her." Garett rubbed his chin. "I don't know how I feel about you mingling with your competitors. Unless, of course, you were trying to get in her head. Psych her out a bit?"

Ace waved him off. "We have a healthy rivalry going, but I'm not trying to get in her head. Ronnie and I are friends."

Garett studied him for a minute, nodding his head. "I get it. Not in her head, just in her pants."

Ace was so taken aback, he didn't deny it. He just gaped at Garett.

He snapped his fingers. "Yeah, that's perfect. We've found our angle."

"What are you talking about?" Ace asked, stepping into his flip-flops.

"I'm talking about the 'showmance,' my friend. The classic reality-TV romance. We let it leak that there may be a little more than competition heating up between you and your competitor, Ms. Veronica Howard. The press will eat it up. They'll be jumping out of trash cans to catch you two sneaking around together."

"Hold on, Garett, that's the last thing I want. You'd better go back to the drawing board, because that angle's not going to work."

Garett slung an arm around Ace's shoulder as they

headed inside the hotel. "So you're denying that you're interested in her?"

"No," Ace said, twisting out from under his friend's arm. "But my interest in her has nothing to do with manufacturing a 'showmance' for the sake of the press."

"Look, if you're going to pursue her anyway, why not kill two birds with one stone? Let your little fling work to our advantage?"

"It's not going to happen, Garett. That's final."

Once Ronnie was safe in her hotel room, she breathed a sigh of relief. Had she and Ace really been flirting with each other?

Never in a million years had she imagined that he could actually see her that way. Of course, circumstances were different now. She'd lost a lot of weight. Now she was finally in the ballpark of being his type.

She didn't know why, but that thought bothered her quite a bit. It was understandable that wearing a smaller size would make her more attractive to a wider pool of men. But she secretly wished she'd been his type *before* she'd lost the weight.

Ronnie hopped into the shower and washed and dried her hair. When she came out of the bathroom, her mind was still whirling with the memory of what had happened at the pool.

What she needed now was a bit of perspective. Picking up her cell phone, she dialed Cara.

"Hello?"

"Greetings from Vegas, baby!"

"Ronnie. You made it." Her friend's voice sounded far away. "If you're calling to check up on Baxter, relax. He's having the time of his life playing with the kids."

"I'm so glad. But I miss my little puppy." At eighty

pounds, her German shepherd was well into adulthood, but Baxter would always be a puppy to Ronnie.

"He misses you, too," Cara said and Ronnie heard an echo in the background.

"Do you have me on speakerphone?"

"Yes, I'm in the car. I'm on my way to pick up the kids from day care. A.J.'s working late today."

"Then I won't keep you. You can call me back later."

"Wait a minute. I know you didn't call just to say hello and good-bye. What's on your mind?"

"I think I'm in trouble," Ronnie said, sinking down on the edge of her bed.

"Oh, no. What kind of trouble?"

"The usual. Man trouble."

"You haven't been in Las Vegas for even twenty-four hours and you already have man trouble…. Good for you!"

"I'm glad you think this is funny."

"It's not funny. It's great. Who's the guy?"

"Ace Brown." Ronnie flopped onto her back, staring up at the ceiling. She felt like a high school girl with a crush. It was embarrassing.

"I should have known. He caught sight of your new hot bod and couldn't resist you."

Ronnie sighed. "Something like that."

"Then what's the problem? You two have been friends for years. He's a good guy. You like him. He's gorgeous. Sounds like a win/win to me."

"Yeah, but he's always been a player. And he never showed any interest in me when I was…pleasantly plump."

"Ahh, I see. I guess I can understand why that would bother you. But, you've got to get over it. Tell me exactly what happened."

"Well, I ran into him at the airport, and he didn't even recognize me. I mean I know I've lost weight, but do I really look that different?"

"No, but you have to give him the benefit of the doubt. It was probably a context thing. You probably caught him off guard. He didn't know how much you've changed. What happened after that?"

Ronnie told her friend about the ride to the hotel and running into Ace at the pool.

"Ooh, steamy. Well, he's clearly into you. You might have actually gotten somewhere with him if you hadn't run away."

"You're not helping me at all here, Cara."

"What? Because I'm not encouraging you to continue your forced celibacy? No one was happier than me when you finally got Andre out of your life. But you can't keep punishing yourself for that mistake."

Sure, if her on-and-off relationship with Andre Roberts had been her only mistake, maybe she could get past it. But every guy she'd dated since high school had treated her poorly. For the longest time she thought that was just how relationships were. And then her best friend found her own soulmate in A. J. Gray, and Ronnie began to realize she deserved more.

"He wasn't the first. I have a pattern of picking guys like Andre. How am I ever supposed to trust my own judgment again?"

"Now that your eyes are wide-open, you'll never let a man take advantage of you like that again. Ronnie, believe me, it's time to get back in the game."

She shook her head at the phone. "No, this isn't the right time. Maybe after the competition is over—"

"There's no time like the present. If you wait until after the competition…well, for one thing, Ace might not be around. And you'll just find another excuse to put this off."

"But I need to stay focused."

"Listen. You're going to win the competition. But that doesn't mean you can't reacquaint yourself with an old friend at the same time. Just go out with him. Have fun. It doesn't have to be a lifetime commitment."

Finally, Ronnie sighed, giving up. "You've got a one-track mind, and that track leads to Ace."

"Why did you call if you didn't want my opinion?"

"Fine. You win. If he asks me out, and that's a big if, I won't say no."

"That's all I can ask for. Okay, I just pulled up to the school. Gotta go. But keep me updated, okay?"

"You've got it. But if this turns out to be a big mistake, I'm not going to miss my chance to say I told you so."

Chapter 5

After Cara's pep talk, Ronnie remembered that she'd wanted this trip to Las Vegas to be fun. She'd promised her best friend that she'd jump back into the dating world, and she knew she'd have to keep that promise eventually, but something was still holding her back.

She wanted to dress up and hit the Strip, but instead she stayed in her hotel room, watching rental movies and ordering from room service. It was a tame, restful evening, and when she woke up the next morning, Ronnie felt like a coward.

She washed her face and stared at her reflection in the mirror. Sometimes it still shocked her to see that her face was no longer perfectly round. It had narrowed, revealing high cheekbones and a defined chin. The transformation moved her on the beauty spectrum, further away from cute and closer to beautiful.

Before, she would embrace her heavier stature and had defied anyone to tell her she wasn't amazing in every way.

Strangely enough, now that she was thin, she'd lost her wall of defense. She constantly felt vulnerable and exposed. She missed sassy, confident Ronnie. But today was a new day. It was time to own the changes she'd made in her life and to stop hiding.

And she couldn't ask for better timing. Today she had a press junket that would take most of the day. What better chance to show the world that she knew what she wanted and planned to take it.

LQ would be arriving in the evening to help her plot out a strategy for whatever GTV would spring on them tomorrow. Maybe she'd be able to convince her sous chef to hit the town with her. She had big plans for her last free night in Vegas.

But before that, she was going to be trapped in a room with reporters. There was also a photo shoot, during which they'd take promotion shots of each chef in their jackets. That meant Ronnie had to take special care with her appearance that morning. Her chef's jacket was tinged pink because Ronnie thought typical white chefs' coats were boring, and she was anything but.

Setting her hair in hot rollers, she took a steamy hot shower, then carefully applied her makeup. A little raspberry lipstick for her full lips and just a hint of sparkling charcoal-gray at her eyes to make them pop. Finally she smoothed her dark curls into gentle waves that framed her face. It was a bit more glamour than she usually wore in the kitchen, but she had to look her best for the photos.

The extra effort wasn't for Ace, she told herself. But if he happened to notice, it couldn't hurt. Unfortunately, as she slipped on her chef's jacket and hustled toward the elevator, Ronnie realized that all that extra attention to her appearance had made her slightly late.

She showed up at the hotel ballroom at the tail end of

the buffet breakfast that GTV had provided. Of course, Ace was the first person she saw as she entered the room.

"There you are. I was starting to wonder if you were going to make it," he said, refilling his coffee cup.

It didn't help matters that he looked delicious. His sleeveless chef's jacket might have been a bit self-indulgent, but as Ronnie took in those giant biceps, she couldn't help wondering what sleeves *could* contain them.

"Better late than never," Ronnie said, filling a small bowl with fruit and pouring herself a cup of black coffee. The cheese Danish was whispering, *Ronnie, Ronnie*, in her ear, but she made it through another breakfast without giving in.

Nodding good-bye to Ace, Ronnie took her food and crossed the room to take a seat. She couldn't risk standing there making awkward conversation. It wouldn't have been long before he'd brought up yesterday's embarrassingly hasty exit. Yes, she had literally run away from him, she thought with a private wince.

Taking a long sip of her coffee, she sat down next to Stewart Compton. Rail thin, with shoulder-length blond hair and a long hooked nose, Stewart was the most flamboyant of the bunch.

Even though they'd never competed against each other, Ronnie had seen him backstage at several studio tapings. He always made bold choices with his food, so it would be interesting to see what he came up with tomorrow.

He looked her up and down before a wide smile broke out on his face. "Check you out, Ms. Thang. You look fabulous."

"Thank you, darling. You're not so bad yourself," she said, admiring his crisp white chef's jacket with navy-and-gold piping on the collar and sleeves. His restaurant logo looked like a family crest with the words Compton Arms stitched below it.

He leaned close to whisper in her ear. "You don't know how glad I am to see your friendly face, sweetie. Everyone in here has their game face on. Especially her," Stewart said, glaring in Ann Le Marche's direction.

In the kitchen, Ann was all business, so it wasn't surprising that she had no appreciation for Stewart's fun-loving, gossipy nature. Whereas Stewart's food was whimsical and bright, hers was sparse and symmetrical.

Ronnie picked up a handful of berries. "I know, I could feel the tension the second I walked in here. I guess the promise of such a huge check has everyone on edge."

"Honey, if Ann was any edgier, she wouldn't need a stone to sharpen her knives."

Ronnie laughed, realizing that Stewart was referring to Ann's style as well as her demeanor. She wore heavy black-rimmed glasses and blood-red lipstick, and her spiky hair was bleached to a shocking platinum blond. Her elaborate tattoos peeked out along the neck and wrists of her black Nehru jacket.

"Ann's tough competition," Ronnie whispered back to Stewart. "But I'm most worried about *her*," she said, nodding toward Etta Foster, who was quietly nibbling the corners of a homemade muffin while crocheting an afghan.

"Ahh, the grand dame herself." Stewart nodded. "She's a veritable culinary mogul. We should be honored just to breathe the same air she does."

Etta had always reminded Ronnie of Betty White with her blonde/white hair curling around her ears and the broad, wholesome smile that puffed out her cheeks. She wore the whitest chef's jacket of everyone, fitted perfectly at the waist with matching pants. Even her logo stitched on the breast of her jacket was white.

Just then, the director came in to give them an overview of how the following weeks would go, and Ronnie had just enough time to gobble down a handful of berries and drain her coffee cup.

After the orientation, all of the chefs were led into a connecting room with tables set up around the perimeter. Ronnie tried not to feel self-conscious as she took in the displays of promotional items filling the tables of the other chefs. Most of them, like Ace, had a line of cookbooks to show off. And Etta Foster's table was so full her tiny face could barely be seen among the stacks of cookbooks, cookware and other merchandise.

Ronnie took a seat at her table. She didn't have a publicist, so she'd had to produce her own promotional item. It was a cardboard foldout of her standing in front of Crave on the right, and her restaurant menu on the left.

It didn't take up as much space as a tower of cookbooks, but she was proud of the glossy piece that showed off her dream-come-true. As she looked out over the room, Ronnie was smacked with the reality of just how big this competition was going to be.

Normally these press gatherings were small, with just a few reporters from the local area looking for human interest pieces. This time, though, the press had more than tripled in number, and they represented all the major news outlets and food publications across the country.

As the press began circulating, Ronnie warmed to it quickly. Sometimes it could get tedious answering the same questions over and over, but Ronnie didn't mind this time. She had fun joking with the reporters and finding new ways to respond to similar questions.

"You've got some heavy-hitting competition in this

All-Star Food Fight. Does that intimidate you at all?" a journalist from *Food and Wine* magazine asked.

"You said it yourself, it's *all*-star. That makes me a star, too, and I plan to blind them with my shine."

Bon Appétit magazine asked, "Would you consider yourself an underdog going into the first round tomorrow?"

"I'm undefeated, just like the other chefs in this competition. All being an underdog means is that no one will be disappointed if I lose. I think that's a great starting position."

Ronnie was having such a good time, she was caught completely off guard when a food critic from her past sat down in front of her.

"Veronica Howard. If I didn't have your name written right in front of me, I wouldn't have believed it was you."

Her temper spiked, bringing a full flush of angry heat to her cheeks. "Andre Roberts. If I hadn't gotten you fired for that libelous review you wrote about me, I wouldn't be so shocked to see you here."

He was her ex-boyfriend, and Ronnie couldn't believe how quickly her day had turned from sweet cream to sour milk.

"Oh, no hard feelings about that, Ronnie. I know we're both adult enough to put all that unpleasantness behind us. Obviously, we've both landed on our feet. Leaving the newspaper turned out to be a good move for me."

Ronnie's eye twitched at his gall. He always found a way to sell his crap as fertilizer.

"Now I've got this sweet gig at *Food Trends* magazine," he continued. "The only downside is that I have to cover cheesy contests like this. But the travel makes it worth it."

Ronnie stared, unblinking, wondering what she'd ever

seen in this jerk. Sure, he was pretty-boy handsome with light skin and gold eyes. He'd chemically processed his hair so it waved against his scalp, and he wore two obnoxious diamond earrings that flaunted money he didn't have.

His looks, like his personality, no longer appealed to her. He was supposed to be interviewing her, but of course all he'd done was talk about himself. And now she could see how he'd used backhanded compliments to keep her down. When they'd dated, he'd had her convinced no other man could want her.

What a fool she'd been.

"I'm sure *Food Trends* isn't paying you to talk about yourself, Andre. So let me help you earn that sweet paycheck. Those gaudy diamonds can't pay for themselves, after all." Before he could respond, she continued. "Yes, I'm an underdog, but I think that works in my favor. No, I'm not intimidated by my competitors. I, too, am undefeated, and I still have a few tricks no one has seen."

As Ronnie talked, Andre grinned at her, making no move to turn on his tape recorder or jot a note down on his pad. "Come on, do you really think you have a shot at winning this thing? I mean, Etta Foster is a legend all by herself."

Ronnie swallowed hard, urging her inner self to remain calm. "Of course I think I have a shot, that's the only reason I'm here—to win. I wouldn't have been invited to compete if I wasn't one of the best."

Andre's brows rose. Clearly he was surprised by the change in her attitude. At that point, he went ahead and asked her a couple of real questions for his magazine.

Relieved that it was almost over, Ronnie answered confidently, pleased to be able to brag a little about her recent success.

"And how does your weight loss factor into your new-found success? Do you think you're a better chef now that you're thin?"

Ronnie felt like she'd been kicked in the gut. She opened her lips to speak, but no words came out. If she could have found anything heavy enough within reach, she would have clobbered him over the head. Instead, all she did was seethe in silence, shooting flames from her eyes.

Laughing, Andre held up a hand. "You don't have to answer that last one."

Hearing his laughter, Ronnie realized she'd given him exactly what he'd wanted. He'd thrown her off her game and made her lose her confidence. That had been his goal all along.

"I've got to move on, but maybe we can catch up later. I'll be in town until tomorrow evening."

Before Ronnie could protest, he walked away, leaving her angry and flustered as the next reporter sat down in his place.

That evening, Ronnie stood in front of her closet. She didn't want to think about seeing her ex-boyfriend or the press conference she'd stumbled through afterward. Tonight she just wanted to get a taste of Vegas and have fun.

She'd promised Cara that she'd give Ace a chance, but she hadn't seen much of him that day. And since he'd always been smooth with the ladies, there was a chance he'd already found company for the evening. But that didn't mean she had to spend another night in her room.

Instead, she pulled out a vibrant green party dress she hadn't yet dared to wear. It was simple in design with spaghetti straps and an A-line silhouette. It fell smoothly over her curves, and the hemline was a lot shorter than anything she normally wore. Yet, it was modest compared to some of the outfits she'd seen the girls in this town wearing.

After slipping into her dress, Ronnie turned her attention to her hair. Outside of work, she loved to be more daring with her styles. She'd become slightly more conservative in the last few years, opting out of the big showy hairdos she'd sported in the past. But she still thought hair was the best way to express her mood.

For tonight, she flat-ironed it straight and sleek, then pulled it back from her face. She added a little extra hair for a long ponytail that would hang to the middle of her back. Ronnie usually went with her own naturally long hair, but this was a special occasion. And sometimes a girl deserved a little extra body.

As soon as Ronnie stepped outside her room, it hit her that she'd be on her own for the night. It seemed a tad sad to be all alone in a party town. Resisting the urge to go back and hide in her room, she headed down to the casino. Despite feeling nervous, she registered for a seat at one of the poker tables. After playing Texas Hold 'Em a few times with her busboys after hours, she felt she might have a chance at holding her own. But several losing rounds quickly sent her back to the familiarity of the slot machines.

Ace found her there twenty minutes later, playing down the last of the twenty-dollar bill she'd fed the machine.

"Hey, big spender," he joked when he saw her playing a nickel machine.

Feeling her heart start to race, Ronnie spun around on her stool. "Hey, Ace."

He grinned at her. "Look at you. You look fantastic."

"Thank you," she said, trying to play off her blush. "I can't help it. It comes naturally."

He nodded in agreement, and Ronnie basked in the pleasure of the genuine attraction in his eyes.

"What are you doing tonight?"

Ronnie's heartbeat thundered. Here it is. He was going to ask her out.

"Nothing much. I was just sitting here killing time—"

Ace opened his mouth to speak, but couldn't utter a sound before a slick gentleman in an expensive suit clapped him on the back. "Ready for dinner, buddy?"

"Yeah, in a minute. Ronnie, this is my publicist, Garett Fontaine. Garett, this is my old friend from culinary school, Veronica Howard."

They shook hands and exchanged greetings, then Ace said, "We're going to have dinner at the hotel's steakhouse. If you don't have plans, why don't you join us?"

As her mouth began to water, Ronnie felt a moment of panic. Steak. She'd like nothing better than to indulge in a thick, juicy prime rib. It was her favorite cut of beef. But she'd already eaten a bland little salad in her room. The salad hadn't done much to fill her stomach, so there was plenty of room left for steak. But if she wanted to keep wearing dresses like the one she had on, she couldn't eat whatever she wanted anymore.

But she didn't want to tell these two handsome men that she couldn't join them because she didn't want to get fat again.

"No, thanks. I'm meeting friends in the V Bar in a few minutes."

Ace frowned. "I didn't know you had friends in town."

"Oh, they're just some people I met earlier. They asked me to hang out with them tonight."

Ace shook his head. "You don't want to spend the evening with strangers. Let two friendly gentlemen treat you to a great meal."

Garett nodded eagerly. "You should definitely join us. It'll give the two of you a chance to catch up. Once the competition starts you become the enemy," he joked.

"That settles it, then, right?"

Ronnie almost gave in. She did promise Cara that she'd go out with Ace if he asked. And lo and behold, he was asking.

Then she pictured herself at the table eating a carrot with a knife and fork while they cut into tender hunks of meat. No, if she went to dinner, she'd get a steak. That meant only one thing.

"Thanks for the invitation. But it really is time for me to get going. Besides, two handsome bachelors like yourselves will have a much better time this evening without me tagging along."

Ronnie cashed out the $2.45 left in the machine, stuffed the claim ticket in her purse and stood. "Maybe I'll run into you guys later."

Ace stared after Ronnie, not believing for a minute that she really had plans for the evening. She was definitely running scared, and he didn't know how he was going to get past her brick walls.

"Sorry, man, I tried to help your cause. Better luck next time." Garett took his arm, dragging him forward. "Let's eat. I'm in the mood for a porterhouse."

Ace walked beside him, ignoring Garett's chatter about the female "talent" he'd spotted during the day. He was still trying to figure out a way through Ronnie's defenses. He'd wanted to make his move tonight. Garett had been right about one thing, though. Once the competition started, she became the opposition.

And as much as he liked her, he still planned to win.

After dinner, Garett wanted to hit the casino, but Ace was tempted to stop by Ronnie's room instead. If her plans were as phony as he suspected, he'd find her there.

"Come on, Ace. You can't leave me hanging like this," Garett said as they left the restaurant.

"You seem to be forgetting that we're here for work, not to party. I have to compete tomorrow, as you keep reminding me."

"Fine, let's compromise. Let me buy you a drink at V Bar. That'll give me some time to find a new companion for the evening. And you won't have to feel guilty about abandoning your best friend."

"You're right. How would I ever have gotten to sleep tonight," Ace said, sarcastically.

They entered the bar and Garett punched him in the arm. "Don't worry about it, buddy. That's why I'm here. To save you from yourself." Then he broke his stride, pausing to stare at a table in the back of the room.

Ace didn't even turn his head. No matter what his friend said, when Garett was on the prowl, he didn't need any help from Ace.

"Hey, isn't that your friend Veronica?"

"What?" Ace swiveled his neck so fast he could have given himself whiplash.

Sure enough, Ronnie was sitting at a table with a rowdy group of girls. One was wearing a short white veil and bending over the table, arms behind her back, to upend a shot using only her mouth. Ronnie and the others were cheering her on.

Surprised, Ace stared in her direction. She must have felt the heat of his gaze because she looked up and caught his eye. Smiling wide, she waved and reluctantly Ace waved back.

He'd been wrong. It seemed she *did* have plans all along.

Feeling a little less sure of himself, he followed Garett to the bar. "I guess I will join you in the casino tonight, Garett. This is Las Vegas, after all."

Ronnie smiled to herself as she watched Ace walk to the bar. He had the perfect butt. Firm, tight, and it filled out his pants beautifully.

Then she blinked in the direction of her thoughts. Sitting up straight, she realized she'd had too many champagne cocktails. She'd had only two, but Ronnie didn't drink much anymore. History had proven that drinking made her... amorous.

One of the girls let out a whoop, bringing Ronnie's attention back to the table. "Okay, we can cross 'get a stranger to buy you a drink' off the list," a tiny blonde said. "We have to leave the bar now and get Jen a body piercing."

Two hours ago, Ronnie had walked into the bar alone, petrified of appearing lonely and desperate. She'd found a table in the back and stared at the drink menu. When she'd been on the verge of creeping back to her room, the bachelorette party had clamored in and swept her up in their celebration.

The girls had a long list of tasks for the bride to complete, and they wanted to borrow Ronnie's lipstick so the bride could kiss the top of a bald man's head. After finding out that Ronnie was on her own for the evening, they'd insisted she join them.

"Wait a minute," one of the girls shouted. "We can't leave until we have another round. Screaming Orgasms for everyone."

* * *

Sometime after midnight, the bachelorette party broke up, and Ronnie found herself teetering toward the hotel elevators with her shoes in her hands.

Still off kilter, Ronnie careened into the side of a man who was already waiting for the elevator.

"Whoa, are you okay, Ronnie?" he said, steadying her on her feet.

"Ace, all I have to do is think about you and you appear." Right now he looked like a giant hot fudge sundae to her and Ronnie knew she was grinning widely at him.

"Sounds like you had a lot of fun with your new friends. You didn't mention that you couldn't join us for dinner because you were attending a bachelorette party."

"Oh, I lied about having plans," Ronnie said, a bit more loose lipped than she had expected. "I met those girls after I got to the bar."

The doors to the elevator opened and Ronnie carefully made her way inside. Ace followed her, laughing under his breath. "I knew it."

Ronnie moved closer to him. "What about you? Did you have fun tonight?"

"It wasn't bad. Obviously I didn't have as much fun as you did. What kind of trouble did you girls get into?"

"Trouble? No trouble." Then a slow grin broke out on her face. "Well, maybe a little."

"That's what I thought."

The elevator chimed and the doors opened on Ronnie's floor. "Aww, our ride is over already."

Ace took her arm and helped her through the doors.

"Ooh, are you on this floor, too?"

"No, but I think I'd better make sure you make it back to your room safely."

She nudged him with her elbow. "What a gentleman," she

said as they stopped in front of her door. "But if you're not too much of a gentleman, you can come in for a while."

He stared at her for a long moment, and Ronnie knew he wanted to say yes.

"That's the best offer I've had all night, but I think we should save that for a time when you're a little less tipsy."

"Then how about a kiss good-night?" Ronnie dropped her purse and shoes on the carpet and pressed herself against him, throwing her arms around his neck.

Their mouths came together in a steamy lip-lock. Ronnie felt like her whole body was floating as she felt the roughness of his light stubble brush against her face.

After a moment, Ace pulled away, setting her back on her feet. Immediately, her foot connected with something round, which rolled under her toes and then started vibrating. "What the—"

With a burst of laughter, Ace reached down. "Looks like you dropped something," he said, handing her the mini-vibrator she'd gotten as a party favor from the bachelorette blowout.

Ronnie giggled, the alcohol in her system taking away her embarrassment. "Oops! I forgot about that."

Ace raised his eyebrows in mock surprise. "I see…."

She dropped it back in her clutch and snapped it shut. "No, you don't, silly. That isn't mine."

"Really? Because it seems to have fallen out of your purse."

"I mean, I didn't buy it. It was a gift. From the party."

"I see." He laughed.

"But, hey, it's just plastic. I prefer the real thing," she said, looking him up and down.

Ace laughed. "Oh, Ronnie, if I thought for a minute you'd feel the same way tomorrow, I'd make good on that suggestion. As it is, I have a feeling you're going to need all the sleep you can get."

He took her purse and found her key card inside. After unlocking her door, he saw her safely inside and then disappeared back into the corridor.

As Ronnie fell back on her bed, her head was spinning. She wasn't sure if it was from the drink or Ace's lips. His face was the last image that floated in her mind as she fell asleep.

Chapter 6

Ronnie woke the next morning with her brain slam-dancing inside her skull. Moaning, she fought to turn off the alarm. Without it, Ronnie wasn't sure she would have awakened before nightfall.

Her eyelids were swollen and the crack of sunlight that made it through the curtains hurt her skewed vision. Clutching her head, she realized this was exactly why she didn't drink.

Swinging her legs off the bed, Ronnie suddenly became aware of a stinging pain coming from her middle. Sending a hand to her abdomen, her fingers ran over something chunky.

Startled, she raced to the bathroom and hiked up the old T-shirt she'd slept in. A simple gold stud was jutting through her navel.

"Oh, no," she moaned, sinking down on the toilet seat before her legs gave out. She hadn't thought she'd had *that* much to drink. But, she now remembered that the bride hadn't wanted to get a piercing unless everyone in the party joined in. Ronnie had tentatively considered a third earring, so how had she ended up with a navel piercing?

Head in her hands, Ronnie considered what the day had in store for her.

Could her brain function properly with this hangover pounding in her head and making her slightly nauseous? She wasn't sure, but she had to at least look like a winner. It didn't matter that she felt terrible—she'd rather die than go on television looking this way.

After a hot shower, ibuprofen and a lot of careful grooming—she slicked her hair back into a ponytail, then braided four sections, which she wove into an elaborate bun at the back of her head—Ronnie showed up at the holding room just in time. She only felt slightly better, but she looked absolutely terrific.

All the chefs and their sous chefs were gathered there before they'd be released to their kitchens to start the competition. As she entered, she found everyone milling around, talking.

"Good morning, Ronnie. How are you feeling?" Ace asked.

As soon as Ronnie saw him, her cheeks started to burn. She'd been so preoccupied that morning, she hadn't taken the time to dwell on her biggest humiliation of the night.

Memories of her tipsy elevator ride, confessing that she was a liar and then throwing herself at Ace all came rushing back.

"Good morning," Ronnie said, hoping that if she pretended not to remember, he might be enough of a gentleman to let the moment pass. "I'm feeling okay," she exaggerated.

He winked at her, leaning down so only she could

hear him. "Got any more goodies tucked away for me to find?"

"Not today," she said through her teeth, as she waved her greetings to the other contestants.

Stewart clapped his hands together. "I hope you came ready to work, people. Because it's going to be tough to beat my authentic French cuisine. I hear Jean Paul Pelletier is one of the judges."

Ann crossed her arms and rolled her eyes. "Oh get off it, Stewart. First of all, I'm more French than you'll ever be. And second, if Jean Paul Pelletier wanted to be fed nothing but French cuisine, he wouldn't have opened a steakhouse in Las Vegas."

Ace laughed out loud. "Besides, this round is about showing off our signature dishes. The judges will be looking to see us do what *we* do best."

Ronnie found herself giggling. "Does that mean you'll be filling the judges up with natural aphrodisiacs, Ace?"

"I don't think it would be a bad idea. They'll be in a really good mood by the time they reach a verdict."

Stewart clapped his hands again, loving to talk trash. "You'll see. I'm classically trained—"

Ann, who was self-taught, shot Stewart a dirty look, freezing the words coming out of his mouth.

"That's enough of all that, now," Etta said, getting up from her seat in the back of the room. "We have to remember that this is still a friendly competition. None of us would be here if we weren't all talented chefs. So let's quiet down now and focus on what's ahead of us."

Etta's voice was as soft and sweet as honey. The room instantly fell silent. Ronnie felt like they'd all just been chastised by their grandmother, so she ducked to the other side of the room to join LQ.

"You don't know how relieved I was to see you walk

through that door," her friend whispered. "You had me in a panic. I called your cell phone three times. I thought you weren't going to show up."

"Are you kidding? This is the big day. I'm ready to win this thing," Ronnie said, trying to sound more confident than she felt.

"All right, boss, that's what I wanted to hear. Should we go over the menu one more time?"

"Go over it in your head. I don't want anyone overhearing our game plan."

Ronnie honestly believed in the integrity of the other chefs in the competition, but something about the intense atmosphere of *this* contest made her wary.

The Las Vegas round of the *All-Star Food Fight* would focus on signature dishes. They would have ninety minutes to create a three-course meal, including a cocktail. The dessert was a no-brainer for Ronnie. Even though she wasn't a pastry chef, she had a knack for desserts. When she worked for the Embassy Plaza hotel, she even made wedding cakes. And in her own restaurant, her chocolate kiss dessert had gotten her a stellar write-up in the *Washington Post*.

Ronnie used a handmade chocolate mold in the shape of lush lips as a frame. Inside, she piped alternating layers of chocolate mousse, crumbled Black Forest cake mixed with a Chambord Liqueur and white-chocolate ganache. Then Ronnie topped the dessert with raspberry puree to make the lips red.

The rest of her menu was carefully designed to complement the dessert. For her cocktail, Ronnie planned to serve a fruity pink drink with coconut rum, pineapple and grenadine. She needed bright, clean flavors to prepare the palate for her rich dessert.

They would start with citrus-glazed scallops for her first

course. Then, for her entrée, she would prepare a lobster tail seasoned with delicate Asian flavors over a crisp cabbage-and-herb salad. She planned to drizzle the plate with just a hint of wasabi oil to add a bit of heat to her dish.

The judges would score them on taste, presentation and originality. On paper, her menu might appear simple, but she'd spent a good deal of time composing the flavors—smoky, citrusy and sweet—so that they unfolded in layers that would keep the judges wanting more.

Ronnie had carefully designed her final plates in her head so that her presentations would have a wow factor. Her scallops and lobster dishes may not score big in originality, but she knew her dessert would bring home all the points she needed in that category.

She and LQ would have to work quickly, in a carefully orchestrated dance to make sure everything was ready on time. But Ronnie believed they could do it. It surprised her how important winning had become over the last few days.

Her confidence would've had a stronger foundation if Ronnie didn't feel sick to her stomach and her belly button didn't sting. What had she been thinking when she'd joined that bachelorette party last night?

Fortunately, there wasn't time to worry over her physical ails as the producer announced that the competition was about to begin. Ronnie and LQ filed out of the holding room and rushed over to their kitchen.

Ronnie knew from past competitions that it was important to stay calm. Cooking under hot studio lights with cameras milling around was a completely different experience from cooking in her own kitchen. Luckily, LQ had done all the previous *Food Fights* with her and knew the drill.

As soon as they got to their kitchen, things started

happening quickly. LQ began pulling together the ingredients for their scallop dish, while Ronnie went right to work on her mold for chocolate lips.

Ronnie had just finished tempering her chocolate when the camera and one of the judges stopped by her kitchen. She raised her head and smiled. As soon as she'd started working, the effects of her hangover were forgotten, and she was in the zone.

"I'm working on my dessert first," she told the camera, "because I need to give the chocolate time to set up in the mold." She went on to describe how she would later fill and present the chocolate kiss when it was ready.

Things were off to a good start, and Ronnie began gaining confidence as she steamed her lobster tails. Then she heard some commotion in the kitchen next to hers.

Over to her left, Stewart beamed as he chattered to the judges about his escargot starter, followed by chateaubriand steak and crème brûlée taken straight off the Compton Arms menu. But the ruckus Ronnie heard originated in Ann Le Marche's kitchen to her right. Ronnie didn't want to get distracted from her own dishes, but Ann was making a fuss that was hard to ignore. Instantly, the camera crew dashed away from Stewart's kitchen to follow Ann.

"Half of my tools are gone," she shouted. Ann was overturning every item in her kitchen, not bothering to stifle her long string of expletives as she stomped around.

Ronnie knew Ann was a student of molecular gastronomy, which relied heavily on science and technology in food preparation. It seemed some of Ann's fancy gadgets had gone missing.

Ronnie just shook her head as she focused on chopping cabbage. Sometimes that happened in competitions. People forgot to pack things or left ingredients off their acquisition list. In times like this, chefs got to prove how well they functioned under pressure.

Just then, LQ leaned over her shoulder. "At the risk of sounding like a copycat…"

Ronnie's back straightened. "What's wrong?"

"Most of our herbs are missing."

"What do you mean? Missing—as in, you forgot to order them?"

"No—as in, I ordered them, but they're not here."

Ronnie resisted the urge to storm around the kitchen, swearing as Ann had just done.

"Okay, this means we're going to have to find another way to flavor the cabbage salad. Take a quick inventory of what we do have, and let's try to put something together."

From there, she and LQ scrambled around the kitchen assessing their options. Ronnie hated to repeat flavors, but they finally agreed that they'd have to use citrus to flavor both the scallops and the cabbage salad that would accompany the lobster. In an effort to switch things up, Ronnie garnished the salad with clementine orange and pink grapefruit supremes.

Even though the colors and flavors were milder than the herb combination she'd planned, Ronnie had to hope she'd done enough to save the dish. Fortunately, her scallop dish was still coming together the way she wanted.

But the clock was ticking down fast, and it was time to check on her chocolate mold. Ronnie knew something was wrong the minute she pulled the refrigerator open.

"LQ, I think it's warm in here." Ronnie pulled out her tray of molds and, sure enough, they were melting all over the pan.

Ronnie heard the cameras zooming in on her station, and

the producer asked her to talk about what was happening. What was happening was that she wanted to cry.

"There seems to be something wrong with my refrigerator. The chocolate lip molds didn't cool, and they're starting to melt."

Ronnie turned to look at LQ, and for the first time in all her years of competing, she wanted to give up and quit. Her chocolate kiss dessert was the star of her meal, and with only fifteen minutes left, there wasn't time to start over from scratch.

Thankfully, LQ remained levelheaded as always. "Okay, we've got to regroup," she said. "What can we do for dessert without the chocolate molds?"

Ronnie inhaled deeply, filling her lungs with air. Suddenly the gears of her mind began to turn. "Find me some cocktail glasses," she told her assistant. "We can still use the filling and make some sort of parfait."

LQ rushed back to her with three martini glasses. Working fast, Ronnie began filling the bottoms of the glasses with chocolate cake. With the refrigerator broken her mousse and ganache were a bit softer than they should be. She just had to hope that the judges would overlook the texture and take the flavors into account.

Topping the desserts with raspberry coulis and chocolate shavings, Ronnie placed them on the serving tray just as the audience counted down to zero.

A loud buzzer sounded, indicating the end of the *Food Fight*. Now they'd each present their dishes to the judges and receive a critique before deliberation and the announcement of the round-one winner.

Ronnie hugged LQ, relieved that, one way or another, it was over. "We made it to the end. Let's just hope we've done enough to make it past this round."

* * *

Ace clapped his assistant, Marcel, on the back. "It was touch-and-go there for a few minutes, buddy, but I think we did our thing."

Marcel slapped his hand, sliding his fingers back into a snap. "We've got this, Ace. I just know we've got this."

Ace was glad to be the first to present his dishes to the judges. Marcel went back to the holding room to watch everything on a big-screen TV with the other chefs, while Ace went to stand on his mark.

The director gave him his cue to start.

"Well, I'm known as the Sexy Chef, so I had to prepare some sexy dishes for you today. To start, I have oysters three ways. The first one is in a half shell flavored with yuzu juice, the second is fried crispy in brown butter and chives and the third is a sweet ceviche."

Ace was really pleased with the way his three courses had turned out, but it didn't happen without a bit of Las Vegas's Lady Luck on his side. A few ingredients were missing and the oven in his kitchen cooked unevenly, but improvisation saved the day.

He hadn't planned on serving a fried oyster, but when he couldn't count on his oven to heat properly, he switched his game plan. The results turned out even better than he'd hoped.

"For the entrée, I've given you a beautiful seared filet of beef with a trio of sauces to dip it in. My specialty is meals for two, but since there are three of you, I've made three the theme for the day."

Ace knew the judges didn't give any points for charm, but he was hoping it wouldn't hurt. Especially since he was afraid his dessert plate was looking a bit empty. It was supposed to be filled with a triple-layer chocolate cake, but again the oven had forced him to change things up.

"And to finish this meal off, I've given you a trio of chocolate truffles. For a bit of variation on the signature cocktail, I decided to offer you a hot coffee shot with brandy and Kahlúa."

Ace kept a smile on his face as the judges sampled his offerings. "The truffles were delicious," said Jean Paul Pelletier. "My only complaint is that I wish there had been more. Perhaps you could have added some coulis or sauce so the plate didn't look so sparse."

The next judge, renowned pastry chef Kari Voegler, told him that his team did the best at regrouping from some major setbacks, and the final judge, Hawaiian restaurateur Sam Lomi, complimented Ace's flavors and his creativity.

Overall, Ace went back into the holding room feeling pretty good. But his heart went out to Ronnie when it was her turn to stand before the judges.

She was his competition, and Ace should have been glad that they were a bit tougher on Ronnie, but he couldn't help but hope she would make it past the first round.

He watched the screen as the cameraman zoomed in on Ronnie's face as Judge Lomi spoke. "I really enjoyed the flavors of your dish. But I can't help thinking it lacked a bit of creativity to have the same flavors in both your appetizer and your entrée."

Ronnie simply nodded. "Yes, of course. I planned to flavor the entrée with an herb salad, but some of our herbs were missing."

"And I'm not sure what this dessert is supposed to be," Judge Voegler said, dissecting the contents of the martini glass with her spoon. "Everything is mushy and running together."

"But you have to admit it does taste good," Judge Pelletier chimed in.

Minutes later, Ronnie walked back into the holding room looking a bit like a deflated balloon. Ace wanted to go over and comfort her, but he had a strong suspicion that any words from him wouldn't be welcome.

"This is BS," Ann Le Marche shouted as she entered the room after her critique. "Did anyone else have supplies missing or appliances that didn't work?"

Everyone in the room raised their hands, which Ann followed with another string of expletives.

"What kind of rinky-dink operation are they running here? This is my fifth *Food Fight* for GTV, and I've never had so many things go wrong."

Stewart shrugged. "Maybe they did it on purpose. You know, to see how we handle the pressure. We all showed up with prepared menus. Maybe they threw a monkey into the works to make the competition more exciting."

"I think the expression is monkey *wrench,* dear," Etta offered.

"Whatever. The point is, either you pulled it off or you didn't. Since we all had some sort of trouble, it's probably safe to assume it was part of the competition."

Ann glared at Stewart from across the room, then threw her hands up. From where he sat, Ace could still hear her cursing the air blue around her.

After all the contestants received their critiques, they would normally line up for the presentation of the award check. But since this competition would continue for two more rounds, each chef was sent back to their kitchens to hear their scores. For the chef with the lowest score, their kitchen would go dark, and they'd be eliminated from the competition.

As Ace stood next to Marcel in his kitchen, he felt pretty good about his chances. It surprised him how concerned he was that Ronnie might not continue to the next round.

"With the highest score in the competition, earning a total of forty-four out of fifty, our round-one leader is Etta Foster." The in-studio audience clapped and cheered.

"Second, with a score of thirty-two out of fifty, is Ace Brown."

Ace felt Marcel patting him on the back, saying, "Hawaii, here we come!"

Ace nodded absently. They were in a pretty good position heading into the next round, but he couldn't keep himself from turning toward Ronnie's kitchen on the other side of Stewart.

The host was just awarding Stewart Compton third place. Suddenly the music in the studio got louder as the spotlights focused on Ronnie and Ann's kitchens.

"One of these remaining contestants will be moving on to the second round in Hawaii, and the other will be going home. The contestant coming in fourth, with a total score of twenty-six out of fifty is Veronica Howard. That means Ann Le Marche has been eliminated from the competition with a total score of twenty-two out of fifty."

Ace watched Ronnie hug LQ and felt more relieved than he should have. But the fact was, he and Ronnie had a lot of unfinished business.

She'd been very tipsy when she'd kissed him last night, but that didn't mean she wasn't expressing all the feelings she kept on lockdown when she was sober. Now that she'd tipped her hand, Ace planned to press that advantage.

Chapter 7

For several minutes after the rankings were announced, Ronnie's heart continued to pound in her chest. She'd been convinced that she and LQ were going home. The judges' comments about her dishes had been disappointing at best. Sure, her dessert was mushy and the flavors in her entrée weren't as unique as they should have been, but she stood behind the fact that everything tasted really good.

"Cheer up," LQ said. "We'll do better next time. At least we made it through to the next round."

"Barely."

"I know you're disappointed in our final score, but this is the *All-Star Food Fight*. It's supposed to be more of a challenge."

"A challenge is one thing. Outright sabotage is another. Do you think the network screwed up our kitchens on purpose?"

LQ shrugged. "Normally, I'd say no. But, since everyone had complaints, it's starting to look that way."

Ronnie shook her head, uncertain what to believe. "Do we have any cocktails left? I could use one."

"Honey, I don't know what you did last night, but judging from the way you were first moving when you got here this morning, you should probably lay off the cocktails."

"I was just kidding," Ronnie said, then suddenly looked up as Ace entered the kitchen.

"Congratulations, ladies."

Ronnie sighed. "Did you come over here to gloat?"

Ace laughed. "It's not time for that yet. I just wanted to invite you two to join Marcel and me for dinner tonight to celebrate."

Ronnie frowned. "You two have reason to celebrate. We don't."

"Oh come on, you made it to Hawaii. That's worth celebrating."

LQ stepped forward. "I can't make it anyway. I have tickets to see the magician at the Monte Carlo tonight. It's a VIP package that includes dinner and a backstage meet-and-greet."

"Then I guess it's just you and me, Ronnie," Ace said.

"What about Marcel?"

"I'd hate to make him feel like a third wheel. Besides, I have tickets to a show, too, and Marcel definitely won't go with me."

Ronnie turned away to gather her things. "No, I think I'd better stay in tonight. I did enough celebrating last night to last me awhile."

"Come on, didn't you say there were three things you wanted to do in Vegas before you left? Tonight is your chance."

"I don't know," she said, packing up her knives. "I'm really not in the mood."

"All the more reason to go. Don't sit around in your

room rehashing the competition. It's over. There's time to focus on what's up ahead tomorrow. Tonight, enjoy Las Vegas."

Ronnie knew everything Ace was saying was true. But, going out on the town last night had made her lose focus for today's competition. Maybe the best thing to do was keep a low profile and stay on track.

"I've cleaned up everything, Ronnie. I'll see you tomorrow," LQ said, interrupting her thoughts. "And, for what it's worth, you *should* go out tonight. Have a nice dinner and put today behind you."

"There it is," Ace said. "LQ agrees with me. You're outnumbered, two against one."

Ronnie threw her hands up in surrender. "Fine. I'll have dinner with you tonight."

Chapter 8

When Ace got back to his hotel room, he felt like he was on top of the world. Not only had he come in second in the *All-Star Food Fight,* he'd gotten Ronnie to agree to go out with him. Now he had just one more detail to take care of, he thought, picking up the phone.

"Fontaine here," Garett answered.

"I need a huge favor."

"Ah, a favor. I love it when you owe me."

"Great, because I need you to get me two really good seats to a show for tonight."

Garett paused for a moment. "Short notice, great seats… This is going to cost you."

"I'm willing to pay. I just need to know if you can do it."

"Depends on the show. What do you want to see?"

Ace shrugged, looking around his room as he tried to remember what was popular. "I don't know. What's hot?"

"Hot? How about *Le Nu?*"

"What's that?"

Garett chuckled. "It's like a cross between a French revue and Cirque du Soleil."

"That sounds perfect. Get me the best seats you can."

"I'll do my best, but first, can I ask just why you want me to bust my hump getting these tickets?"

Ace smiled. "I have a date tonight."

"Let me guess. It's with one Ms. Veronica Howard?"

"That's right."

"You should let me make the most of this occasion. You get to impress Ronnie with great seats to a hot show, and I can get a little free publicity to promote your new cookbook. It's win-win."

Ace shook his head. "What are you talking about?"

"I'll tip off a couple of photographers and tomorrow on TMZ everyone will be talking about the celebrity chef who's having a bit of a showmance on the set of GTV's *All-Star Food Fight.*"

"There you go again. What does 'showmance' even mean?"

"Just what it sounds like. A romance on the set of a reality show."

Ace rolled his eyes. "I hardly think the press would take an interest in anything going on between a couple of chefs from Gourmet TV. It's a bad idea on so many levels."

"Why don't you let me be the judge of that?"

Ace's thoughts were already moving on to dinner reservations. "What I want you to do is get me those tickets. That's all I need right now."

He hung up with Garett and, just as he'd hoped, twenty minutes later he received a text message confirming that the tickets would be waiting for him at the box office.

Now he just had to confirm the evening's plans with Ronnie, he thought, dialing her room number.

"Why don't we meet in the lobby at six so we can have dinner," Ace suggested when Ronnie picked up the phone.

"Actually, I think it might be best if I stay in tonight."

"Stay in? But I have front-row seats to one of the hottest shows in town."

Ronnie sighed. "Well, the problem is that I only brought one party dress, and I wore it last night. I'm not exaggerating when I say I have nothing to wear. Unless you want to set a new fashion trend of chefs' jackets as evening wear."

"You don't have anything to wear? Is that the only problem?"

Ronnie hesitated. "Well, yeah…"

"Fine, that's easily remedied. Let's go shopping at Caesars."

"*Let's?* You actually want to go with me? I'm sure I could pick something out myself. I just don't know if it's worth the effort."

"Why not?"

"Because I hate shopping."

Ace laughed. "You're the first woman I've ever heard say that."

"Well, it's true. I think I would rather wear my chef's jacket than skulk around a mall trying to find something to wear," she said grimly.

"Then consider me your personal shopper. I promise to make it fun."

"Thanks for the offer," she said, and Ace could hear that he was losing her. "But, I really should stay in tonight."

"Come on. I'll make the experience as painless as

possible," he said, refusing to take no for an answer. "Meet me in the lobby in fifteen minutes."

Before Ronnie could protest again, Ace hung up the phone.

As soon as she put down the phone, Ronnie began pacing her hotel room. Shopping? With Ace? She felt anxiety rising in her chest.

Even though she no longer wore plus-size clothes, all the memories of fluorescent lights and unflattering mirror images came rushing back to her. She wouldn't even have had her one party dress if Cara hadn't insisted that she pick out a goal outfit that she wanted to fit into when she lost weight.

Despite her worries over going shopping, there was one strong feeling overpowering that fear. And it was the desire to spend time with Ace.

She was completely embarrassed by her behavior the night before, but Ace didn't seem to be the least bit put off by it. In fact, now that she'd made a fool of herself gushing over him, he seemed even more determined to spend time with her.

It would have been nice if Ace could have shown this kind of interest in her when she was overweight, but she wasn't going to dwell on that now. She couldn't blame him for preferring the skinnier Ronnie over the heavier version. After all, she had no trouble appreciating his buff physique then or now.

Realizing that she would be running late if she continued to wallow in her emotions, she picked up her purse and headed to the lobby.

Ace had been right about one thing. Sitting in her room fretting over all the things that had gone wrong that day wouldn't do her any good. As she rode the elevator down to the lobby, she vowed to live in the moment and enjoy her night out. The shopping? That still remained to be seen.

Ace and Ronnie walked over to the mall in Caesars Palace hotel, and he directed her to an upscale women's clothing store.

As soon as they crossed the threshold, Ronnie felt her heartbeat pick up speed. She took in all the skinny metallic mannequins and felt certain that nothing in the store would look good on her. How was she going to get out of this? But before she could make a break for the door, Ace had already motioned for a sales clerk to come over.

"May I help you?"

"Yes, this beautiful lady needs a dress for an evening on the town. Can you offer her some suggestions?"

Immediately Ronnie felt like her cheeks were on fire. She expected the saleswoman to turn a disapproving look in her direction and laugh her out of the store. To make matters worse, the woman had the nerve to ask the dreaded question.

"What size do you wear?"

Ronnie swallowed hard. "Uh...I...um—" Her old dress size formed on her lips and she stumbled over the number as she realized she didn't wear double digits anymore.

"You look like a four. Let me pull some dresses for you."

"No, I don't think...four?"

"If the fours are too big, I'll bring you a smaller size."

Ronnie was shaking her head as the saleswoman returned with three dresses and led her over to a dressing room. Taking the dresses Ronnie entered the room feeling like a caged animal. In a few minutes she'd have to come back out and admit that none of the dresses fit her. Worse yet, she'd have to admit this truth in front of Ace.

At a loss for any other option, Ronnie took the first dress off the rack in the fitting room. It was a red sheath that made her cringe in anticipation. But because it didn't have any belts and wasn't cinched at the waist, she tried to pull it over her head.

To her shock the dress slid over her figure with room to spare. Before Ronnie could turn to check the mirror, Ace's voice came through the door.

"Come out and let me see it."

Ronnie's eyes went wide and she spun to look in the mirror. She blinked, not recognizing the thin but curvy woman looking back at her.

A woman who wore a size four.

The dress hung from a beaded halter at the neck to skim over her hips, ending just above her knees. Stepping forward, Ronnie opened the dressing-room door just enough for Ace to catch a glimpse of the dress.

"I can't see you. Step all the way out."

Tiptoeing forward, Ronnie watched his eyes light up as he took her in. He was already nodding as he motioned for her to spin around. Ronnie started to protest, but he looked so pleased by the sight of her, she couldn't resist.

"Very sexy."

Ronnie's cheeks were on fire once again, but this time for a different reason. She'd never had a man tell her she was sexy before.

Feeling almost giddy, Ronnie disappeared into the dressing room and put on the next dress. This one was a royal-blue strapless that hid nothing from breast to hip. The fabric was beautifully draped with ruching at the waist, but Ronnie feared it was too revealing.

As soon as she stepped out of the dressing room, Ace and the sales girl began oohing and ahhing.

"Ronnie, you look incredible in that dress."

"That's the perfect color for you," the sales girl said, "and it really compliments your figure."

Ronnie immediately discounted the clerk's opinion because Ronnie knew the girl wanted to make a sale. But Ace's appreciation was written all over his face. He looked like he wanted to scoop Ronnie up and rush her back to his room.

Suddenly this shopping experience had taken a turn for the better. Ronnie went back into the dressing room and put on dress number three. It was a black lacy number with spaghetti straps and a frilled hemline.

"This dress looks great," Ace said when she came out of the dressing room, "but the blue one's my favorite. It, um, showed off your best assets."

Ronnie eyed him up and down. "My best assets? And what would those be?" she teased, enjoying watching him squirm.

For a second she saw him racking his brain for a politically correct answer until he saw the evil glint in her eye. They both laughed.

She put her hand on her hip. "I don't know. The blue dress may be dangerous to my virtue. Maybe I ought to shop around for something more conservative?"

Ace waved off that suggestion. "Nah, you hate shopping. The blue dress is perfect. If you don't buy it for yourself, I'm buying it for you."

Ronnie felt her heart float with feminine pride. "You like it that much, huh?"

He winked at her and she suddenly felt as though she was standing before him naked. "Okay, fine, I'll buy the blue dress."

"Maybe you should get the red and black, too. After all, I'm going to want to take you out in Hawaii and Paris."

Ronnie sighed. Not only was he making it clear that he planned to spend a lot of time with her in the future, he was also expressing confidence that she'd make it to the final round of *Food Fight*.

She was riding so high from all the positive feedback, Ronnie decided she would buy the other dresses, as well. After all, it couldn't hurt to be prepared.

Ace walked her back to the hotel and they parted ways to get ready for the evening. She'd been so consumed by the shopping trip that she hadn't even asked him what show they'd be going to see.

Later, as Ronnie slipped into her blue dress, she thought about her most recent dating history. It had been a long time since she'd been on a date. But now that she'd allowed herself the indulgence, she was going to make sure she enjoyed it.

Seeing Andre at the press junket yesterday had reminded her of what a fool she'd been. But what she saw in the mirror today reminded her that she wasn't that person anymore. Why couldn't she have a good time with an old friend? Sure, he was a notorious player, but she wasn't ready for anything long term anyway.

Ronnie decided she was going to revel in this relationship for as long as she lasted in the competition. She'd enjoyed watching Ace's eyes pop out of his head when he'd seen her in that blue dress.

Leaning forward, she applied a hint of sparkle to her eyelids. Tonight she wasn't above tempting him a little further. And if things progressed between them, she wasn't going to hold herself back.

Ace waited in the lobby for Ronnie, anxious to get the night started. When she stepped off the elevator, he suddenly sucked his lungs full of air, as if he'd just been punched in the gut. Even though he'd seen her try on the dress in the store, nothing had prepared him for the full effect with hair and makeup. She'd pulled just enough hair back from her face to show off her bright, shimmering eyes and a pair of glittering earrings. The rest of her hair curled down her back in soft waves, just above her shoulders.

Without any other jewelry to disrupt his view, his eyes traveled down her bare neck to her ample cleavage and got lost there. A second later, Ronnie snapped her fingers in front of his face.

"Hey, Ace, my eyes are up here."

"Yes, but I've seen *those* before." Then his skin heated as he realized he wasn't acting like the gentleman he'd set out to be. "I'm sorry," he chuckled. "I wasn't supposed to say that out loud."

Fortunately, when he raised his eyes to hers, he saw that she didn't look angry. In fact, her eyes held a flirtatious glimmer as she reached up and touched his cheek.

"Getting fresh on the first date?" she asked.

He leaned down and kissed her on the cheek, inhaling her soft floral scent. "You can't blame a guy for trying. I mean, look at you. It's not my fault that I temporarily lost control of my common sense."

Ronnie laughed. "Saved by the charm once again."

Ace took Ronnie to the brand-new luxury hotel on the Strip where the show *Le Nu* was playing. He'd had the concierge make reservations at the five-star restaurant there.

As the host led them to their table, Ronnie turned to look at Ace, her eyes flashing with anticipation. "I've heard so much about the chef of this restaurant. I've been dying to try his seafood risotto. You must be really connected to get last-minute reservations."

Instantly, Ace knew he had a way to redeem himself for his lecherous behavior earlier. When Ronnie went to the ladies' room, he signaled the waiter to send a message to the chef.

When she returned, they shared a crab cake appetizer and found themselves laughing about Ann Le Marche's cursing fit during the competition.

When it was time for their entrées to be served, Ace could barely hide his smile as he saw Chef Telloni headed in their direction.

Ronnie's back straightened and her eyes opened wide as the chef stopped at their table. "I hear you would like to try my seafood risotto," he said, after introducing himself to her.

"Yes, I would." She looked across to Ace. "How did you know?"

Chef Telloni clapped Ace on the back. "Ace and I are old friends. And he tells me you're a remarkable chef yourself."

"Does he, now? I can never get him to admit it to me, but I'm glad to hear that he knows it."

"Come this way, and I will give you the VIP tour."

The chef led Ronnie back into the kitchen, put her in an apron and showed them how he made his seafood risotto. Of course, with some of the ingredients already prepped, his real secrets remained intact. But Ace knew Ronnie was thrilled with the experience.

When they returned to their table, the waiter served them the very dishes they had just watched Chef Telloni prepare, and Ronnie was on cloud nine.

"Do you have room for dessert?"

Ronnie looked wistfully at the menu. "I'm going to have to get up early and work out twice as hard if I do."

"Come on, a little chocolate never hurt anyone."

She shook her head. "Speak for yourself. A little chocolate here and a little chocolate there, and picture me eighty pounds heavier."

Ace knew she was probably sensitive about her weight, so he wasn't sure of the best way to respond. Fortunately, she continued on her own.

"I'm sure you understand. You didn't get that buff in your sleep, did you? If you tell me your muscles just sprout out of nowhere because of your naturally fast metabolism, I'm going to get up and leave."

"No, you're right. I try to do some form of exercise every day. I slacked a little while I was traveling, and I had to spend more than a couple of weeks in the gym to get back into shape."

She smiled. "After all, the Sexy Chef has a lot to live up to."

"How about I make you a deal? We'll split a dessert, and I'll work out with you in the morning."

"You'll work out with me, huh? Just what kind of exercise did you have in mind?"

Ace grinned. She was flirting with him again. "Any kind you think you can handle."

Then the waiter came and interrupted them before things got out of hand. Ace ordered a fruit-and-sorbet platter for them to share.

Before the waiter could walk away, she said to Ace, "Wait a minute. I thought you wanted a little chocolate."

He gave her a puzzled look. "I thought you wanted to be health conscious."

"But this restaurant is famous for its Grand Marnier cake and chocolate gelato."

He gestured to the waiter and changed their order.

Ronnie shrugged. "If I'm going to have to double my workout, I may as well make sure it's worth it."

Minutes later the waiter returned with their dessert and the two of them wasted no time tucking into it.

"Uh, Ace, you have whipped cream on your cheek."

He winked at her. "Want to lick it off for me?"

Her nose instantly wrinkled. "I'm sorry, but you may as well know, despite the fact that I'm a chef, I don't go for all that licking food off body parts. It grosses me out."

Ace wiped his cheek with his napkin. "Are you kidding me? You don't like a little chocolate and whipped cream in the bedroom?"

She wrinkled her face again, shaking her head vigorously.

"You don't know what you're missing," he said, licking his fork clean.

"I'm sorry but food tastes best when eaten off plates. Once you mix in salty skin, the whole recipe is thrown off."

"Maybe you just haven't tried the right combination of person and food."

Ace hadn't meant to let his thoughts go there, but suddenly in his mind's eye he saw Ronnie spread out and covered with whipped cream, chocolate and strawberries, and his entire body went hot. He had to focus on his breathing so he wouldn't start panting and give his thoughts away.

"I have too much respect for food to treat it that way."

His eyes narrowed with skepticism. "You're making it sound like you've never even tried it."

"I don't have to. When I was seventeen, my best friend Cara and I snuck into this racy movie that was famous for its sexy love scenes. Well, in one of them, the guy puts the girl on the floor in front of the refrigerator and just starts pulling stuff out and smearing it all over her."

Ronnie absently licked her fork as she spoke passionately. "Trust me when I tell you, it was *not* sexy."

Tell that to my pants, Ace thought, chewing on the inside of his mouth to rein in his libido.

Not only were her words sexy to him, she wasn't even aware of the way she'd taken a bite of cake and then licked every speck of chocolate off her fork with the tip of her tongue. Even the most proper gentlemen would have had trouble resisting that image.

"And," Ronnie continued, "if I'm reading your face correctly, let me just warn you now, do not take my words as a personal challenge. You'll never convince me otherwise. The whole idea makes me sick."

Caught in the act, Ace made a show of looking at his watch. "The show will be starting soon. We'd better finish up."

Grateful to have a safe topic to focus on, his amorous thoughts eventually began to abate. After starting off this date with such a sexually charged conversation, it would be a great relief to clear his mind for a couple of hours during the show.

Ronnie walked with Ace through the hotel to the theater where the show would take place. As they approached the doors, she saw a series of posters with performers covered in elaborate body paint inside flaming rings, suspended in swings and walking tightropes.

"Le Nu?" she asked. "I don't think I've heard anything about this show. What's it about?"

"Honestly, I'm not sure. But Garett said that it's the hottest ticket in town."

She shrugged. "I guess I haven't heard anything about it because it's a new production."

An usher escorted them to their seats three rows from

the stage. "These *are* great seats. I guess it's all about who you know."

"In that case, I know Garett, and he knows everyone else."

Ronnie laughed and relaxed back into her seat. It amazed her how easy this date was. Normally, even when she tried her best to relax, she found relationships to be a lot of work. Granted, they were only a few hours into the date, but Ace was courteous, complimentary and seemed genuinely attracted to her. There was no chance that at the end of this date he would tell her he just wanted to be friends.

On the contrary, the sexual tension between them seemed to be mounting quickly. She couldn't believe that they'd gotten comfortable enough to actually talk about sex. Thank goodness they had this show to keep their minds on neutral ground for an hour or two.

After several minutes, the theater went dark and a ringmaster stepped through the curtain to begin the show. As he began introducing performers, Ronnie started to realize that, despite the fancy body paint, all the performers were naked.

The body art was done tastefully, and the circus acts required skill and training, but the nudity created a sensuality that was normally absent from similar performances she'd seen in the past.

Ace leaned toward her and whispered in her ear, "I'm sorry. I didn't know."

Ronnie felt her skin flushing profusely. "It's okay."

"I just heard the guy next to me tell his wife that *le nu* means *the naked* in French. I'm going to kill Garett when I see him."

"Really, it's okay. The show isn't raunchy or tasteless. Let's just enjoy it."

But as the show went on, Ronnie found it increasingly

difficult to focus on the performance. Instead she was excruciatingly aware of Ace's every move beside her. Anytime his hand or arm brushed hers she felt her skin burn.

On the stage, a male and a female with perfectly sculpted bodies entwined and contorted as they swept around in a sultry dance.

Ronnie felt like her entire body was on alert. Finally, it was clear that Ace had given up pretending he wasn't affected by the titillating sights before them. He slipped his arm around her and began caressing her shoulder.

She leaned into him as much as she could despite the armrest separating them. Her nipples had constricted so tightly they were almost painful.

As she concentrated on not moaning in pleasure at his caress, his fingers glided up from her bare shoulder to slip beneath her hair. He rubbed her neck in soft little circles that caused her eyelids to close involuntarily.

It seemed like an eternity passed before the show was over. Ronnie watched, half-distracted by Ace's presence as a sensual array of music and beautiful bodies assaulted her senses.

Neither of them said a word as they left the theater. Ace hailed a cab back to their hotel, and during the short ride, they sat close to each other, still barely speaking.

Even though it had been hours since she'd had any wine, Ronnie felt drunk. Her entire body was heavy, from her eyelids to her legs. They felt as though they'd been weighed down with lead.

They walked through the lobby and rode the elevator together. Ronnie punched in her floor, and Ace made no move to choose his own.

Her heart began to pound in her chest with anticipation. Part of her felt like she should slow things down, or weigh the pros and cons of the moment, but that part of her was receding tonight.

Ronnie pulled out her key, and Ace followed her into the room. Before she could get too far, he lifted her against his body and crushed his mouth over hers in a long, deep kiss.

Chapter 9

When the kiss broke, Ace smiled and said, "I've been wanting to do that all day."

Ronnie leaned into him. "Then next time, don't wait so long," she said, running her tongue across her upper lip. Their kiss had ended her fast and now she wanted more.

She lifted her face to his, but his head was already lowering again. This time, his lips pressed hers at a much less urgent pace. Inviting his slow exploration, she let her lips part naturally so his tongue could slip between them.

Hunger fully awakened, Ronnie *was* feeling a sense of urgency. These kisses were just an aperitif, and she wanted to skip to the main course. Three years of celibacy were now working against her as her supersensitive skin tingled for his touch.

Ace's mouth continued its slow, gentle brushes against hers. Pressing back with more force, Ronnie had to restrain herself from devouring him like a woman famished.

Reaching up to hook her arms around his neck, she let her fingers trace upward to his cleanly shaven head. The movement pulled her body tighter against his. The material of her gown scraped her aching nipples as her generous breasts threatened to pull free from the dress.

But suddenly her clothes no longer mattered. Ace was fingering the zipper under her right arm. With a quick downward flick, the dress fell to her feet, leaving Ronnie in nothing but a pair of panties and heels.

She hadn't been stripped bare before a man since she'd lost weight. Resisting the urge to cover herself, instead she splayed her arms as though she were an all-you-can-eat buffet. Whether Ace liked what he saw or not, it was too late for her to make any changes. And she had too much pride to cower under his heated gaze.

Lifting her chin to bolster confidence, she raised her eyes to take in his reaction. To Ronnie's relief, if she were an all-you-can-eat buffet, Ace was a man with a hearty appetite.

His eyes drank her in and his lips parted as though his mouth watered for the taste of her. A guttural sound escaped his throat. "My God, you're sexy," he growled.

Ronnie, trembled slightly, wobbling on her heels. Could it be that this beefy hunk of man really wanted her?

As his hooded gaze burned over her, the bulge in his slacks grew, confirming the truth of his words.

Ronnie had never felt so beautiful or powerful.

He reached out and touched the jewelry in her belly button. "This is a surprise."

"To me, too. A little souvenir from the bachelorette party," she whispered.

"I like it," he whispered back.

Feeling bold, she stripped off her underwear. The scrap

of fabric had barely hit the floor before Ace lunged forward and swung her up into his arms.

He carried her to the bedroom and placed her gently on the bed. Ace tore away his coat and shirt, but he didn't pause for her to take in each ripple of muscle or the dark-roasted-coffee color of his skin. His hands worked quickly to satisfy the raw need that was etched out on his features. Off came his pants and underwear before Ace went in search of protection.

Once he found it, he crawled onto the bed, raising himself up on his knees before her. Finally, Ronnie could take in the feast.

The only light was the twinkling city shimmer streaming in through the windows. But it was enough for her to see that Ace had a lot to be proud of. He was broad and solid, from his linebacker torso to his powerful thighs.

Then his hard, heavy form came down on top of her, as Ace slowly entered her, gently yielding to allow her to fully accommodate his size.

Ronnie stretched her fingers and came into contact with the soft, springy hair on the hard planes of his chest. She let her nails flick his small, peaked nipples before striking out to explore his slatted abs.

Ace took her mouth in hungry bites, first a corner, then a lip. Then their tongues found each other. Meanwhile, his hands were sampling the buffet, cupping her breasts, stroking her waist, caressing her hips.

Ronnie's thoughts became hazy as sensations began to layer like the flavors of a rich sauce. She tasted his salty-sweet skin from his neck to his toes. Her eyes feasted on his physical perfection.

As Ace's caresses became more intimate, she remembered how long it had been since she'd been with a man like this.

Then he whispered, "I want you so badly," while sipping at her neck. Folded against his larger, muscular body, Ronnie felt petite and dainty. And she knew she'd never been with a man quite like this. He was focused on her pleasure, each touch attentive and loving. He made her feel like the only woman in his world.

Her hands roamed his broad back, while his large hands molded the cheeks of her round derriere, pulling her close until there was no more space between them. Their bodies paired like a filet and fine wine, each bringing out the best in the other.

Ronnie heard her breath coming heavily as her anticipation mounted. An ache began to grow in her core, and she craved more of Ace, unable to get enough of him.

"Ace, please," she pleaded against his mouth.

He continued to feed her lust with quick, hard strokes. She bit her lip, as he turned up the heat. Then, just as Ronnie thought she could take no more, she reached her boiling point. The pressure inside her released like steam in a kettle, and Ace followed seconds after.

After a moment, their bodies began to cool, and Ace withdrew, kissing her gently on the cheek.

With a sigh, Ronnie fell back against the pillows, her appetite fully satisfied.

Ace watched Ronnie come awake. Before her eyes opened, her body uncurled and she stretched one arm above her head. Then her lashes fluttered, and he found himself staring into her dark brown eyes.

There was a moment of disorientation, then a slow smile curved her lips as she focused on his face.

"Good morning," he said jovially, leaning forward to press his lips against hers.

Ronnie accepted the kiss then glanced away shyly. "Good morning. I feel like I slept like the dead. What time is it?"

"Almost noon," he answered, laughing, watching her expression change from shy to startled.

She sat up straight in bed. "Noon? I'm a morning person. I never sleep this late."

Ace was neither a morning nor a night person. He'd actually been a bit of an insomniac lately, waking early and going to bed late. But with Ronnie in his arms, he couldn't remember the last time he'd slept so soundly.

"I guess I really wore you out," he teased.

She grinned at him. "I think I gave as good as I got."

He nodded. Ace was in a fantastic mood and Ronnie was one hundred percent the reason. And he wanted to let her know that.

"Seriously, Ronnie. Last night was incredible. I've wanted to be with you for so long."

She snorted. "So long? A whole three days?"

"No, not just three days. I've wanted to be with you since culinary school."

Ronnie scoffed. "Come on, Ace. You don't have to do this. I don't need you to throw me a line or pretend this means more than it does. You gave me just what I needed. It was great. We can leave it at that."

Ace frowned, stunned at her reaction. "Wait a minute. I don't think you're hearing me."

"I hear you. And I'm letting you off the hook. I'm done looking at relationships through rose-colored glasses. We had fun. Now the only thing I need to know is how this is going to affect the next leg of the competition. You're not going to go all soft just because we slept together, are you?"

Ace's spine straightened. He wanted to argue. He'd had

feelings for Ronnie from the very beginning, but she didn't want to believe it. He knew she had a rocky history with men. Trying to convince her that he really cared about her was probably futile at this point.

The only way to let Ronnie know how he felt would be to show her. And he was more than willing to put forth the effort.

"Do me a favor," he said, "and don't mention *soft* and *sleeping together* in the same breath. And you don't have to worry about the competition. I always bring my A game. I expect you to do the same."

"Don't worry, I will. And don't get complacent just because I'm in fourth place right now. You haven't seen the best of me yet."

Ace laughed, thinking back to all of the trash-talking they used to do in school. "I'm sure that's true. The problem is, even your best isn't as good as my worst."

Her eyes went wide. "Oh, is that so? It's been many years since we've cooked in the same kitchen. You have no idea what new tricks I've learned."

He lay back on the pillows folding his arms behind his head, feeling confident. "That's true. I've seen how you cook in the bedroom, and I have no complaints there. But you have to remember, I've sharpened my knives in kitchens around the world. You haven't seen all *my* best moves either, in the kitchen or the bedroom."

She narrowed her eyes at him. "Oh, you'll be lucky if you get a repeat performance in the bedroom."

Ace sat up, clutching the sheets to his chest in mock outrage. "You're not telling me this was just a one-night stand, are you? I think you should know I'm not that kind of guy!"

Ronnie picked up her pillow and bonked him on the head. "Stop being so silly," she said, glancing at the clock.

"Oh, no, the day is getting away from me. I have to hit the gym and then get back here to pack for the flight to Hawaii this evening. When are you leaving?"

"First thing tomorrow morning."

She started to climb out of bed, and Ace, realizing he wasn't ready to leave her presence, took her wrist and pulled her close. "Are you sure I can't persuade you to stay here in bed with me?"

"I don't know."

He leaned down, dropping kisses on her neck.

"It is a tempting offer."

He started massaging her shoulders.

She squirmed in his embrace. "You have to stop that. I can hardly think straight."

"That's the idea."

"You don't understand. Cara's going to call and ask me if I made it to the gym while I was here, and if I can't honestly tell her that I did, she won't leave me alone."

"Some might consider what we did last night a workout," he said, placing a kiss on her throat.

She hit him in the stomach with her pillow.

"Never mind. How about you sleep in with me and just tell her you worked out."

"There's a good reason I did so poorly at the poker tables the other night. Apparently, I have a tell and Cara's very familiar with it."

"A tell, huh?" Ronnie could be hard to read. So if she had a reliable habit that tipped her hand, Ace needed to identify it. "What is it?"

"Oh, no, I'm not telling you. You're just going to have to figure that one out on your own."

"Fine. If you won't join me, I'll join you in the gym just like I promised. Afterward maybe we can grab a late lunch."

"I wouldn't mind having a workout buddy, but I can't do lunch. I have to meet up with LQ later. I'll probably just order room service to eat while I pack."

"All right, then why don't we have dinner together tomorrow night in Kauai?"

Ronnie hesitated.

He wagged his finger at her. "If you don't go out with me again, I'm going to feel used."

"Fine, you big baby. Dinner, but don't count on dessert. We'll have to see about that."

Chapter 10

Ronnie dressed in her sweats and took the elevator to the gym to meet Ace. As soon as she set foot inside the pristine high-tech gym, she regretted agreeing to let Ace join her.

While the gym itself was amazing, offering a huge selection of fancy machines, free bottled water and indoor rock-climbing, the atmosphere was already making her want to run back to her room.

All the women were scantily clad hard-bodies that made her wish she'd done more than throw on a baggy T-shirt and frumpy cutoff sweatpants. And her ponytail wasn't cutting it either. If you wanted to work out in this gym, you needed full hair and makeup to match your designer workout clothes.

Ronnie might have bailed out completely if Ace hadn't chosen that very moment to come up behind her. "There you are. Ready to break a sweat?"

She turned to see Ace dressed in a sleeveless gray T-shirt

and long white basketball shorts. The outfit was nothing special, but he definitely made it look good. Maybe they should have slept in after all.

"Yeah, but I don't know how long I'm going to stay. Maybe I'll just run on the treadmill for a few minutes."

"Sounds good. Let's do it."

Ronnie programmed her machine, watching as he matched her settings. "Um, don't let me hold you back. I concentrate on fat burning rather than cardio." She winced. Did she really just say *fat burning* out loud? That was just great. Remind him that she had a lot of fat to burn. Not sexy at all.

"No problem. This is a great warm-up and we'll still be able to talk to each other."

Wishing the treadmill would allow her to run away rather than stay in one spot, Ronnie started a light jog. Just as she was beginning to recover from her awkward confession, two bikini-clad blondes got on the stationary bikes that faced them.

"Okay now, that's just ridiculous. It's got to be against the rules to work out in just bikinis. It seems unsanitary."

Ace grinned, barely breaking a sweat. "I don't know. This is Vegas. I'm sure it's not the most shocking thing that's taken place in here."

Ronnie thought for a minute and a private smile crossed her face. "Yeah, I guess you're right."

"Wait a minute. I saw the look you just had on your face. What was that all about?"

"Nothing. I just remembered something. You're probably right."

"What did you remember?"

She shook her head. "It's not my story to tell."

"Then don't name names, but you have to spill it. Now."

She didn't need much prodding. Ronnie had never been able to resist a good piece of gossip. "Okay, back home, I knew someone that had a little after-hours workout in the gym that we belong to."

Ace was silent for a moment, then his eyes went wide. "Oh, no, are you telling me that Cara had sex in the gym?"

Ronnie almost lost her footing. "I never said it was Cara."

"I know you didn't. I'm just putting two and two together. She used to be a fitness trainer. She probably had keys to the place to sneak in and get busy on the bench-press machine or something."

"She'd kill me if she ever found out that you knew. You have to keep that to yourself."

Ace laughed. "No problem. I know how to keep a secret. I'm just shocked, really. I always thought she sounded like she was a bit…conservative."

"She was, but I guess she loosened up when she met her husband-to-be."

"Now tell me this, where's the freakiest place you've had sex?"

"That's a nosy question," she said, looking around to make sure no one was eavesdropping on them.

"You can say that to me after last night?"

"I can say that because I don't really have a good answer. I'm kind of a regular girl when it comes to that stuff. It's always been indoors and on a bed."

"Unbelievable. If I'd been laying odds on it, I would have bet you were the adventurous type."

"That's why it's a gamble," she said. "And you would've bet wrong." To take the attention away from herself, she asked, "What about you? Are you adventurous?"

He flashed all his teeth in a devilish smile. "Maybe."

"So? Are you going to tell me?"

He thought for a few seconds. "I guess I'd have to say the car wash."

"What?" Ronnie stopped running for a moment to stare at him.

"You know, the kind that lets you stay in the car while it drives itself through the brushes and sprays."

"Oh," she said, resuming her pace. "Wait a minute. Don't those car washes have big viewing windows where people can watch?"

"If anyone was watching, all they saw was me sitting in the driver's seat."

She stopped again. "I don't understand."

"Of course, my girlfriend was missing from view. I was getting a little wash and polish of my own."

"Oooh!" Blushing, Ronnie started running faster on the treadmill. Great. Now Ace probably thought she was boring.

After that, Ace tried to continue the conversation, but Ronnie kept increasing the pace until they were both panting too hard to talk.

When the timer sounded on her machine, she jumped off. "I'm going to hit the shower. So much to do today. See you in Kauai tomorrow."

"But, Ronnie, don't you want to— Okay, bye."

Ace shook his head as he watched Ronnie walk away while he tried to catch his breath. He always managed to push things to the point that she ran away. Everything had been going so well between them. Had he ruined it by sharing too much too soon?

For every two steps forward with Ronnie, Ace took one step back. Long-term relationships were foreign to him, and here he was pursuing one with a woman who might not be ready for it.

How could he even be sure that he was ready for it? He didn't exactly have a long track record with serious relationships. After watching the slow death of his parents' marriage, for a long time he hadn't even believed true love really existed.

But being with Ronnie felt really good. She told him this morning that they were just having fun. Maybe he had to stop focusing on getting serious and just concentrate on the fun.

Ace smiled to himself. Just because she hadn't been sexually adventurous in the past didn't mean they couldn't change that. An idea began to formulate for their date the next night in Kauai.

"Well, that's an evil grin if I ever saw one," Garett said, coming up next to him.

Ace laughed at his friend, who was better dressed for the tennis court than the gym, in his white polo and shorts. "I don't know what you're talking about."

"Oh, I think you do. Wasn't that Veronica I just saw leaving?"

"If you knew her at all, you'd know she hates to be called Veronica."

He shrugged. "She looks more like a Veronica than a Ronnie to me. So how was your date last night?"

"It went surprisingly well, considering that dirty trick you pulled."

"Dirty trick?" Garett said with feigned innocence. "I don't know of any dirty tricks. But you don't have to thank me for the tickets. Just knowing you're satisfied is thanks enough."

"Thank you? I should sock you. If Ronnie hadn't been such a good sport, you could have ruined everything."

"But I didn't, did I? Dare I ask where you slept last night?"

"You can dare, but you won't get an answer."

Garett laughed. "That's okay. I don't need an answer. I called your room several times this morning and you weren't there. So actually, I take it back. You really *should* thank me."

Ace rolled his eyes. Garett wasn't ever going to change and it was useless to try to reason with him. "Whatever. I have to go shower."

"Stop by the front desk on your way up to your room. I left a clipping for you."

Ace stopped in his tracks. "What kind of clipping?"

"I was able to work my magic and get you mentioned in the local paper. I wanted to get you in something national but it was short notice."

Feeling a tingle of suspicion sneak up his neck, Ace all but ran to the front desk. The woman behind the counter handed him an envelope, and Ace stepped on the elevator and pulled out the clipping.

It was a very small article but it carried a powerful impact.

The Sexy Chef Makes Good On His Name With Fellow Reality Show Contestant.

The article went on to describe their date and the racy show they'd attended last night. Suddenly sweat was pouring down his back that had nothing to do with his workout.

Hopefully, Ronnie would board her flight before anyone could show her the local paper, Ace thought, hastily stuffing the clipping back into the envelope. If she found out that this story had originated with his publicist, their romance really would be just a one-night stand.

Chapter 11

Ronnie boarded the plane feeling her usual preflight jitters, coupled with second thoughts about her night with Ace. It was time to admit that she'd gotten in over her head. She'd planned on merely dipping her toe into the dating pool. Instead, she'd done a cannonball straight into the deep end. It was time to get out before she drowned.

Ace was a great friend and an amazing chef. But their conversation at the gym reminded her that he was in a different league.

In school, when he'd been a big fish in a little pond, women had clamored to reel him in. Now that he was a big fish in a big pond, Ace was catch of the day on every girl's menu.

Ronnie knew she'd never be able to compete with the beautiful, experienced women Ace was used to dating. They'd had one incredible night together, but what if that was just an average night for him?

She didn't need that kind of pressure. Not when she had to shoulder the weight of moving up from behind in the next round of the *Food Fight*.

Trying to calm her frenetic thoughts, Ronnie settled into her roomy seat with a glass of wine, next to LQ.

"I guess you had a good time on your date last night," LQ said. "I thought you and Ace were just friends."

"What do you mean?" Had LQ somehow figured out that Ronnie had slept with Ace? Could LQ read it on Ronnie's face?

"I'm talking about the article in the *Vegas Review*."

Ronnie's heart leaped. "We were mentioned in the *Vegas Review?*"

"You didn't see it? My husband saw it online and called to tell me about it. I assumed someone already told you. Here. I have a printout of it in my purse. They say no press is bad press."

Her adrenaline spiked. That didn't sound good.

Sure enough, there they were. A blush instantly crept up Ronnie's neck as she read the headline.

"So, you're dating the competition," LQ said, unable to hide the note of judgment in her voice. "I hope it's to throw him off his game and not the other way around."

Ronnie tightened up, not yet feeling the calming effects of the wine. "LQ, Ace and I are old friends. We respect each other too much to let anything personal get in the way of our work."

"I'm glad to hear that, because the Sexy Chef is a notorious player. I had a friend who—"

"Don't worry." Ronnie wasn't in the mood for a lecture. "I don't think Ace and I will have another night like last night. I'm not going to let a man steal my focus. If anything, my desire to beat him is stronger than ever."

"Good," LQ said, clearly relieved. "I need that prize

money to buy a new house. I'm not raising a family in that chichi Georgetown apartment we have now."

As embarrassing as it was to have her friend questioning her judgment, something else was bothering Ronnie. "I just can't believe such a small local paper cares anything about two chefs out on the town."

"Celebrity chefs. You're going to have to get used to this kind of thing from now on. Gourmet TV has a lot of viewers and food competitions get big ratings."

"I guess I didn't realize that." All the more reason to keep things strictly business with Ace. It was bad enough to make a mistake, but it was worse still to do it with the whole world watching.

The combination of white wine and not getting enough rest the night before put Ronnie to sleep shortly after the plane took off. She awoke sometime later at the plane's sudden lurching dip and a smattering of startled gasps. Disoriented, Ronnie looked at LQ, who was wide-eyed and gripping the armrest tightly.

The fasten seat belts sign dinged and the captain's voice came on over the loudspeaker. "We're flying into a thunderstorm and will be experiencing some heavy turbulence for the next several minutes. Please stay in your seats until I turn off the fasten seat belts sign. Flight attendants, please take your seats, as well."

Ronnie caught her breath. She was a reluctant flyer at best, at times like this she considered giving it up all together.

The plane continued to bob in the air, and Ronnie could hear the rain pummeling the aircraft. Swallowing hard, she couldn't help thinking that they might actually crash.

Throughout the plane she heard nervous laughter and several frightened shrieks with each jerk and dip. In the back of the plane, a baby was wailing inconsolably, and

Ronnie had to fight the urge to do the same. If she started screaming over a little turbulence, security might carry her off the plane when they landed in Hawaii.

Trying to keep her nerves in check, Ronnie closed her eyes and clutched the armrest. Where was that wine when she needed it? Of course, it would take an entire bottle to dull her anxiety right now.

That's when her worst fear was realized.

The oxygen masks dropped from their panel. Physically shaking, Ronnie reached for the mask, fumbling to fit it over her mouth.

LQ, mask over her mouth, was audibly praying and crossing herself. Ronnie decided it was time for her to do the same.

Aloud she said, "Dear God, please don't let this plane crash."

When her plane landed safely in Kauai, Ronnie had never been so happy to see the ground. LQ immediately pulled out her cell phone to call her husband. And Ronnie, who was just glad to be alive, was stuck in a daze as she went through the motions of claiming her baggage and picking up her rental car.

When she finally got into the convertible and started the drive to her hotel, her mood began to brighten. The scenery was like nothing she'd ever seen before. Where Las Vegas had been all lights and architectural whimsy, Kauai was flora and tropical fantasy.

As Ronnie drove toward her hotel, the sun was beginning to set over the mountains. On impulse, she pulled over and parked on the side of the road so she could take in the view. For those few minutes, though they'd seemed like hours, when the wind had batted the plane around like a kitten with a ball of yarn, Ronnie had thought she'd never see a sight like this one again.

As she watched the wind ripple through the palm trees, she realized something important. She was being foolish about Ace.

He'd made it clear that he wanted to be with her, and she really wanted to be with him. What else mattered?

She could continue to get hung up on his past, or she could enjoy the present. After that harrowing flight, she knew life was too short not to enjoy it.

Besides, Ace was nothing like any man she'd dated before. Looking back, she could see that there had been a dozen warning signs with men like Andre. She'd known Ace as a friend for so long, she already knew that he cared about her.

It was time to stop holding back and let herself enjoy being in a romance again. Enjoying the company of a handsome man didn't mean she had to be stupid about it. There wasn't anything wrong with a little competition fling. Once the *All-Star Food Fight* was over, they'd be returning to their old lives in separate states.

And letting herself trust Ace a little bit didn't mean she was blind to reality. As LQ had reminded her, he'd always been a bit of a player. He wasn't heartless, but he didn't stay with one woman for long. Because they were friends, Ronnie believed she was more than just another notch on his headboard. But that didn't mean he wouldn't eventually go looking for his next seduction.

If she entered the relationship with her eyes wide open for a change, maybe she could avoid getting hurt.

Ronnie got back into her car and drove to the Hyatt Regency Hotel in Poipu, where she was greeted with a cool drink and a Hawaiian lei.

As she entered the open-air hotel, she could hear the

blowing of a conch shell and a native drumbeat. Torches were being lit on the back of the property. Ronnie felt like she was stepping into another world.

This is a new beginning, she thought to herself. *I'm going to stop living like a fat girl.*

She hadn't lived like one when she *was* one, so why was she stifling herself now that she was thin? It was time to get reacquainted with the old Ronnie who had no worries or fears. What would *that* Ronnie do next? That was easy.

Go big, or go home!

Chapter 12

It was nearly noon when Ace pulled his rental car up to the hotel. He'd expected the bellhop to reach for his luggage, and he'd even expected a lei greeting.

But instead, as he walked toward the opening, three women dressed in hula skirts lined up to dance for him.

Instantly, his mouth curved with male appreciation as his gaze skimmed over the trio of shaking hips and swaying arms. "Now, this is what I call VIP treatment."

Traditional Hawaiian hula dancers—

Wait a minute. His eyes skidded back to the dancer in the middle. "Ronnie!" He clapped his hands together in surprise. "This is fantastic."

Like the two others, Ronnie was dressed in a grass skirt, a floral halter and a headpiece made from purple orchids. He watched her hips roll and sway with new appreciation. As her body moved, he saw the little stud in her navel glint in the sunlight.

The dancers circled him, and as they swayed by, they each put a lei over his head.

Ronnie gave him her lei last, leaning forward to kiss him on the cheek. Ace laughed out loud. "This is amazing."

She pulled away, looking embarrassed. "Oh my God, they're everywhere."

Ace looked over his shoulder and saw a photographer standing a few feet away, snapping pictures. This had to be Garett's doing. If his friend hadn't flown out last night, Ace would have had the chance to call off this media circus Garett was orchestrating.

"Don't worry, he probably works for the hotel," Ace said, trying to downplay the photographer's presence. "Someone will probably try to sell us a copy of that picture later today."

As soon as he got inside, he'd wring Garett's neck and make sure that picture never saw the light of day. Until then, he didn't want her to worry. "This is the best greeting I've ever gotten. How did you set this up?"

Ronnie's eyes were bright with mischief. "I took a hula lesson this morning. The girls teaching the class were so nice. They agreed to come out here and help me give you a special welcome."

Ace's heart was light in his chest. He'd left Las Vegas wondering if Ronnie was going to start pulling away. And here she was arranging this incredible surprise for him. Maybe she *did* share his feelings.

"LQ and I are going on a tour of the botanical gardens this afternoon, so I knew I wouldn't see you until dinner. This is just my way of saying hello."

Ace leaned down, circling her bare waist with his hands. "Well, hello," he said, pressing his lips against hers.

He knew he was giving the photographer a show, but

he was going to have to deal with that later. Right now he just wanted to feel Ronnie close to him.

He took his time, letting his lips sip at hers. Her lips parted slightly, and he teased the opening with his tongue. When the kiss finally broke, they were both out of breath.

Ronnie sighed. "I thought my hello was pretty good. But yours is better."

Ace was reluctant to let her go. "Dinner at eight?"

"Don't kid yourself, we're both from the East Coast, and there's a six-hour time difference. At eight o'clock we'll both be snoring. Let's make it six."

"Six it is. Meet me in the lobby. I'll take care of the rest."

After he and Ronnie parted ways, it took Ace a few minutes to check in. Then he called Garett to meet him for lunch. His friend showed up to the poolside grill without a clue as to how upset Ace was.

"We need to talk," he said as soon as Garett pulled up a chair.

"What's on your mind, buddy?"

"Did you sic a reporter on me this morning?"

Garett laughed, crossing his legs. "No, not at all."

Ace sank back into his chair in relief. "Thank God, because Ronnie set up an amazing hula greeting and—"

"He wasn't a reporter," Garett continued. "He's just a photographer I hired. I wasn't happy with the coverage we got in Vegas. I thought we could stimulate some national press if we leaked some juicy photos."

"Oh geez, it *was* you," Ace said, pounding the table with his fist. "I thought I told you to kill the whole showmance thing. I don't want photographers popping up every time I'm alone with Ronnie."

"That's what you think. But just that little article in the

Vegas Review has caused the preorders for your cookbook to go up on Amazon."

"Garett, I want to make this crystal clear. Fire the photographer you hired and kill the photos. If I see that shot of Ronnie kissing me in a hula skirt in a newspaper, you'll regret it."

Garett held up his hand as if he were swearing on the Bible. "Okay, fine. I promise to fire the photographer. You definitely won't see that photo in the paper, okay? Now, let's order. I'm starving."

"Thank you," Ace said, opening his menu. Now he could plan his romantic date without any worries.

At six o'clock Ronnie met Ace in the lobby as promised. Taking her new attitude to heart, she'd gone shopping after seeing the botanical gardens and bought several sexy new outfits.

Today she was wearing a white orchid-print sarong dress that knotted at her breasts, with a pair of high-heeled sandals. She wore her hair down with a white plumeria flower by her ear.

Ace, wearing his own bamboo-print Hawaiian shirt with tan slacks, took her arm. "You look perfect for what I have planned this evening."

He escorted her to his car and they drove toward the mountains.

Normally Ronnie didn't like to ride with the convertible top down. Her hair would whip around her face and she'd end up looking like a bedraggled mop by the time the ride was over. But this evening there was just enough breeze to blow through her curls without tousling them.

The late-spring air in Kauai was cool enough to be refreshing and warm enough to be comfortable. They were surrounded by breathtaking views at every turn. Colors seemed more brilliant in Kauai. The grass was a deep emerald, the flowers were bright enough to paint a rainbow and the sky framed it all in a dreamy blue.

"I feel like we're living in a fantasy right now. If we didn't have to compete in three days, I'd never want to leave."

"Fantasy is the theme for this date. For now, forget about the competition and everyone else. This evening is just for us."

"Where are we going?" She studied the smirk on his face. "You're not going to tell me, are you?"

"No, but I don't think you'll be disappointed."

They continued up the mountain, across tiny one-lane bridges and beside steep drop-offs. Ace pulled over a couple of times so they could enjoy the unexpected waterfalls trickling down the mountains, and chickens running wild on the side of the road.

Finally they pulled into the parking lot of a tiny building. Ronnie read the sign on the window. "Helicopter tours?"

"This is the best way to see Kauai. I came here once a few years ago, and the helicopter tour was the highlight of my visit."

Ronnie's heart started to race. "I didn't have a chance to mention this, but I had a really bad flight. I'm not sure I'm ready to get into another aircraft so soon. Especially one so small."

Ace came around to her side of the car and pulled her door open. She still wasn't convinced that she wanted to get out.

"Do you trust me?"

She took a deep breath. He'd never given her a reason not to. "Yes."

"Then know that I wouldn't put you in danger. This

company is the best. And I'll be right beside you to hold your hand. Believe me. You don't want to miss this."

Hadn't she decided to stop holding herself back? Even though the thought of getting in that tiny aircraft gave her the shakes, she couldn't give up flying. If she made it through this next *Food Fight* round, she'd have to fly to Paris. And even if she didn't, she'd still have to fly home. Now was her chance to lay her fears to rest.

"Okay, let's do it," she said, finally.

They entered the building, filled out their release forms, which did nothing to assuage her fears, and were escorted out to the helicopter.

They put on headphones so the pilot could speak to them above the noise of helicopter blades, and Ace took her hand. Ronnie held her breath as the helicopter lifted off. She soon forgot her reservations as she got caught up in the incredible sights below her.

They flew over the colorful fingers of Nā Pali Coast and over more waterfalls than she could count. The pilot pointed out the falls from the old TV show *Fantasy Island* and the movie *Jurassic Park*. Ace squeezed her hand as they looked down into the stunning gorge of Waimea Canyon.

Between the Hawaiian music the pilot played for ambience and his funny commentary, Ronnie realized that she was having the time of her life. And she would have missed it if she hadn't allowed herself to trust Ace.

After they'd been in the air for nearly an hour, Ronnie was shocked to see the helicopter descending in the middle of an open field. Immediately, her heart started hammering. "Is there something wrong with the helicopter? Why are we landing?"

"This is your final destination," the pilot said, and Ronnie looked at Ace in confusion.

He just smiled cryptically and helped her out of the helicopter. He led her through a path of trees that opened to a gorgeous lagoon where a table for two had been set up. It was surrounded by tiki torches and two covered platters sat at each place setting.

Ronnie felt her eyes welling with tears. No one had ever gone to this much effort for her. She was always the one who planned Valentine's Day and birthday surprises. She'd practically come to the decision that romance was something men only practiced in the movies.

Trying not to blubber like a fool, Ronnie wobbled in the grass on her heeled sandals. "Why don't you take those off," Ace said, kneeling to unfasten the straps for her.

As soon as his big hands touched her ankle, her knees almost buckled. It must have been her rush of emotion that overwhelmed her. Because suddenly Ronnie wanted Ace with a passion she'd never experienced before.

He took her arm and helped her get seated at the table. Finally she could trust her voice to speak. "This is the most romantic thing anyone's ever done for me. Thank you."

Ace smiled. "Believe me, Ronnie, you deserve it. It may not be my place to say this, but, I caught a glimpse of how Andre used to treat you, and it always bothered me. I want you to know that not all men are like that."

Feeling embarrassed, Ronnie stared at her covered platter. She knew the incident Ace was talking about.

A couple of years ago, she'd surprised Andre with a weekend in New York City. She took him to dinner at one of Ace's restaurants. When Ace had come to the table to greet them, instead of complimenting the food, Andre had joked about how a big girl like her could always be counted on to clear her plate.

She hadn't appreciated it at the time, but Ace had stared Andre down as if he wanted to punch him.

Not wanting to spoil the night with bad memories, she pushed that thought aside. "What's for dinner?"

Ace reached over and uncovered both dishes, revealing a grilled fish with a tropical salsa and steamed vegetables. It looked both healthy and delicious. "Taste it and you tell me."

Ronnie took a forkful of the fish and the salsa together. "Mmm, this tastes like mahimahi with a light herb and—" She tasted it again. "Macadamia nut crust?" Ronnie looked at him suspiciously. "You didn't make this, did you?"

"No, I didn't. I had it delivered. I told the chef to surprise me and make sure it was a local dish."

"Well, he outdid himself. This salsa is fantastic. I taste star fruit, mango and papaya."

"And there's a bit of citrus and lime. Maybe grape-fruit?"

They went back and forth throughout the meal picking out the ingredients and trying to guess the cooking methods of the dish.

Finally, Ace reached into a picnic basket under the table and pulled out their desserts. A giant slab of chocolate cake garnished with fresh fruit, and one fork.

Since their first date, Ronnie hadn't been as faithful to her diet as she'd wanted, but she promised herself that she'd make up for it later.

She couldn't pass up being fed the delectable chocolate dessert by her even more delectable chocolate date.

As Ace fed her the last bite, Ronnie's mind returned to her earlier amorous thoughts. "Did you say we're all alone out here?"

"Not a soul for miles."

Her back straightened. "Then how are we getting back to the hotel?"

"Don't worry about that until it's time. I've taken care

of everything. In fact, I thought you might want to take a dip in the lagoon."

"You should have told me. I would've brought my suit."

He grinned. "You don't need a suit. Besides, I'd do anything to keep you from putting on that frumpy black thing you call a bathing suit. I thought we could go skinny-dipping."

Ronnie frowned, almost starting to protest. But as she glanced at the inviting pool of water, her mind began to change. The sun was just beginning to set, casting the water with a vibrant pink glow. They were surrounded by lush trees blooming with tropical flowers from hibiscus to plumeria. She may never get this chance again. And with the setting sun and the cover of trees, she really *did* feel as though they were all alone in the world.

"I've never gone skinny-dipping before. But you might be able to talk me into it."

"You need some persuading?"

Before Ronnie could answer, Ace got out of his seat to pull her against him. Lowering his face to hers, he gave her a deep, stirring kiss.

"I'd love to make love to you surrounded by all of this beauty," he whispered.

Then he reached for the knot between her breasts that held her sarong together and let it fall to the ground. Underneath she wore a cream slip-dress, which quickly followed her sarong.

Ronnie unbuttoned Ace's Hawaiian shirt and shoved it off his shoulders. He helped push his slacks down over his large, muscular thighs.

By the time they were both nude, the last thing on Ronnie's mind was swimming. So when he lifted her into his arms, she stared into his eyes, anticipating the feel of his hands on her body.

Instead, his arms disappeared and she was falling. Cool water instantly surrounded her. With a flashback to the pool in Las Vegas, she surfaced, sputtering.

This time, Ace stayed close, pulling her against him with one hand, and wiping her face clear of water with the other.

Before she could say anything to kill the mood, his lips were on hers again. Moments ago the water had been a shocking cold. Now, with their bodies pressed together, they could have made it boil.

Ace's dark, wet skin shone like polished onyx. Ronnie felt like the luckiest woman in the world to have such a handsome hunk all to herself.

Instead of Frank Sinatra on the stereo, they had the night sounds of birds and insects chittering their mood music. Instead of candlelight they had the amber glow of the setting sun. There were no bedsheets to drape their bodies—instead they were blanketed in teal-blue water and evening mist.

As they kissed, Ronnie could feel Ace's arousal. She would finally have a romantic adventure to file away in her memories. She was fulfilling a fantasy she didn't even know she'd had.

With strong arms, Ace began to lift her out of the water, and her legs instinctively encircled his waist. It was exciting to have a man burly enough to hold her without complaint. With Ace, she felt like the most delicate flower.

Though her eyes were closed, she sensed a flash of light. Her eyes snapped open. "Was that lightning?"

Ace's eyes were hooded and distracted. "What do you mean?"

"I saw a flash of—there it is again." This time she could

see it was coming from the trees. And it was followed by several more.

Ace lowered her into the water. "It's a camera."

Immediately Ronnie sank into the water up to her neck. "Someone's watching us?" She remembered the article in the *Las Vegas Review*. Maybe that photographer at the hotel had been with the paparazzi, too. "Oh, no!"

"Stay down," Ace ordered in a no-nonsense tone. Then he charged out of the water, barely pausing to grab his pants.

Ronnie huddled in the water, hoping it was dark enough to hide her body. Ace, as bold as ever, ran for the trees while pulling on his pants.

She saw more flashes and heard some shouting before Ace reappeared. Grabbing a towel from under their table, he stood with open arms, motioning to her that it was safe to leave the water.

Starting to shiver with both chill and adrenaline, Ronnie skittered into Ace's arms, where he wrapped the towel around her and helped her dress.

"What happened?" She bent over to slip on her shoes.

"It seems a reporter showed up to photograph us," he answered tersely, his brows knit in anger.

Ronnie shook her head. "Are you kidding me? Are Brad and Angelina in the area? Because I can't imagine why the paparazzi would care about a couple of chefs. Especially when they would have had to go to such lengths to find us out here."

Ace looked tense. "You're right. This shouldn't have happened," he said, vehemently.

Ronnie still couldn't wrap her mind around it. "I don't mean to sound skeptical, because I know you're popular with your fans. But are you really so famous that the paparazzi stalk you?"

With them both fully dressed now, Ace wrapped his arms around her shoulders and started guiding her out of the clearing. "No, I'm not. And I never wanted to be. I'm going to have to find a way to put a stop to this."

Ronnie saw that they were approaching the main road where a limo was waiting. She had to admit that she was relieved not to be getting into a helicopter again. Looking at Ace's profile, he seemed genuinely upset.

She squeezed his shoulder before climbing into the limo. "I'm sorry your romantic evening was interrupted, but all is not lost. We can finish what we started back at the hotel."

He climbed in beside her. "This is all my fault. I don't know what kind of pictures that photographer got, but I'll do whatever I can to make sure they don't make it into the paper."

Ronnie laughed. "Could it be that they got a bogus tip? Maybe they thought we were Beyoncé and Jay-Z."

Ace just shook his head, refusing to pick up her light mood. She wasn't thrilled about their romantic tryst getting interrupted by a photographer. And if she really took the time to think about it, she'd be mortified. But Ace was taking it harder.

She could only imagine the time and money he'd spent trying to make the evening special for her. Obviously he felt that everything was ruined now. Apparently, it would be up to her to salvage the night.

In the lobby, Ronnie tugged on Ace's arm. "Come back to my room with me. I think I know how to cheer you up."

He gave her hand a squeeze as he pulled away. "Not tonight. I have a headache."

She laughed. "Are you a suburban housewife now? 'Not tonight, I have a headache'?"

He shook his head. "Seriously, I think I'm just going to take some aspirin and go to sleep. I'll see you tomorrow."

Disappointed, Ronnie went back to her room. Too wired to go to sleep, she dialed LQ's cell phone. "What are you up to?"

LQ yawned. "I was getting ready for bed. I thought you'd be doing the same. I stopped by your room earlier, but you didn't answer."

Ronnie sighed. LQ would think she was nuts after their conversation on the plane yesterday, but LQ was bound to find out eventually that Ronnie was still dating Ace. "I had a date. With Ace."

There was a long pause. "Really? But, what about—"

"I know what you're thinking, but the time we're spending together has nothing to do with the competition. He's a great guy, and I think I deserve to be with a great guy for a change."

"How can you be sure he's as great as you think he is?"

"He planned the most romantic date for us tonight." Ronnie told LQ about the helicopter tour and gourmet meal beside the lagoon. "It would have been perfect if those crazy paparazzi photographers hadn't interrupted us."

LQ sighed heavily. "Ronnie, this just doesn't sound right to me. How do you know that Ace didn't set this whole thing up for publicity?"

Ronnie scoffed. "If you'd seen how angry Ace was, you wouldn't even question it."

"That could be an act. I tried to tell you before. One of my girlfriends who used to model in New York used to date Ace. She had a really bad experience."

Ronnie stiffened. "What happened?"

"She said he used her to get free publicity for his

restaurant. He took advantage of her rising fame. They were photographed together all over town, then after his big opening, he dumped her."

"Come on, LQ. That doesn't sound like Ace at all. I'm sure your friend misunderstood the reason for their breakup. He doesn't need to use cheap tricks like that. His food speaks for itself."

"Fine, it's your life. You can believe what you want. But I'd be careful if I were you."

Ronnie hung up the phone feeling sick to her stomach. Was it true? Could Ace be responsible for the press suddenly taking an interest in the two of them?

She remembered his miserable expression on the limo ride home. There was no way he was faking that. Getting to her feet, Ronnie pushed LQ's words aside. Ace was so distraught over how the evening had ended he'd given himself a headache. She shouldn't have let him go back to his room alone.

Smiling to herself, she went to her closet. It wasn't too late for her to nurse him back to health.

Chapter 13

Walking back to his room, Ace knew he hadn't been good company. But he just couldn't let his anger go. Garett had gone too far. Hadn't he made it clear that he didn't want to turn his relationship with Ronnie into a media spectacle?

Even though he'd rather be with Ronnie, he wouldn't be able to focus on romance until he found Garett and tore him a new one. He'd gone to great lengths to win Ronnie's trust and make the evening one she'd never forget. Now, once again, Garett's schemes could ruin everything.

If nude photos of them frolicking in the lagoon showed up in the morning paper, how could he ever look Ronnie in the eye again? Garett was responsible for this and he worked for Ace. She'd never believe that Ace hadn't put him up to it.

What made things worse was that he hadn't told anyone his plans. Especially not Garett.

Sure, Garett had been known to ignore his wishes in the

past, but only on trivial matters. They'd been friends for many years, but if Ace couldn't get through to him, he'd have to fire him.

Ace paced his room, dialing Garett's number on his cell phone every two minutes. The coward wouldn't answer. He probably had his ringer turned off.

He decided to call the front desk to connect him to Garett's room. Even if he wasn't there now, he'd have to show up at some point. And Ace would ring the line every two minutes. If Garett wanted to sleep that night, he'd have to talk to Ace first.

Before he could hit the keypad, there was a knock at his door. Ace dropped the phone and stalked to the door. Maybe Garett had realized Ace was trying to reach him and had decided to face the music in person.

When Ace jerked open the door, he got a surprise.

Ronnie was smiling at him from the hallway, holding a large banana split.

Mouth agape, Ace just stood there with the door open. She squeezed past him into his room.

"Shut the door, Ace. I want to show you something." She was wearing a short lavender raincoat and her high-heeled sandals. It wasn't raining.

Unable to form words, he did as he was told.

She put the sundae on the table. Untying her belt, Ronnie pulled open the raincoat to reveal a simple black bra and panties. "I thought you needed something sweet to make you feel better."

Her honey-colored skin looked tasty enough to eat. He took a step toward her, and she dropped the raincoat on the floor and picked up the sundae.

"I know what I said about food in the bedroom, but I thought you might be able to change my mind." Ronnie took a cherry and placed it between her glossy lips. Then she crooked her finger for him to come and get it.

Still unable to speak, Ace just nodded. Leaning over, he sucked the cherry from her lips into his mouth. He ate the cherry, tasting the sweet juice and her soft lips all at once.

Ronnie led him over to the bed, pushed him down and began taking off his clothes. "Do you still need an aspirin?"

Ace dipped his finger first into the hot fudge and then into her cleavage. "No, I think I found my cure," he said, leaning forward to lick the fudge away.

Still on East Coast time, Ace woke up at 6:00 a.m. to find Ronnie staring at him. "You're already awake," he whispered, realizing his voice was a bit hoarse.

"Yes, I've been awake since five thirty. Jet lag, I guess."

"Good. Since we're both awake, why don't we have breakfast in the hotel restaurant overlooking the ocean?"

Ronnie levered herself up on one arm. "I don't know. Do you think it's safe to be seen together? Now I feel like there are photographers hiding in every bush. We've already had one article in the paper and there might be another one today." She cringed.

Ace's stomach turned over. For a short while, he'd been able to forget about the paparazzi. Ronnie's surprise seduction had cleared his mind of everything but her.

But, he hadn't caught up with Garett yet, which meant anything could happen today. He had to get through to him before things got further out of control.

Trying to downplay how much it still bothered him, Ace said, "I'm offended that you're ashamed to be seen with me.

But, if it will put your mind at ease, we could always order room service. My balcony overlooks the ocean, too."

"That's not a bad idea. I'm starving."

After breakfast in Ace's room, Ronnie allowed him to talk her into going down to the beach for a surfing lesson. So she went back to her room to change and promised to meet him on the beach.

Even though staying in had felt a bit like hiding out, Ronnie preferred to think of it in a more romantic light. They weren't sneaking around. They were having a clandestine rendezvous.

Donning her standard black tank suit, Ronnie threw a T-shirt and shorts on top of it. Then she heard a knock at her door.

"LQ, what are you—"

Her friend bounded into the room with her laptop under her arm. "Where have you been all morning? I got something important to show you."

Ronnie felt heat creeping up her neck. "I was— Last night I—"

LQ held up a hand to halt Ronnie's stammering. "Don't say any more. I can guess."

She set up her laptop on the bed and flipped open the screen. "These pictures showed up online this morning."

Ronnie leaned forward, then clasped her hands to her face. A well-known gossip website had two pictures of Ronnie and Ace. One had been taken in front of the hotel yesterday when she was kissing him on the cheek in her hula outfit. The other was dark and blurry, but it was two people standing in a lagoon kissing.

Thankfully, it was impossible to make out who the two people were, but the gossip columnist speculated that it was Ronnie and Ace.

"I can't believe this is happening," Ronnie said, sinking to her knees in front of the computer.

LQ had her hand on her hip and was shaking her head. "I warned you this could happen. I still think Ace has the most to gain in this situation."

Ronnie shook her head. "No, he's as unhappy about this as I am. It's not his fault the press have glommed on to this story. He—"

She was interrupted by a knock at the door. It was a member of the hotel staff holding a bag from the gift shop.

"What's this?" she asked him.

The man smiled at her. "It's a gift courtesy of Ace Brown."

After closing the door, Ronnie dug into the bag. Her fingers connected with some fabric and string. Pulling her hand out of the bag, she found herself holding a tiny bikini.

LQ rolled her eyes. "You see? He's dressing you again."

Ronnie narrowed her eyes at her friend. "What are you talking about?"

"He took you shopping for a sexy dress in Las Vegas and then suddenly you show up in a newspaper article wearing it. Now there are photos of you half-naked online. If you put on that bikini, where do you think those photos will show up?"

"I think you're giving Ace too much credit. He doesn't think that far ahead. Elaborate schemes really aren't his style. I've been friends with him for many years, and I know he wouldn't—"

Exasperated, LQ cut her off. "Ronnie, do you really think he'd be dating you if you were still fat?"

Ronnie froze and so did LQ.

Her friend's face went pale as she realized she'd crossed a line. "Ronnie, I didn't mean to—"

"Actually, LQ, I have to go. I'm supposed to meet Ace on the beach." She crossed to the door and held it open for LQ.

Looking miserable, LQ left without another world.

Later, on the beach with Ace, Ronnie decided to block out all the stress of the morning. She didn't mention the photos to Ace because she knew the news would upset him. And for a little while, Ronnie just wanted to enjoy herself.

The surfing lesson was more fun that Ronnie ever would have anticipated. During the last thirty years of her life, no one ever would have accused her of being athletic. But the last several months in the gym had changed that.

She turned out to be a much better surfer than Ace, who kept wiping out in the waves.

"You're top-heavy," Ronnie called as he finally surfaced after another brutal fall. "For once all those big muscles are working against you."

He glared at her, clearing the water from his eyes. "I'm done with this," he said, heading for the beach.

Ronnie followed him, dropping her board in the sand beside his. "Honey, don't be such a sore loser. This should be good practice for the next *Food Fight*. You're going down hard."

"Such big talk for fourth place. You've got a lot of ground to make up. You might want to save face and focus on not getting sent home."

Pursing her lips, Ronnie struggled not to stoop to name-calling. "You'll see," she finally retorted.

After drying off and changing, they headed to the

hotel grill to share some overpriced hamburgers by the exotic pool.

"I wish they'd let me in that kitchen. I could really hook this burger up. A little asiago cheese and some cayenne pepper. You've never had a better burger."

Ace frowned at her. "Is everything a competition with you? Now you've got to show up the poor fry cook at the grill? Why don't you relax and save your energy for the real competition. Enjoy letting someone else cook for you."

She shrugged. "I do enjoy it. But don't you ever eat a meal and think, 'this food would be perfect if it just had...'"

"Only if it's a bad meal," he said, laughing. "This is a perfectly good hamburger. Stop talking and eat it."

Ronnie stuck her tongue out at him and took another bite.

He winked at her. "Don't show me your tongue unless you're going to come over here and put it to good use."

"Fine, I'll be quiet. But first there's something I've always wanted to know about you."

"And what is that?" Ace asked, wiping his hands on his napkin.

"Why did you become a chef? You're clearly athletic and you've always had a lot of hobbies. You could have done anything you wanted. Why cook?"

"It's a calling. I've always been a natural cook. Putting flavors together until they pop. That's what gives me satisfaction."

The words rolled out of his mouth almost without any thought.

Ronnie groaned. "No. That's your slick TV response. I've heard you say almost those exact words a thousand times. What's the real reason?"

Ace wadded up the napkin and dropped it on his plate. "You don't want to know the real reason."

"Yes, I do. Are you afraid to tell me?"

He shrugged. "I'm not afraid to talk about it. It's just not the cute story that makes good TV. That's why I've never told it to anyone before."

Ronnie hesitated. She hadn't meant to push him into uncomfortable territory. She was just about to let him off the hook when he began to speak.

"Cooking was the only way I could get my parents to stay in the same room."

"What do you mean? They're divorced, aren't they?"

"Now they are. But they stayed together for years, even though they could barely tolerate each other."

"So, where did the cooking come in?"

"When I was fourteen, we learned to make coq au vin in home economics. I came home and made a big production of making it for them. They sat through the meal for my benefit and even managed some small talk. That's when I convinced myself that I could make them love each other again, if I could keep them in the same room long enough."

Ronnie put her hand to her chest, feeling a deep sympathy for the teenager who felt responsible for keeping his parents together.

"I went through every cookbook in the house looking for romantic-sounding dishes. I made beef Wellington, chicken cordon bleu, and eventually, I even learned to make a crown roast of lamb."

"Did it work at the time?" Ronnie asked, knowing how the story eventually ended.

Ace shook his head, and Ronnie could see there was some lingering pain in his eyes. "No, only a kid would think romantic meals could unite two people who'd given up on their marriage years ago. They sat through the first few dinners but, after a while, I think they caught on to my plan. Suddenly my dad had to 'work late' several nights a week."

Ronnie touched his hand. "Maybe his workload *had* picked up."

"Yeah." Ace laughed, bitterly. "A few months later I found out that his workload's name was Sabrina."

"Oh, no!"

"Don't feel bad," Ace said, waving off her sympathy. "Turns out my little sister and I were much happier once our parents got divorced. It was the strain of their pretending that made everyone miserable. Plus, I discovered that I really do love cooking."

"Wow, that's some story." Ronnie sighed. "I'm sorry I made you go into it."

"It's okay. It doesn't hurt anymore, and both of my parents are happily married to other people."

"Oh, your dad married Sabrina?"

"Yeah. And Amber and Kelly. Turns out he's not so good with commitments."

Then Ace's cell phone rang, but he didn't move to answer it.

"Do you need to get that?"

He pulled out the phone and looked at the screen. "No. It's just Garett. I'll talk to him later. The conversation we need to have may take a while."

"Oh, if you have business—"

He shoved the phone back into his pocket. "No, I'd rather be here with you. The competition starts tomorrow, and we'll have to retreat to our respective corners. For now, I just want to enjoy our time together."

Ronnie felt herself warm. Ace wasn't holding anything back. He seemed genuinely into her. Maybe after the competition, there would be a chance for them to have something more serious.

She blinked as LQ's stinging words hit her again. *Do you really think he'd be dating you if you were still fat?*

Her skin lost its warmth. Was she falling back into her old ways? Here she was eating a hamburger instead of something healthy. Was she slacking on her common sense the way she'd been slacking on her diet?

When LQ had told Ronnie about her model friend's experience with Ace, Ronnie had defended him. When LQ accused Ace of leaking photos to the press, she'd defended him. The last time she'd defended a man against the concerns of her friends, she'd made a fool of herself. What if she just wasn't able to make smart judgments when it came to men?

Should she guard her heart? After what Ace had just told her about his parents, it was quite possible that he wasn't any better at commitments than his father. Or should she take a chance? His story also told her that he was a romantic. He focused on cooking for lovers because, once upon a time, he'd tried to rekindle his parents' love.

"So, now are you going to tell me what made you become a chef?" Ace asked, breaking into her heavy thoughts.

Ronnie laughed, relieved to let go of her worries until another time. "You already know the reason.... I cook because I like food."

Ace shook his head. "No chef worth his salt doesn't like to eat."

"You don't understand. It's not about liking to eat. It's about the food. The smells, the textures, the combination of flavors... I love all of it. Do you know how excited I can get over a basket of fresh strawberries or a cut of pork loin? When I see really good ingredients, my skin tingles. The possibilities are endless."

"I see." Ace smiled, leaning forward. "Fresh food is to Ronnie as a palette of paint is to an artist."

"I guess that's right," Ronnie said. "That's why winning this *Food Fight* is so important to me. It's an opportunity to realize a dream. If I win this, I can open another restaurant, and share my food with more people. When I was a kid, my mother, grandmother and I used to spend all day Sunday cooking. We'd bake fresh biscuits with honey, shell peas, batter and fry chicken with gravy...."

Ace closed his eyes. "Stop it. You're making me hungry all over again."

She laughed. "I know you're thinking the best part of the day was eating it all. But, believe it or not, the best part was the three of us talking and cooking in the kitchen all day. Those are some of the best memories of my life."

With those words, a memory hit her at once. Her father had disappeared on them when she was only eight, and she'd never met her grandfather. A lot of those talks over a hot stove had revolved around their troubles with men.

Ronnie swallowed hard. Until recently, she'd been repeating the pattern that her mother and grandmother had started. No wonder she always picked the wrong man. She'd been trained to think that was how it was supposed to be.

"You just got really quiet on me. Are you okay?"

Ronnie brought herself back into the moment. "Yes, I was just thinking how much I learned during those cooking sessions." Looking away, she added, "The tricky part now is not allowing my relationship with food to affect my clothing size."

"Trust me, Ronnie, you look good no matter what size you wear."

She felt her smile fade a bit. It was a nice line. But unfortunately, she knew it was nothing more than that.

Smooth talkers like Ace always knew the right thing to say, but she didn't need pretty lies.

The one thing she still believed was that men lied. They'd lied to her grandmother, they'd lied to her mother and they'd certainly lied to her. Ace might seem different on the surface, but she knew his flattery, however harmless, was still just a lie. After all, Ace hadn't been interested when she'd worn a larger size.

"I don't know about you, but this time in the sun has made me tired. I think I'll go upstairs for a nap."

Ace raised a wicked brow. "Care for some company?"

"No, thanks. Because of all your *company,* I haven't had a decent night's rest in days."

He leaned back in his chair. "I can't argue with that. You definitely need your rest. Tomorrow we duke it out."

Ronnie nodded. "Yeah, I want to get up early and check my kitchen setup. I don't want to have the same problems I had in Las Vegas."

Ace shook his head. "I don't think we're getting full kitchens."

She frowned. "What do you mean?"

"I mean that our stations will probably be set up outside. Think about it. The Hawaiian scenery will make a great backdrop, and I don't think this hotel has the indoor space we'd need. My guess is that we'll be set up in the same area as tonight's luau. The crew wouldn't even have to change much, since it will already be decorated."

Ronnie chewed her lip. That made a lot of sense. In fact, it was such a clever deduction, she wasn't quite sure why he was willing to share the information. A chef prepared to cook outside in the heat would strategize differently than one who expected to cook in an air-conditioned building.

"You're probably right. If you'd kept that theory to yourself, you could have had a big advantage over me."

Ace shrugged. "I guess so. But, you're a good chef. That kind of an edge wouldn't have helped me much. I plan to bring my A game, and I know you will, too."

Just as quickly as the dark cloud had settled over her thoughts, Ace had brought on the sunshine. She really wanted to trust him. And he was giving her reason after reason to give him a chance.

"If you're going to take a nap, I guess I'll go back to my room and do the same. You're going to be my date for the luau tonight, aren't you?"

His smile was so engaging. Ronnie had to remind herself not to let her heart get carried away. When the competition was over, they'd have to go back to their old lives. But for now, they were still having fun.

"Absolutely. I'm looking forward to it."

Ace laughed and clapped his hands as two hula dancers led Ronnie and several other audience members to the stage to dance with them.

She looked stunning in her pink sundress and lei of purple orchids. Again she wore her hair long and curly, framing her lovely face.

The drummers started a rousing, rhythmic beat, and Ronnie began to copy the hip shaking of the other hula dancers. Ace stared with appreciation as she moved her voluptuous curves in time to the beat. He felt like she was giving him a private show that he'd be sure to have her repeat when they were alone.

Even though they were supposed to get a good night's sleep before the next *Food Fight* round, Ace was determined to convince her to spend the night in his bed anyway. These last couple of days had been better than he could have imagined. He just hoped they both made it through tomorrow, so their time wouldn't come to an end.

Minutes later, Ronnie returned to the table beaming and out of breath. "That was so much fun. I'm going to have to teach those moves to Cara when I get home. Maybe I can convince her that hula is a better workout than the treadmill. Lord knows I hate that machine."

"You're welcome to hula for me anytime. You're a natural. And I love to watch those hips shake."

She threw her napkin at him. "Behave yourself, now."

Ace felt a buzzing in his shorts pocket. Pulling out his cell phone, he saw a text from Garett: BEEN LOOKING 4 U ALL DAY. WHAT TABLE R U AT? WILL COME OVER.

He felt his adrenaline spike. He'd been having such a good time, he'd almost managed to forget the paparazzi drama. He'd tried to call Garett again before the luau but hadn't had any luck. He couldn't speak to Garett now, in front of Ronnie. But Ace needed a chance to find out what was going on with these lame publicity stunts.

Ace typed: NEED 2 TALK. MY ROOM 5 MINS.

Ronnie leaned forward. "What are you doing?"

He pushed his chair back. "I have to run to my room for a minute. I'll be right back."

She gave him a puzzled look. "You have to go right now?"

"I won't be long," he said, getting up.

"Oh…okay."

Ace jogged back into the hotel, hating that he felt like he was up to no good. At least he could clear the air with Ronnie after he set Garett straight.

As soon as Ace rounded the corner and headed down the corridor toward his room, he saw Garett was already waiting outside.

"You have got to be the toughest guy to reach today. I woke up to a ton of messages from you this morning, but when I tried to return your calls, you wouldn't pick up."

"I was with Ronnie all day. And I didn't want to chew you out in front of her. Especially since your little stunt with the photographers last night almost ruined everything. Didn't I tell you to call off the press?"

"I did, but this thing has taken on a life of its own. Thanks to those steamy lagoon shots, your showmance with Ronnie is starting to generate some real interest. I have six calls from news outlets wanting quotes or an interview with you."

"You've got to put a stop to this. If Ronnie finds out you were behind this—"

"Look. The showmance angle is boosting the buzz about your cookbook. I don't see how Ronnie can object. She was a virtual nobody before this."

Ace rubbed his temples. "I don't think she's going to see it that way."

He gestured toward the door. "Are we going to go into your suite or not?"

"No, I don't even have time to get into this with you right now. Ronnie is waiting for me at the luau. I just need you to make all of this go away."

"No can do, buddy. This is a speeding train. All I did was start the engine, it has a destination all its own."

"Garett, this isn't over. I have to get back to Ronnie, but I'm not done talking about this."

"Relax. Just because the focus is on you and Ronnie right now doesn't mean that you're stuck with her. It's not going to interfere with you dating other women."

Ace released an exasperated sigh. "You're a piece of work, you know that?" he said, heading back down the hall.

Hearing Garett and Ace's voices coming closer, Ronnie ran back to the elevator. Fortunately, a family of four was just getting out, and she could jump in and jab the door-close button.

When she was safe behind the metal doors and the elevator was headed down to her floor, she let her face fall into her hands. A showmance?

Her fling with Ace had just been a publicity stunt planned by his publicist? LQ had tried to tell her Ace was responsible for the paparazzi shots, and Ronnie had defended him. She never would have known what was really going on if she hadn't gone to his room to tell him the luau was over.

Feeling tears welling in her eyes, Ronnie got off the elevator and walked liked a zombie back to her room. She thought she'd finally stopped playing the fool.

Turned out she was wrong.

Chapter 14

Ronnie sat on her bed staring at the carpet for several minutes. Tears made hot trails down her cheeks until they dripped off her chin. Leaning over, she watched them fall to the floor. Then she began to get angry.

Here she was crying over a man yet again. As always, the signs had been there and she'd ignored them. She'd also convinced herself that if she kept things light and fun, no man could hurt her. Wrong again.

As she always did when things like this happened, Ronnie picked up her cell phone and dialed Cara's number. After several rings she heard a groggy "Hello?"

Not picking up on her friend's sleepy voice, Ronnie said, "It happened again," without preamble.

"Before I ask you what happened, I just want to make sure you know that it's three a.m. here."

Ronnie's eyes went wide and she smacked her forehead. "Oh, no! I'm so sorry. Go back to bed." Embarrassed, she hung up the phone.

Seconds later, her cell phone rang. "Ronnie, I'm awake now. Tell me what happened."

"Do you think they need chefs in convents? Because I think the safest place for me is an environment without men."

"What happened with Ace? I just saw a story about the two of you on the entertainment news channel. It looked like you two were getting along great."

"Well, that news story is the problem. He and his publicist cooked up a plan to start a showmance with me so they could get extra press for his new cookbook."

"Wait a minute... He told you this?"

"No, I overheard them." Ronnie told Cara how she'd left the luau to find Ace and heard him talking with Garett.

Cara was quiet for a moment. "I don't believe it. Ace is a great guy. You know him. Are you sure he was in on the plan? Maybe his publicist realized the two of you were dating and took it upon himself to capitalize on that fact."

"That's not how it sounded. I heard Garett say he told Ace to get involved with me. Then he had to reassure him that he wasn't stuck with me if Ace wanted to date other girls."

"It's hard to believe Ace would go along with this. Have you talked to him?"

"No, and I don't plan to. LQ tried to warn me. She said he did something similar to a model friend of hers. But like you, I couldn't believe he'd stoop that low."

Cara sighed heavily. "Wow. Are you going to be okay, Ronnie?"

She lifted her chin. "Yes. Tomorrow is round two of the *Food Fight*. Now I don't just want to beat him. I need to. I have to show him that he can't hurt me."

"Good for you. Don't let this stand in the way of your

goals. For what it's worth, Ronnie, you shouldn't beat yourself up over this. Nobody could have anticipated this. It doesn't mean you'll never find true love."

Ronnie shook her head bitterly. "I'm glad you found it, Cara, but I'm starting to realize that it may not be for everyone. The women in my family seem to be magnets for the wrong men. We seem to do much better when we give up and go it alone."

She could tell her friend wanted to talk about it further, but Ronnie had wasted enough time thinking about Ace. From here on out, it was about winning and nothing else.

The morning of the competition, all the chefs were herded to an outdoor canopy where they would be told the terms of the second round. Just as Ace had suspected, they were going to be cooking outside in the tropical sun all day.

When he spotted Ronnie, he immediately rushed to her side. He'd been trying to reach her since the night before. She'd disappeared from the luau and hadn't answered her phone. Finally, Ace had decided she'd gotten tired and had gone to sleep early to rest for today's competition.

"There you are. I couldn't find you last night," he said, greeting Ronnie with a smile.

"I went to bed early," she said coldly, without looking up at him.

Puzzled, his eyes strayed to LQ who glared in his direction.

"That's what I figured. I'm sorry if I disappeared for too long," he said, wondering if she'd gotten upset when he'd left so suddenly. "I did come back to look for you. I at least wanted to tell you good-night."

Ronnie shrugged without looking at him, clearly indifferent to his presence. Ace bristled. He knew she'd be in the zone today, but did she have to act like he didn't exist? Ace stared in disbelief at her profile, but there really wasn't anything more to say. The host announced that they'd be getting started soon, and he had to join Marcel.

"Okay, well, good luck today."

Ronnie finally raised her eyes to meet his, and they were as cold as shards of ice. "I won't need it. But you will."

Ace almost physically shivered. Muttering under his breath, he crossed over to Marcel. His sous chef, picking up the vibe said, "Did you two have a falling out or does she just have her game face on?"

Ace sighed. "I don't know, but I can't worry about it. It's all about the food now."

The show's host took his mark, and the producer cued the camera operators. To Ace's surprise, the host was going to tell them the day's challenge on camera.

"Welcome to round two of the *All-Star Food Fight* here on Gourmet TV. In just a few minutes we're going to release our remaining competitors to their workstations to prepare a tropical feast."

Ace watched the monitor and saw the camera pan to four kitchen setups on the grounds where soon the afternoon sun would be beating directly down on them.

"The catch is that each chef is going to have three mystery ingredients that are popular in Hawaii that they *must* use in their dishes," the host continued. "One will be a protein, one will be produce and the final ingredient will be a spice. And to make sure we're taking things to the next level, each contestant is responsible for providing a carved fruit centerpiece to help showcase their dish."

Ace smacked Marcel on the back. The fruit sculpture was the only part of the challenge they'd been made aware of ahead of time. Marcel would be in charge of that section of the contest while Ace focused on the main course. He couldn't wait to find out what his ingredients would be. As soon as he saw them, he'd have to work fast to compose a winning dish.

The rest of the host's spiel was standard to the other *Food Fights* Ace had participated in. The host introduced the judges and talked about how they'd be scoring based on taste, presentation and originality.

"Okay, chefs. You will have one hour to complete your tropical feast for the judges, and your time begins now."

Four teams of chefs began running across the lawn. Ace got to his kitchen first and found a giant box sitting on his cutting board.

Pulling the lid off the box, he began to unload it. His first ingredient was a large portion of ahi tuna. A smile overtook his face right away. In preparation for this round of the competition, he'd been studying Hawaiian cuisine, and there were more than a few mentions of ahi tuna. Several dishes came to mind.

The next thing out of the box was jicama, a root vegetable with a creamy white interior similar to a potato. Ace nodded, thinking things were off to a great start.

Reaching down into the box he pulled out a pork loin. Confused, he studied it for several minutes. He turned to Marcel who was already gathering fruit from the shared pantry for his sculpture. "I thought we were only getting one protein."

Marcel shrugged, already concentrating on his task.

Then he saw the cameras running from Etta's station, where they'd been watching her unpack her box, to Ronnie's station next to Ace's. He looked over and saw her waving the judges to her workspace.

"I have no protein. Instead I have taro, wasabi and huli-huli sauce. Produce and two spices."

Hearing that, Ace figured it was a good time for him

to speak up. "There must have been some mix-up with the boxes. I have two proteins and no spice. Should we swap?"

Ace caught Ronnie's eye and she glared at him. He splayed his hands palm up to her, trying to communicate that he'd had nothing to do with it. But she just averted her eyes while the judges huddled to make a decision.

After visiting all the kitchens, the judges determined that Ace's and Ronnie's boxes were the only ones that were mixed up. The judges and the two chefs involved gathered in front of their workstations.

"How do you want to decide which ingredients go to which chef?" the host asked.

"Let's just make it easy," Ace volunteered. "Ronnie can choose which protein she wants and which spice to give me."

One of the judges, Chef Lomi, frowned at Ace. "Are you sure you want to put your fate in your competitor's hands?"

"Yeah, it's no problem. We just need to get this resolved so we can get back to our kitchens and start cooking."

He was also hoping that by taking the high road, he'd get Ronnie to stop glaring at him. It was one thing to take the competition seriously, but it was another thing to make it into an all-out war.

"Fine," Ronnie said, showing no signs of lightening up. "I want the ahi and he can have the wasabi."

Ace's heart sank. It wasn't until she took the tuna that he realized how much he'd wanted it. He could have made an amazing ahi poke. The raw-fish salad was a delicacy in Hawaii and would have been light and refreshing on such a hot day. But they'd lost so much time already that Ace didn't have the luxury to mourn his loss. Instead he had to regroup quickly and try to make a decent dish out of his jicama, pork and wasabi. Marcel was already elbow deep into his pineapple carving, so that was the one thing Ace didn't have to worry about.

Looking at the clock, Ace began to panic for the first time. He realized that he'd let his relationship with Ronnie interfere with his drive to win. Had he really just given up the best ingredients just so she wouldn't be angry with him? And for what? Her mood toward him still seemed to be as sour as ever.

Ace stared at his ingredients but nothing was coming together in his head. For the first time since he agreed to compete, he was worried that he might not make it any further.

Ronnie stood before the judges confidently. Despite her rocky start, she and LQ had remained focused and had worked together like a well-oiled machine. Instinctively, Ronnie knew she was about to present the best dish she'd made in a *Food Fight* challenge to date.

"Welcome, Ronnie," the host said as the camera panned over her presentation. "Would you please explain to the judges what you've prepared for them today?"

As soon as she'd had the taro, ahi and the huli-huli sauce laid out before her, a dish began to formulate in her mind.

"I seared the ahi and flavored it with a spicy fruit salsa and stacked it on a bed of crunchy taro chips. I like to call them huli-huli chips because they'll make you want to do the hula-hula," she said, swaying her hips in a hula dance.

The judges nodded, starting to sample her dish. Kari Voegler looked up and smiled. "Ronnie, after the mix-up with the ingredients, you had the opportunity to choose which protein and spice you wanted to keep. You made a risky choice by keeping the huli-huli sauce with the tuna instead of the pork. What made you decide to do that?"

"Huli-huli sauce is a marinade of ginger and soy sauce that's similar to teriyaki, so yes, it would have been a brilliant match with the pork. But my other option was wasabi, which I'd used in my first-round dishes. I chose the huli-huli sauce because I didn't want you all to accuse me of being a one-trick pony. Taking the ahi was a no-brainer. It was a beautiful cut, and I was excited to use it."

Chef Sam Lomi spoke next. "I love the huli-huli chips you made from the taro."

Taro, a purple root used in the traditional Hawaiian poi, was known to be gluey and bland. It would have been easy for Ronnie to panic when she saw it in her box. Instead of using the sauce on her fish, Ronnie chose to slice the taro thin, marinate it with huli-huli and deep-fry it into crispy chips.

"Taro is a tough ingredient to use," Chef Lomi continued, "and I'm impressed with your creativity as well as your flavors. Making the chips sweet instead of salty was an inspired choice. The contrast of the crunchy chips and the tender fish is delightful."

Ronnie breathed a sigh of relief. Her salt and sugar had been mislabeled, and the sweet instead of savory chips were a happy accident.

"I'd like to talk about your fruit carving," Chef Pelletier said.

Framing the fish platter were LQ's painstakingly carved tropical flowers made from mangos, melons, starfruit and pineapples.

"The carvings your sous chef created are bright and colorful. It's not overly complex, but they are beautiful and complement your plate."

Ronnie thanked the judges and headed back to the

canopied area where the other chefs were waiting. "This time, I'm not going to be at the bottom," she told herself.

Ace couldn't believe he was in the bottom two and now facing elimination. Once again, Etta Foster had come in first, and Ronnie, in a valiant comeback, had placed second with only two points keeping her from the top spot.

Sweat beaded on his brow as the host recapped the judges' comments. "Ace, the judges thought your spicy wasabi pulled pork and jicama salad were good but lacked creativity, but your tiki statue carved out of pineapples was impressive."

He shot Marcel a grateful look. If they made it out of this round, Marcel would get all the credit. They'd managed to dodge another disaster when they'd discovered that two of the feet on the base they'd brought for the sculpture had broken off. Thankfully, Marcel was able to think on his feet and prop up the base with carved fruit.

As for his part, Ace just hadn't been able to get his thoughts together fast enough to create a dish he could be proud of.

The host turned to Stewart's workstation. "Stewart, your ingredients were breadfruit, dried beef and soy sauce. The judges thought your presentation was beautiful but your flavors were overpowered by too many components.

"The question of the day is, Who will be going home, and who will move on to compete in Paris against Etta Foster and Veronica Howard?"

Ace held his breath as the announcer paused during what had to be the longest thirty seconds of his life. He'd never once imagined that he would mess up so completely. If he was sent home—

"Stewart Compton, you've been knocked out and will not move on in the *All-star Food Fight*."

Stewart let out a dramatic shriek. But all Ace could hear was his own breath pouring out of his lungs in one long, relieved sigh. He didn't ever want to feel this way again.

It was okay to lose. If he wasn't as good as his competitors, he was man enough to face that. But today he'd nearly defeated himself. He'd let his emotions stand in the way of doing his best, and he couldn't afford to let that happen again.

He looked across the yard at Ronnie, where she was standing with Etta Foster and their sous chefs. Ronnie still wouldn't look at Ace.

"That was a close one, buddy." Garett had jogged over to clap him on the back. "I have to admit, you had me sweating there for a minute."

Looking into his friend's eyes, a sinking sensation washed over Ace. Was it possible that Ronnie had overheard him speaking with Garett last night? They'd been talking in the hallway outside his room. If she'd decided to come after him—

He shook his head at Garett. "Oh man, Ronnie's not speaking to me, and I think it may be all your fault."

His friend blanched. "Me? What did I do? I haven't even spoken to her."

"I couldn't find her after we talked last night, and she's been giving me the cold shoulder all day. I think she might have overheard us in the hallway."

Garett shrugged. "So? What could we have said that was so bad?"

"Are you kidding me? I was telling you to call off the publicity stunts, and you were talking about showmances and me being free to date other women. Now she probably thinks our entire relationship was nothing but a publicity stunt cooked up by you."

Garett grimaced. "Yeah, that sounds like something I would do. Well, all you have to do is set her straight."

Ace chewed his lower lip. "It's going to be nearly impossible to convince her to see me at this point."

"Then cut your losses. To be honest, after your piss-poor performance today, it's clear that this relationship is nothing but a distraction. She's the enemy, for heaven's sake. If you want to get it on with her, you should wait until the competition is over."

"That's what I've been trying to tell him," Marcel chimed in as he cleared off their workstation.

Ace rubbed his temples. Things would be so much simpler if he just wrote the whole thing off. But he wasn't ready to do that. And the thought of letting her think he'd been playing her this entire time made him feel sick.

"I know what you both think, but I have to clear the air with her. Regardless of what goes on between us, from now on nothing is going to stand in the way of my winning this competition. I can promise you both that much."

Both men gave him skeptical grumbles, but Ace's mind had already moved on. How was he going to get Ronnie to listen to him, and more importantly, believe him?

He'd already spent half the previous evening and part of the morning calling her. If she wouldn't answer then, she wasn't going to answer now. And that made it a safe bet that she wouldn't open the door to him if he knocked.

Suddenly, an unconventional solution came to mind. Perhaps what he needed was a little hair of the dog that bit him.

Ace turned to Garett. "Do you think you can use your powers for good instead of evil?"

His friend shook his head. "Hmm, it's not really my area of expertise."

Grabbing Garett by the arm, he said, "It is now. I need your help."

Back in her room that evening, Ronnie tried not to think about Ace as she packed her bag. Tomorrow the remaining chefs in the competition would fly to the GTV studio in California to do the voice-overs for the first two rounds of the *All-Star Food Fight*.

The final round in Paris would tape live next week after a special double episode of the first two rounds aired that weekend.

Ronnie took the last three dresses out of her closet and placed them in her garment bag. She'd avoided packing them until now because they were the ones Ace had helped her pick out in Las Vegas. Now, staring at the empty closet, she'd been tempted to leave them hanging there. But they'd cost her too much money for that. But the bikini, which she hadn't paid for, was in the trash can.

The phone in her room rang and Ronnie didn't answer it. It was probably Ace again, and she had nothing to say to him. Seconds later, her cell phone rang. She saw Cara's picture and tapped the answer button.

"Hi, Cara."

"Ronnie," her friend said. "You've got to go online. There's something you've got to see."

Cara had always been a computer geek, but Ronnie had never gotten too involved with them herself. "Girl, you know I don't have a computer here. Why don't you just describe it to me? What is it—dancing babies or some talking animals on YouTube?"

"I can't describe it. You have to see it for yourself. And

trust me, you don't want to miss this. Just go look. Your phone has internet access."

Confused but curious, Ronnie sat down and let her friend talk her through the process of pulling up an internet video on her phone.

"Okay, now we have to hang up while you watch it," Cara instructed. "But call me when you're done."

Ronnie navigated to the link Cara had told her to and found herself watching streaming video on the Entertainment News channel. A reporter was holding a microphone out to Ace, and Ronnie caught her breath.

"This can't be good," she muttered.

"There's been a lot of buzz in the last few days about a budding romance between you and one of the chefs you're competing with on Gourmet TV's *All-Star Food Fight*. Are you finally ready to comment on this?"

"Yes, actually, I have a lot to say on this topic because the press and my overzealous publicist have joined together to get me in trouble with my lady. She seems to think our romance is just an elaborate publicity stunt. Right now, I want to tell her, and the world, that I'm in love with her. My feelings for her are real, and I'm hoping that she'll talk to me and give me a chance to explain things in person."

Unsure what to make of this spontaneous confession, all Ronnie could do was stare at the screen and blink. He loved her? Then why had he thought doing an online interview would be the appropriate way to tell her? Wasn't this just more promotion for his book?

Apparently, the reporter thought so. "You do have a new cookbook coming out soon, don't you?"

Ace shrugged. "Actually, I've said all I came to say. Thanks for your time." Then he walked off camera.

As Ronnie sat, shaking her head in disbelief, there was

a knock at the door. Still deep in her thoughts, she absently stood to open the door.

"Can we talk?" Ace said, from the hallway.

Ronnie frowned, looking back at the phone. "I thought you were online."

"I taped that in the hotel lobby two hours ago," he said, walking over to her.

Ace pushed her open suitcase aside and sat down on the edge of her bed. "Look. When you disappeared last night and wouldn't return my calls, I realized you must have overheard me talking to Garett in the hallway last night. Is that right?"

Ronnie nodded. "That's right. I heard him admit that you got involved with me just for the publicity."

"That conversation was out of context. From the beginning he could see that I was attracted to you. He started joking, I *thought,* that a showmance would be a great press angle. I kept telling him to forget about it, but Garett is headstrong, and because he's a friend, I guess I've always given him too much freedom when it comes to my career. Once we got together, he started leaking it to the press. I didn't even know what he was doing until it was too late."

Ronnie sighed. "And when was that? When you didn't say anything to me about it in Las Vegas? Or when you didn't say anything about it to me at the lagoon?"

"You're right," he said, running his hands over his bald head. "I should have told you what was going on when I figured out what Garett was up to. But I wanted to set him straight first. We started playing telephone tag and then I finally tracked him down last night. That's why I left you to go meet him. When I came back, I was going to tell you everything. Unfortunately, you were already gone."

Ronnie shrugged. "Whatever."

"Whatever?" He frowned at her. "Is that all you have to say?"

"Yeah. Whatever. There's nothing more for me to say."

"I meant what I said today, Ronnie. I love you. My feelings for you are real. They always have been."

Ronnie looked into his eyes, and she wanted to believe him. "You sound convincing, but the truth is, all along you've been trying to make me into something that I'm not. The real me was never good enough for you."

"What are you talking about?"

"You've been dressing me up like some doll, picking out sexy outfits and skimpy bikinis, so I'll be more like the girls you usually date. Maybe that's just not who I am. What about that?"

Ace threw up his hands. "That's crazy. I wasn't trying to make you over. Picking those clothes was an innocent gesture."

"Maybe it was, maybe it wasn't, but until this competition is over, I can't continue to worry about this."

He rolled his eyes. "This competition is really all you care about, isn't it. Is winning really the only thing that matters? I can't help wondering what you wouldn't do to win this thing."

Ronnie's spine snapped straight. "What are you implying?"

"Oh, nothing. Just that maybe all the mishaps in the kitchen ultimately worked to your advantage today."

"Are you accusing me of sabotage?" she scoffed. "That's funny, since you're the one who ended up with two proteins. You didn't even speak up about it until I complained. Maybe you were hoping to keep your advantage."

"That wasn't an advantage, and I *was* going to speak up when the judges got to my table."

"By then it may have been too late to make adjustments. Were you also the one who switched the salt and sugar in my station?"

"Listen, I don't need to stoop to petty tricks to beat you in this competition, Ronnie. I've proven that many times over. Maybe you're the one who broke the stand for our fruit carving. It wasn't damaged until today."

Ronnie was so angry all she could do was stare daggers in Ace's direction. "This conversation isn't getting us anywhere. But one thing is clear. We don't trust each other. And that's certainly not a foundation for any kind of relationship. I think you should leave now."

Ace stared at her in openmouthed silence as if waiting for something to change. Finally, when nothing did, he stood and walked out the door.

Chapter 15

Ace felt like a caged animal. In a few minutes, their plane from Kauai to California would be taking off, and he had nowhere to run. He was in a left aisle seat and Ronnie was across the aisle in the right window seat.

Of course he was seated near the last person he wanted to see. That's how his luck was going these days.

He refused to look in her direction. He didn't have to look to know she was going out of her way to ignore his existence. Their argument last night had been one of the worst he'd ever had with anyone. And after watching his parents bicker and take petty shots at each other when he was young, he'd made it a point to avoid that kind of bitter confrontation.

Picking up the in-flight magazine, Ace blindly flipped through the pages. Maybe this failed attempt at a real relationship was just confirmation that he wasn't cut out for one.

His grand gesture, confessing his love for her on the internet, had backfired. She'd rejected him outright. Ronnie was so focused on winning the *Food Fight* that she hadn't wanted to work things out.

Now, for his trouble, he had fallen into last place in the competition. Did he really believe that she'd tried to sabotage his kitchen? No. But it had been the only thing he could say to lash out at her. It hurt that she cared more about winning than she cared about him.

For all he knew, she really believed he was capable of the things she'd accused him of. But they'd been friends for years—she should know him better than that.

Friends. Now they didn't even have that between them. How had things gone so terribly wrong?

Ace closed his eyes, wishing this plane was headed home to New York.

Normally, Ronnie would have been completely preoccupied with the fact that Ace was sitting just a couple of feet away. But, as the plane began to taxi down the runway, she realized she had a much bigger problem to deal with.

Somewhere between Washington, D.C., and Hawaii, she'd developed a very real fear of flying. She'd never been comfortable with air travel, but now she was facing full-on panic.

The businessman in the seat next to her had taken the armrest, and while Ronnie wasn't normally rude, this was an emergency.

She moved her arm over until she could clutch the armrest as tight as possible. The man turned his head sharply to stare at her, but she ignored him. He should have been glad she hadn't grabbed his arm for support. In a crisis, personal boundaries were null and void.

She heard the roar of the engine and knew the plane

was about to take off. Ronnie could feel the sweat beading on her forehead, and she suddenly felt as though it was a struggle to breathe. Her chest constricted in pain as though someone were stabbing her. Anxiety attack, her mind told her. She'd had a roommate in college who'd had them all the time.

Not wanting to start screaming hysterically, she pressed her eyes closed and began repeating reassuring thoughts in her head.

Ronnie hadn't realized that she'd been mumbling "You're not going to die," out loud until she felt a hand cover hers on the armrest and a deep voice whispering, "It's going to be okay."

Startled, Ronnie looked up and found herself staring at Ace. Looking across the aisle she saw the businessman sitting in the seat Ace had vacated.

Ace squeezed her fingers, "I know you're afraid of flying. I'll help you through this...if you want me to."

Too scared for pride, Ronnie swallowed hard and nodded. The plane was still angled upward into the sky. This was always the worst part for her. It was like the painstakingly slow climb up the incline on a roller coaster. Once they leveled out, and the ride was underway, she'd be fine. At least she hoped so.

"Don't worry. Nothing's going to go wrong. And just think, even in the unlikely event that the plane did go down, the three of us are all here together," he said, nodding to the front row where Etta Foster and her grandson and sous chef, Adrian, were seated. "Nobody could win the *Food Fight.*"

It shouldn't have made her laugh, but it did. Ace continued to talk to her, never letting go of her hand. Half the time, Ronnie didn't even know what he was saying. She just focused on his voice and the firm grip of his fingers.

A few moments later, the pilot told them they'd reached their cruising altitude, and Ronnie began to relax. Realizing that she was doing better, Ace let go of her hand.

Ronnie immediately missed his touch. It was an overwhelmingly kind gesture for him to come to her when she needed him. Especially after the horrible things they'd said to each other the night before.

"Ace, thank you for—"

"You don't have to thank me."

"No, really, I do. I was seconds away from having a complete breakdown."

"No problem. I wouldn't sit by and watch you suffer—no matter what kind of person you think I am." He tried to lighten his tone with a laugh, but it fell short of the mark.

Heat spread over Ronnie's face. Now she regretted some of the things she'd said. They'd been friends for many years. He'd deserved the benefit of the doubt.

"I'm sorry. Last night, I didn't mean to say—"

He held up his hand. "We both said things that we regret. I think the pressure of the competition has gotten the best of both of us."

Reaching up, she took his hand just as he'd done when she was having her panic attack. She squeezed his fingers gently until he finally turned to look at her.

"I hate the idea of us not being friends anymore. Is it too late to go back?"

"I don't know. It's hard not to think of you as more than a friend."

"I was scared," she whispered. "Too scared to believe you when you said you loved me. Too scared to trust you. But, most of all, too scared to trust myself. I'm starting to fall for you, too, but with my track record, that can only mean one thing. And that's to run as fast as I can in the opposite direction."

Ace's eyes softened. "I'm sorry if I was rushing you. I guess I felt I had to step things up because I felt you slipping away. Maybe cooling things off is best for both of us. I do still want to be your friend."

Ronnie sighed with relief. "I'm so glad to hear that. Maybe, after the competition—"

"You don't have to say any more. After I came in last in the second round, I had to promise Marcel and Garett that I'd keep my head in the game. No more getting distracted by my beautiful competition."

She smiled, then hesitated. There was still one more thing she needed to know before the air would be clear between them.

"At the risk of ruining things again, there's still something bothering me."

Ace sighed. "Go ahead. Get it off your chest."

After their difficult conversation, Ronnie found it even harder to get the words out. She hoped asking wouldn't make things worse. "LQ told me that you used to date one of her model friends from New York. She says that you used her fame to get free publicity for your restaurant, and then, after your opening, you dumped her. Is that true?"

Ace snorted. "You must be talking about Mariah. What actually happened was that GTV was hiring models as background for my show. She thought I had some influence in who they chose. When she found out that I didn't, she dumped me."

Ronnie frowned. "Then why would she tell LQ that you dumped her?"

Ace shrugged. "If I knew why women did anything, I'd be a rich man. You may not believe me, but *The Sexy Chef* was just getting ready to air when my second restaurant was opening. I really didn't need the reputation of a model to promote it."

She nodded. His explanation made perfect sense. Now she was sorry she'd even asked. But it was too late for her to take it back. And so much had gone on between them over the last two weeks.

Ronnie hoped that they'd be able to salvage some sort of friendship from the wreckage, but as Ace put headphones in his ears and closed his eyes, she couldn't help wondering if it was too late for that, too.

Chapter 16

After the studio taping in California, the chefs had a couple of days off before traveling to Paris for the final round in the *Food Fight* competition.

Ronnie had never been to Paris, so she planned to fly over early with Cara and do some sightseeing. But first she went home for two days to play with her dog, Baxter, check in on Crave and visit her family.

On her last day home, Ronnie drove to her mother's house in Maryland where she'd grown up. Her mother, Sadie, and her 87-year-old grandma, Patsy, lived there. Ronnie often worried about the two of them alone there together, but somehow they managed.

As soon as she let herself into the house she could smell fresh-baked cherry pie, her favorite, fried chicken and corn bread. Her stomach growled in excitement. Coming home was hands-down the toughest part of maintaining her diet.

Ronnie walked through the house toward the kitchen, calling, "Mom? Grandma? I'm home."

When she entered the kitchen she found the two little old ladies sitting at the table peeling potatoes. Her mother eyed her from across the table. "Veronica, it's about time you came home. Nowadays we have to turn on the TV if we want to see you."

Ronnie leaned over to kiss her grandma on the cheek and the woman grabbed her wrist. "Child, you're skin and bones. You can't let yourself waste away to nothing. Now sit down and eat."

The Howard women were traditionally full-figured, and ever since Ronnie had lost weight her mother and grandmother had never let her hear the end of it.

"Actually, Grandma, I think I gained five pounds while I was traveling. I have to be very strict with my diet while I'm here."

"Five pounds," her mother scoffed. "I've never heard such nonsense. The mashed potatoes aren't ready yet, but there's plenty of chicken and corn bread. Grab yourself a plate."

It was futile to argue, so Ronnie put a sliver of corn bread and one drumstick on her plate. Grandma Patsy pulled down her glasses to stare at Ronnie's portion. "We don't keep any birds in here, Veronica. Go back and get yourself a human-size portion."

Laughing, Ronnie shook her head. They went around and around like this every time. "Human-size? Look at all those potatoes you two are peeling. I hope you all are expecting more company because you've got enough to feed an army."

"Give up, Ma," Sadie told her mother. "Veronica's one of those modern women now that don't believe in eating.

At least we can be sure that we taught her to cook properly. Tell us about the competition, sweetie."

As Ronnie peeled the skin off her drumstick under the glaring eyes of the two women, she described the whirlwind of activity surrounding the first two rounds. She purposely left out the parts involving Ace, which made Ronnie realize just how much he'd become a part of her life. She studied her two mentors sitting across the table from her.

"Mom? Grandma? Do you two ever regret not remarrying after your husbands left?"

Sadie rolled her eyes. "Lord, no. I can do bad all by myself. I don't need the help of a man."

Grandma Patsy nodded. "That's right. They're all liars and cheaters."

Ronnie nodded, staring down at her hands. "I guess it is easier to be on your own. A strong woman doesn't need a man."

Both women stopped peeling potatoes to stare at her. "What?" Ronnie asked, looking back at them.

"We didn't mean for you, child," Grandma Patsy said. "You're too young to give up on men."

"That's right," her mother said, shaking her peeler at her. "I need grandbabies. I don't care what kind of modern woman you are, you'll need a man for that."

"Huh? But, the two of you have always said—"

"Oh, Veronica," her mother said with a sigh. "We talk a lot of mess, but that's just talk. Do you think I don't wish for a man every time the lawn needs mowing?"

"And somebody to warm your feet under the covers when it's cold outside," Grandma Patsy said.

Ronnie shook her head in shock. In all her years growing up in that house, she'd never once heard her mothers admit that they missed the companionship of a man.

Her mother looked her in the eye. "Listen, Veronica, just

because our marriages didn't work out doesn't mean that you won't find a good man one day. We may have forgotten to mention it, but the truth is, they do exist."

Grandma Patsy nodded.

"They're hard to find, though," Sadie continued. "So when you come across one, you'd better hold on to him."

"And ask if he has a single grandfather for me," Grandma Patsy said, laughing.

"Cara, I can't believe you're eating hamburgers in Paris. You should be eating something more French, like croissants or vichyssoise."

"Here, this is French," Cara said, shoving a French fry in her mouth.

They were sitting at a café close to the Eiffel Tower. Unfortunately, the trip wasn't the week-long girlfriend bonding time she'd expected. When Cara told her that she wanted to bring her husband and kids to Paris with her, Ronnie couldn't say no.

As it was, during the last three days they'd been in France, Cara had sent A.J. and her children off on their own as much as she could so that she and Ronnie could have girl time. But this was the most romantic city on earth, and Ronnie didn't want to keep her friend from experiencing it with her husband.

"Besides," Cara said, "you've forced me to have rich French food for three days straight. I practically have crème brûlée coming out of my ears. This morning the hotel even served it with breakfast."

"And you combat rich French food with a hamburger and fries?"

"It's comfort food. It reminds me of home." Cara paused, making a face at her. "Have we switched bodies? I'm usually hassling you about eating burgers and fries.

I'm impressed with how dedicated you've been to your diet. But when I get home I'm going to have to lose a few pounds."

Ronnie rolled her eyes. "Don't worry, fat doesn't dare stick to your skinny frame. You've scared it away permanently from your years of cardio."

Cara finished her hamburger and wiped her hands on her napkin. "How are you holding up? Are you still upset about Ace?"

Ronnie waved off her friend. "I'm fine. Like I told you, we cleared the air on the plane. We probably won't be as close as we once were, but we've agreed to be friends."

"That's a start."

Ronnie shook her head. "Or maybe it's a finish. I won't know until we see each other again. But what matters now is getting through this last leg of the *Food Fight*."

Even as she said the words she didn't quite believe them. Something felt very empty inside her since she'd broken things off with Ace. And ever since the startling revelation that her mothers didn't hate men as much as they pretended, Ronnie had been more confused than ever.

The truth was, these last few days in Paris had been lonely. Sure, Cara had made a point to spend a day at the spa with her getting massaged with chocolate-infused oils. They'd shopped on the Avenue des Champs-Élysées, and that morning they'd gone to the top of the Eiffel Tower.

But the rest of the time Ronnie had insisted that Cara do things with her family. They always invited Ronnie to tag along, but after eating dinner with them the first night, she realized that it was less painful to order room service in her hotel room.

Seeing the happy family looking picture perfect made her realize that she was over thirty and without a family of her own. In the past she'd spent a lot of time with Cara's family and that fact had never bothered her. But somehow things were different now.

In order to keep her friend from feeling sorry for her, she always claimed she was going to do something with LQ. There had been some tension between Ronnie and her sous chef at first, but after a long talk over lunch, things had lightened up between them. Still, when LQ asked her to spend time with her and her husband, she didn't always go. Right now, it was tough to be a third wheel.

Most of the time Ronnie was on her own—window shopping, sightseeing and sampling French cuisine. While she *was* lonely, she took the time to sort through her emotions. Her friends meant well, but she didn't want to have to pretend to be upbeat when she wasn't.

The competition was in three days, and she'd spent a lot of time thinking about what the judges might ask them to prepare. No one knew what the final *Food Fight* challenge would be, but Ronnie made sure she was prepared.

She studied French recipe books, visited restaurants and spoke with the chefs, keeping her mind focused on the things she knew she could do best.

When it was time to compete, Ronnie knew she'd be ready. But for the moment, she just wished she could have a little taste of the romance Paris seemed to demand.

Ace got off the elevator and entered the hotel lobby after spending most of the day sleeping. He was in Paris a few days early, but he wished he wasn't. Unfortunately, he'd taken a leap of faith and booked his plane tickets months in advance, not knowing he'd be so reluctant to tour the city.

It had been only three months since his last visit, and while he'd had a great time tasting the local flavors and meeting new people, he hadn't forgotten how lonely the place had made him feel.

He wasn't looking forward to dining alone in spots better suited to couples or strolling along the Seine by himself. Taking out his phone, he searched for Marcel's number. He knew he'd brought Simone along for the final leg of the competition, but at this point, being a third wheel would be better than being on his own.

As he scrolled through his contact list, he almost ran into someone headed toward the elevators. *"Excusez-moi,"* he muttered without looking up.

"My, aren't you fancy, with the French just rolling off your tongue."

Surprised at the familiar female voice, he looked up to see Ronnie standing before him. Immediately, his spirits lifted. "Ronnie, I'm sorry. I didn't see you there. Where are you headed?"

"Back to my room to order room service." She held up a shopping bag. "I was out buying souvenirs for my staff back home."

Ace felt like a teenager, with his heart hammering in his chest at the sight of her. "I'm headed out to find some place to eat. I—" He swallowed, almost changing his mind. "I don't suppose you'd like to join me?"

With the words out, he braced himself for her rejection.

"Uh, sure. Do you mind waiting while I dump this stuff in my room and freshen up a bit?"

She said yes! "No problem. I'll wait for you here," he said, almost feeling giddy.

To his relief, Ronnie was only gone only a few moments. Because during that time he'd managed to convince himself that she wasn't coming back. When had he become so vulnerable?

Coming toward him she looked great in her dark denim jeans, purple camisole and long black sweater. Her hair was pulled back from her face, but fell long around her shoulders. She looked soft and pretty.

He wanted to kiss her.

Blinking rapidly, he pushed those thoughts aside. Just because she'd agreed to have dinner with him didn't mean she would let him kiss her. She'd made it clear that all she wanted from him was friendship.

"So where are we going for dinner?" she asked when she reached his side.

"When I was here a few months ago, I found some great places we could try. What are you in the mood for?"

"Why don't you surprise me?"

They left the hotel, and Ace hailed a cab. He enjoyed the chance to show off his French. He instructed the driver to take them to a little bistro owned by a well-known French chef.

If Ace was afraid the dinner conversation would be awkward after all they'd been through recently, he was wrong. They'd fallen back into the rhythm of the lighthearted banter they'd shared in culinary school.

The food was amazing, the company was wonderful and Ace felt happier than he had in a while. The only thing hanging over him on the cab ride back to the hotel was that it would be over soon.

The sky was darkening and they were nearing the Eiffel Tower. "Have you been to the Eiffel Tower yet?"

She nodded. "Yeah, Cara and I went this morning."

"Have you seen it at night?"

"No," Ronnie said, laughing. "Is there much to see at night?"

"They light it up. Do you want to see?"

She shrugged. "Yeah, okay."

Ace told the cab driver where to go. There was a concrete viewing area between two buildings across the way from the Eiffel Tower. From there they had a perfect view of the tower twinkling at night with white sparkling lights.

"This is a great view," Ronnie said. "I never would have guessed that it would be worth seeing at night even more than during the day. Thanks for not letting me miss this."

"You're welcome," he said, standing a bit behind her. For a moment they just stood silently, staring at the twinkling tower. This was one of the romantic activities that he'd had to do alone the last time he was here.

He wanted to wrap his arms around her and rest his chin on the top of her head. But he also didn't want to ruin the moment by doing something she didn't want him to do. Still, the urge in him was strong. Inching forward, he moved up until her back was against his chest. She didn't move away.

Taking a deep breath, he slipped his arms around her waist. He felt her lean back on him, covering his hands with hers. Smiling, Ace tightened his arms around her, letting his chin drop onto her head.

They stood there watching the Eiffel Tower sparkle for several more minutes. Finally, he pulled back and Ronnie turned in his arms. Then, as if it were the most natural thing in the world, Ace leaned down and kissed her.

When the kiss broke, he said, "We can probably walk back to the hotel from here. Do you want to?"

She smiled up at him. "Let's do it."

As they entered their hotel lobby, Ronnie's heart began to race. She'd had a wonderful evening with Ace and she wasn't ready for it to end.

For the last couple of hours she hadn't had to think

about the competition or relationships. And best of all, she'd finally been able to appreciate the inherently romantic atmosphere that Paris had to offer.

They walked back to their hotel, holding hands while Ace tried to teach her key phrases in French. Soon they were back at the hotel and the only thing left to do was say good-bye.

Ace hit the up button on the elevator and they stepped inside.

"Do you want to come up to my room for a little while?" Ronnie asked. "The hotel gave me a complimentary bottle of champagne."

A wide smile broke out on Ace's face. "Yes, I'd like that."

Ronnie let Ace into her room, knowing in the back of her mind that she was treading on dangerous territory. But she ignored that nagging feeling because being with Ace felt so good at the moment. And after so many days of feeling bad, she wasn't ready to give that up.

If she stopped to examine the situation, she'd be forced to admit that this was her old pattern. She chose what felt good over what was good for her. That's how she'd woken up and found herself overweight one day.

But that was a problem for another time.

Ronnie opened her minibar and pulled out the champagne. She turned to find Ace standing over her. He took the bottle out of her hand and placed it on top of the bar.

"I missed you," he said simply, and Ronnie felt herself break.

"I missed you, too," she said. Then their mouths came together urgently.

Chapter 17

Ace slid his hand behind Ronnie's neck, tilting her face so he could deepen their kiss. His other arm locked around her waist, holding her tight and close.

He slipped his tongue between her lips. He'd missed the heat of her mouth. His hands slid down her body. He'd missed her soft, supple curves. She moaned his name.

Afraid a false move or stray word would shatter this fragile moment, Ace pulled Ronnie over to the bed and began undressing her. But as her fingers burrowed under his T-shirt to help him pull it off over his head, he saw no sign of second thoughts in her eyes.

Ace didn't waste time questioning this unexpected good fortune. He lay back on the bed and lifted Ronnie over him. He wanted her to take the lead.

Relishing the opportunity, she surprised him by leaning over until her lips grazed his chest. Then they made a whisper-soft trail over the planes of his stomach. His abdomen contracted as her tongue circled his navel and continued downward.

When she reached the apex of his thighs, she cupped him in her hands and lowered her mouth over him. Ace squirmed against the sheets as she licked from the base to the tip like an ice cream cone on a summer day.

Ronnie worked him with her lips and tongue until Ace thought he'd go out of his head. Hoping to take back control, he dragged her up his body, groaning at the torturous friction.

Rolling her beneath him, he began his own assault on her senses. First he used his teeth to lightly nip at her breasts, then soothed his bites with the suction of his mouth. Before long she was writhing against the bed just as he'd done moments earlier. But Ace wasn't done with his sensual torment.

Taking the same journey down Ronnie's body that she'd taken over his, he found her sensitive folds. Lovingly, he kissed and licked her until she was nearly screaming his name. Despite her protests, he didn't quit until he felt her body quiver with pleasure.

Then, knowing he'd held on as long as his body could, he put on protection and buried himself inside her. Their bodies rocked together in several long strokes, and Ace knew he was about to fall over the edge.

Thankfully, Ronnie began to tremble, freeing him to enjoy his own release. Exhausted, they fell asleep in each other's arms.

Ronnie awoke in the middle of the night disoriented. She shivered, not sure if it was a bad dream or something else that had caused her to sit straight up in bed.

Then it was as if all her demons and insecurities came to haunt her at once—worries over the competition, pressure to stay thin while surrounded by some of the most decadent food in the world, questions about whether it had been a mistake to be with Ace again.

Ronnie shifted to climb out of bed and a pair of steel arms slipped around her. Ace pulled her close, letting her rest her back against his chest as he held her.

"What's wrong? Did you have a bad dream?"

Ronnie felt like a fool. She couldn't find the words to express the fears that plagued her, so she shook her head.

"It wasn't a dream? Are you just overwhelmed?"

Sighing, Ronnie nodded.

He squeezed her tighter. "I know the feeling, but you can't let this competition get to you. It's just food. In the grand scheme of life, how much is this really going to matter down the road?"

She leaned back against his chest. "Probably not much."

"That's right. And I'm sure your mom and your grandma Patsy are proud of what you've achieved so far."

"Yeah, I think they are."

"Then take a deep breath and relax. You're an amazing, funny, beautiful woman and a talented chef. That's all you need to remember."

Ronnie sighed again. "Thanks, Ace. You always were good with words."

He laughed, squeezing her again. "Good with words, good with food, good with the ladies. You need to recognize... you're in the presence of greatness right now."

His words were so cocky and out of the blue, Ronnie found herself laughing out loud.

"That's more like it," he continued. "Stop and think about where you are right now. You're in Paris, France. About to cook in a television competition with two other world-class chefs. You're one of the best. How many people get opportunities like we have right now?"

"I know you're right. And I've tried to take it all in. I've toured the city, I ate in some of the most amazing restaurants, I talked with the chefs…. But there must be something wrong with me, because it left me kind of cold."

Actually the first time she'd begun to feel like she was truly enjoying herself was tonight. Having a simple meal with a man she liked, visiting the Eiffel Tower and strolling home made her finally feel a part of the romance of Paris.

"I know exactly what you're talking about. The last time I was here researching my cookbook, I was on my own. Suddenly everything seemed made for couples. It's much easier to appreciate this beautiful city when you have someone to share it with."

Ronnie nodded, feeling her heart rate picking up. She didn't want to think about how much she was letting herself lean on Ace. She didn't want to acknowledge the feelings that were chipping away at the walls around her heart.

"I have an idea," he said suddenly.

"Yes?"

"Why don't I show you Paris tomorrow. Now, before you tell me that you've already seen it, let me show you Paris my way. Some of the funky little places you may not have seen yet. We can do some of the things that I couldn't do on my own last time I was here."

Ronnie felt warm and safe in Ace's arms. And for now, she didn't want it to end. She'd just have to face the consequences later.

"That sounds like fun," she whispered. Then they both laid back and eventually drifted off to sleep, wrapped in each other's arms.

* * *

Ace woke up early the next morning, realizing that he'd have to work fast if he wanted to make good on his promises to Ronnie. He carefully climbed out of bed, trying not to disturb her in her sleep. As he pulled his pants back on, he couldn't help but watch as she lay peacefully on the bed.

She always came off confident and strong, and seeing her so upset made him want to cheer her up. He wanted today to be special. Their relationship was at a tenuous point. They'd agreed to keep things casual, and it hadn't taken long for them to push that aside.

Ace was well aware of the fact that she could back away from him again, if he gave her the chance.

He scrawled a note on the hotel pad, left it on his pillow and crept out of her room. He had several ideas for making it a fun day, but he was going to need some help from the hotel concierge to make everything come together.

Two hours later, after showering and changing into navy walking shorts and a gray polo shirt, he met Ronnie in the hotel lobby. The concierge had been very helpful, and Ace was excited to show Ronnie his first surprise.

She walked over to him and splayed her arms. "Am I dressed appropriately?"

Ace thought she looked cute in her khaki shorts, black tank and matching sweater. "Yeah, you look great. Are those shoes comfortable?" he asked, eyeing her black leather sandals.

"Yes, they have padded soles. Why, what are we doing?"

"You'll see as soon as we get outside."

Taking her hand, he led Ronnie through the hotel entrance. A red Vespa was parked at the curb. "This is our transportation for the morning."

Ronnie clapped her hands in delight. "This is great. I've always wanted to ride one of these. But is it safe?"

"I drove one all over the city last time I was here. There's a bit of a learning curve, but I'm an old pro with it now. I promise to take care of you."

"Okay, let's do it," Ronnie said, putting on the helmet he offered her.

She got on behind him and they took off. Ace gave her a brief tour of the city through his eyes, stopping frequently to share bits of trivia he'd picked up. Ronnie added in her own anecdotes, and they had a wonderful time.

After an amazing morning, Ronnie was stunned when Ace took her to a private room in the wine cellar of a French château for a wine-and-cheese tasting lunch.

"This is the most beautiful place I've ever visited," she said to Ace as their sommelier, Phillipe, poured them a glass of white wine and served them some rich, sharp cheeses with a baguette.

"I'm glad you like it. I have to admit, I'm pretty pleased I was able to pull this off on such short notice."

The sommelier poured five different wines for them over the course of the lunch, serving different meats, cheeses, fruits and breads that paired well with them.

After he was done with his presentation, Phillipe left them alone to help themselves to what remained.

"Uh-oh," Ronnie said, giggling.

Ace wiped his lips with his napkin. "What's wrong?"

"I think I may have drank too much. I'm feeling a little tipsy."

"That's okay. We don't have to leave right away. And I'm having a car pick us up, so you don't have to worry about getting back on the Vespa."

She shook her head. "That's not my problem."

He frowned. "What is it?"

"I don't usually drink much because wine...um, puts me in the mood."

"In the mood for—oh, I get it now. If I'd known that's all I had to do, we could have just stayed in the hotel room with a bottle of wine."

"How long will it take us to get back there?" she asked, circling the rim of her glass with her finger.

"Too long," he said. "We don't have to go back right away. We've got this room all to ourselves. No one will interrupt us."

"Are you sure? What about Phillipe?"

"He's not coming back. Come here."

Ronnie got out of her seat and walked over to straddle Ace. "Phillipe forgot to tell you what goes best with Château Margaux," she whispered.

"Oh, yeah? What?" he asked, slipping his hands around her waist.

Wrapping her arms around his neck, she sucked on his earlobe, then whispered softly, "Me."

Ronnie bent over to pick up her sweater from the cellar floor, then stood.

Ace gave her a sexy smile. "Are you ready to go?"

Even though she was no longer tipsy, Ronnie still felt giddy. "Yes," she said, giggling.

Taking her hand, Ace led her over to the heavy oak door of the cellar. It took two hands to pull it open.

They stepped through the opening and saw a tour group standing in the corridor admiring a long hall of tapestries while the guide described them.

Shocked, the two of them just stood there for a second. Ronnie, remembering her loud moans, felt an embarrassed heat rushing up her neck. Some of the tourists, having spotted them, were starting to snicker. Both of them realized at once that they had been overheard.

Ace grabbed her arm and they began weaving their way around the tourists until they could reach the stairs and make their exit.

Safely in the car, they headed back to their hotel, Ronnie buried her head in Ace's broad shoulder. "I still can't believe we just did that. When I saw all of those people standing out there, I thought I was going to die of embarrassment."

Ace laughed. "Who cares if they could hear us. We'll never see those people again. Besides, now you can't claim that you're not sexually adventurous. I think we've added a couple of daring escapades to your list."

"That's true."

Her time in Paris with Ace would make for some of the best memories of her life. Too bad they had to get back to reality when the competition started up again the next day. It had been wonderful to live in the fantasy for the last day and a half.

And after the competition was over... Well, she didn't even want to think about that. She and Ace didn't even live in the same state. There were so many reasons why they couldn't make this a long-term thing.

"You've grown quiet on me. What's wrong?"

"Nothing. I was just thinking about how much I enjoyed this day together."

"The day's not over yet."

"You can't possibly top what we did this afternoon," she said, resisting the urge to giggle again.

"Why don't you let me try?"

They walked into the lobby of their hotel hand in

hand, but as soon as the desk clerk saw them, she waved them over.

"We've been trying to reach you two. Your cooking competition is starting early. It will begin in two hours. You must dress and meet in the ballroom at six o'clock," she said, handing them envelopes from the Gourmet TV Network.

Ronnie and Ace exchanged harried looks. "We'd better go track down our sous chefs," Ace said.

"See you in the ballroom."

Without time to process the change in plans, they both got on the elevator and went their separate ways.

Back in her room, Ronnie called LQ's cell phone. LQ picked up with a panicked tone. "There you are. Did you get the message from Gourmet TV?"

"Yes, that's why I'm calling. Do you know what's going on?"

"Only that we're all meeting at six to find out. Where have you been? I've been calling your cell phone for the last hour."

"I was sightseeing. I must have had my ringer off."

"Okay, I guess it doesn't matter now. You got back in time. I'll see you there."

Ronnie hung up. It was just beginning to sink in how close she'd come to missing the start of the final leg of the *All-Star Food Fight*. Of course, Ace would have missed it, too.

What were they thinking giving them notice at the last minute? They wouldn't have been able to move forward without two of their contestants, would they? It wouldn't have been good television to let Etta Foster win by default.

Even though Etta was in the lead, Ronnie had to believe that she still had a shot at winning. There was still a chance that Etta could have an off day. Of course, the kitchen mishaps never seemed to rock Etta the way they had messed up her and Ace.

Swallowing hard, a terrible feeling washed over Ronnie. What if it wasn't a coincidence? Why were all the chefs plagued by mishaps with the exception of Etta Foster?

As the thought popped into her mind, she tried to push it out. It was hard to picture the grandmotherly figure doing anything sneaky or unethical. Of course, just because it was hard to believe didn't make it impossible.

Taking out the information packet sent by Gourmet TV, Ronnie found the producer's number on the bottom and dialed it.

"Ed Sims speaking," the producer answered.

"Hi, Ed, this is Ronnie."

"Hi, Ronnie, what can I do for you?"

"I have a question about the competition."

"I can't tell you what the next challenge is until to-night."

"My question isn't about tonight, it's about the previous rounds. Was GTV purposely messing up our equipment and ingredients to make the show more interesting?"

"No, those were just the realities of a live television show. It might not be a bad idea for future *Food Fights,* though. It's been a lot of fun watching you guys cook yourselves out of a corner."

"So you're saying that the missing or broken things that every chef has had are just coincidences."

"Yeah, of course. What else would it be?"

"Sabotage."

The man laughed. "Yeah, I guess it wouldn't be the first time."

"What? Are you serious?"

"I'm not saying anything for sure. I'm just saying it's

not the first time someone has blamed a problem in the kitchen on sabotage. Before the *Food Fights* we used to do an annual pie bake-off. One year the lead contender's stove went haywire and she never stopped claiming that she'd been sabotaged."

Ronnie's heart began to pound in her chest. "I used to watch that show. Wasn't that the year Etta Foster won for the first time? Her career really took off after that win."

Ed laughed. "Hey, you're right. I'd forgotten that she'd participated."

"Don't you think it's a bit of a coincidence that she's in the lead now after all the rest of us have been complaining of so many things going wrong? She hasn't seemed to have any problems at all."

Ed sighed. "I understand what you're saying, but there isn't much I can do about it. We don't have any proof. And just between you and me, I suggest you don't even bring this up again. Etta Foster is beloved by everyone at the network. If you start making accusations against her, it's just going to look like sour grapes. They'll think you're picking on a sweet old lady."

"You won't even investigate the possibility?"

"Investigate? How? Etta doesn't know what's coming up tonight just like the rest of you. Even if you believe she's been doing something to your kitchens in the past, there's no way she can sabotage you this time. I suggest you put your energy toward doing your best in this leg, and let your food speak for itself."

Ronnie hung up the phone steaming mad. The more she thought about it, the more she was convinced that Etta was behind these kitchen mix-ups. The chefs may not know what was ahead now, but that didn't mean Etta wouldn't find some way to mess them up before the entire thing was over.

Ronnie wasn't afraid to match her skills with Etta Foster or Ace. But she did want to make sure she started with a level playing field.

Picking up the phone she dialed Ace's number. "Can you and Marcel meet me in my room in ten minutes? I think we have a problem."

Chapter 18

Ace, Marcel and LQ all compared notes in Ronnie's room. It was clear now that Etta Foster wasn't the sweet grandmotherly type everyone believed her to be.

The question now was, how did they prove it?

"Now that I've talked to Ed on the phone, it's pretty obvious that, even if they suspect Etta themselves, they're not inclined to do anything about it without a lot of proof. They can't bring themselves to accuse a sweet little old lady of such crimes."

Ace nodded, deep in thought. "Then we're going to have to get our own proof."

LQ frowned at him. "How? There's no time. Apparently the competition is going to start in just over an hour."

Marcel nodded. "We don't even know what the competition is. Maybe it will be something she can't cheat at."

Ace shrugged. "There's got to be something we can do. We may have to wait until the competition is officially underway, but I don't think she's done messing us up."

Ronnie looked at the other chefs in the room. "We're just going to have to play it by ear. She can't make her move until she hears what the challenge is. And when she does try something, we're going to be ready for her."

The four of them tossed some ideas around and then went their separate ways to get ready.

Ronnie, LQ and the other chefs entered the ballroom to find out the next challenge. Everything was set up, but there was no live audience. The chefs had been told the live audience taping would be tomorrow.

The three chefs and their sous chefs were sent to their kitchens, and the cameras started rolling.

"We're here the day before our final *All-Star Food Fight* with our top three chefs for a special pre-round challenge. Right now, our chefs are going to find out for the first time exactly what their final challenge is. Are you all ready?"

The lights flashed in the studio, and Ronnie's heartbeat sped up. She crossed her fingers that it would be a challenge she could handle.

"The final round is a cake inspired by a landmark in Paris. We have cars parked outside our studio to take our chefs to any landmark they wish to use. If two chefs pick the same landmark, the first one to arrive there gets to use it. Once at the landmark, the chefs will be asked to sketch their cake design. Then they'll be brought back to the studio tonight to start baking the cakes they'll use to build their design in the studio tomorrow."

As soon as the host finished describing the challenge, Ronnie knew which landmark she wanted. The Eiffel Tower. She was afraid it might be a popular choice, so as soon as she, LQ and the cameraman climbed into their car, she instructed the driver to go.

As they were driving, Ronnie was asked to talk to the

camera about her choice and the reason behind it. She kept seeing an image in her mind of the Eiffel Tower sparkling with lights at night, and Ace kissing her in front of it.

She couldn't say any of that to the camera, so instead she said, "I think I'm going to make a wedding cake. Before I opened my restaurant, Crave, I used to make wedding cakes for the hotel where I worked. The Eiffel Tower may seem like an obvious choice, but I'm choosing it because it's Paris's most romantic icon. That's why it would be the perfect symbol of the vow between two people to spend the rest of their lives together."

Etta Foster had climbed into her car behind Ronnie, and glancing out the window, Ronnie realized Etta's car was following hers, turn for turn. As the Eiffel Tower came into view, Etta's car began to pass them.

"Vite, vite, s'il vous plaît." She told the driver to go faster, using the limited French she'd learned from Ace.

The driver nodded and their car surged forward, edging in front of Etta's as they crossed through traffic trying to get close to the tower. As Ronnie's car pulled over, Etta's car sped away.

Ronnie looked back to LQ as she climbed out of the car. "I guess she knew it was pointless to get into a footrace with me."

Back at the set, Ace had just started pouring his cake batter into rectangular pans as the cameras came over to his kitchen. He'd had no competition traveling to the Arc de Triomphe, the large arch in the middle of Paris.

"My cake is going to be more of an architectural structure rather than just a cake. I'm going to bake oversized bricks that I can use to build the arch. I'm not a pastry chef, so I am a bit out of my element, but I think this is something I can do."

Ace tried to sound confident, but there was a lot to be done and he needed everything to go well if he was going to bring his vision to life. That meant he couldn't afford any inconvenient mishaps in this round.

Since they were baking the cakes tonight, he had a strong feeling that if anything were going to be sabotaged, it would occur overnight. They were going to have to find a way to make sure their cakes stayed untouched.

But there wasn't much time to strategize about that when he and Marcel had so much baking to do. They also mixed up a huge batch of icing to use on the crumb coating that would go beneath the fondant.

The Arc de Triomphe was a simple structure compared to Ronnie's Eiffel Tower and Etta Foster's Cathédrale Notre Dame, but Ace felt it was something he could do cleanly in the allotted time. If he was able to execute the cake well, maybe he could win this.

It was nearing midnight when all the chefs had finished baking their cakes and finally left the ballroom. Ronnie waited for Ace near the elevators and stepped inside with him.

"So, do you have a plan?"

Ace nodded. "Yes, I do. I had Marcel text Garett while we were baking. In a little while he's going to place video cameras in each of our kitchens so we'll be able to see if the cakes we baked are contaminated."

"When he recovers the cameras tomorrow, won't that be too late?"

"No, he'll be able to monitor the cameras on a live feed from his laptop. That way we don't have to lose sleep before the final leg of the competition. He'll call if he sees something shady."

Ronnie realized that with the rest of this sting operation

in Ace's hands, she was going to have to trust both him
and Garett. It was an uncomfortable feeling, but she didn't
have a lot of choices anymore.

"Okay, call me if anything turns up," she told him as
Ace got off on his floor.

Around two thirty in the morning, Ronnie's telephone
rang. Startled into full wakefulness, she grabbed the phone.
"Yes?"

"We have some action in the kitchens," Ace said.
"Someone came in and started tampering with your cakes
and my royal icing. Etta's products weren't touched."

"Who was it?"

"We're not sure."

"I'll be right there." She started to climb out of bed.

"You don't have to come down now."

"But my cakes. I have to bake new ones."

"No, you don't. Garett is taking care of everything right
now."

Ronnie blinked, still sleepy. "He's going to bake more
cake for me?"

"No. It seems you and Etta are both doing round layer
cakes. Her cakes are the same as yours. So he's switching
your tampered cakes with her fresh ones and doing the
same with her royal icing and mine."

Ronnie frowned. "Is that the right thing to do? Maybe
we should just report the whole thing and let the judges
decide how to handle it."

"We can do that. But I'm in favor of giving Etta Foster
a little taste of her own medicine. When she walks into her
kitchen tomorrow, she'll find the contaminated products
she tried to make us use. Let's see if she's the star chef she
thinks she is."

"I don't know."

"Look. You and I were able to make it through this competition despite working against the odds. If she's going to beat us fair and square, that's fine, but if she really deserves to win, she can triumph over the same odds we did."

"You've got a point there. But are you sure Garett can handle all of this by himself?"

Ronnie didn't like where her mind was going, but the thoughts came anyway. What if Garett only fixed Ace's problem and left her at a disadvantage with Etta. Then Garett's client, and his only real concern, Ace, would be a sure thing for the win.

"I know you must be worried, Ronnie. But I promise, neither he or I would screw you over just to win. I've never worked that way, and despite his obvious flaws, Garett doesn't either. I'll make sure of it."

"Okay," Ronnie replied, still not completely comfortable with the fact that everything was in Garett's hands now.

"Besides, if everything isn't just how it should be in your kitchen tomorrow, you can cry foul, and I'll back you up," Ace added. "We'll take our chances with the judges and let them sort it out. But I hope you can trust me."

"It's easier for me to trust you than it is for me to trust Garett."

"I know we don't have the best track record, but I wouldn't want to win if I had to do so at your expense. We've always had a *friendly* rivalry between us. I wouldn't stoop to dirty tricks now. I'm not afraid to lose to you, Ronnie. If you make the best cake tomorrow, I'll congratulate you. The fact that I plan to win doesn't take away from that fact."

Ronnie smiled. Ace hadn't ever shied away from a challenge in his life. Win or lose, he always fought hard.

And even though he could talk a lot of trash, he'd never been a sore loser.

She was going to have to trust him, because not doing so could cost her sleep, and she needed to put her best foot forward in the morning.

"I believe you, Ace. See you in the morning. You're going to need a good night's rest to handle the butt-whooping I'm going to hand you tomorrow."

The morning of the competition was a blur of activity for Ronnie. The first thing she and LQ did was inspect their prebaked cakes. They were light, fluffy and perfect. If Ronnie hadn't known better, she would have thought they were the cakes she'd baked herself.

There was some commotion in Etta's kitchen initially. She'd never seen a white-haired woman swear up such a blue streak.

"They've been switched. Someone switched my cakes. Look at them. They're falling apart."

Ronnie and LQ continued to work, and when the cameras arrived at her kitchen for her reaction to the accusations Etta was making, she played innocent.

"It seems Etta didn't bake a dense enough cake and now they're falling apart. I wish her luck. It's going to eat up a lot of her time if she has to start baking new cakes."

As the day went on, Ronnie heard that the judges had allowed Etta's sous chef, her grandson Adrian, to purchase new cakes at the market for her to use in the competition.

Beyond that, Ronnie didn't have time to worry about what was going on in the other kitchens. She wanted her Eiffel Tower wedding cake to be a showstopper.

At that moment, LQ was busy hand-pouring chocolate into the lattice shape of the top spire of the tower. Once the four sides of the candy pieces dried in the cooler, they would be constructed on top of the cake as the topper.

Ronnie planned to paint the rest of the towers by hand on the four round tiers below. The hand-painting would be the most time consuming portion of the cake, but if she could do clean work, she knew the judges would appreciate the detail. Especially Kari Voegler, who was a stickler for craftsmanship.

Now that all of her cake tiers were covered in smooth white fondant, she had a perfect blank canvas to showcase her artistry. Ronnie thought she had a genuine advantage in this leg of the competition, and she was excited to finally show what she could do under fair circumstances.

Ace had finished constructing and carving the shape of his arch for the Arc de Triomphe, and now that he'd covered it in fondant it was time to start carving the sculptures that were all around the archway.

If Ace had had more time, he would have special-ordered molds to fill with white chocolate to give a more authentic feel to his cake. Unfortunately, he didn't have that opportunity, so he was going to have to get creative.

He didn't have dainty little fingers to make the sculptures freehand out of chocolate, so he had to use modeling chocolate to form the general shape of the relief sculpture and then paint on the details. The result was that some of the elements would appear flat instead of raised. But it was the best he could do in the time he had left.

When the judges and the cameraman came around to his station, he had some tough questions to answer.

Kari Voegler, one of the *Food Fight*'s toughest judges, asked him, "In the other kitchens we have the Cathédrale Notre Dame and the Eiffel Tower. Do you think you've chosen a landmark that's complex enough?"

Ace smiled at Kari, but continued to work. "I'm not a pastry chef, so I chose something I thought I could do cleanly and completely in the allotted time. Hopefully, when you see my finished product, you'll like what I've done."

It didn't hurt to hope someone else in the competition messed up. There had been many cake challenges for the *Food Fight* where contestants didn't complete their cakes, or only vaguely represented the sketch they'd started with.

Ace and Marcel were working hard, so Ace had to hope *that,* along with the scores from his previous rounds, would be enough to put him over the edge.

From the quick look he'd given Ronnie's kitchen on his right, he could see that she was bringing her A game. He'd heard the interview she'd given about her chocolate spire at the top of the Eiffel Tower. With the delicate hand-painting she was doing on the cake, she was definitely the one to beat.

He didn't want to underestimate Etta Foster, but from the looks of her cake, she was grossly behind schedule. She had shed her grandmotherly image and was barking snide orders to her grandson. There were so many curse words flying out of her mouth, the producers had to warn her more than once.

She'd constantly complained about her cakes and her royal icing, and at this late stage in the competition, her cake barely resembled the Cathédrale Notre Dame.

But considering the fact that she'd won the first two rounds of the competition, it was possible that she'd take the top prize simply for completing her cake.

If that happened, he was worried that Ronnie may regret her decision to go along with his plan to let Etta drink her own medicine instead of trying to get her disqualified for cheating. But it was too late to turn back now.

There were only two hours left before they'd have their answer. Ace and Marcel just had to keep working.

Ronnie heard the audience counting down the clock just as she and LQ were trying to attach the chocolate spire to her Eiffel Tower cake. If they dropped it now, there was no time to make repairs.

The last leg of the spire was glued to the cake with royal icing and Ronnie instructed LQ to let go. They both stood back from the cake just as the buzzer sounded.

With a lump of pride in her throat, Ronnie surveyed her work. She'd carved the legs of the tower out of her round cake tiers, so that with all the layers stacked together, the Eiffel Tower appeared to be standing out from a round wedding cake. She'd meticulously piped the latticework of the tower's rails in chocolate so that it blended with the chocolate spire at the top. She'd decorated the rest of the wedding cake with traditional white icing decorations so that the tower was the main focus of the cake.

She'd never been more pleased with her work. She and LQ gave each other a high five. Now if she and LQ could just move the cake from their kitchen to the display table, Ronnie would be able to rest easy with the outcome of this competition, whatever it turned out to be.

It was a safe bet that Etta Foster wouldn't win this round. Her unfinished cake was being moved to the table as Ronnie awaited her own turn. Only half the elements in Etta's cake had made it onto her finished product. There were gaps and drooping frosting on the cake.

Ronnie watched as Etta and her grandson began to move their cake to the table. Etta was wearing a scowl that had been on her face since the start of this round. She was still muttering under her breath as they approached the table.

Adrian lifted his edge of the cake to move it over to the display table, but Etta seemed to give up at that point. A corner slipped out of her hand, and the cake dropped to the floor.

There was a startled gasp in the audience, and the announcer continued. "Etta Foster's entry is now just a pile of frosting on the floor. It's hard not to wonder if the perfectionist in Etta just wouldn't allow her to show an unfinished cake. Now we move to Ace Brown's kitchen where he'll be moving his Arc de Triomphe cake to the table."

With two strong men in that kitchen, no one was surprised when Ace and Marcel easily moved their showpiece to the table.

Now the final round would definitely go to either Ace or Ronnie. All she had to do was move her cake without incident, and she'd be in the running to win one hundred thousand dollars.

She and LQ each took two corners of the cake board and began to slide it off the counter. As soon as they began moving, her spire began to sway.

As if their minds were connected telepathically, both she and LQ froze. "Slowly, LQ. Very slowly. Let's move."

It was a delicate balancing act, but they took baby step after baby step toward the cake table. After what seemed like an eternity, Ronnie and LQ gingerly placed their cake on the table.

When the board was in place, Ronnie clutched her chest in relief and the audience exploded with applause.

Ronnie was riding a wave of elation as she and LQ entered the green room. It had been a long day, and after three very tough rounds, this competition was finally about to be over.

The last to place her cake, Ronnie was also the last to enter the green room. As she came in, she was surprised to find Etta Foster yelling at Ace.

Ace was sitting calmly as Etta ranted from across the room about her cake and icing being switched.

Ronnie glared at the woman. "Etta, you may as well admit that you cheated. Everyone in this room knows that you did. There are no cameras in here. Just admit it."

Etta glared back at her in surprise.

"It's true," Ace added. "Besides, how could you be so certain that your cake and icing had been switched, if you weren't expecting our kitchens to have the contaminated products? We saw Adrian on camera, Etta. If you don't want to admit the truth here in private, maybe you'd like to explain to the judges why Adrian was in our kitchens messing with our supplies last night."

Etta waved him off. "All right, all right. Why do you need me to say it out loud? You already know the truth."

Ronnie shook her head, confused. "I'd just like to know why a woman with your reputation in this industry would have to stoop to such low tactics. You're world famous and practically the face of GTV. Why didn't you go up against us fairly?"

She snorted. "The face of GTV? Maybe I used to be. But when it was time to renew my show's contract last month, the network told me they were going in a new direction. They want to pull in a younger demographic. Apparently I'm no longer relevant."

Ace tsked. "I'm sorry to hear that, Etta. But how does cheating to win help you stay relevant?"

"I can't afford to lose when they've already cancelled my show. I have to show that I *can* compete with you hotshot young chefs. I was planning to leverage this win into a pitch for a new show where I travel the country challenging young chefs to a cook-off."

Ronnie frowned. "Etta, if you feel you had to cheat in this competition, how were you planning to manage in your future challenges? Were you going to try to cheat your way through those, too? You're a talented chef. I'm sure you could have won without the underhanded tactics."

The older woman scowled. "We'll never know now. I guess it's time for me to retire anyway. All this travel has made me realize that I'd rather be at home."

Before they could discuss the matter further, the chefs were being called back out for the announcement of the winner.

Giving LQ a big hug, Ronnie left her with the other sous chefs backstage and lined up next to Ace and Etta for the announcement.

The host began to recap their scores from the previous rounds, and discussed the judges' comments on their cake presentations that day. Ronnie had received the highest praise of the day, but her scores going into this round were slightly below Ace's. With Etta receiving no points for this round, it was mathematically impossible for her to win.

Swallowing hard, Ronnie's mouth went dry as she waited for the verdict.

"The winner of Gourmet TV's *All-Star Food Fight...*" The announcer paused for effect.

Ace took Ronnie's hand and squeezed. They exchanged tense looks, but still managed to share a smile.

"With a final-round score just five points above the other chef, the winner of one hundred thousand dollars is Veronica Howard."

Chapter 19

Her win didn't start to sink in until LQ came out and a gold medal was placed over Ronnie's and LQ's heads, and they were presented with a giant check in the amount of one hundred thousand dollars.

She gave LQ a tight squeeze, and then she felt someone's hand on her back. It was Ace.

"As soon as I saw that amazing cake you made, I knew you'd win. Congratulations. You deserve this," he said, pulling her into a gentle hug.

She hugged Ace back, not letting herself savor it the way she'd like to because the cameras were still rolling. "Thanks, Ace. You made me work for it."

Cara and her family came out of the audience to share hugs and kisses with her and LQ. "I knew you could do it! See, the next time I make a prediction, you're going to have to listen to me."

A.J., Cara's husband, kissed her on the cheek. "Now you

can come back home and the kids can have their favorite babysitter back."

At A.J.'s words, Ronnie realized that the fantasy was over. It hadn't been all blue skies and roses, but it had been the best adventure of her life. But now it was over. And that meant it was time to face the realities of her relationship with Ace.

Ronnie handed Cara's baby girl back to her. In a few minutes she and LQ were due for follow-up interviews in the press room. She wanted to touch up her hair and makeup.

As she turned away from her friends, Ronnie was pulled into a hug. "Congratulations, Ronnie."

"Andre. What the—" She pulled away, backing out of his arms.

"I always knew you were a winner. How about dinner to celebrate your big win? On you, of course. You're the one with a hundred thousand dollars," he said, laughing as though he'd just told the funniest joke in the world.

Ronnie scoffed. "You're kidding me, right? You and I aren't friends. Why would I go to dinner with you?"

He leaned in and deepened his voice in the way that used to make her melt. "We *could* be friends again."

Now that tone just made her skin crawl. "No, thanks. Tonight I have my choice of dinner dates, and you're not on the list."

His eyes became cold, and Ronnie braced herself. Finally, she recognized what a cruel person Andre had always been. Whatever he had to stay, she could handle.

"Your choice, huh? I suppose your referring to the Sexy Chef himself. Are you two really a thing? I thought that was just some publicity stunt."

"Whatever we are to each other, it's certainly none of your business."

"Sure, now that you're skinny you can get a guy like that. But you're a chef and you like to eat. Let's be real. You probably won't always be that slim. Where will he be when you gain all the weight back?"

She swallowed hard. "I'm not going to—"

"Maybe you will, maybe you won't. But maybe you should be nicer to me. I'm the only one who wanted you when you were fat."

Feeling her face flash hot with anger, Ronnie opened her mouth, but before she could get any words out, Cara stepped to her side.

"What are you doing here, Andre? Isn't there a rock you should be crawling under?"

Then an arm slid around her waist. It was Ace's. He kissed her on the cheek. And when she turned to look up at him, he kissed her full on the mouth. "Are you ready to go out and celebrate your win? We can do it up big, inviting one and all, or we can make it more of an intimate celebration, courtesy of me, the Sexy Chef," he said with a grin.

Andre rolled his eyes and walked away.

Cara released a big sigh of relief. "Thank God that loser slithered away. I almost died when I saw him over here talking to you. What did he say?"

Ronnie waved him off. "Nothing important. You know Andre, he's full of shitake. Mushrooms, I mean."

"I always hated that guy," Ace said to Ronnie. "Your taste in men has improved a great deal since him."

They all shared a laugh, but inside Ronnie felt a niggling of fear.

She knew that Andre's words had been intended to make her feel insecure. It had been an old tactic he'd relied on in the past to keep her from leaving him. Even though she saw through him now, it didn't keep his words from hurting her.

People who lost a lot of weight often fluctuated or even gained it all back. She couldn't promise that she'd never be fat again. Would Ace still want her if she did gain it all back?

Ace sat in the hotel bar with Marcel and Garett. They'd insisted on buying him a drink, just in case he felt like drowning his sorrows.

"Honestly, guys, I don't feel that badly about the loss. Sure, I would have loved that prize money, but I don't think I stood a chance in the last round. I'm not much of a pastry chef. That area is where Ronnie has always been strong. You saw that cake she made. Mine was okay, but hers was spectacular."

Garett curled his upper lip. "You're just saying that because you *love* her," he said in a mocking tone. "I miss the days when you were a hunter and no one woman was enough for you."

Marcel clapped Ace on the back. "Sorry, buddy, but Ace has finally come over to my side. Team monogamy. One of these days you're going to have to join us."

Garett crossed his arms. "Never. It's not going to happen. All the qualities I need to keep me interested don't exist in one woman. I'm doing them a favor by spreading my love around."

Ace shrugged. "Just make sure whatever you're spreading isn't contagious."

Garett downed the last of his drink and stood up. "All right, you guys don't appreciate me, but I think I see a sexy Parisian girl in the lobby who might."

Marcel stood up next. "Well, brother, we can't win them all. Tomorrow morning Simone and I are getting on a train for Rome, where we're going to gorge ourselves with pasta for three days. See you back in the Big Apple."

They exchanged a handshake and then Ace was alone. Not hearing his name called to win the big check had stung a bit, but he knew just how much that win meant to Ronnie. The look on her face had been worth a hundred thousand dollars.

Maybe now that the competition was finally behind them, they could focus on their relationship. They'd made fantastic memories in Las Vegas, Kauai and now Paris, but he was anxious to see how they would do once they were back home.

They were from two different cities, but Manhattan was only a four-hour drive and a sixty-minute flight from Washington, D.C. That was a workable distance until they could figure out something more permanent.

He didn't want to pressure her right away. Ronnie knew how he felt about her. That was going to have to be enough for him until she grew confident in her own feelings.

Ace headed back to his room, looking forward to calling Ronnie when he got there. He hoped she'd want to stay in tonight. While he loved a good party, after all the stress of the last couple of weeks, a more private party was starting to look good to him.

As he got off the elevator, he saw Ronnie slipping something under his door.

"Hey, Ronnie. What are you doing? Slipping me a love note?" he asked with a smile.

She looked up, startled and somber, and instantly Ace's heart began to sink. Her expression told him that it definitely wasn't a love note.

"Oh! I—I tried to call your room, but you weren't in, so I thought I'd leave a note."

Ace steeled himself. "I'm here now. You can tell me what's on your mind face-to-face."

Chewing her lower lip, she stepped back for him to unlock his door, then followed him inside.

Ace took a seat, realizing he probably wasn't going to like whatever she was planning to say. "Go ahead. What's in the note?"

Ronnie picked it up from the floor. "Do you just want to read it?"

He shook his head. "No, I'm not going to make it easy for you. I want to hear you say the words."

Her brow wrinkled. "What words?"

"That you're dumping me. Right? Isn't that the gist of the note?"

"I'm not *dumping* you," she started, and Ace felt a twinge of hope. "I'm not certain we were ever anything officially anyway."

"Really? It has to be official? How much more official does it get than my telling you that I love you, anyway?"

Ronnie covered her face. "I'm just afraid we're making a big mess of this. The competition is over. We have to go back to our real lives now. I live in D.C. You live in New York. There are so many reasons why we shouldn't drag this out."

"Drag it out? I thought we cared about each other. You already know that I'm in love with you." Watching her face, he saw the skepticism pass over it. "Oh, I see what the problem is. You don't believe that I love you. Listen. I'm thirty-two years old. Don't you think I know my own mind by now?"

"It's not that I don't think you know your own mind. I'm just not sure you want *me*. Sure, I'm thin now. But I wasn't always this way, and I may not always be thin. Will you still love me if I get bigger again?"

"Of course."

She shook her head. "You answered that too quickly. You didn't even take the time to think about it."

"Why do I have to think about it? I love you. It's not a passing fancy. I've known you for years. Do you really think I wasn't attracted to you when you were heavier?"

"No, I don't think you were."

"Ronnie, the last time I saw you before this competition, you were in a relationship. I would have tried to date you, but you were never available. It wasn't your weight that stood in our way."

"Look, thanks for trying to make me feel better, but that's not really what this is about. I've got to stop making the same mistakes over and over."

"You can't possibly be comparing my relationship with you to your relationship with Andre. I know I've always tried to treat you well. Don't you trust me?"

She sighed. "I don't know if I trust *me*. I just can't tell if I've finished all the work I need to do on myself. I'm not sure if I'm ready to be in a relationship. I'm still confusing the wrong things with love."

"So you *do* love me? Ronnie, if you love me, I'm not going to just sit here and let you walk out of my life."

She froze for a second.

"I never said I loved you."

"Are you saying that you don't love me?" Ace asked, watching her carefully.

"Yes, that's what I'm saying."

He should have been hurt, but in that instant, he knew that she was lying. But if she wasn't ready to admit that, then he'd just have to wait. If their love was as real as he felt it was, he knew she'd come back to him.

He'd enter every *Food Fight* that came up to keep her in his life if he had to. But for now, there was nothing more to say. There was only one thing to do. Let her go.

Chapter 20

Ronnie got on the plane to fly home the next day. This time she didn't have time to focus on her fear of flying—she was too entrenched in her own heartache.

Saying good-bye to Ace hurt more than anything she'd ever experienced before. But like the burn of a vigorous workout, Ronnie kept telling herself that the pain was good for her.

Didn't this almost physical pain in her chest where her heart was supposed to be mean that she was growing? In the past, she'd stayed with men in order to avoid this terrible feeling. The fact that she was willing to suffer like this had to mean that she'd finally started doing what was best for her instead of what felt good.

In a few days this pain would fade, she told herself.

In the meantime, she had the glow from a big win to bask in and a huge check burning a hole in her bank account. She could start planning to open another restaurant now. All she had to do was choose a location and a concept.

But as Ronnie returned home and fit herself back into her old routine, she couldn't focus on her dream. It was all she'd wanted when she'd started out in the *All-Star Food Fight,* and now that she'd won the biggest prize of the competition, all she could think about was how lonely she was.

"Come sit down with me for a minute," LQ said, pulling her into a booth before Crave opened for dinner one evening.

Ronnie took in a deep breath. All she could hope was that LQ hadn't found another job. She didn't know what she would do without her.

"What's on your mind?"

"The real question of the day is what's on your mind. You won the *Food Fight,* but you haven't been the same since. We were all prepared to handle you if the fame went to your head, but what do we do now that you've been in a funk for the last week?"

Ronnie gasped. She thought she'd been doing a good job of hiding her feelings. "Has everyone noticed?"

"Of course. It's all anyone talks about when you leave the room. Is it Ace? I thought you were the one who dumped him. Are you having second thoughts?"

She shrugged, trying to make it seem like it wasn't a big deal. "It's natural for it to hurt a bit at first. I'll be fine."

LQ made a face at her. "What are you talking about? You dumped him. Why did you do that if you want to be with him?"

"Because it can't last. We're from different cities. We have different priorities. It just won't work."

"Look, I know I was hard on him at first," LQ said. "But he's kind of proven to be a deeper guy than we all thought. Aren't you supposed to wait for it to *stop* working to decide that it's not going to work?"

"That's been my problem in the past. I wait too long to see that something doesn't have a future. I'm trying to learn from those mistakes."

"You poor mixed-up thing. You've been screwed over so many times you don't know a good man when you find one."

"I know Ace is a good man. But that doesn't mean he's a good man for me. I don't know if I'm really his type. There may come a time, down the road, when he might find me disappointing."

"What on earth are you talking about?"

"Some men love women who are thin. He never showed much interest in me when I was heavy. Who knows what would happen if I gain the weight back one day. I don't plan on it, but it could happen. I don't want that constantly hanging over my head."

"Ronnie, the man told you he's in love with you. Do you honestly think that can be undone by a couple of pounds? Don't you think he's well past that with you?"

"I don't know."

"Can you tell me one thing?"

"What?"

"Do you love him?"

Ronnie swallowed hard. She'd gone out of her way not to say the words out loud. If she said them, she'd have to deal with them.

"I don't know."

"Don't play coy with me, Ronnie. What's the truth?"

Taking a deep breath, she said. "Yes. I love him."

"Then you have to take a chance."

"Why don't you let me fix you up with someone," Garett whispered in Ace's ear as he filled his table with another stack of cookbooks. Ace was at a major Manhattan bookstore chain to sign that day.

"My PDA is full of potential dates for you. All you have to do is tell me what you like. Models, business professionals, a girl-next-door type…just name your poison," his friend continued.

Ace shook his head, then signed his cookbook for an elderly woman who claimed she'd prepared every recipe in his last book. As the woman walked away, Ace craned his neck to glare at Garett.

"I've already told you that I don't want to date anyone in your contact list."

"You don't have to worry. They aren't all women I've dated. Some of them I just got numbers from but never called."

Ace rolled his eyes, then put a big smile on his face for a pair of housewives that were giggling as they approached him. Ace signed their books and joked with them a bit, then turned back to Garett.

"I'm not interested. Let's just leave it at that."

"You've got to get back on the horse. It'll help you forget about Veronica."

Ace rubbed his temples. "I don't want to forget about Ronnie."

"It's over, man. It's time to move on."

"I'm not so convinced about that. But you don't have to concern yourself with my love life one way or the other. Besides, it works better when you stay out of it."

"You say that now, but you're known as the Sexy Chef. That means you have a reputation to live up to."

"You're the only one who thinks so. I don't think my career would suffer at all if I were to get married or have a couple of kids."

Garett pretended that Ace had just stabbed him in the

heart. "Don't do it. It's bad enough that you've been on this monogamy kick lately. Our friendship will die a quick death if you go ahead and get married."

Ace shrugged. "Your day will come. Eventually one of these girls you date is going to get you on the hook. Then there won't be any turning back."

"Stop cursing me. Look how miserable you are. You'd wish that on me?"

"I may be miserable now. But I honestly believe it's temporary. Ronnie just needs a little time to realize that she's ready. I think she's going to come back to me."

Garett paused. "What makes you so sure? What do you know that you're not telling me?"

"That's going to have to remain my secret for now. Maybe when she comes back to me, I'll let you know."

Ronnie was still thinking about LQ's words when she went to the gym the next morning. She'd never been more confused in her life.

Of course she had feelings for Ace. But she'd also had feelings for all the other jerks she'd dated in the past. And staying with them until they ruined her life had been her mistake.

She'd spent so much time distrusting men, it was hard to know when it was the right time to take a chance. Would Ace be like all the rest and break her heart one day?

"You worked out like a madwoman today," Cara said, when they sat down together at the Big Squeeze. "What was motivating all that intense energy?"

Ronnie didn't feel like talking about it so she tepidly said, "My zeal for good health?"

Cara scoffed. "You know I'm not going to let you get away with that. Try again."

Ronnie shrugged.

"It's Ace, isn't it?" her friend asked. "You've been a complete mess ever since you came back from Paris. Maybe you should call him. Talk things out."

"There's nothing to talk about."

"Really? You can talk about why the two of you broke up. Didn't he say or do something to upset you?"

Up until now, Ronnie had been avoiding this topic with Cara. She'd been front and center to all of Ronnie's disastrous relationships in the past. All she'd wanted Cara to see this time was how strong she was being, resisting the urge to go back to a dead-end relationship.

"No, actually he didn't."

Cara's brow furrowed. "Then why did you break up with him? He seemed perfect for you."

Ronnie reared back. "Perfect for me? Weren't you the one warning me off him when I was in Hawaii?"

"That was before we found out what was really going on. You two have always been friends, and now the two of you have fallen in love. Sometimes there's no better way to find your soulmate."

"Now you think he's my soulmate?"

"He could be. Why not?"

"Because there's too much standing between us. There are a lot of obstacles. Maybe we never should have let things leave the neighborhood of friendship in the first place."

"Ronnie, is that how you really feel?"

"The only thing I know is that it wouldn't hurt to be apart from him now if we'd never gotten started in the first place."

"All relationships are a risk. Look, I know better than anyone why you'd be afraid to start over. But just because you've been hurt doesn't mean you can't find true love. Look at A.J. and me. I was so afraid that all men would be like the ones in my life that did me wrong, that I almost ruined things between us. I really made it hard for him. But he was the right guy so he stuck it out. Maybe Ace is the right guy."

Ronnie shook her head. "I'm so confused. I don't know what the right thing to do is. There are a few things that are still bothering me."

"What things?"

"Maybe they're my own baggage or maybe they're real concerns—I don't know how to find out."

"If you care enough about him, you'll go ahead and take the leap."

Ronnie frowned at Cara. "I'm the queen of taking the leap. That's been my problem, remember? I've always given my boyfriends second and third chances to show me that they're the one. That's why I don't know what to do. If I go crawling after Ace, how is that different from all the times when I was a fool for love?"

"The difference is that Ace hasn't broken your heart. You're punishing him for what all the men in your life have done to you in the past. Maybe you're the one breaking his heart."

Ronnie's body went still. Was it possible that she'd broken his heart? He was the one who had told her he loved her, and she had never really said it in return. Was she the villain here?

What if she did try to contact Ace and he didn't want to speak to her? What if she'd hurt him so badly that he'd have nothing to do with her?

For the first time, Ronnie realized that there were more feelings involved in this relationship than just her own. She'd already hurt Ace. She couldn't risk hurting him again when she didn't even know what she really wanted.

Chapter 21

As Ronnie started work the next night, she felt as though she were under a microscope. Was everyone she knew monitoring her moods?

With that in mind, she went out of her way to put on a happy face. But inside she'd never been more confused. Part of her wondered if talking to Ace would help her sort out her feelings. But they weren't going to casually run into each other. They lived four hours apart in separate states. She'd have to make a very deliberate and long trip if she decided she wanted to talk to him again. Talking on the telephone wasn't likely to help her answer any questions for herself.

Dinner service at Crave was going even better than usual, so Ronnie felt good that at least one area of her life was starting to come together. Since the airing of her *Food Fight* win, there had been several write-ups on her restaurant in local papers.

Just as she was in the midst of reverie, her host, Callie, came to the back and whispered to Ronnie. "There's a special diner who's asked to give her compliments to the chef."

Immediately, Ronnie's nerves kicked in. "Special diner? Who is it?"

"Sharon Vincent. She's a writer for *Taste* magazine."

Wiping her hands on her kitchen towel, Ronnie followed Callie into the dining room.

"Ms. Vincent, this is our executive chef and the owner of Crave, Veronica Howard."

Ronnie shook hands with the woman. "Welcome to Crave. I hope you enjoyed your dinner."

Sharon Vincent was a lovely brown-skinned woman with a round face and a slightly plump figure. She was dressed in expensive designer clothes "It's an honor to meet you, Chef Howard. Everything I tried was mouthwatering and delicious, but hands down the best thing I've ever put in my mouth was your chocolate kiss dessert. I wish I didn't live so far away because I'd be back every night for that one."

"Thank you so much. That dessert is our signature dish. I'm so glad you liked it. Where are you from, Ms. Vincent?"

"Please, call me Sharon. I'm from New York City. Any chance you'll be opening a restaurant in the Big Apple?"

Ace flashed in Ronnie's mind. That's where he lived. If she opened a restaurant there, she'd have an excuse to see him all the time. Pushing those crazy thoughts aside, she smiled at Sharon.

"I do plan to open up another restaurant, but I haven't decided on a location yet."

"Oh! I thought for sure you'd come to New York to be close to your boyfriend."

Ronnie blanched. "My boyfriend?"

"Ace Brown, the Sexy Chef. I followed your romance in the tabloids. You'll never find a better guy. I shouldn't have let him get away."

"Get away? Did you date him?"

"You don't have to worry. It's been over for a long time. I'm a married woman now. But, yes, we dated awhile back before he left for his world tour. He left a man who didn't want to settle down and came back looking for a commitment. Of course, I'd moved on by then. But we're still friends. I think you two make a wonderful couple."

Ronnie's mind reeled as she took in Sharon's words. It was highly unlikely that Sharon had put on the extra pounds she carried in the time that she and Ace had been apart. That meant that Ace had dated a woman who was a bit overweight much the same way she had been.

Clearly, Sharon misread Ronnie's stunned expression for jealousy, because the woman was bending over backwards to reassure her. "Seriously, it never would have worked out with Ace and me. The only thing he and I really had in common was a love of food."

"Um, Ace and I aren't together right now."

Sharon's face fell. "That's a shame. I thought I saw a real spark between you when you were on camera together. It didn't work out? Girl, what am I thinking trying to mind your business like this. Don't mind me."

"Actually, we may get back together. I'm hoping we do."

"That's right. Go get your man. You don't want to let that one get away. He's built to last, you know what I mean?"

Ronnie spent some more time speaking with Sharon and walked away from her table that night with more than just the promise of some good publicity for her restaurant. She now had hope for her future with Ace.

She felt like a fool as it dawned on her that she'd almost let her ex-boyfriend ruin her life once again. He'd gotten in her head and found just the right button to push to amplify her insecurities with Ace.

Now she had to find out if there was any chance that he'd still want her. It was possible that she'd already ruined things between them. Or worse yet, maybe he'd already moved on to someone else.

Heading back into the kitchen, Ronnie made a decision. She couldn't afford to waste any more time. Tomorrow was her day off. She had to go see Ace.

Sunday morning Ace had trouble getting out of bed. For the past couple of weeks he'd been putting on a brave face, but today, his false bravado was starting to wear thin.

Maybe he'd been wrong and Ronnie really didn't love him. Perhaps he shouldn't have made it so easy for her to walk away. He'd been able to do it because he'd been so confident that she'd come to her senses. But now he was starting to have doubts.

Dragging himself to the shower, he tried to plan his day. His best friends would be coming over later for dinner, but if he kept feeling the way he did now, he was tempted to cancel. There wasn't anything he liked better than making good food for the people he cared most about. But without Ronnie among those people, he wasn't really in the mood to do it.

Maybe it was time to stop waiting for her to come around and talk to her. Should he call? He wouldn't be able to see her face over the phone. He needed to look in her eyes as well as hear her voice.

Perhaps the best thing to do was jump in the car and just show up on her doorstep. He didn't care if it made him look needy. At this point that's exactly how he was feeling.

He didn't know if he could move on without trying to get through to her one more time.

With a new plan formulating in his brain, adrenaline began to pump through him. Suddenly highly motivated, he started getting dressed. He'd have to cancel his plans with his friends before he left, but at least this way he'd be doing more than sitting home waiting.

Ace had just finished tying his sneaker laces when his doorbell rang. He wasn't expecting anyone, so he looked through the peephole of his door.

Ronnie was standing on the other side, looking decidedly nervous.

He felt as though his knees might give out, and sweat immediately began to bead on his upper lip as his heart rate picked up. Excited, he jerked open the door.

"Ronnie! What are you doing here?"

"Is this a bad time? If it's a bad time I can—"

"What? Come back later? Ronnie, you live four hours away. It's the perfect time. Come in."

She looked amazing, wearing a pair of sexy dark jeans and a turquoise camisole top. Her hair was pretty and framed her face. All Ace wanted to do was pull her into his arms and give her a big kiss.

But he had to hear what she'd come to say first. He believed it was good news. She wouldn't drive four hours to dump him a second time. But she had to say the words.

Ronnie walked into his apartment and took a seat on the sofa. He offered her a drink or a snack, but she was clearly too nervous for any of that.

"I'm sorry to barge in on you like this, but I think I owe you an apology."

He frowned. "For what?"

"I didn't give you a fair chance. I let a lot of things that didn't have anything to do with you, but had everything to do with my own baggage, stand between us. Now I'm just hoping this isn't too little, too late."

"I'm listening," Ace said.

"The first thing I want to tell you is that I *do* love you. I was lying in Paris when I said I didn't."

Ace laughed and Ronnie looked hurt.

"I'm sorry. I'm not laughing at you. I'm laughing because I knew you were lying."

"You knew? Then why didn't you say anything?"

"Because you clearly needed time to work things out for yourself. I was hoping that when you were ready you'd come to me."

"Then I'm not too late? You haven't found somebody else?"

"Somebody else? How could I find somebody else when all I can think about is you? I still love you."

"Then there's hope for us. You want to try to make this work between us?"

"Yes, absolutely."

Ronnie jumped up and threw her arms around Ace's neck. "I'm so glad to hear you say that. I could barely sleep last night wondering if I'd permanently jinxed things with us."

Ace answered by doing the thing he'd wanted to do the second she'd stepped into his apartment. He lowered his mouth to hers, giving her a long, deep kiss.

Suddenly Ronnie pulled her mouth away from his. "Wait a minute."

"What's wrong?" he asked, trying to kiss her again.

"How did you know I was lying in Paris?"

"Remember when you told me you couldn't lie to Cara because you have a tell?"

"Yes?"

"Well, I figured out what that tell is."

Her eyes widened. "What is it?"

"When you try to lie you twist the earring in your left ear."

"Really? Ha! Cara would never tell me what it was."

Ronnie laughed and he laughed along with her.

"So, you were confident that I'd come running back to you, huh?"

"I was at first. But to be honest with you, that confidence was fading fast. In fact, I was just about to get into my car and drive to D.C. to see you. If you'd shown up an hour later, I would have been there and you would have been here."

Ronnie shook her head. "Then I got here just in the nick of time."

Ace pulled her back into his arms.

"I just have one question for you," Ronnie asked, tentatively.

"You can ask me anything," Ace said, concerned.

"What do you think about opening a restaurant together here in New York?"

Ace smiled wide and leaned in to answer her question with a kiss.

* * * * *

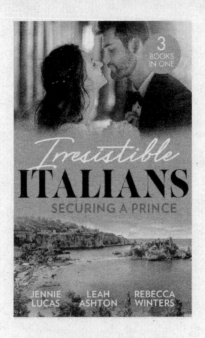

OUT NOW!

Available at
millsandboon.co.uk

MILLS & BOON

MILLS & BOON
MODERN
Power and Passion

Prepare to be swept off your feet by sophisticated, sexy and seductive heroes, in some of the world's most glamourous and romantic locations, where power and passion collide.

Julia James

Heiress's
PREGNANCY
SCANDAL

Jennie Lucas

Chosen as the
SHEIKH'S ROYAL
BRIDE

Kim Lawrence

A WEDDING
at the
ITALIAN'S DEMAND

Sharon Kendrick

The
SHEIKH'S
SECRET BABY

MILLS & BOON

THE HEART OF ROMANCE

A ROMANCE FOR EVERY READER

MODERN

Prepare to be swept off your feet by sophisticated, sexy and seductive heroes, in some of the world's most glamourous and romantic locations, where power and passion collide.

HISTORICAL

Escape with historical heroes from time gone by. Whether your passion is for wicked Regency Rakes, muscled Vikings or rugged Highlanders, awake the romance of the past.

MEDICAL

Set your pulse racing with dedicated, delectable doctors in the high-pressure world of medicine, where emotions run high and passion, comfort and love are the best medicine.

True Love

Celebrate true love with tender stories of heartfelt romance, from the rush of falling in love to the joy a new baby can bring, and a focus on the emotional heart of a relationship.

Desire

Indulge in secrets and scandal, intense drama and plenty of sizzling hot action with powerful and passionate heroes who have it all: wealth, status, good looks…everything but the right woman.

HEROES

Experience all the excitement of a gripping thriller, with an intense romance at its heart. Resourceful, true-to-life women and strong, fearless men face danger and desire - a killer combination!

To see which titles are coming soon, please visit

millsandboon.co.uk/nextmonth